ALDEMERE'S DILEMMA

By The Same Author

Jester-Knight (Book 1 of the Ambir Dragon Tales)

*Minor Confessions of an Angel Falling Upward

*Three Gothic Doctors and Their Sons

*Sherlock Holmes and the Mystery of M

*The Cannon and the Quill, Book One: We All be Jacobites Here

*The Cannon and the Quill, Book Two: Princes of the World

*The Cannon and the Quill, Book Three: How to Be a Proper Pyrate

*The Cannon and the Quill, Book Four: All the Devils Are Here

*The Icarus Continuum (Short Story Anthology)

Watch Out For the Hallway: Our Two-Year Investigation of the Most Haunted Library in North Carolina (with Tonya Madia)

Roommates from Beyond: How to Live in a Haunted Home (with Tonya Madia)

Every Day Is a Story All Its Own: A Triadic Approach to Storytelling

*Part of the Stanton Chronicles

ALDEMERE'S DILEMMA

‡

BOOK TWO OF THE AMBIR DRAGON TALES

JOEY MADIA

New Mystics Enterprises
Leavittsburg, Ohio

Aldemere's Dilemma

Published by New Mystics Enterprises, Leavittsburg, OH 44430
www.newmystics.com

ACKNOWLEDGMENTS

Dr. Richard Wertime, who taught me to write well and never stop challenging myself.

Sue Ernst, who has championed this story from the start.

Knight and Kate, whose lives are about books. Thank you for caring about and championing mine.

Jolie, who created the Mynoweth map and building floor plans.

Annette, Gerry, Marc, Laurie, and Ron, who all were taken too soon. Your influence fills these pages and infallibly guides my path.

DEDICATION

To Tonya, Daniel, Jeremy, and Jolie—you are the center of my world.

I love you.

PART ONE

CHAPTER ONE

Sir Aldemere, captainguard of Glittereye, was falling to his death.

Seconds before, he had been holding fast near the top of the desolate mountain that had been his targeted destination for endless weeks when his foot had slipped on an unseen patch of moss.

He was suddenly falling backwards.

The frigid air through which he fell was like thousands of needles entering his skin. He could feel the weight of accumulating ice crystals putting pressure on his neck as they formed in his tangled, shoulder-length hair.

Below him, a frozen lake eager to splinter his bones awaited.

As he passed an outcrop, he tried his best to grab it, but its slick edges would not offer him their aid.

As he fell, he thought, *Where did I get this ring?*

Before he could hazard a guess, the frozen lake was filling his field of vision, pulling his attention to his reflection in the ice.

Just before he hit, he saw he was an Elf.

"Aldemere—are you alright?"

The voice, so familiar, so comforting, seemed to come from just beyond the edge of the ice as his bones began to break.

Then Aldemere was awake, gasping hard for air.

"It's alright, my love," he heard through the rush of the blood in his ears. "It was just a nightmare. Just a nightmare. You are safe at Castle Silveth."

Blinking his eyes in an attempt to clear his head, Aldemere recognized in the early morning light his wife of six months, Anastasia, beside him in their bed.

"You look worried," he whispered, wiping the sweat from his forehead with the sleeve of his homespun nightshirt. "I am sorry I woke you. Those with child need their rest."

"As do future fathers," the princess replied with a smile, laying her head on his trembling shoulder. "That one seemed particularly vivid…"

In lieu of an answer, Aldemere stroked Anastasia's hair, its scent—lavender and rose—and the rhythmic motion of his fingers working to calm his heart.

"They are getting more life-like every night. Kal-Gadras never should have gone to Ferrukkla alone. I should have gone as well."

"Do you believe he has met his death?"

Anastasia's concern for her husband's closest friend was palpable, a result in part of the complicated, mystical life-bond the Elf and Human shared.

It was six weeks after the wedding, while Aldemere was making a morning inspection as part of his daily routine as captainguard, that he first began to the realize the soul connection that he and Kal-Gadras had forged during their journey to find the Ambir Dragon was further entwining their lives.

"Is everything well with you, Captainguard?" one of the Watch Tower guards had asked.

"I am fine, Sir Gadwin—why?"

"Your temple is bleeding, Sir."

More than a month would pass before Aldemere fully understood the implications of the mysterious laceration. Kal-Gadras had traveled with Petror, governing head of Marlooq Fer, to the castle for the blessing of the new tower constructed to honor the Ambir Dragon and the strengthening alliance between the Humans and Elves.

Aldemere had been waiting for him at the gates.

"Friend Kal-Gadras, as captainguard of Glittereye, I welcome you to Castle Silveth." As his childhood friend dismounted, Aldemere noticed a nearly healed wound on the warrior's left temple. "Did you injure yourself?"

"About a month ago," Kal-Gadras answered, tracing the fading cut with his finger. "A silly mistake involving a rather sharp axe and an underestimation of my strength."

In response, Aldemere ran a finger along his exactly matching wound. "It was just before dawn, was it not?"

Examining Aldemere's temple, Kal-Gadras raised a brow. "After the ceremony at the tower, we must find somewhere to talk."

On the morning that followed Anastasia and Aldemere's wedding, after the Elven delegation had departed for Marlooq Fer, Dylwyn, third king of Glittereye, summoned the five barons, the Council of Elders, the Seven Lord Seers, and his chief advisor, the jester Elde, to Castle Silveth's courtyard.

"My friends," he began, "thank you all for joining me. I apologize for the earliness of the hour after a night of drinking and merriment, but I wanted to talk to you all before we went our separate ways. I know as well that it is most unusual to forego the warmth and formality of the throne room for a gathering of this size, but I have made an important decision and, once you hear what I desire, I think you will understand.

"During the Festival of Eyeclear and the wedding ceremony that followed—which I appreciate you all attending despite the pressing business that awaits you in the baronies—I was struck with the need to mark for ourselves and even more so for our children the journey we have taken these past many months. I have decided on the construction of a monument, so that none shall ever forget the price of the recent rebellion, or what it nearly cost us, including our Alliance with the Elves.

"An inspired notion, Sire," remarked the eldest Seer. "What do you have in mind?"

"A tower, Dictus. In the courtyard in which we stand. A tower topped with a polished ambir gem. Aligned so precisely that during the Feast of Summerwelcome the sun shines through its many facets, illuminating the symbol of Glittereye carved upon the castle's wall. I further propose we name it the Dragon's Tower, in honor of the journey made by Captainguard Aldemere and the Elven Lord Kal-Gadras."

Dylwyn listened with pleasure to the ripples of applause.

Such unification amongst this lot had once been all too rare.

"On behalf of the Council of Elders," said Talorous, the most senior of the kingdom's scholars, and former tutor to the king, "may I say, Your Highness, that this is a most impressive course of action. It is both wise and well to honor the Ambir Dragon."

"Your blessing is appreciated, Master Teacher," Dylwyn answered. "I will leave it to you to make the proper calculations for the height and width of the tower and the placement of the ambir, if you would be so kind."

If I did not know any better, Elde the Jester thought, *I would swear the king is blushing.*

"And when will construction begin?" asked Baron Chrystan, recently appointed head of the Central Barony.

"As quickly as possible," Dylwyn answered, "so that the tower can be ready for the ambir to be placed upon it as soon as the northern passages allow a suitable specimen to be delivered. Baron Ciloto—"

"Yes, Your Highness?"

"As head of the Northern Barony, I will leave it to you to meet with Master Talorous and our chief artisans on the dimensions and other requirements necessary to prepare the ambir for the tower."

3   *Aldemere's Dilemma*

"It will be my honor, Sire."

King Dylwyn allowed himself to smile wider than he had in years.

Father and grandfather, he thought, raising his eyes to the brightening sky, *I hope that you are proud.*

The following few months passed uneventfully and well, as the new barons learned their lands and the needs of their people, and life at Castle Silveth returned to the peace it had known in the days of kings Paquom and Vagan.

Baron Chrystan and Master Talorous supervised the construction of the Dragon's Tower, while Ciloto worked with his brother Milani—the captain of the northern mines—to extract a perfect piece of ambir to meet the artisans' needs.

Blessed with an early thaw and ideally warm and rainy spring (a clear blessing by the Deities, as Dictus and the other Lord Seers piously remarked), the gem was delivered and secured upon the top of the tower the third week in March. King Dylwyn sent word across the kingdom and south to the Elves that the dedication ceremony would take place at the end of the month.

"Thank you all for coming," Dylwyn began, addressing the immense crowd gathered in the castle's courtyard in a deep and regal voice. "Especially our friends, Lords Petror and Kal-Gadras."

"It gives us great pleasure to be here on this important day, friend Dylwyn," Petror answered with a bow. "Nemmerle sends her deepest regrets that she could not make the journey with her son. But she is here in spirit, as are all the Elves of Marlooq Fer."

"I do feel her presence all around us, friend Petror," Dylwyn answered, returning the bow. "And I am grateful that she blesses this event. So let us now begin."

Vitus, chief incantor of the Seven Lord Seers, stepped forward as Dictus had instructed him at the previous evening's rehearsal. Raising his arms to the heavens, he intoned, "May the Gods and Goddesses watch over us this day and every day as we dedicate the Dragon's Tower. May it stand as a symbol of the cooperation between Human and Elf, between Mortal and Deity, and between the five baronies of this young and resilient kingdom."

Taking his place to Vitus's right, Dictus lit a censer of incense, saying, "I bless now this tower, rising fifty feet in height—five being the number of Deities and baronies that we all are born to serve."

Talorous, oldest and wisest of the scholars of Glittereye, made the final dedication. "Let us not forget that the gem of ambir that rests atop this tower is there to honor Ambirgondrad, the Ambir Dragon, called by the Elves Abyr-Goon-Draad, who watches over us all. May the oldest of Mynoweth's creatures serve as a reminder that we are never far from the shadow and always near to the light."

"Thus do I declare this Mass of the New Light ended," Dylwyn said, bowing his head. "In the years to come, we shall make the Dragon's Tower the focus of the three-day Festival of Eyeclear, which shall commence at dawn on the Biad—the shortest day of the year—that its eye of ambir may never lose its clarity and strength. Let us reflect upon the future for the next several moments before we say our goodbyes and each of us turns to the unfinished work that awaits."

After giving Kal-Gadras and High Lord Petror a tour of the castle's new defenses (as both a show of trust—the king's idea—as well as a demonstration of his ability to handle the complex duties of captainguard), Aldemere left the High Lord in the Throne Room with his father and the king. He and Kal-Gadras then made their way to the Hall of Books and Ancestries, where they found an inviting fire awaiting them.

"So, about our matching head wounds..." Aldemere began, setting a pair of chairs upon the edge of the hearth. "I'm sure you have a theory."

"It is more than just a theory, friend Aldemere," Kal-Gadras answered, declining the offered chair. "You and I endured many trials on our quest to find Abyr-Goon-Draad. It has forged an undeniable, inescapable bond of blood between us. Mother had foreseen it, but had not shared that portion of her vision with me until the knuckles of my left hand began to burst open and bleed for no apparent reason one day as we sat at our morning meal. You had no doubt lost your temper and struck a defenseless wall, yes?"

Aldemere felt his cheeks begin to flush. "Close. It was a *well*, my friend, not a *wall*. The one at the stables. I daresay, given the damage to our hands, not altogether defenseless. I had lost my grip on the rope and had to begin again. I was due to make inspection, to which I wound up being late." Looking at the floor, he added, "How far does this connection between us go?"

"Do you mean, is it a death-bond?"

Aldemere lifted his head, but could not meet his old friend's gaze.

"There is no way to know for sure. Well, one way." Kal-Gadras put his foot upon the chair. "But I am sure you are no more eager to test it than am I."

5   *Aldemere's Dilemma*

"This is an opportunity for our races," Aldemere said, rising and pacing before the fire. "It shall allow the Elves and Humans to come together in a way they never have before. We should make an announcement immediately! I wish your mother had come..."

Kal-Gadras gripped the captainguard's arm. "Easy, my friend. Your heart is overriding your head, as it did when we were boys."

Aldemere shook his head. "Not this time. It all makes perfect sense..."

"Perhaps if the world were different. If almost everything were different," Kal-Gadras said, releasing Aldemere's arm and sliding into his chair. "But we still each have our enemies, and they could use this bond between us to very destructive ends. There is another matter as well. The matter of my mother not being able to make the journey..."

"Has she fallen ill?" Aldemere asked, pulling his chair close to the one occupied by the Elf.

"Our bond, it seems, is not just physical," the Elven lord whispered, his voice heavy with emotion. "She is, in truth—and in strictest confidence—fighting for her life."

"This is terrible news, friend Petror. I am most aggrieved." Dylwyn ran his hands over the arms of his chair, not daring to make eye contact with the Elf or with Elde as his eyes grew heavy with tears.

"Is there anything we can do?" Elde the Jester asked, buying the king a moment. "I do not presume to think that our scholars and physicians could succeed where your own have thus far not, but if there is anything you require..."

"Just your ceaseless prayers," Petror answered. "Kal-Gadras and I must soon return to Marlooq Fer. Hir Marlooq has chosen him to undertake a most important task. One that might very well be our only hope for keeping Nemmerle alive."

"Will he once more seek the council of the mighty Ambirgondrad?" Dylwyn asked, ready to offer any help the Elven warrior might require.

"Perhaps, if he shows himself once more worthy, Abyr-Goon-Draad will deign to assist him," Petror answered. "But that is not the primary path he is chosen to take. He must go to the island of Ferrukkla, in the Sea of Silence, to the east, to seek the favor of the witch that is rumored to reside there."

"You speak of Caecaelev, do you not?" This came from Elde the jester, whose extensive knowledge of Elven lore earned him great respect amongst their races.

"I do indeed," answered Petror with a scowl. "And if there were any other way, I would readily pursue it."

"There is much not known about Caecaelev the witch," Kal-Gadras began, adding several thick logs to the fire in the Hall of Books and Ancestries, signaling to Aldemere that the story would take some time. "She was born to a Human in the Forest of Everrain almost two and a half centuries ago."

"Impossible," Aldemere said with a shake of his head. "Two hundred and fifty years is well beyond the lifespan of a hu—"

"Her father was an Elf," Kal-Gadras whispered, producing and lighting a long-stemmed pipe, letting his words linger in the air with his first exhale of thick, blue, fragrant smoke.

"I was unaware that such a thing was even possible," Aldemere said, raising a brow.

"Possible, my friend, but not at all preferable."

"Nor permissible—although neither side would admit it."

Talorous, head of the Council of Elders of Glittereye and Aldemere's former tutor, had entered the room unnoticed, as was the scholar's habit.

"True enough, friend Talorous," Kal-Gadras answered. "And all the more problematic considering the Alliance had yet to be forged. She was a special child, with astounding powers to heal and the ability to predict without error storms, floods, and droughts. She also warned of future wars that would engulf our races for years in death and blood. The Elves—devoted to my mother in her role as Hir Marlooq—deemed the child's insights to be unnatural, and the Humans, just by the mere aberration of her being partly Elven, proclaimed her dangerous and cursed."

"So what became of her?" Aldemere enquired, from deep within the story.

"Through a conspiracy between the leaders of our races, Caecaelev and her mother were banished to the Forest of the Black Light. No one knows when her mother died, but as the century passed and the chieftains were amassing their factions and preparing for a definitive war in the Centerlands, they sent representatives to seek out the one they had banished, leaving gifts and slaughtered livestock outside her door in hopeful payment."

"Because her visions were coming true."

"It's all too typical of our people," Talorous said, before lighting his pipe with a stick from the fire and sitting beside the warriors.

Aldemere's Dilemma

"Ignore the warnings and then desperately scramble for information once the wheel is set in motion."

"She spoke with them in time, sharing her visions of victories and misery, and suffering at their hands when it was not what they wished to hear." Knocking the dottle from his pipe into the fire, Kal-Gadras packed his bowl with fresh tobacco, staring into the twisted strands as though he were reading tea leaves. "She tried to speak with my mother, but Izmen and the other scholars turned her brutally away. It was not for many years that my mother was made aware that Caecaelev had even tried."

"Nemmerle spoke to me of it once," Talorous said, almost to himself. "And of the tragic day of the blinding."

Kal-Gadras nodded, prodding the fire with a poker. "It is said that in the second year of the Unity Wars, one of her visions was so terrible that she cut out both her eyes, which were the primary source of her magic. Some time later she was taken to the island of Ferrukkla, which lies south from the Forest of Tombal in the midst of the Sea of Silence, where she is believed to remain to this day."

"Ferrukkla... the 'Place of Flames,'" Talorous muttered. "Unless I have lapsed in my knowledge of the language of the Elves."

"Your memory, as always, is flawless, Honored Teacher," Kal-Gadras replied.

Aldemere, overwhelmed by the endless tragedy, threw a bulbous root he had been passing from hand to hand into the raging fire, sending up a shower of sparks. "How does a blind woman, witch or not, navigate a boat by herself?"

"I see my once student is still given to ill-timed and unnecessary questions now and again," Talorous said in a tone only a little bit unkind. Feeding bits of dried fruit to his constant companion, the raven Nigredo, he answered Aldemere's question. "She was taken to Ferrukkla by her father, who was no doubt motivated by his guilt over abandoning her and her mother long before."

"That is thought to be most likely," Kal-Gadras confirmed. "Although who her father is and if he truly was the one who took her to Ferrukkla are still matters of speculation amongst the Elves."

"Regardless of the whos and hows, you must travel to Ferrukkla," Talorous said, relighting his pipe and offering the glowing stick he used to light it to Kal-Gadras, who gladly accepted. "If I was younger, I would want to go along."

"You would be most welcome," Kal-Gadras said, his eyes asparkle, "but before I journey to Ferrukkla I must locate a legendary tree beside the River Skillen in the Forest of the Black

Light. Within its trunk lives the Firegem, which I must take to the witch."

"What can this Firegem do?" Aldemere asked, doing his best to ignore Talorous's derisive glare and exhalation of frustrated air.

"When Caecaelev removed her eyes, they fused together and lived," Kal-Gadras answered. "I am going to retrieve them and return them to her in payment for saving my mother's life."

Aldemere sat in the Hall of Books and Ancestries for many hours after the Elven delegation had departed, watching with heavy eyes as the fire burned to coals and then to ash. Long after Mynoweth's twin moons, the Night Guardians, had taken their place in the sky, Anastasia entered, sitting silently by his side.

"I am not going with him," Aldemere whispered, taking his wife's hand without turning his head to meet her gaze.

"I am grateful," she answered, placing her free hand upon her stomach. "As is our child. Did you tell Kal-Gadras our happy news?"

"I wished to, but the timing was poor. Nemmerle is dying. It shall keep until he returns."

Anastasia placed her head on Aldemere's shoulder. "You did not want to use my pregnancy as an excuse. You are as good a husband as you are a friend and captainguard. My father was certain you would wish to go and was ready to grant his approval."

"My first loyalty is to you and to our child. This kingdom, this castle, the alliance with the Elves—I will fight for them when I must, as I have pledged, but things have changed for me. You must not ever doubt that."

As the princess rose and embraced him goodnight, Aldemere closed his eyes and tried his best to push his feelings of failing his closest friend from the center of his mind.

Upon arriving in Marlooq Fer, Kal-Gadras left the stable boy to care for his horse, named Hir, something he never had done before, so anxious was he to see his mother.

Crossing the suspension bridge leading to Nemmerle's chambers, nestled twenty feet above the ground within a stand of ancient oaks, the Lord of the South Shore ran his fingers over a spot on his neck called the Mark of Gal-Rashand. As he entered his mother's bedroom, his heart began to race with the pain he had suppressed while he was gone.

"Come to me, my son." Nemmerle's voice, always but a whisper of summer wind, was even fainter than usual.

9   *Aldemere's Dilemma*

Time was growing short.

"I sense the dedication of the Dragon's Tower has well-pleased ancient Abyr-Goon-Draad, and Marlooq Fer as well. How is your friend?"

"He is well," Kal-Gadras said, taking her hand and kneeling beside the bed. "Aldemere prays for you, as does the king and all the court. Mother—I feel any further delay in my going to the Forest of the Black Light…"

"Things will be as they are destined to be, Kal-Gadras," Nemmerle whispered. "You will go there soon enough. Do not fear for me."

"I should already be on my way to Ferrukkla!" Kal-Gadras yelled, standing in his frustration. "High Lord Petror could have adequately represented Marlooq Fer at the dedication. My accompanying him was an unnecessary and dangerous delay."

Nemmerle rose from the pillows beneath her so she could look her son in the eye. "Do not forget yourself, Kal-Gadras. You are a great warrior and the blood of Gal-Rashand, first of the Elves, runs like quicksilver through your veins, but it is not your place nor within your considerable capabilities to know what is *unnecessary* and *dangerous* where I am concerned. Your going to Silveth was what your mother, and our sacred mother, desired. Do you dare to question Marlooq Fer?"

Kal-Gadras averted his eyes in shame. "I would never question either of y—"

"And yet you already have," Nemmerle said with a smile, lowering herself with an exhale back onto the bed. "Do not let your love for me cloud your vision. You must see farther than those around you. You know the visions I have had, what I have seen of Aldemere and yourself, and what the fates will come to demand. Your journey has already started. Even if I wanted to delay you, I could not."

"Then let me proceed to the Forest of the Black Light."

As he leaned over to kiss Nemmerle goodbye, Kal-Gadras felt the Mark begin to throb, as though a dragon were nearby.

Convinced the Ambir Dragon was hovering somewhere close, Kal-Gadras was determined to find it. As he rode at a gallop toward the eastern forest, he scanned the sky for a glimpse of the constellation.

He could not find it anywhere in the sky.

By the time he approached the River Skillen the following afternoon, the Mark of Gal-Rashand had ceased its throbbing, and the Elven warrior's sense of Abyr-Goon-Draad had all but left him.

A quarter mile from the river's steeply sloping banks, Kal-Gadras patted the neck of his horse. "We must proceed with caution, Hir," he whispered to his lifelong companion. "The ground near the water is dotted with pits of livesand, and Aldemere is not here to save me as he did when we were boys. I shall trust in you to direct us."

As they proceeded to the river, a stinging rain began to fall, accompanied by an unrelenting wind, which made it impossible for them to see more than a couple of feet ahead.

"We have suffered through worse than this," Kal-Gadras said aloud, as much for his own benefit as Hir's. "The River Skillen shall be a wicked challenge to navigate."

An understatement to say the least. The foreboding sable waters were churning, and the powerful storm, coupled with the recent thaw, had raised the river's level, giving it an added unpredictability.

Climbing down from the palomino, Kal-Gadras made a series of quick decisions. The first was perhaps the hardest. Elven warhorse though he was, Hir would not be able to enter the river.

"I cannot risk your being injured," Kal-Gadras explained as the palomino whinnied his frustration at being unsaddled and tied to a tree. "The water is full of broken branches and other hazards to your legs. I need you to take me to the South Shore once I have found the Firegem."

The rest of his decisions were more a matter of necessity than any conscious, considered plan. Draping a long length of Elven rope over his shoulder before taking in a girding breath of air, Kal-Gadras entered the icy water, sinking to his waist in the deep, mysterious river. Within minutes, his hands and feet were numb. As he swam toward the bald cypress the wisest of the Elven historians and scholars believed was the hiding place of the disembodied eyes of Caecaelev the witch, his arms and legs began to ache.

After a few more minutes in the frigid, churning waters, they would cease to work at all.

Standing like a sentinel on the far bank of the river, the ancient cypress took the rain and wind without complaint, its thick, curving roots entering and exiting the ground as though they were segments of a primordial black-grey snake. Its trunk, which rose more than thirty feet in the air, where it erupted in a mass of gnarled and knotted limbs, was deeply gashed almost exactly halfway up. Deep within the split, Kal-Gadras noticed a faint yet powerful reddish glow.

Aldemere's Dilemma

Although his legs screamed in protest and he could no longer feel his feet, Kal-Gadras willed his limbs to propel him faster toward the tree. Concentrating on the light emanating from the trunk as his arms refused to paddle and the swirling water began to pull him into its depths, the determined Elven warrior cursed his body's limitations.

Gathering his last bit of strength, he launched himself toward the bank, hooking his arms through a section of root before the river could claim him for good. Inching his torso into a more secure and stable position, Kal-Gadras gave into the needs of his exhausted, near-broken body, falling within minutes into a feverish, uneasy sleep.

"There is to be no worry about that moody man of yours while you are carrying his child, do you understand me, Anastasia?"

Glenna Gravanal, the ageless and venerated senior midwife of Castle Silveth, was cleaning up her ointments and instruments in the Birthing Room as the princess lowered and adjusted her skirts.

"You might as well order the Night Guardians to refuse to rise in the evening as ask that of my daughter, Glenna," Queen Cecile answered, fussing with the lace trim on the bodice of Anastasia's dress. "Isn't that right, my dear Arianna?"

Aldemere's mother, not quite used to the growing familiarity between she and the queen, raised a brow and nodded. "The Deities know my son invites more than his fair share of worry and concern."

"No one knows his nature better than I," Glenna replied with a growl. "After all—I was the one that delivered him. Moody he was and moodier he shall be." Turning her attention back to the princess, she added, "I delivered you as well—so you best be minding my words!"

"I certainly shall try, Glenna Midwife," Anastasia answered. "Although perhaps a stern talking to from the likes of you is just what my worrisome husband needs."

"If I hear one more word from Glenna Midwife about not needlessly upsetting Anastasia through the duration of her pregnancy, I will have to resign my appointment as captainguard and take up knitting, Father!"

Aldemere, comfortable in plain dress in his parents' private chambers, sprawled himself out on the floor as he used to as a child.

What simpler times they had been.

"No one seems to understand one plain and simple fact. I have so much to live up to—my predecessor was the greatest champion of the field and ablest leader of men this kingdom has yet to see. Not to mention the thousand achievements of my namesake, Alde the Jester…"

Elde put down the half-finished torso of a wooden horse he was carving and gazed upon his offspring with a sigh.

"You have aged so much, my son, since that memorable morning nearly nine years ago when Sir Laurel first took you from these chambers to claim you as his squire. You have overcome all manner of obstacles, seen things and places no other man in Glittereye has, yet you continue to concern yourself with the names and reputations of those who have come before you."

"The past is not all that concerns me, Father."

"I did not think it was. A visit from you has become a rare and precious thing. Speak what is on your mind."

"Where do I begin? I am to be a father. That is foremost on my mind. But then there is Kal-Gadras…"

"You feel as though you should have accompanied him on his quest." Elde was working his knife into what would soon be one of the lower leg joints of the exquisitely carved wooden horse.

Aldemere nodded, watching the delicate but firm way in which his father handled his task. "He did not invite me, but what if it was only because he did not wish to put me in the position of saying no?"

"Does Kal-Gadras know you are soon to be a father?" Elde enquired, although he already knew the answer.

"I do not think so, but we share so much between us—more than I am able to understand—that he might very well have sensed it. I am confused and frightened, Father. How does one balance his duties to his wife and child, his greatest friend, his soldiers, and his kingdom? How have you managed this impossible, vexing thing?"

"There are times I almost have not. I very nearly failed you, your mother, the king, and this kingdom, not so long ago."

"And yet you managed it all when it counted," Aldemere replied. Standing up and stretching, he asked, "How do I balance upon so many precarious positions without falling to my death?"

"That, my son," Elde the Jester began, popping a small wooden pin into the place where the two sections of the wooden horse's leg seamlessly fit together, "is the question that has most concerned leaders like you and the king from the earliest moments of time.

Follow your heart in this, as you have in all of your endeavors, and you are sure to find your way."

By the time Kal-Gadras was able to open his eyes and move his arms—which screamed in protest with even the smallest of movements—it was evening. The rain had stopped, and the sky was a glittering blanket of stars. Sitting up despite the sharp pain coursing through his limbs, Nemmerle's son tracked his eyes up the trunk of the ancient cypress until he was able to focus them on the faint reddish glow some thirty feet above. Knowing he needed another day or more to recover before he could make the climb to retrieve what he hoped against hope was the Firegem, Kal-Gadras buried his hands in his tunic and adjusted his position into one of meditation. Unable to light a fire in the saturated expanse that surrounded him, he did the next best thing.

He imagined one.

It shall have to do, he told his battered, shivering body, as he drifted back to sleep.

"Excuse us, Captainguard... may we have a word?"

Aldemere looked up from the duty lists he was refining for the castle's new defenses to find Sir Eric and Sir Lan, two of his newly appointed lieutenants, standing at painfully stiff attention.

"Is it absolutely urgent that you interrupt my work?" he asked in return, suppressing the desire to smile at the level of their discomfort.

"Well, Sir Aldemere, Lan certainly thought it was," Eric began, instantly seeing his error.

"You were in agreement at the time," Lan said, as though his whispered voice were an arrow and Eric's inner ear its target.

Aldemere arose from his chair and took up position behind them.

"What is the primary responsibility of a lieutenant in the King's Guard?" he asked them, his voice a bladed, weakness-seeking whisper.

Squaring his shoulders and saluting, Sir Eric answered, "To protect the king and his castle," the seeming surety in his tone betrayed only by the briefest hesitation.

"What about you, Sir Lan? Do you align with Eric's position? You would be wise to answer carefully—your father was one of our most senior and distinguished members."

"Well, Sir... yes—it is as sound of an answer as any I could muster."

Returning to his original position, Aldemere did his best to maintain the façade of the terrible taskmaster. "You are partially correct, Sir Eric. First and foremost, a member of the King's Guard must be loyal to its members—especially a pair of lieutenants such as yourselves. We are a unit, only as strong as the loyalty that binds each of us to the others. Lan's father gave his life during the Rebellion so our king could keep his throne and Glittereye would continue to be a beacon of hope and light. I do not ever again want to hear one of you betraying the other to try and save his skin—am I making myself clear?"

His two lieutenants saluted in acknowledgment.

"I meant no offense to your father," Eric said to Lan. "And certainly none to you."

Only then did Aldemere smile.

"I am sure that Sir Lan is satisfied with your apology, Eric—as am I. Now... Why have you come to see me?"

Awakening to the brightening rays of the early morning sun, Kal-Gadras reached for the bundle of Elven rope that had served as his headrest during the night. Willing his still- aching fingers to unfasten and unloop its intricately woven length, he fixed his eyes on a thick branch protruding just a few feet above the persistent glow of the Firegem.

"That shall do quite nicely," he said, addressing a small, blue bird that had alit on a bush to his left as the Elven warrior tied one end of the rope securely around the hilt of his dagger.

Throwing the ten-inch dagger up and over the branch so that the rope hung with an almost perfect evenness from either of its sides, Kal-Gadras allowed himself permission to smile. After wrapping the dangling length of rope that held the dagger three times around its partner, he tugged on the free end, watching the dagger's hilt slide against the rope until it locked itself securely on a diagonal at the place where the branch met the trunk. Giving the rope a tug, and satisfied it was secure, he began to climb, focusing all of his considerable concentration on willing his still-aching arms, legs, feet, and hands to do their needed work.

It took several minutes more than it would have under less adverse conditions, but Kal-Gadras at last found himself at eye level with the Firegem. Although he did not wish them to, so beautiful was the sight, he found his eyes closing against the brilliance of the sacred object before him. Placing his hand upon it, he immediately

Aldemere's Dilemma

felt the blood begin to flow with greater strength through his arm and into his hand, allowing him to grip the Firegem considerably tighter.

"Praise Nemmerle," he whispered, gently pulling it from the space where it had rested for so many years. As he held it, its insistent, subtle pulsing soothed and strengthened his muscles. Switching hands, he let the Firegem heat and heal the remainder of his body before placing it in a pouch fastened to his belt.

Tying off the rope and dislodging the knife from its snug companionship with the branch, he slid quickly to the ground. The small, blue bird began to sing and bob its head in approval.

"Your blessing is welcome, friend songbird," Kal-Gadras answered with a head-bob of his own. "I mean no offense taking the Firegem from this cypress. But my mother is desperately ill, and this is my only hope to heal her."

Crouching at the foot of the tree, Kal-Gadras removed the Firegem from the pouch, holding it tightly in both of his hands for several minutes until he felt his strength restored. Gripping it tightly in his fist, he entered the river and swam with ease toward the spot where his patient palomino stood awaiting him.

"A most pleasant day to you, friend Hir," Kal-Gadras said with a smile, shaking the water from his hair and clothes. As Hir began to nuzzle his master's neck, the Elven warrior added, "I see you missed me! Are you ready to move like the lightning?"

"Did you concede to their request?"

Baron Ralin of the Western Barony found himself more than a little surprised by what his childhood friend—and blessedly brief enemy—had just revealed.

"I did," answered Aldemere, pouring two goblets of hazelnut mead for him and his guest. "Their argument was sound, and their larger concerns my own. They will leave with you at first light for the trade meeting in the Eastern Barony."

"We are all a bit on edge about this first meeting of the Trade Council outside of Castle Silveth since the Rebellion and the Endless Winter," Ralin answered, draining half his goblet, "but the place of the King's Guard is here with the king. If I were concerned with my safety—or the safety of any of the barons—or the baroness—I would have asked Eric's father to join me, as would be his duty as Chief Knight of the Western Barony."

"Since you brought him up, I am surprised that Sir Prima chose to remain at Spiltrow—I thought he would be eager to see how his son is faring in his duties."

"I promised I would check on him," Ralin answered, finishing his drink and extending the empty goblet for a refill. "It was not so awfully long ago that I was a young man alone in this castle. Now it seems I will have plenty of opportunity to observe him. Would it be rude of me to ask you for another? I am *parched*."

"Not at all." Aldemere drained his own before filling the goblets again. "Baron Chrystan assures me there is much good mead stored here at the castle, and plenty for trading as well."

"Then all should go as planned. The Endless Winter was rough on each of the baronies, so we all should be eager to cooperate. That certainly seemed to be the spirit at the dedication of the Tower—so I hear, as I was not invited."

"None of the barons were invited, *per se*," answered Aldemere. "Chrystan was here because of where he lives. Not even Ciloto returned after delivering the ambir for the top of the tower. You no doubt had much to do during the time of the ceremony, as did the rest of the barons."

"And the baron*ess*," Ralin added, finishing his second goblet.

"Is there some difficulty you are having with Baroness Ashlin, Ralin?"

"Not *per se*, my friend," Ralin said, the effects of the hazelnut mead becoming apparent in his manner and demeanor. "But I need not remind you that the Eastern Barony was where all the trouble started. And I know I played a part, so do not even—"

"I would not think of doing so," Aldemere answered. "The past, as Talorous always taught us, is best left to the historians until we find ourselves repeating it."

Ralin's voice got suddenly quiet yet hard. "Perhaps, in some small way, by the king choosing the Eastern Barony as the site of the first Trade Council since all the new appointments, we are, in fact, repeating it."

Aldemere shook his head. "It is more a boon to Ashlin after the death of her brother and her new position than any sort of pointed political statement. Colar—before Garamin made his play—was a highly respected baron. Surely you do not question the king's decision?"

Ralin sat silent for a moment before sliding his goblet toward the captainguard. "If I did, Prima would not be waiting at Spiltrow for news of his son. I think all of this business about an escort is a wagonload of nonsense. What did you say? That there have been reports from our scouts of unfamiliar faces in the eastern forests?"

"Lan has several friends assigned to our eastern garrison."

Aldemere's Dilemma

Ralin slapped his hand upon the table. "Well, then, we had better not take chances. If Lan and his comrades say." He motioned to his goblet. "How about another? The mead here is splendid—do I also detect a subtle kiss of lemon?"

"You shall have to ask the meadmeister," Aldemere said, bringing Ralin's goblet to the mead barrel, although he left his own behind. "I believe his name is Richard. I am just a simple soldier."

"Perhaps I shall," Ralin said, letting out a belch. "It might be worth a bit more oil when we trade."

"Here you are." Aldemere said, returning to the table with Ralin's newly filled goblet. "Just... do not overdo it."

"Have no fear," Ralin said, taking the goblet and draining it in one long, sloppy swallow. "I am sure your eager new lieutenants will catch me if I fall."

The following afternoon, as Kal-Gadras and Hir approached the sentries stationed on the near side of the suspension bridge that led to his mother's elevated chambers, the Lord of the South Shore noticed his hand pulling his cloak over the triply knotted leather pouch that contained the pulsing Firegem.

It has a dangerous power, he thought. *Even Elves of kind and steadfast heart will attempt to possess it if they can.*

"Lord Kal-Gadras," one of the pair of sentries said, saluting his superior in the manner of the Elves. "Was your journey a success?"

"The part that I have thus far undertaken has proven to be so, yes," he answered, dismounting. He noticed an inner agitation over what he perceived as a needless, probing question from a witless bore of an Elf. "What news of my mother?"

"There has been no change. High Lord Petror is with her. She was calling out your name a handful of minutes ago."

"Then I will go to her immediately. See that the stable boy pays extra attention to Hir. He has served me well." Running his hand along the palomino's sweaty neck, he whispered, "Thank you, my trusted friend."

Running across the bridge as much to keep the Firegem from the peering eyes of the sentries as to all the more quickly relieve his mother's mind, he entered the bedroom, where High Lord Petror held vigil beside her bed.

"It is good to see you, friend Kal-Gadras," Petror whispered without changing his position. "Your mother has been concerned. Is your task complete?"

"It is," answered Kal-Gadras, kneeling beside the bed. "I am here, Mother. The Firegem is with me."

"You have done very well, my son," Nemmerle whispered, lifting her hand with considerable effort to touch Kal-Gadras's cheek. "Though you shall have no time for rest. I feel my strength diminishing. You must journey to Ferrukkla as quickly as you can."

"I would not stay a moment longer, even if you were to demand it of me, Mother." Turning to Petror, Kal-Gadras asked, "Is the boat prepared?"

"It is. Provisioned exactly as I instructed. A horse awaits you in the stables."

Kal-Gadras nodded, filled with further sadness. "I know that Hir is not of sufficient strength after our recent journey to come with me to Ferrukkla, as much as I hoped he would be. He has been my kind companion on many an adventure. It will be strange to not be with him on the most important mission for which I have yet been chosen."

"The horse I have selected is intelligent and strong."

"Then all has been arranged, and I will leave you for my task."

As he turned to go, Kal-Gadras felt Petror's powerful fingers close around his bicep. "Before you take your leave—I was hoping I could see it. Just for a moment or two."

Nodding in agreement, Kal-Gadras pushed aside the folds of his cloak to access more easily the leather pouch that held the Firegem. As he began to untie the pouch's fastenings, his fingers ceased to work.

"Is something the matter?" Petror asked.

Something is *the matter!* Kal-Gadras heard within his head. *It is not yours to see or touch. I nearly died in the River Skillen attempting to retrieve it. Why then should you, or anyone else, behold it!*

Because he is the High Lord of the Elves, another voice instructed.

Why are you acting so human? a third voice asked.

"Why must you insult me?" Kal-Gadras hissed.

"I only asked if something is wrong," Petror replied.

Shaking his head in answer—and to silence the unwelcome voices—Kal-Gadras produced an excuse. "The pouch strings have a knot. Just give me a moment to undo it."

"Take all the time you need."

Aldemere's Dilemma

Undoing the strings, Kal-Gadras tried his best to ignore the surge of power he felt in his hand and arm as his fingers gripped the Firegem.

Handing it to Petror—although relinquishing the powerful totem was not at all what he wished to do—Kal-Gadras turned his thoughts to the trials ahead, for it would not be the crossing to Ferrukkla or the harsh terrain that would test him the most, but the possessive power of the Firegem itself.

He prayed he could soon get rid of it.

Soon… but not just yet.

Although Petror held it for only a moment, fully aware of its danger, it felt to the Lord of the South Shore as though half a day had passed before it was once more in the pouch.

"What worries you, my husband?" Anastasia asked as Aldemere removed his cloak and readied himself for bed.

"Nothing of dire consequence," Aldemere answered, joining his wife beneath the covers. "And even if something were, I am under strict orders from Glenna Midwife not to agitate you or the baby."

"I swear I shall not tell her," Anastasia whispered, pushing Aldemere's hair from his eyes. "I see that you are more filled with worry than you were before Ralin's arrival and your meeting."

"He is still so angry and bitter about all too many things," Aldemere answered, laying his cheek on the princess' shoulder. "And he may be using drink to try and mask it. He said some things about the location of the trade meetings and the eastern baroness specifically that raise in me concern."

"That is one of the problems with an over-fondness for drink—it utterly fails to mask. It accentuates and amplifies. Ralin's father was proof enough of that."

Aldemere sat up with a scowl. "Baron Vellom was a drinker?"

"I would not say that drunkenness was his habit," Anastasia answered, annoyed at the conversation. "But at weddings and feasts, he and Filgrith would get noticeably intoxicated. Father would sometimes have them escorted to their rooms. There were nights I listened to them emptying their stomachs into pails across the hall. I pitied the servants their work."

"Do such habits run in families? I mean by that, father to son?" Aldemere enquired, settling back beneath the covers.

"No more or less than any other family habits," Anastasia answered, not knowing that this was the very answer her husband had feared the most.

CHAPTER TWO

The horse I have selected is intelligent and strong.

Petror's words were as exacting and true as one would expect of an Elf of the High Lord's age and standing.

Grazing serenely in a stall just inside the stable's entrance was the most magnificent horse Kal-Gadras had ever had the pleasure of grooming.

For, up until now, no one but High Lord Petror had ever sat astride her.

The horse was Petror's own.

Her name was Lightning Stride, in Elvish Lethir-na.

"She is ready to depart as soon as you wish, my Lord," one of the stable boys whispered, feeling as humbled to be in the presence of the heir of Gal-Rashand as Kal-Gadras was to be riding Petror's horse.

"Just look at this pair of idiots! Kiss and get it over with."

Kal-Gadras pursed his lips.

Although he would only be conscious of it later, he pulled his riding cloak tighter over the pouch that held the Firegem.

"Master Izmen—how nice of you to come to see me off."

"See you off?" Kal-Gadras's boyhood teacher asked with a particularly un-Elven scowl. "See you off? I am here to dissuade you from this foolish, meaningless task. Your mother is daft with fever and Petror's desperate to save her... But you... you must have a bit more sense than to trust them and their plan."

Checking the provisions in his saddlebags, Kal-Gadras did his best to avoid eye contact with the crotchety old Elf.

It was his only hope of not striking him where he stood.

"As sharp as you may be, my aged and wizened shrew, I find it surprising that even you would dare to contradict the orders of my mother and High Lord Petror. And, surprised as I am, it pushes incredulity even further when I hear you would expect of *me* to do the same." Kal-Gadras climbed into the saddle and spurred the mare into motion.

"I beg of you," Izmen shrieked, grabbing the bridle and bringing the horse to a halt. "You must hear me out!"

Breathing deeply, as he would to keep from squashing an insect flitting in and out of his ears, Kal-Gadras dismounted with a growl.

Aldemere's Dilemma

"Very well, but you had better make it quick. Should High Lord Petror discover I have lingered for even a moment to listen to your nonsense..."

"Awaken from your ignorance, you lout!" Izmen shouted, keeping his grip on the bridle. "You have more power and say than you know. But here it is, in as few syllables as I can muster. Caecaelev is both clever and malicious. She must have been mad to pull her own two eyes from their sockets! If you insist on doing this—and I see in your own eyes you are—you must not try to speak to her. Do what you must and leave. The mixing of Elven and Human blood enhances the worst of both. Do not let her draw you in, do not let her entrance you. Her mother must have been a cursed and villainous vixen to seduce so maliciously a confused and helpless Elf. Why else would he betray his own and do the heinous thing he did?"

Kal-Gadras retook the saddle, yanking hard upon the reins, forcing Izmen to release them. "Are you through? Have you said your say? Daylight shall not last, and I have much to do."

Izmen's eyes went suddenly wide. "Do you have the Firegem?"

Finally out of patience, Kal-Gadras turned Lethir-na in Izmen's direction and yelled, "Out of the way, my embittered old teacher, or I will drag you along behind me."

Not looking back as he spurred the horse to a gallop, Kal-Gadras could hear Izmen kicking at the stable posts and cursing in Elven, Human, and Ereti. Such an outburst would normally make him laugh.

He did not even smile.

"All of our preparations are made," Baron Chrystan reported, standing before the king. "Baron Ralin and I shall be departing upon the dawn."

Dylwyn nodded his approval. "I think it will be productive for you and him to speak before the negotiations amongst the Trade Council, Chrystan. You have a knight's sense of character. I want to know what he is thinking. He walks the halls as though he wished to own them."

"I am sure Sir Aldemere could offer you some insight..."

"If I were to ask him, I have no doubt that he would," Dylywn replied, "although it would be hard for him to do so. Our new captainguard is a man of honor, like his predecessor and yourself. He and Ralin are like brothers."

"I see that Laurel's crest is at last to grace this room." Chrystan motioned toward an artist from the Herald's Guild, who was deep in concentration as he drew upon the mortared western wall the outline of a sea dragon within the suggestion of a wreath.

"Enough time has passed since his death for us to do so," answered Dylwyn, a glint of curiosity in his wise and weathered eyes. "I detect a sense of melancholy in your voice that goes well beyond what you must feel for your fallen comrade. Do you regret your de-commission?"

The knight turned baron genuflected. "I cannot conceal the truth from you, my king. It is far harder to be a knight no longer than I had first imagined. I think that watching the tournament games from the seats at the Feast of Summerwelcome will be unbearably bittersweet. Laurel was a friend, a comrade in arms, and I would have liked to have had the chance to honor him by vying for Champion of the Field in his memory."

Alighting from the dais, Dylwyn leaned in close, so only Chrystan could hear. "You may no longer be a knight in title, my friend, but I need you to be one in spirit and in action. There is far more at stake than the winning of tournament games. I expect a full report of what is happening with the baronies upon your return, and I do not mean the facts and figures of the season's trade agreements."

Chrystan nodded in understanding and wordlessly rose to depart.

Sir Lan was polishing his vambraces and greaves as though he was due to stand inspection. His mother had been pleased to hear that he would be accompanying Chrystan and Ralin on their journey to the eastern barony.

"It is opportunities such as this that help a knight to distinguish himself," she had said. "Your father always felt you did not seize upon them enough. While others were forging themselves into heroes, you were standing guard at the throne room door. Do not let this pass without giving it your best. You have all the promise in the world. One day, when Aldemere is king, you might just rise to captainguard. How pleased your father will be as he stands to the right of the Deities looking down upon you. Make the most of this, my son."

Taking his sword to the whetstone, the 30-year-old lieutenant drifted back in time to the moments of his selection as squire, the day of his knighthood, his father's burial, and his appointment to lieutenant in the King's Guard. Aldemere was not just showing respect when he had referred to Lan's father as one of the most

Aldemere's Dilemma

distinguished members of their unit. He had been one of Sir Laurel's chief advisors. His death was as noble and grand as any knight could wish it to be.

How could Lan do better? He had been afraid to be a squire and content to be a knight. It was more than he had ever thought he would achieve as a child, playing with his little wooden soldiers as his father rose in the ranks.

Then the appointment to the King's Guard, unexpected and even unwelcome. Endless duty at the throne room door. Yet he was happy in the role.

His father's death had allowed for his promotion. Too high a price to pay for a position he did not desire. Although there was no saying no. Not to Aldemere, nor the king, nor the ghost of his fallen father.

It was Eric's idea to offer their services as escorts to Baron Ralin. Of course it was Eric's idea—his father, Sir Prima, was ambitious and well liked, and Eric was exactly like him.

Maybe that is not all it takes, Lan mused, although he struggled to produce an example. Aldemere, Ralin, Garamin, Eric—they had all received their appointments because they matched and at times surpassed the achievements of their fathers.

Or they took what they wanted by force.

"Are you sharpening that sword or trying to whittle it down to a food-skewer, Lieutenant?"

Lan looked down and saw the edge of the sword glowing ever so faintly from too many minutes of repetitious friction. He had neglected to use any water.

"I guess I got lost in my thoughts, Pemby," he answered. "I have got some pressing affairs coming my way. How are things with you?"

"I am about to go blind from the shine on your greaves," the junior Stable Master answered, covering his eyes with a laugh. "I think the captainguard is having too fine an effect on you. Did he ever tell you about the time he let me wear Sir Laurel's tabard? Heady times, my friend."

Lan, sheathing his sword and gathering up his armor, shook his head. "I doubt he ever will. A knight's tabard is not for stable hands to sport."

"That, my Shiny Knight, is the truth," Pemby answered, selecting tools for the late-day's work. "If you are not the son of somebody, you keep on being nobody."

Kal-Gadras never once permitted Lethir-na to waver from a gallop as he journeyed through the lush Elven landscape to the docks on the southernmost shore of Marlooq Fer.

When he arrived in the early evening, it was to a fine meal and fully provisioned boat—the single-masted vessel he had purchased from the Vaelportians for the sum of two sizable lumps of Elven false-gold—iron ore converted by a secret process of alchemy which certain disreputable Humans were desperate to discover.

Kal-Gadras let out a hearty laugh thinking about his adventure with Aldemere at Vaelsport.

"The sails are secured and all is ready for your departure, my Lord," an Elven sailing master said with a salute as Kal-Gadras approached the docks after dinner. "It is good to have you back, if only for an evening."

"I am honored to be here on the shores that my mother and High Lord Petror have charged me with protecting. I regret that so many pressing duties have kept me from what should be my full-time home. I look forward to remedying my neglect quickly upon my return. I appreciate your service in readying this vessel. I must see to Petror's horse and attempt to get some rest. I have a week and a half's arduous journey ahead of me, and I must be at my best."

"The Elves of the Southern Shore are praying for your safe return and the restoration to health of Hir Marlooq," the sailing master answered, speaking the name that most of the Elves used when referring to Kal-Gadras's mother.

"I will not fail our Mother's Heart," Kal-Gadras whispered, more for his own sake than that of the sailing master. "I shall not let her die."

An hour's ride from Castle Silveth, in an open field surrounded by free-grazing cattle, stands the Temple of the Seers, the modest stone structure built adjacent to the burial grounds of the Central Barony—row upon row of cairns marking the gravesites of fallen heroes, merchants, and the more modest inhabitants of the castle and its surrounding farmsteads and dwellings.

Constructed in the time of King Paquom at the insistence of the mad mystic Manthes Fragenoar—who quoted from ancient scrolls he permitted no one else to see about the necessity of the separation of the religious from the political—the temple was the home of the Seven Lord Seers of Glittereye. Before the time of Manthes Fragenoar, and the building of Castle Silveth, the Seers had been residents in the village complex, enjoying all the rights and privileges of their station. Their daily interactions with the leaders of the village that became the Central Barony allowed them to have a hand—fourteen of them, to be exact—in shaping policies and ensuring that the will of the five Deities—which were, in many ways, five distinctive, at times conflicting, wills—were brought to bear on the people and their politics.

Which is why Manthes had them moved.

Nearly a hundred years had passed since the completion of the Temple, and it was already in disrepair. The Seven Lord Seers, devoted as they were to acts of service to the Deities and the pursuit of greater spiritual wisdom and grace—as well as tending the gardens and livestock—did not have the time nor the skills to keep the building up.

It is a blessing from Taplah and Cirrah that there is no rain today, thought Farvon, Keeper of the Scrolls and the most learned of the seven, *or our guests would be dodging waterfalls while they ate*.

Beyond the door to his modest library—only a third the size of the Hall of Books and Ancestries and with a mere tenth the collection of scrolls, maps, and volumes—Farvon could hear the representative of the Academic Council conversing with Dictus and Vitus.

"This should be an interesting day, indeed," he said to himself, gathering the last of the materials his superiors had requested and pulling tight the strings of the threadbare sack that held them. "I will no doubt be asked to speak much and say what amounts to nothing. So be it," he said with a sigh.

Entering the atrium and once more praising the God Taplah who allowed the sun to shine through its filthy, chipped glass ceiling, Farvon could not help but smile at the sight of the old taskmaster, Talorous.

As well as the beautiful woman beside him.

"Wise and Learned Teacher," Dictus was gushing, "it is a rare and momentous honor to have a visit from one such as you. Cortus and Sullus have worked through the night preparing a meal worthy of your knowledgeable palate."

"There is no need for any fuss on my account," Talorous answered with an overly formal bow.

He truly is a master, Farvon thought.

"I accepted your invitation because I agree there is much to discuss. Which is why I requested my longtime student, Laurianna, to join me." Talorous paused a moment to allow all seven of the Seers a chance to nod, stoop, and bow to him and his companion.

"I am honored to be here," answered Laurianna, the sunlight streaming through the atrium ceiling creating a halo effect around her blue-black raven hair. "I am hoping to spend some time after dinner browsing the shelves of your library."

Answering a little too loudly, a little too enthusiastically, Farvon answered, "It would be my pleasure to show you!"

"Well then," Dictus said, placing a firm hand upon the librarian's forearm as if to keep him from floating to the ceiling and further damaging the glass, "we should begin. If you will join us in the dining hall—which also serves as our place of meeting—we can set our heads together on a host of important items."

The Firegem longed to be home.

It was the only explanation Kal-Gadras could manage as a fine, prevailing wind swept the single-masted ship along—almost as if being pushed—on flat, glassy seas. With a full sail and even keel, the Elven lord had little else to do but man the tiller and marvel at the ingenious design and impeccable craftsmanship of the sleek Eretian vessel.

As able as the Elven boatwrights were—especially those on the southern shore— there was a clear difference between the new navigational assembly they had crafted to replace the Eretian one so heavily damaged on the approach to the Isle of the Nine Perpetual Winds and the rest of the vessel.

The Ereti reigned supreme when it came to surviving the seas.

On the morning of his second day, still within sight of the shoreline of the southern border, Kal-Gadras watched the wild horses of Ahkete-Val—the Valley of the Horses—as they ran free across the sand and along the cliffs above. He could hear the racing heart of Lethir-na as she looked with longing on the place where she was born.

"I know how you feel, my friend," Kal-Gadras whispered in her ear. "I too am often far from home." He thought about Hir and how he wished his stalwart palomino could be with him here to see this, and of Poet, Aldemere's magnificent ivory stallion, a gift from Nemmerle when the son of a jester had saved her sole son's life.

For four more days, the steady sailing vessel made its way across the Sea of Silence. Each evening, Kal-Gadras would scan the cloudless, star-filled sky for some sign of Abyr-Goon-Draad, but the stardragon did not yet choose to honor him with its presence.

Then, on the seventh day, the Mark of Gal-Rashand began to itch and soon began to burn.

Aldemere's Dilemma

Shielding his eyes against the blinding brightness of the sun, Kal-Gadras searched the skies for the elusive Ambir Dragon.

The ship began to rock, and the once-unbroken sea began to part with the fury of an undersea explosion, although this was no mere shifting of the seafloor. Kal-Gadras readied his shield and his spear as the tips of two great wings broke the surface of the sea.

Before him was a sea dragon, and he knew why it had come.

Reining Poet toward Castle Silveth, Aldemere cursed the fog around the Minor Sentinel Lake, which obscured his view of the castle. A dangerous natural condition unforeseen by those who had designed it, this fog, which rose up thick each morning, had nearly handed Garamin a victory in the Rebellion.

Aldemere had worked closely with Sir Linead, knight-marshal of the Combined Armies of Glittereye, to ensure that an enemy would never again be able to use that to his advantage. At the northern and southern tips of both the Minor and Major Sentinel Lakes, guardposts had been constructed, complete with a complicated signal system using fire and glass designed by Master Talorous. In each guardpost were stationed a pair of knights, with a third continually scouting the perimeter.

To offer added protection to the interior of the castle, Aldemere had ordered the construction of additional lookout and archer stations as well as a thick oak door with a triple-lock system for the armory. Before anyone could open the door, the guard on duty, the Chief Knight of the Central Barony, and Aldemere all had to insert their keys into the locks and release their mechanisms at the same moment. Several of the highest-ranking knights had offered arguments against and conjured half a dozen scenarios to try to dissuade the captainguard from such a complicated system, but he refused to allow rebels and other enemies to have access to the castle's weaponry ever again.

All of the added defenses had necessitated a greater number of knights be stationed in and around the castle, and Aldemere had assigned several to draw up and maintain what had become long lengths of duty lists, all of which he had to review and approve at the beginning of each new week.

Aldemere also made it his habit to visit once daily the guardposts at either the Major or Minor Sentinel. As he headed for the castle after visiting the knights who guarded the Minor Sentinel, he heard the hooves of a fast-approaching horse. Drawing his sword at the same instant the guards drew theirs, he rocked back in the saddle, driving his heels deeper into the stirrups. Positioning his shield across his chest, he yelled into the fog, "Come no closer! Identify yourself!"

He heard the grunt of the horse as its rider pulled hard on the reins not thirty feet before him.

"Sir Aldemere, is that you? It is Sir Peecwyl—I come with urgent news."

"Remain where you are," Aldemere replied, signaling Poet into a trot. "I shall come to you."

Aldemere willed himself to breathe evenly as he approached the not yet visible rider. It had sounded like Sir Peecwyl—they had fought for many months together in the northern mountains—but he could not make assumptions.

Then he saw Peecwyl's shield with its familiar lion and crossbow charges and the leather patch the veteran knight used to cover the place where his eye used to be. He was running a gloved finger up and down the scar that ran beneath it.

"Spoiling for a fight, are we?" he said with a laugh.

"I will not be fooled out here. We must always be alert. I expect every man under my command—and under yours as Chief Knight of the barony—to do the same."

"Sheath your sword and drop your shield, old friend," Peecwyl said, saluting his former commander. "Now that you know it is me, I find it unsettling that you still sit there so aggressively poised for a fight. We saw much in the mountains, you and me. It has made you a capable commander and strategist, but it has also darkened your heart."

When the campaign in the north had gone on to the point where Aldemere had ordered the assassination of two tribal kings, Peecwyl had been the one to argue most forcefully against it. He carried a deep admiration for Elde the Jester's son. He had been Aldemere's vicious protector when the young knight had lain unconscious outside the gates of Silveth in the final hours of the Rebellion.

So much treachery and fighting had turned a mischievous boy into a shadow-laden man.

"I mean no offense, Sir Peecwyl," Aldemere replied, sheathing the short sword Crow Feather and lowering his shield. "The Deities know I owe you my life. You said you have urgent news…"

"Corvit sent this with one of the messengers accompanying the northern delegation to the Trade Council meetings in the east," Peecwyl replied, handing over a scroll, which Aldemere promptly scanned.

29   *Aldemere's Dilemma*

"Has Sir Linead read this yet?" Aldemere asked, rolling the scroll and placing it in his saddlebag.

Shaking his head, Peecwyl replied, "Sir Linead is inspecting the southern army and will not return for several days. I take it you are in agreement with my concerns?"

"You see more with your one eye than most knights do with two," Aldemere said, urging Poet into a gallop. "I am glad you are by my side."

"Surrender to me the witch's eyes, and I will end you quickly!" the sea dragon screamed, holding station in the air twenty feet above Kal-Gadras's little vessel. "If you choose to deny what I demand, I will take you piece by piece in the course of many days."

"And if you try to fight me," Kal-Gadras answered, his voice amplified by the activated Mark upon his neck, "I shall inflict upon you the same."

"Listen to me, Elf!" the dragon screamed, rearing back as if preparing to release a stream of fire. "I am the sea dragon Borrenax, brother to Flemvemor whom the traitorous dragon slew, and to Diette and Simnac, who met their end at the hands of your Human companion. I shall grant to you no mercy. Give me what I want!"

He is not coming closer, Kal-Gadras observed. *If he had the fire-gift, he would have already used it.*

It was then he noticed the poor condition of its wings, and the scarred and vulnerable spaces along the dragon's torso where layers of scales should be.

He is old, Kal-Gadras thought, *and does not want to fight, although he cannot resist the Firegem*.

"I am waiting, Elf!" Borrenax hissed, although his voice was noticeably weaker. "I shall not ask again."

"You do not want to fight me," Kal-Gadras answered. "I can see that you are old, and you are tired. The power of the witch's eyes is compelling you. Sink once more beneath the sea. I do not wish to kill you—and you know that I shall. I carry within me the power of Gal-Rashand, first of the Elves and slayer of the mighty dragon Rilvax. My quest is sacred and time is of the essence. I command you, let me pass."

Kal-Gadras could sense the hesitation in the ancient dragon's eyes, but the Firegem's force was strong in its power to lure. A subtle twitch in Borrenax's battered body cued his intent to attack.

"Abyr-Goon-Draad, forgive me," the Lord of the South Shore whispered as the sea dragon aimed its dull and yellowed claws at his chest as it started its descent. "I take no joy in this."

In an instant, it was over. Borrenax's wings, tattered and torn, made him veer as he attacked, exposing his chest to the tip of the tempered Elven spear as he hovered for an instant just off the starboard side of the vessel. In order to spare him any more than a moment's pain, Kal-Gadras made a powerful upward thrust, aiming dead center to ensure he would pierce the creature's heart.

Kal-Gadras could swear that, as Borrenax's body sank into the sea amidst torrents of blood and bile, the sea dragon kept his dying eyes affixed on the pouch that held the witch's eyes.

The Firegem.

It began to pulse with a steady, insistent beat as the Mark of Gal-Rashand once more went to sleep.

"I must hasten to Ferrukkla," Kal-Gadras said to the sky, dropping his shield and rinsing the spear in the water. "If this cursed object holds such irresistible power that an aged, defenseless dragon would give its life in a quest to possess it, what chance has an Elf such as me?"

As if in response to his words, the winds began to blow, and the ship resumed its course.

Taking hold of the tiller, Kal-Gadras watched with sadness as the last few inches of the fallen dragon's wings sank beneath the sea.

After a simple but capably prepared meal of boiled chicken, steamed vegetables, and fried potatoes in broth—eaten in contemplative silence, as was the Seers way—Sullus and Cortus quietly cleared the bowls and plates. Once the dining table was empty, the remaining five Seers rotated it one hundred and eighty degrees to signify the hall had now become a place of meeting and council, where they would not only permit speaking, but also encourage it.

Standing in his place at the head of table, Dictus placed his hands in the sleeves of his robes and bowed his head. Knowing their traditions, Talorous and Laurianna rose and did the same in coordination with the others. "If our guests would so permit," Dictus began, his voice resonant in its solemnity, "I would ask our chief incantor, Vitus, to offer a song of prayer to the Five Deities of Mynoweth, that they may guide us in our talks."

"You honor us by asking, Lord Dictus," Talorous answered, not looking up, "although I would not presume to question any act undertaken in the Gods and Goddesses' names."

"Well spoken, Master Teacher," Dictus replied, motioning with a movement of his head toward Vitus that he should now begin his song.

> All honor to our Deities, Five for whom we live
> Fair favor from our Deities, this is what we ask
> Iryah, who gives sun and moon, who lights our days and
nights
> Taplah, who brings rain and snow, water, wind, and sleet
> Cirrah, god of skyblankets, shrouder of the skies
> Liosah, who made stones, mountains, hills, and ores
> Aklah, queen of birds and beasts, weaver of our souls
> Bless us with your bounties that we may serve you well

When the song was ended, all who were gathered whispered, "May we serve you well."

"Let us take our seats, for the meeting has begun," Dictus said, opening wide his arms in a gesture of welcome and blessing. "And let us speak with truth, that none may doubt our hearts. Brother Ayron—as Keeper of the Rites, it seems wise that you should start."

Brother Ayron—short in stature and wide in girth and not used to speaking before anyone but the Seers (and rarely enough to them)—took a sip of water and tried to clear his throat.

"I have not much to say on the matter of the kingdom's ad… adherence to the rites established by the first of our Order, thousands of years ago. King Dylwyn is a wise and pious ruler. He has demonstrated this in his—um, excuse me… just another sip of water… his continued observance of the Festival of Eyeclear and his maintenance of the Chapel of the Trying Soul in Castle Silveth. Yes. He is pious. He is…"

Sensing the terrible awkwardness created by his having to address the Seers' guests, Dictus motioned for Ayron to sit.

"Brother Ayron—yes, that is the simple remedy, have another sip of water—have you any concern about the Dragon's Tower, and its honoring of the stardragon?"

"I do not. It was Aklah who made the dragons, and it is a not… not unpopular… belief amongst the masses, yes—the people as it were—that the Ambir Dragon brought to a close the Long Winter, clearly as Aklah's emissary. As long as we honor the dragon, we are honoring the goddess."

"Let us not forget that the Long Winter was thrust upon our world as a punishment for the actions of rebellion forced upon the people by elite, embittered barons and their angry, ambitious sons. Just look upon the cairns that were not there before the recent uprising and you shall fast remember."

This came from Amilus, the Lord of Burial Rites.

"No one shall forget," Vitus said, grasping Amilus's shoulder. "We are all aware of Talorous's position on the matter of the Long Winter, and the Ambir Dragon's role in ending it. We heard enough about it and of his friends the Elves as we were engaged in prayer and supplication in order to do our rather considerable part in bringing it to an end."

"Now, Brother Vitus," began Dictus, a cautionary tone in his voice.

"No need to have him temper his tone on my account," Talorous said, smiling. "Vitus and I have been differing in our views since I was apprenticed to the heralds by Renald the Jester and he was shining silver in the Chapel of the Trying Soul. Come to that, you and I have had our own disagreements, have we not, Brother Dictus? Surely, you agree that how and why the Long Winter ended is far less important than our making sure it never happens again. Is that not correct, Brother Vitus? Is that not why we have come together?"

"Yes. Yes of course," Vitus mumbled, knowing Talorous had outmatched him.

Cortus, who, in addition to his duties in the kitchen, was responsible for maintaining the five wooden statues in the atrium with a daily application of oils, was next to offer his thoughts. "Then let us speak of how we do so in the midst of larger armies, a greater show of military might in and around the castle, and a group of barons that were either there when it started or are related to those that were?"

"One of whom is a former knight himself!" Vitus shouted.

"And another who *proclaimed* himself a knight after his dismissal from the squirehood," Amilus added.

"Brothers! Brothers, please!" Talorous shouted in a voice that stopped them cold. "This is getting out of hand. I assure you—I share almost all of your concerns. It is true that our beloved Glittereye has become ever more steadily a kingdom of military might whose barons enjoy an admittedly problematic level of

Aldemere's Dilemma

prosperity that goes more than a measure beyond simply meeting their basic needs. But as a student of history—a pursuit shared to greater and lesser degrees by you all—I know that this has always been the fatal flaw of men. Revisit the tales in the First Book of Ancestry and they will surely remind you that the ungoverned massing of power and riches was the bud that bloomed into Glittereye. Vitus scowls at the mention of our allies the Elves, and their belief in a single goddess, but they watch us from afar, hoping our leaders have learned from their mistakes. We cannot thrive without them, and Dylwyn knows this well."

The scowl on Vitus's face deepened at the mention of the First Book of Ancestry. "How dare you speak of the great blasphemer at our table, within our very own walls!" the chief incantor bellowed. "Manthes Fragenoar was the one who banished us here, to sleep and eat with the cows!"

"Brother Vitus," Talorous said, with as disarming a smile as the old man could muster. "I did not speak his name. You did."

Before Vitus could answer, he felt Dictus's hand upon his arm, forcing him to swallow his words along with a steaming mouthful of broth.

"What are we to do?" asked Sullus, the gentle temple gardener and keeper of the beasts, just to break the thick-as-butter silence.

"Brother Farvon can speak to that," Dictus answered, motioning to the Keeper of the Scrolls. "Have you readied your lists and histories? I see by your sack you have... Well then—share with us the tales of what other Seers did, in the days when chieftains ruled and our place at their table was prime."

"How many more miles to Eerbell?" Baron Ralin asked, packing his provisions and readying his horse after spending the night in the rain. "I have done very little but ride since I departed from Spiltrow more than a week ago, and I crave some hospitality!"

"If we push the horses, we can be there by early afternoon, even with the mud," Baron Chrystan answered. "Baroness Ashlin should have Eerbell well prepared for our arrival. I had occasion to visit her and Baron Colar several years ago and although he was head of house, she clearly ran the home."

"I am ecstatic to know it," Ralin answered, taking the saddle. "I hear she brews a potent walnut beer. It will make the miles and all the lousy rain and hardship worth it."

You have been on your best behavior, Chrystan thought. *I have to wonder what a few stiff mugs might bring.*

They had been traveling for two days, mostly in the rain and in no mood to speak. Eric and Lan rode with hoods up and heads down, wondering silently to themselves and with the occasional look to one another just why it was they had volunteered to come.

As for Ralin, he had said little to nothing of interest to Chrystan or, by extension, to the king. *I wonder if he trusts me*, Chrystan considered, knowing that Vellom's son was almost certainly wondering the same of him.

Two and a half hours into the morning ride, the road became so bad it forced them to walk the horses or risk a fall. Ralin pulled a flask from his saddlebag and, pulling the cork with a gleam in his eye, took a long, deep, and clearly needed swallow.

"Anyone care for a swig?" he asked, offering the libation to each of his companions in turn. "I filled a few flasks with the hazelnut mead from the castle—so that some of the other barons—and the baroness—might have a sample before considering placing an order. It will no doubt fetch a more than fair price at the trade negotiations."

"As head of the Central Barony, I thank you for supporting our interests," Chrystan said with a nod, declining a taste of the mead with a dismissive upraised hand. "We are new to this game of coin and commerce, Ralin. At least, I am. If we stick together, we might just come out with favorable trades for us all."

"We shall best be served by watching Tooras and Ciloto," Ralin answered, taking another long pull on the flask after Eric and Lan declined. "They are old and crafty, and they will try to make a play. Tooras has no doubt lost some standing with the Elves, despite the daily patrols King Dylwyn makes him ride. Who is to say how favorably or not the Elves shall react to a woman being charged with the running of the eastern forests."

"I think you forget, old friend," Eric said with a laugh, "that the whole of Marlooq Fer is governed by a woman. Baroness Ashlin might be their favorite!"

"You forget *yourself*, Sir Eric," Ralin said, not returning the mirth. "Yes, we were squires together, and had our share of laughs, but you are only a knight, and I am now a baron. Perhaps you should keep your eye out for bandits and refrain from speaking on things of which you do not know."

"Yes, my baron," Eric said, his tone devoid of sarcasm. "You are of course correct. I will ride ahead a hundred yards and see what I can see."

Aldemere's Dilemma

Not wanting to be an additional target of Ralin's insults and jabs, Sir Lan volunteered, "And I will drop back fifty yards and make sure we are not being followed."

"You do that," Ralin said as the pair mounted and rode away. "Usefulness is what makes a man a necessary part of any endeavor. And, as much as I would like to, Chrystan, I am not sure it is wise to speak any further about our making any alliances. I wish to keep my options as open as my mind. I am sure you understand."

"I do indeed," Chrystan said with a smile.

Better than you think.

"You need not show me the library if you are not up to it," Laurianna said to Farvon when Talorous and the other six Seers had excused themselves for bed. "Dictus had you speak the evening away. I am sure that must be tiring."

Packing away the last of his materials into the threadbare sack from which he had pulled them, one by one, as the night drug mercilessly on, Farvon shook his head. "All the talking has left me wide awake. I would welcome the company while I put these scrolls away. But if *you* are too tired…"

"Not at all," Laurianna answered, opening the door that led to the atrium, which was the only way of getting to the library other than through the dormitory.

"Thank you," Farvon said, making sure to keep from smiling. "If there is anything you would like to know about the history of the five statues or the layout of the atrium, I shall be honored to enlighten you."

After passing the statue of Iryah on their way to the library entrance, which sat between the statues of Taplah and Cirrah, Laurianna said in a whisper, "Questions… I do. I understand why Iryah stands alone, for she is queen among the Deities. But why do the other goddesses stand there near the wall adjoining the chapel, while the gods are over here, adjoining the wall of the library? And why is Cirrah not nearer to his sister, Iryah?"

"True to your academic bent," Farvon said, putting down his sack, "you ask shrewd and probing questions no other visitors have ever asked. At least, not of me."

"Are you too tired to answer?" asked Laurianna, a hint of a smile on her lips.

"Not at all. Let me take your second question first, as it is the easiest to answer, although I must venture a question of my own to do so. Have you any siblings?"

"A brother and a sister."

"Older? Younger?"

"I am the eldest. My sister is the youngest."

Farvon spread his arms. "And how did you get on, you and your younger sister? Were you seated next to one another at the family table?"

"Very clever, Brother Farvon." Laurianna laughed. "In fact, we were not. Our brother sat between us, so we would not quarrel and ruin the meal. What of the other question?"

"Take your pick of answers," Farvon said with a shrug. "Some say that males are the keepers of our knowledge, so the two gods guard the library. But then you ask yourself, if the goddesses guard the chapel, are the goddesses all supreme?"

Laurianna leaned in close. "And what is it *you* think, Brother Farvon?"

"Me?" asked the junior Seer, his voice cracking as he did so. "I think that supreme goddesses are all well and good for Elves, but that our Deities are more equitable in their rule than such a notion implies. And as far as the males all being the keepers of the knowledge, you are living proof that this is not steadfastly so."

"Does that make you uncomfortable, Brother Farvon?" Laurianna asked, as the Keeper of the Scrolls abruptly entered the library.

Opening his bag and putting his attention on the work he had before him, Farvon answered, "Not at all. If I may speak freely, what I said about goddesses being favored only by the Elves… that is more my superiors' words than mine. There is much about our ways, and the running of this temple, with which I disagree."

"If you wish you speak of it," Laurianna whispered, scanning the shelves to see what materials they contained, "I am more than happy to listen. I noticed right away that you are different from the others. Talorous and I agree that if there is to be any progress between the academics and priests in aiding the king while protecting our own separate interests, individually and collectively, in this new era we are entering that it will not be made with Dictus and Vitus."

After emptying his sack and lighting several candles, Farvon pulled two chairs to a table piled with scrolls and motioned for Laurianna to sit. "There is much on my mind. These are complex times, and I could use a friend."

As the Night Guardians, the two moons of Mynoweth, began their slow descent, Farvon spoke his thoughts, as he never had before. Laurianna listened attentively, adding ideas of her own. When at

Aldemere's Dilemma

last they parted ways, mere minutes before a brother rang the bell to summon the Seers to chapel, Farvon knew what he must do.

Although how he was going to manage it, he could not begin to guess.

For four days more the winds blew fair and the seas maintained their calm as the single-masted ship brought its cargo of Elf, horse, and Firegem toward the island of the witch. Scanning the skies and waters for any signs of dragons, Kal-Gadras stayed fixed to the tiller as Caecaelev's eyes, which he had stowed in the bow of the ship soon after his slaying of Borrenax when their ever-increasing pulse began to strain his heart—glowed ever brighter with the miles.

As the craft approached the western shore of the forbidding and mysterious island his people called Ferrukkla, the reasoning behind its name—the Place of Flames—became immediately, abundantly clear.

Ringing the island for as far as he could see was an unbroken wall of blue-green flame the height of a full-grown Elf. Half a mile beyond it, at the foot of an ash-grey mountain rising steeply through the clouds, was a matching ring of fire.

Through the shimmering disturbance of air that it produced, he noticed a semicircular shadow that indicated a cave.

Kal-Gadras's instincts told him the witch was waiting for him within it.

Securing the ship to an outcropping fifty feet from shore, for he dared not bring it closer—the heat of the flames was already flushing his cheeks—the Elven lord secured the rudder, dropped the sail, and gathered his sword and shield. Securing the pouch with the Firegem to the pommel of his saddle, he readied Lethir-na to leave the ship.

"I am glad to have you with me," he whispered in her ear, as they entered the heated water and began the swim to shore.

Keeping one hand on the pouch and the other on the bridle, Kal-Gadras began to wonder how he would make it through the fire.

Hold the Firegem to your heart, and the flames will let you pass.

Although he could not see the speaker, Kal-Gadras knew the voice.

"Abyr-Goon-Draad," he said, as the Mark began to pulse.

Before exiting the water, Kal-Gadras gripped the Firegem and held it to his heart. As he stood upon the beach, mere inches from the fire, he no longer felt its heat, although the mare was not so blessed. From the saddle and her flanks, steam began to rise.

Keep your hand upon her heart and your horse shall not be harmed.

Doing as the voice instructed and holding the Firegem, which glowed a brilliant red, even tighter to his chest, Kal-Gadras walked steadily toward the flames.

"I shall not be afraid," he whispered, although in truth he was.

Willing his eyes not to close, Kal-Gadras stepped within the fire, watching in awe as the blue-green flames leapt forth, intermingling with the erupting radiance of the Firegem to produce an aura of purple protective light around him and Lethir-na.

It energized his body and filled him full of strength.

"Blessed be," he cried, passing through the flames unscathed.

Finding himself aching to once again experience the invigorating energy produced by the alchemical combination of Firegem and flame (for the purple aura had been extinguished within an eye-blink of his passage) Kal-Gadras took his hand from Lethir-na and broken into a run, eager to enter the flames that danced at the foot of the mountain.

Crossing the fiery threshold with neither fear nor hesitation, he pressed the radiant Firegem hard against his breast, welcoming the aura as it once again engulfed him. The minute he felt its energy, he stood fast in the flames, not wanting to let the feelings of strength and safety go.

Remember why you stand here. Remember Hir Marlooq. Others were tested. Others were tried. All of them destroyed. Do not let your guard down. Do not lose your way.

Not fully understanding Abyr-Goon-Draad's ominous warning, but knowing he must not question the words that he had heard, Kal-Gadras exited the flames, feeling his eyes fill with tears as the purple aura once more disappeared.

Gazing upon the mountain, Kal-Gadras dropped to his knees as its cold, forbidding façade revealed its endless dangers.

There were myriad shards of ice, all of them reflecting, as though daring him to climb them, the merciless frozen lake upon which he now stood.

Talorous had been riding the road back to Silveth for over an hour with Laurianna by his side after four days of conference—argument, mostly—with the Seven Lord Seers before he decided to speak.

"What are your thoughts about our pious, punctilious hosts?" he asked, pulling a bit of dried fruit from his satchel and scanning the sky for Nigredo, whom he had left with a constable of his fellow ravens so as not to subject him to the comments and stares of the staid and humorless Seers.

"They are each as different as the five Deities they are devoting their lives to serve," Laurianna began, as Nigredo descended from the clouds to perch on his master's arm. "Yet their alliances to each other and their individual and collective aspirations overpower their devotion. Dictus and Vitus are clearly in control, although their views are as antiquated as the vows they took in their youth. Amilus, seeing the fields of the dead extended all around him, is rightfully bitter about the Rebellion. In time, his anger will fade. Ayron, Sullus, and Cortus are content to follow orders. They are at peace with their simple, unburdened lives. They are meek. Ayron especially—he is Keeper of the Rites in title only. It is Dictus and Vitus who wholly set their course."

"Accurate, although obvious," Talorous answered, his mood brightening at the return of Nigredo, despite his less than pleased reply. "And what of Brother Farvon?"

"Farvon is the reason you asked me to attend."

Talorous nodded in approval. "Accurate and not so obvious. I have been observing him for years. In truth, I had hoped to persuade his father to allow him to study under the tutelage of the Council of Elders as a child, but it was not to be. I believe that he is the key to considerable change when it comes to the role of the Seers in the kingdom, and mark my words, Laurianna—things most certainly need to change."

"Accurate, although obvious," Laurianna said with a raise of her brow, willing to risk a scowl from her teacher in order to assert her right of place on the path she saw unfolding. "Subjecting poor Farvon to a vomiting of their history for the better part of an evening to make a case for an enhanced position in the kingdom—and the castle—as the best solution to our present problems proved the age-old adage that one retreats into the old ways when they are set against the new."

"So how do we best help both ourselves and your new friend Farvon?" Talorous asked with a grin, nudging his horse into a trot.

"I do have some ideas," Laurianna answered, matching her teacher's pace. "Though, at least for the foreseeable future, I think that it is best that he is left to help himself."

Although he had been climbing for hours, Kal-Gadras felt alert and full of energy. Having bound the Firegem securely to his chest with his sash and a length of rope, the Elven warrior ascended the mountain with a surety and confidence he knew was far too strong to be coming from inside of him.

Will you be able to part with the Firegem?

Will you bargain with the witch?

Will you succumb to its power, as did Borrenax, although it means your life?

Although it may mean Hir Marlooq's?

Pushing the voices from his head (which he realized were his own, as they had been when he had resisted High Lord Petror), Kal-Gadras climbed a little faster toward the entrance to the cave.

Then he had a revelation.

His existence was constant parallels.

From the second he had started on his quest to reach the witch's island, Kal-Gadras had been treading familiar, well-worn paths.

His rescue by Aldemere from the Livesand in their youth.

His rite of passage with the water asp on the shores of the Sea of Silence.

The deadly fight for the Alliance.

The quest to find Abyr-Goon-Draad.

His mission to save his mother.

So many difficult ascents. So many treacherous journeys.

Why must it be him? Why must he bear the Mark? Be the son of Hir Marlooq?

Suddenly there he was, at the entrance to the cave.

Peering through the darkness, Kal-Gadras loosened his sash. He lay the Firegem in his palm.

"Caecaelev!" he shouted, before he changed his mind.

Only an echo returned in answer, and that voice was full of fear.

Adjusting his eyes to the darkness, he stepped inside the mouth of the mountain, resisting the impulse to unsheathe his sword and raise his shield.

What he saw there made his heart fall.

There was no fire, nor bones, nor refuse—no pile of brush and moss that might serve as a simple bed.

Caecaelev was not inside.

Perhaps she never had been.

Despite the bustle and din of the morning chores taking place in the Great Hall of the castle, Aldemere insisted that Peecwyl and Linead meet him there to talk.

"I think better in the room where I first slept amongst pages and squires," he explained amid their protests, "and it is good for these future knights to see us meeting under peaceful, cooperative conditions rather than solely on the battle and tournament fields."

"Speaking of," Sir Linead responded, "when will you pick a squire? You should ask Sir Eva's for recommendations. Surely even the great Jester-Knight of Glittereye will not strap on his own armor and wash the mud from his horse when the tournament day arrives?"

Such ribbing was part of the way of life with knights of high station, and Aldemere fought the urge to make a blunt, defensive reply to the burly, black-haired knight who took a seat beside him. Sir Linead had fought with distinction during the suppression of the Rebellion and had more than earned his commission as knight-marshal of the Combined Armies of Glittereye. He did not report to the captainguard and held a superior rank to the chief knights of the baronies, such as Peecwyl.

Tread carefully, Aldemere told himself. *Now is not the time to make enemies of allies.*

"I have been preoccupied with my new duties and refining the castle's defenses, but I know the stables are abuzz with anticipation regarding my selection of a squire." He looked around the room at the determined faces of the young boys stacking wood, sharpening blades, and polishing armor, thinking back to when he had worked and studied beside those who came before them. "If it pushes them all the harder, it is best to let them wait as long as I possibly can."

In truth, Aldemere had little interest in the tournaments in which half the kingdom expected him to not only participate but also win. Sir Laurel had been champion of many in succession, setting a precedent his replacement could not hope to match.

I am about to have a child, he thought with a sudden ache in his gut. *How many children shall I take beneath my wing?*

"With all due respect to you both," Peecwyl interjected, motioning to the report he had given to Aldemere several days before, "we must carefully consider the ramifications of Corvit's news from the north. I have been most impatient for you to return from the south so we could discuss this with you, Linead."

"You were wise to share with me this news," the knight-marshal replied, slowly re-scanning the parchment. "I of course never served in the mountains, but I have studied well the tactics and habits of the three nomadic tribes that constantly threaten the population who make their homes and livelihoods in the north. I know what you both endured. I have read both of your accounts of your time there, and I have heard many of Sir Evas's stories—I appreciate that you must have left more than just your eye upon those frozen fields, Sir Peecwyl, and you have my utmost respect."

Admission of respect for fellow fighters was also as deeply an aspect of a veteran knight's existence as the ribbing they gave and got. If Aldemere had harbored any doubt as to why Chrystan had chosen Linead for his successor, he knew he never would again.

"Your kind words do me honor," Peecwyl replied with a salute, "and I am more confident than ever that you understand how important it is that we not let those cannibal bastards ever again get the slightest upper hand. If they are up to something—if that is why they are thus far so inactive, so silent, as Corvit has reported—then we must find out why, and do so with all haste."

Anyone who had spent time in the northern mountains, civilian or military, knew that, once the snows stopped, the Riverskabs, Caveraiders, and Krags would begin their raids on the outlying settlements in the mountains south of the Unsettled Wilderness after holing up all winter with little to sustain them. Although the assassination of the Riverskab and Caveraider chieftains following the death in battle of the leader of the Krags ended the war in the north, no one had expected the tribes to stop their raiding.

The fact that all three tribes had thus far refrained from doing so was an ominous bit of mystery to any martial mind.

"I shall select a scouting party to depart within the hour," Linead said with a tone that made it clear he was not seeking approval to do so. "They will head to the north of the mines and see what they can find. In the meantime, I will send word to all Chief Knights to increase the intensity of their units' daily drills. If we need to go to war, do not doubt that we are ready."

The wind was beating ever more harshly upon his exhausted body as Kal-Gadras began his descent. Although he had refastened the Firegem to his breast, it protected him no longer.

It had gone dormant, as though the disappointment the Elf had felt had put the eyes of the witch to sleep.

"I cannot believe it is all a lie," he said aloud, offering them both a shred of hope.

It was not enough.

Concentrate, he thought, as his foot sought some security on a sharp, thin angle of ice. *You are completely on your own.*

It was then that he started to fall.

Absurd as it seemed, his eyes tracked to a patch of moss, slick with diamondlike flecks of ice, which stood out from the bluish

43   *Aldemere's Dilemma*

expanse of mountain where his foot had been resting just a handful of seconds before.

The frigid air through which he fell was like thousands of needles entering his skin and assaulting his tendons and bones. He could feel the weight of accumulating ice crystals tugging at him as they formed in his long, straight hair.

Below him, the frozen lake awaited, ready to splinter his bones.

Kal-Gadras, Lord of the South Shore and bearer of the Mark of Gal-Rashand, was falling to his death.

As he passed a jagged outcrop, he tried his best to grab it, but its mossy edges would not offer him their aid.

Mother... I am sorry that I have failed you. I am sorry beyond words.

In an instant the lake was there, throwing his handsome reflection back at him just before it crushed his delicate features beyond all recognition or chance of survival.

As the surface began to crack, the surrounding world went dark.

Assuring Anastasia he was fine, and that Kal-Gadras was most likely fine as well, despite his nightmare of the fall, Aldemere quickly dressed and headed out barefoot and unarmed into the hallway, hurrying past the Chapel of the Trying Soul and the castle's interior guest quarters to the Great Hall's open doors.

Entering quietly so as not to disturb the pages, squires, and lesser knights who slept there, he took a seat beneath the massive woodhart's head that was the Great Hall's central feature.

The magnitude of the great and terrible events Ralin's fascination with that prize had set into motion, Aldemere was still attempting to process.

Symbols, badges, and prizes. How empty they all seemed, yet so many wished to amass them.

Kal-Gadras was not dead. Aldemere felt it in his heart. Nevertheless, his friend was surely in trouble and no matter how intertwined was their bond, there was no way he could help.

Despite his quests and accolades and the titles he possessed, at this moment, in this room, Aldemere felt as useless as a squire who had forgotten his master's shield just prior to inspection.

Finding an empty bed of straw in the corner he once inhabited, he looked across the distance into the woodhart's lifeless eyes and willed himself to sleep.

Kal-Gadras awoke to the foul smell of a fire built of smoldering seaweed and driftwood.

"The ice!" he yelled, raising his aching torso from a spongy bed of moss.

"Cannot hurt you. Never could. For it was only in your mind."

Focusing his eyes, Kal-Gadras peered across the sputtering blue-green flames of the fire toward the source of the cryptic words.

Caecaelev was sitting in the shadows just beyond.

She was laughing and clapping her hands

"You are truly a wonder, My Lord. Having journeyed all this way to find me, you seem truly surprised I am here!" Adding a handful of sage to the fire, Caecaelev ceased her cackling. "I expected more from you, Kal-Gadras. *Infinitely* more, in truth."

"Can you sense the Mark?"

"Same as it senses me. The Mark and its ageless roots—hidden deep inside you. I can even see your face, although blind to its outer features. Care to quench your thirst and liven up your hunger?"

Without waiting for an answer, she produced a bowl of steaming, watery soup and thrust it toward her guest.

He took it without hesitation and began to slurp it down.

"Easy there, My Lord. You have been through more than you know. My soup works well in *sips*, not so much in *slugs*."

"I know that I was falling…" Kal-Gadras whispered, placing the near-empty bowl beside him. "I should have fallen through the ice. Or, more likely, been burst like a pumpkin *against* it."

"And so you were—in a manner of speaking." Caecaelev leaned close to the fire, illuminating the singular mix of Elven and Human features her parents' forbidden love had conspired to create. Although she had no eyes, and her face and hands betrayed her age, her beauty was unmarred. "There are boundaries, my child. Nameless barriers with false façades. There are also places of depth, such as here, where you now sit. The only acceptable place for a creature such as me. Some are our own creations—the Humans excel at those—and there are others that Marlooq Fer places as needed around us, to keep us safe from harm, and those who would inflict it. Ferrukkla is a mystical mix of each. It tests, and it protects. It sets out obstacles and opens doors. I sense surprise from you still, young Elf," she said with a clap of her hands. "I would think your time chasing Abyr-Goon-Draad would make such paradoxical puzzles easy for you to fathom."

Aldemere's Dilemma

"Perhaps another time, without pressing matters at hand," Kal-Gadras answered, grasping the bowl and gulping down the last of the invigorating soup despite the witch's advice.

"You speak of your Mother's struggles," Caecaelev replied, making no offer to give him seconds. "Have you brought sufficient payment?"

"I have done what was required."

Do not hesitate! Kal-Gadras told himself, placing his hands upon his sash and feeling the power pulsing beneath them.

"I have suffered to bring it here."

Yet he could not find the will to release it.

"There have been others, you know," Caecaelev said with a sigh. "They sat in the ancient cypress clinging to the 'Gem with no other hope in their hearts than finding a way to keep it. To use it for their gain."

"What became of them, and how was it always returned?"

"They died just where they sat. Some of dehydration. Many of slow starvation. Some succumbed to the cold. Others to the heat. The 'Gem knows its way back to its nest high up in the ancient cypress. It never had far to go. Before you managed to claim it, half a dozen feet was all one Elf could muster. Your sitting here before me is truly the rarest of feats. Your mother was right to send you. *If* you can give it up."

"Of course I can give it up," Kal-Gadras answered, unfastening the sash that bound the Firegem to his breast.

He was surprised at the speed with which he grasped it, and the tightness of his grip as he held it in his hand.

"You must give it to me freely. If you have the slightest hesitation, if you even think that you are the Firegem's owner, it shall be of no use to me, and I will not cure your mother. You have but a single chance. The 'Gem and I will know. Do not doubt that for a moment."

Calling silently to his mother, and to the Ambir Dragon for strength to overcome his attraction to the Firegem, Kal-Gadras brought his arm slowly forward toward the witch.

"I shall not fall prey to its curse," Kal-Gadras said in a voice not quite his own. "I am Kal-Gadras of the South Shore. Bearer of the Mark of Gal-Rashand. I give you back your eyes."

Caecaelev leaned closer, until the fire singed her hair. "And you give them to me freely? Without hesitation or qualm?"

Kal-Gadras willed himself to nod. The Mark began to pulse.

"I do!"

In an instant, his hands were empty.

Kal-Gadras collapsed and cried.

Placing her eyes beside her, Caecaelev sat in silence while he sobbed.

When at last his tears had ebbed, she began to tell her story, talking far into the night.

Sailing for the South Shore the following afternoon, Kal-Gadras thought deeply upon all the witch had told him—of her visions and the future.

War was on the wind. He would play his part in the carnage and pain it would bring.

Hearing the two tolls from the bell in the castle's eastern tower that signaled the approach of one or more visitors to Silveth, Aldemere hurried from his borrowed bed of straw in the Great Hall, doing his best to avoid the stares of the squires and pages as he passed.

"Known or not?" he asked the twelve members of the King's Guard already assembled near the castle's innermost gate.

"Unknown at present, Sir Aldemere," answered the unit's commander. "He bears no shield or pennant. But the rider is alone, so the portcullises and outer gates have been opened and a unit of knights dispatched."

Aldemere could not help but feel some pride in the quick action and proper procedures undertaken by his men. Ordering a pair of soldiers to raise the inner gate and the unit to stay where they were, Aldemere felt a hand upon his bicep as he headed for the courtyard.

Reaching for his sword and then his dagger and realizing he was only in pants and shirt, Aldemere turned with a fierce look upon his face to see who was trying to stop him.

"I am sorry to touch you, Sir," one of the younger members of the unit whispered, retreating several steps. "But you are not wearing boots. Perhaps you want me to fetch some, Sir. And perhaps your sword and tabard…"

Before the lesser knight's immediate superior could unleash the torrent of angry words the captainguard could imagine marching up his throat, Aldemere raised his hand to stop him. "It is fine, Commander. Your man is right. This is no way to greet a visitor— especially one unknown. If he does not offer resistance, bring him into the guardhouse, and I shall converse with him there. I want all of the gates and portcullises closed as soon as possible."

As Aldemere turned to go, half a dozen additional knights, each with his sword in hand, entered hurriedly from the courtyard. In their

Aldemere's Dilemma

midst he saw the unexpected stranger, whose visage he remembered but could not place.

"He insisted on speaking with you immediately, Sir," the newly arriving unit's commander reported. "And his weapons were left with his horse without prompting."

Holding his hands before him to show he was unarmed, the stranger let out a laugh unnervingly at odds with his current situation. "Do not dress on my account, Captainguard Aldemere. I have pressing things to tell you, and boots are not required."

CHAPTER THREE

Thaker Ungerfil looked out across the still, blue waters of the Sea of Nau from the officers' lounge at the Admiralty-Mast in Llafen Eret. Try though he might to cease his hands from shaking, he was having little success.

After three long years of intensive training in all things nautical—from basic ship design, to sail configuration and navigation, to shipping laws, and management of crew—Thaker, in just a few hours, would be made a captain of a ship of his own, as his father, and so many of his ancestors, had before him. Turning his attention to a beautiful three-masted vessel moored at the entrance of the harbor he felt his heart begin to race. Surrounded by an ever-moving mass of harbormen, the *Salt-Serpent*, the flagship of the Eretian fleet, and soon to be his, was the center of attention of a group of stevedores loading her with supplies bound for Vaelsport. Beside her sat the *Sea-Sprite*, another fine three-master, whose destination was the same.

It was two days earlier that Hathom, Thaker's older brother, had been promoted to undersecretary to the warden of the waters, a gruff but shrewd engineer and capable sailor in his own right, named Kiegan Hefflar.

"Nervous?" Hathom asked, joining him at the window. "Because you look a little nervous."

"Of course I am nervous," Thaker replied, buttoning the top two buttons of his tunic and straightening—for at least the twelfth time in the past forty-five minutes—his sash. "I am about to be made captain of the pride of our fleet. Although, just before, I shall be escorted into the inner temple by the sea-shaman and allowed to commune with the Stone of the Ruenai. Would you not be nervous, my brother?"

Hathom nodded and frowned. "Why do you think I opted for administration?"

"Because you do not know the difference between a bilge, a berth, and abeam."

Which was, of course, only the usual teasing between brothers. Hathom, in order to hold his newly appointed position, had to learn as much or more than Thaker. He had already been through two years of Admiralty-Mast, the officers' training school, when the warden had chosen him for an internship positon on his staff fifteen years before.

"Maybe not," Hathom answered, indulging his brother on his admittedly important day, "but I would be wise enough to do whatever I could to prevent father from seeing your hands rattling like a busted winch. He is liable to give the captaincy to Silbern."

"I tell you, brother," Thaker replied, tugging on his tunic and straightening his sash for the thirteenth and fourteenth times, "he can have it."

"Have what?"

Thaker groaned as Silbern Skarling, his soon to be first officer, approached.

Standing just over five feet tall—which made him almost a full head taller than most Eretian males—Silbern made a fine-looking sailor in his new uniform, which was accentuated by three newly knotted beard braids, which hung to his belt, in the style of the Dwarves whose country he would soon have the chance to see.

"He wants to give you the *Salt-Serpent*," Hathom answered, laughing.

"As if your father would permit it," Silbern said, slipping his well-muscled hands into a pair of pristine gloves. "There has never been anyone but an Ungerfil in command of the *Salt-Serpent*, and I am betting there never will be. I am honored enough, Thaker, to be serving as your second in command. I mean that."

Thaker knew he did. "Rumor has it you were offered the *Sea-Sprite*," he said, hoping his own white gloves were not calling even more attention to his "rattling" hands, as Hathom had described them. "You should have taken it. Do I need to remind you that your own ancestor, Altear, was her first captain and his brother was her navigator? You and I battled to a tie in almost every area of proficiency—and you outscored me in the others—as my brother is fond of reminding me… So why did you turn her down?"

"For the same reason *your* hands are shaking and mine are not. Our ancestors' sea-shoes are impossible to fill. I have no intention to try. Dorrin Waelsbun is an excellent fit for captain of the *Sea-Sprite*. And his family is almost as important as yours."

"We should be going," Hathom said, motioning toward the door. "I heartily suggest you leave all your doubt and the charming but inappropriate self-deprecation in this room, the both of you. Like it or not, you are about to be made officers in the Eretian fleet, and a wee touch of arrogance and the proper worth in your walk are both admired and expected. Dorrin and the rest will be looking to you now. You were at the top of your class. Act like it."

"Yes, Mister Undersecretary," Thaker replied, with a quick salute and one last tug upon his tunic and his sash. "We will not let you down."

Appropriately dressed in light mail, a newly polished breastplate, and his cleanest pair of boots, Aldemere hurried down the hall to the Guard House, where Linead and Peecwyl were watching over Silveth's unnamed visitor. Unconsciously touching the Garter of Glittereye buckled around his right thigh and the Clausmer of the Jester-Knight hanging around his neck—on the same leather thong he had worn since his decision to combine his lineage and destiny half a decade ago—Aldemere studied the stranger.

Try as he might, Aldemere could not recall how he knew him, although there was no question that he did.

"You cut quite the impressive figure," the man said as Aldemere entered. "You are now the warrior I remember."

"You claim that you know me," Aldemere answered, suddenly wishing he had opted for a tunic and vest instead of his formal uniform. "In truth, I know your face as well—though I do not know from where."

"That has been the point," the stranger replied with a smile. "I have been tasked with looking after you, Sir Aldemere. Although I cannot say by whom, or share with you the why. Your fame runs far and wide—but certainly you know that."

"That has never been my aim."

"And that, my friend, is a fact as well known as your name."

"Enough of your endless riddles!" Peecwyl erupted, growing weary of the stranger's games. "It is true that our captainguard has earned a certain fame, and that there are many who wish him dead. How do we know you are not a spy or an assassin?"

"If I wanted your captainguard dead," the stranger replied, clearly undaunted by the one-eyed knight's display of anger, "he would be so, and I would be gone without you knowing I was here. There are half a dozen places one could enter this castle undetected."

"That is a lie!" Peecwyl yelled, grabbing the stranger by his collar and lifting him from his chair.

"That is enough, Peecwyl!" Aldemere countered, surprising himself with the strength of his impulse to jump to the nameless stranger's defense.

Peecwyl tightened his grip. "I am chief knight of the Central Barony," he said, his remaining eye an arrow aimed for Aldemere's throat. "This man passed, *uninvited*, through the lands that I am

Aldemere's Dilemma

responsible for protecting. He did so fully armed. Now he says he can breach the castle, which is *your* responsibility. How can you defend him? Because he knows your name and you once passed one another sauntering in some hall or trotting on some hill?"

"You need not feel so slighted, Sir Peecwyl," the stranger said, still undaunted by his now assailant. "I am also well aware of *your* heroism in the northern mountains. Many others are as well. As we are of the great strength and capable leadership of Sir Linead, knight-marshal of the Combined Armies of Glittereye. You are, all of you, accomplished, seasoned warriors. Which is why I have traveled across the northern lands to allow you all to abuse me."

"Peecwyl, let him go," Linead ordered, keeping his hand upon the pommel of his sword until his subordinate followed his order. He then approached the stranger. "Let us begin again. Starting with who you are, now that you have told us from where it is you come. If such a claim can be believed…"

Spreading his arms wide in a show of supplication, the stranger answered, "I am known as Frederick. To tell you of my lineage, or to reveal my family name, would entail the telling of a tale the length and breadth for which none of us has the time."

"Very well then, *Frederick*," Peecwyl said, the tone in his voice making it clear that he was out of patience, "give us a clear, riddleless accounting of why the captainguard knows your face and we may indulge you further."

"I fought as a mercenary in Sir Corvit's employ in the northern mountains when you defeated the cannibal clans. Aldemere no doubt saw me several times. You may have as well. I certainly saw much of him, as he transformed from a green soldier who knew nothing of battle other than what he had learned on the tournament field and in the books the squires skim into an inspiring leader and capable tactician. A warrior of virtue and of violence."

"Welcome then, to Glittereye, Frederick," Aldemere said in response, trying his best not to be lulled by the compliments. "Anyone who fought with us in the mountains is worthy of our trust. At least for the present moment."

"Do you take him at his word?" Peecwyl enquired, incredulity straining his voice. "I shall dispatch a hawk to Corvit, asking for confirmation. I do not recall him mentioning any *mercenaries* in his employ. All who fought for Glittereye fought for honor, not for coin. If you recall, Corvit's camps were in tatters, with reeking water and the men eating horseflesh to survive. Would he waste his precious currency on one the likes of *him*?"

"Send the hawk as soon as you can," Aldemere answered, concerned at how tightly Peecwyl was gripping the hilt of his sword. He then turned back to Frederick. "I trust you do not object to our taking steps to confirm your story. When did you last speak with Corvit? Is there any news from the north?"

Frederick shook his head. "I have no objections, Captainguard. As to Corvit, I have not seen him in many months. I have been busy further north—and in the forests to the east. There are enemies all around you, Jester-Knight. Some are closer than you think."

Protruding from the northeast shore of Llafen Eret, as though an ancient race of giants had beached their colossal craft, The Vessel of the Ruenai, the high holy temple of the Ereti, sat in solemn silence as her insides were filled with those attending the ceremony known as the Conferring of the Captaincy.

Built to the specifications of a three-masted Eretian sailing ship, the Vessel was the sacred location where the Ereti paid homage to their triad of deities, the Ruenai.

Hathom, Thaker, and Silbern found almost all of the six pairs of rough-hewn pews in the edifice already occupied when they arrived.

"Punctuality is the lifeblood of our officers," Admiral Ungerfil barked, glaring at Thaker through his bushy red brows. "And the same can be said of the undersecretary to the warden of shipping, Hathom. Kiegan Hefflar is not as patient as I am."

"I shall find him directly, Father," Hathom said, never losing his self-assured smile although Thaker noticed his shoulders ever so slightly drop.

"He is in conference with Ambassador Waelsbun—who, I might add, is due to sail with the timber ships headed for Mettlec tomorrow morning." It seemed to Hathom that the admiral's eyebrows were growing ever more bristly with his deteriorating demeanor. "They are inspecting the *Sea-Seeker*, which sits low in the water with a full load of provisions for the occupants of Vaelsport, just like the *Sea-Sprite* and my... I mean, Thaker's... ship."

"Old habits do die hard, Father," Hathom said, taking his leave. "I am confident Thaker feels no offense. See you after the ceremony, brother."

"Where are we to wait, Father?" Thaker asked, cursing his brother's ease and his own barely contained agitation. "I do not see Dorrin Waelsbun."

"You shall wait right here with me," the admiral answered, adjusting Thaker's sash. "Dorrin is attending to a minor problem with

Aldemere's Dilemma

the *Sea-Sprite*. He should be finished well before the Conferring ceremony begins."

"I hope it is nothing serious," Silbern offered, secretly hoping it was. Far from being grateful to his classmate for passing up a captaincy, Dorrin had taken his appointment as a second-best situation and a slight. The past few weeks of their working together had not been close to congenial.

The admiral shook his head. "Not serious as far as fixability, but serious when one considers the sloppiness shown by a crew that neglects to furl the sails when a storm is passing through. Technically the ship was not yet Dorrin's, but because her former captain has already assumed his post with the Tribunal of the Seas, she was Dorrin's responsibility. Come and take your seats. The Ruen-Eret shall soon begin their procession."

As if on cue with the admiral's words, all heads turned to the aft section of the Vessel as a pair of junior officers opened the tall oak doors, revealing the six priestesses and sea-shaman who held the responsibility for the care of the Vessel and all of the rituals that took place within its main expanse and Inner Temple. As they passed the fountain a dozen feet from the entrance, the assembly stood in unison as an eight-foot jet of saltwater shot upward from its center.

"We thank Vael, god of the sea, for blessing us with water," the gathered masses intoned.

The procession next arrived at a pool of water in the center of the temple upon which floated a polished metal brazier, filled with wood. As the sea-shaman poured oil over the wood and set it alight, the assembly said in unison, "We thank Xaer, lady of the forests, for granting us her children so we may build our ships and heat our homes."

Processing to the altar of oak and ash—which, like the Vessel itself, was shaped and outfitted like an Eretian ship with its masts removed—four of the priestesses lit candles. Two others filled a pair of bowls with water, pouring it over the miniature oak tree that grew in the spot where the central mast would be.

As the Ruen-Eret knelt as one before the altar, the assembly said in a single voice, "We thank Braen, lady of the wind, who breathes life into our sails."

When the ceremony was complete—a simplified form of the ritual normally enacted three times a day away from the public's eyes and every ninth day for anyone wishing to attend—the six priestesses and sea-shaman rose and took their seats behind the altar, which was positioned ten feet in front of the doors to the Inner Temple.

After a nod of the head from the sea-shaman, Grand Admiral Athes Ungerfil scanned the room to make sure that Dorrin, Hathom, the Warden, and the Ambassador to Mettlec were all present and at the ready. He then motioned for the assemblage to sit and to the attendants to close and lock the oaken doors of the Vessel.

"As always," he began, turning to the seven seated behind the altar, "we thank the Ruen-Eret for your continued service to the Ereti. It is through your devotion that the Ruenai are honored and appeased, and we are perpetually blessed with calm waters, ample woods, and favorable winds."

"Water, wood, and wind," the congregation said in unison.

When the room was once more silent, after a moment's extra reflection, Admiral Ungerfil continued. "We are brought together today for the Conferring of the Captaincy upon two of the best and brightest to have ever gone through the rigors of the Admiralty-Mast—Dorrin Waelsbun, who shall captain the *Sea-Sprite*—and Thaker Ungerfil—my second son—at the top of his class and appointed to command the flagship of the Eretian fleet, the *Salt-Serpent*. Dorrin, Thaker—please come forward with your first officers and your navigators."

As the six new officers took their places in front of the admiral, Athes saluted each in turn. "To confer upon your key officers their titles, I call upon the Tribunal of the Seas—Janzalon Waelsbun, Ammon Mastmin, and Sorva Kaelhul."

The trio of tribunes—dressed in blue, brown, and white robes to represent the three sacred elements of water, wood, and wind—stood and proceeded forward, two of them holding four pairs of silver epaulets in their white-gloved hands.

"Dorrin Waelsbun," Janzalon, his father, began, "whom do you choose as your first officer and navigator?"

"Gorish Bront shall be my first officer and Fagan Ronng, our navigator," came the reply.

"You choose both wisely and well," Janzalon replied, nodding to his fellow tribunes, who efficiently affixed the appropriate epaulets upon the shoulders of Dorrin's selections.

"And you, Thaker Ungerfil—whom do you choose as your first officer and navigator?" Janzalon asked.

"Silbern Skarling for first officer and Corbit Neergarn for navigator."

After the tribunes had affixed their epaulets, the newly commissioned officers took their seats, and Janzalon and his fellow tribunes returned to their places as well.

Aldemere's Dilemma

"The captain of a ship wields a mighty power," the grand admiral said, fixing his eyes upon Dorrin and Thaker. "In our earliest days of sailing the seas, power was abused and the Ruenai punished our ancestors. It was only through the intervention of the first of the Ruen-Eret, the sea-shaman Ettana, that the gods saw fit to place their trust in us again. Just as I, as grand admiral of the Eretian fleet, must consider not just myself but the needs of the fleet and of our country, so too must you navigate the rigging between courage and cowardice, between heroism and folly, between knowing when to consult your fellow officers or when it is wisest to seek solely your own council.

"You shall be tested," Athes continued, the slightest hint of emotion in his voice, "and the decisions you will be called upon to make will determine the fates of all of those around you." Pausing for a moment to clear his throat, the admiral let the gravity of what he was saying sink in. Then he added, "To ensure this is our practice, I—and all of the captains beneath me—must answer to the Grand Admiralty—and its head, Warden of the Waters Kiegan Hefflar."

Rising from his seat at the mention of his name, Warden Hefflar introduced, one by one, the eleven wealthy and venerable shippers, shipbuilders, and timber barons that comprised the Grand Admiralty, who stood as he spoke their names.

After they were seated, Athes said to the newly commissioned officers, "Remember their faces—the warmth and kindness in their eyes. May you never stand before them when they are otherwise than this." Slightly softening his tone to one less grave, with just a touch of pride, he continued, as the tribunes once more approached. "It is now time for the Conferring of the Captaincy."

"Dorrin Waelsbun," Janzalon began, "do you accept that the Ruenai govern the water, wood, and wind?"

"I do," answered Dorrin.

"Do you further accept that the Ruen-Eret are their flesh-and-blood representatives by whose ministrations we owe our prowess on the seas?"

"I do," Dorrin repeated.

"Do you therefore agree to abide by the rules of conduct set forth by not only the Ruen-Eret, but by the members of the Grand Admiralty, and to execute your duties as captain in full faith and trust in our traditions and our laws?"

"I do."

Janzalon could not help but smile as he said, "Then I do hereby confer upon you the title of captain of the *Sea-Sprite*."

As Janzalon spoke these final words, the other two tribunes fastened the captain's gold epaulets to the shoulders of Dorrin's tunic.

Janzalon then asked Thaker the same trio of questions. Following his final "I do," the tribunes completed the Conferring of the Captaincy through affixing the gold epaulets to the shoulders of his uniform.

It was at this time that the sea-shaman, Carra, motioned for the two newly commissioned captains to join her before the doors of the Inner Temple.

"As you are all aware," she said to the congregation, "it is not only the skills learned at the Admiralty-Mast that make Eretian captains masters of the ship and the sea—it is the goodness and grace of Vael, Xaer, and Braen—theirs is the water, wood, and wind. Your part of the ceremony is complete, but for captains Waelsbun and Ungerfil, they now begin their training with the Ruen-Eret and will soon see and study what so few ever have—the sacred Stone of the Ruenai."

The congregation was silent as they processed out of the Vessel, although they erupted in a cacophony of opinions, comments, and questions regarding the Stone as soon as the attendants closed and locked the doors.

"Makes no sense to me why first officers and navigators are not taught the ways of the Stone," Corbit exclaimed as he, Silbern, Gorish, and Fagan broke off by themselves. "Or why they wait until *after* we are graduated from the Admiralty-Mast to show it to the captains…"

"Agreed," Fagan said with a whisper. "Although I would not proclaim it so loudly. If the Grand Admiralty or the tribunes were to hear you…"

"They would bring me up on charges," Corbit said, lowering his voice. "Or the Ruen-Eret might kill me outright. Which would be a pleasurable enough way to go…"

"Stow the chatter, Navigator Neergarn," Gorish barked, seizing the opportunity to exercise his new rank while Dorrin remained in the Vessel. "And you as well, Navigator Ronng. One would think you would be more circumspect after the disappearance of your uncle two years ago."

"Understood, Sir," Fagan answered, making the angle of his salute as precise as possible to appease his superior officer.

Aldemere's Dilemma

"Have they no news of your uncle Millet, Fagan?" Silbern asked, not as concerned about an update as his sympathetic tone suggested. It was either change the subject or confront Gorish Bront for dressing down a fellow shipmate.

"None," Fagan answered, shaking his head. "Eret's best shipwright and a member of the Grand Admiralty disappears on the same night as the Mellyan ambassador leaves in a huff for home and no one seems to care. Not a single eyebrow raised. It serves as a reminder of how fickle the Ruenai can be..."

Taking Fagan by the arm, Gorish saluted Silbern. "If you will excuse us, First Officer Skarling, it seems the *Sea-Sprite*'s new navigator needs to calibrate his instruments without delay. The voyage to Vaelsport is far from a sail 'round the harbor." Looking Corbit in the eyes, he added, "Do you see what questioning the laws and rites of the Ruenai invites? Only doubt and pain. Neither of which has any place upon the deck of a ship. Water, wood, and wind."

"Water, wood, and wind," the other three replied.

"I apologize, Silbern," Corbit said when Gorish and Fagan were out of earshot. "I let my feelings get the best of me. It is just that I would like to have a look at that Stone."

"Bront has always kept his duty to the Ruenai foremost in his manner," Silbern replied with a smile. "Perhaps he is right to do so. Let us attend to the *Salt-Serpent*'s needs. Thaker's concern is the Stone. It has nothing to do with us."

After composing a note to Sir Corvit requesting confirmation or denial of what Frederick had told him and his companions earlier in the day, and securing it to a messenger hawk trained to fly due north, Sir Peecwyl headed for the Great Hall, where Aldemere and Linead had escorted their "guest" to get some food.

"What do you know of the lands beyond the Topmost Mountains?" Peecwyl heard Frederick ask of Aldemere and Linead as he entered the half-full hall.

As Frederick awaited their answer, Peecwyl watched with rising anger as he sunk his teeth into a hunk of roasted woodhart.

May the Deities make you choke, Peecwyl thought with a scowl.

As the one-eyed warrior approached, Frederick gave him a grease-ringed smile.

"Only what is told in the First Book of Ancestries by a monk called Manthes Fragenoar," Aldemere answered, digging into his own plate of roasted meat and buttered vegetables.

"Although we are aware that most of it is rot," Peecwyl interjected, sitting beside Linead and directly across from Frederick. "He was a crazy old zealot who happened to stumble upon the scrolls of some obliterated clan. Scrolls full of gibberish we are told. Gibberish he outlandishly interpreted to further his selfish aims."

"Who even knows if the Fragenoars existed," Linead contributed, pouring Aldemere and Peecwyl each a cup of mead. "There is not a word about that family in the book that Manthes scribed."

"I assure you they existed," answered Frederick, spitting a hunk of bone and grizzle onto the edge of his plate. "And all that Manthes wrote—despite his less than honorable actions and admittedly fractured mind—was accurate and true. Have any of you heard of a country once called Lyseum?"

"Has it to do with the peak we call Mount Lyse?" asked Aldemere, his belief in Frederick growing and his interest fully piqued.

"Where you fought and defeated the dragons Diette and Simnac," Frederick replied with a nod. "Mount Lyse was sacred to the Lyseans. They recorded their story—and many others—upon its walls. It was the place where Lysean warriors initiated their youngsters into manhood. Or so I hear..."

"You have been there, Frederick!" Aldemere surmised aloud.

"If Aldemere is correct, then why did you not just say it?" Peecwyl demanded, the miniscule amount of trust he had managed to muster in this stranger quickly disappearing. Then to his companions, and a good portion of the hall, he yelled, "This stranger is not to be trusted! Just like the mad monk himself!"

"Perhaps a wee touch of civility and a lowering of the voice, Sir Peecwyl," Linead commanded, keeping his own voice low. "Give him a chance to explain."

Frederick, after nodding his thanks to Linead, focused his eyes on his main detractor. "You are correct in part, Sir Peecwyl, as is Sir Aldemere, of course. I have been to the cave on Mount Lyse. Several times, going back to my youth—although now is not the time to elaborate. That is why I dissembled. We have already wasted too much time with your distrust and my ill-played methods of communication. Time is of the essence."

"What of this country called Lyseum?" Aldemere asked. "Does it still exist?"

"Only as a weakening memory," Frederick answered, pushing aside his empty plate. "What was once a thriving country is now a dying idea. Do you recall the drawings in the cave that were not like

59   *Aldemere's Dilemma*

the battles and chaos of the others? The scenes of thriving ports and peaceful villages? *That* was Lyseum and her allies. Lyseum was a place of tranquility and learning, with wise, benevolent rulers who chose to be *regents* rather than chieftains and kings. They worshipped the same gods and goddesses as does Glittereye. Many of their customs were no different from yours, passed down from generation to generation from a time now lost to the mists. They traded peacefully with the Eretians and Dwarves far to the north, across the Sea of Natere."

"Dwarves!" Peecwyl exclaimed, laughing in Frederick's face. "Another fairy tale told to us as children and forgotten by the time our beards began to grow."

"I assure you, they are real," Frederick replied, blinking his eyes to clear them of the sting of Peecwyl's pungent breath but otherwise keeping still. "And if we are fortunate, they shall agree to be our allies in the coming war. They are small, but immensely strong. There are no better warriors or skilled metalworkers in the vast expanses of Mynoweth."

Linead leaned forward with a frown. "As knight-marshal of the Combined Armies of Glittereye, I demand you tell us all you know. No more games, no more patience, Frederick, or I swear I shall clasp you in irons and put you in a cell. If you are any different than Manthes Fragenoar, who also spoke of coming wars, this is your chance to prove it."

Raising his hands in a show of complete surrender, Frederick replied, "That has been my intention from the start. Spies, assassins, and treachery undid Lyseum. Her borders once ran from Mount Lyse in the west to the seas to the north and east. Her southern border was the River Wythe. The regents left the Unsettled Wilderness and its warring clans to pursue a destiny of their own, until such a time as the increasing fighting amongst the chieftains threatened the Lysean way of life. It was then that they sent an emissary to bring the clans together."

"Alde the First was a Lysean!" Aldemere interjected, quickly dropping his voice as the heads of dozens of squires and knights once more turned toward where they sat. "And so was Manthes Fragenoar..."

"As am I, at least by ancestry," Frederick answered, "although the land once known as Lyseum has not existed since the end of what your scholars call the Unity Wars."

"Can this be true?" Peecwyl muttered, shaking his head. "Aldemere. Your teacher—Talorous, if I recall—surely he would know if at least some of what this man has told us is true."

Frederick put his hand on Aldemere's forearm. "I shall happily speak with your venerated tutor, Captainguard, although no one is aware of the true history of Lyseum but those of us north of the mountains. It is solely an oral tradition. Those who conspired in her undoing ruthlessly destroyed her records when the government was unseated. They consolidated, militarized, and renamed the country as Mellya. And it is Mellya, and her self-proclaimed cliffprince, a man of immeasurable ambition named Nadrim, that presently threatens your borders and in truth the whole of our world."

In the heavily guarded war chamber of Mellya, in the capital city of Amdar, sat the "man of immeasurable ambition," the self-proclaimed cliffprince, Nadrim Damonessa. He could not help but smile, as he sat upon the goose-feather and velvet cushion of his richly adorned and intricately carved throne—the one outward sign of good fortune and deep wealth the otherwise austere cliffprince allowed himself. Such austerity was the pride and practice of Mellya, despite the fact that the Lyseans had been expert traders and oh, so industrious, and had filled Mellya's coffers and coin rooms to bursting before they met their end.

Nadrim dressed the part of the warrior that he was. His tunic was studded, double-layered course-weave, the same as his pants. His knee-high riding boots sported extra-thick heels and several spiked buckles. Over the top of his tunic, he wore a horsehide vest trimmed in Dwarven triple-linked ringmail to protect his shoulders, sternum, and groin. From the broad belt at his waist hung two sheathed daggers—one long and slender for finding the gaps in plate and ringmail such as his, the other short and wide for the efficient slitting of throats.

Upon the blood-red wall-coverings and emblazoned upon his tunic was his crest—a three-taloned falcon, clutching sword, lance, and fire.

Nadrim believed that the circumstances dictated the weapon, so he learned to use them all. Smile he could, and smile he did, for all was going well. He had three dozen single-masted ships already built and ready to sail and thirteen three-masted warships near to completion in his newly finished harbor.

Soon enough, he would have the means to let them sail.

Aldemere's Dilemma

Seven years he had plotted and planned, building his strength within and without the military state over which he ruled. Pieces had fallen from the board, but that was the way of the game. All strategic sacrifices, all as he decreed.

All but one, he thought with a sneer, gripping the arm of his throne. Garamin of the Centerlands was potentially more than a pawn, yet ultimately not the puppet king Nadrim had hoped.

Upon the final tally, Garamin had scarcely proven to be a knight.

Nadrim's agents had stolen the failed rebel's remains before their enemies—Garamin's *and* Nadrim's—could discover the tattoo of allegiance inked on the knight's left calf.

A tattoo of a falcon, clutching sword, lance, and fire.

"Is this absolutely necessary?" Garamin had asked Nadrim's agent, as the tattooer prepped his inks. "What if it is seen?"

"If you do what you are told—what you say that you are able," the hooded man had replied, "when the kingdom is taken, it will be there for *all* to see. And if you cannot accomplish what we ask..."

"Then it is no matter," Nadrim said with a sarcastic sigh, turning to grasp the wineskin on the table next to his throne as he let the memory pass. "You did your best to serve me, my boy. Indeed—you serve me still." Nadrim could not help but laugh at his wit as he ran his fingers over the faded and slightly stretched tattoo, taken with the skin of Garamin's leg, from which his artisans had made the wineskin.

"Talking to ghosts again, my brother?"

Ignoring the source of the question, Nadrim drank deeply from the wineskin, enjoying the feel of a few errant drops of the rich, red liquid running down his clean-shaven chin. Tossing the vessel on the table, he sighed again—this time to signal his boredom with his visitor.

"What is it you want of me, Calrain?" he asked, looking at his deformed and limping brother as he would a pile of maggots.

"Some attention and respect," Calrain replied, grasping his twisted leg as he approached. "And an explanation as to why you talk to ghosts like the half-mad kings in the Lysean dramas..."

"See now, my crickbacked brother," Nadrim said, waggling his finger to help him make his point, "that is why our great-grandfather had the Lysean libraries burned. No good comes of reading anything but manuals of war—and maps of the world you plan to conquer."

Coming closer, until his thin, pointed nose was nearly touching Nadrim's finger, Calrain answered, "Great-grandfather must have retained some of the folios for a reason. Father was fond of them as well. He read them to me at bedtime." Wincing in pain, but too proud to ask for permission to sit, Calrain continued. "You never had any interest in the stories that they tell, and, as a result, I think you are missing something necessary to a capable ruler."

"Really, Crickback," Nadrim said, running a pointed fingernail across the tip of his brother's nose, forcing him to pull away, "fantasy stories are for little girls and the misshapen, strengthless boys whose bodies continue to grow long after their brains have stopped at idiocy."

Giving into his pain despite his will to ignore it and answer his brother's rebuke, Calrain asked instead, "May I sit for a bit, my brother? The curve in my back puts undo pressure on my knees."

"Sit if you must, Brother Crickback," Nadrim answered, motioning to a spot on the floor a man's-length from the throne. "It is not like you are actually standing when you are standing, if you take my meaning."

When he had found a somewhat comfortable—if not completely painless—position, Calrain asked, as pleasantly and nonthreateningly as he could manage, "Would you please not call me Crickback? It is fast becoming all the rage for Amdarian nobles and their sons, who comprise the officer corps in your armies, to do so. Everywhere I go I hear the taunt of 'Calrain Crickback.' Father never let you—"

"And now our father is dead. *Seven years* a corpse." Nadrim's volume was increasing in perfect proportion with his incremental loss of patience with his sibling. "And yet you, my malformed, *crickbacked* brother, talk of *him* more than you do of *me*!" Nadrim rose from his throne, pulling a gauntlet of studded leather from his belt to strike the cowering Calrain as a way to make his point.

As he raised his well-muscled arm, he heard the war chamber's double doors as they opened, revealing Captain Davus Purloch, head of the guards of Amdar, which thoroughly ruined the moment.

Seeing what was about to take place and cursing his terrible timing, Purloch averted his eyes and said, "I am sorry for the interruption, My Cliffprince. The nomad chiefs are impatiently awaiting an audience."

Dropping his arm but holding tight to the gauntlet, Nadrim asked, "Why apologize, Captain Purloch? Are you not just following orders? The orders I, myself, have given? Is that not your greatest strength?" Letting out a frustrated huff of air, he added, "By all means, let them in—that is, after you have helped my dear, disabled brother into a comfortable chair."

"We have been here for ten frustrating days, and we are no closer to an agreement!"

The mood in the Trade Hall at Eerbell in the Eastern Barony had been at a simmer for days. Ralin's latest—and noticeably slurred-speech—remark was bringing it to boil.

"These are delicate matters," Baron Tooras answered, the growing din preventing the other attendees from hearing his aged and weary voice.

"We have no need to rush," Ciloto, baron of the north, chimed in, although no one heard him but his old friend Tooras and a pair of serving maids.

Watching the moving mouths of the two eldest barons from his spot across the room, but unable to hear what they were saying, Baron Chrystan stood upon his chair, dropping a large pewter pitcher full of water on the center of the table as he did so.

Taking advantage of the split second of silence that followed the initial expletives of surprise and anger at the dousing the pitcher had given to those in its proximity—Ralin included—Chrystan spoke with the strength and intent of one used to commanding a unit of strong-willed knights. "If you would settle down… Please! I agree with Baron Ralin that progress has been slow."

"You have a strange way of showing it," Ralin answered, wiping water from his tailored suede jerkin with one hand while motioning to one of the serving maids for a refill of his mead mug with the other. "But I thank you nonetheless."

"But how he has stated his case…" Chrystan continued, acknowledging neither the interruption nor the baron's continued drinking. "We are tasked with a serious responsibility. The two amongst us with the most experience—barons Tooras and Ciloto—cannot make themselves heard over the shouting, posturing, and threats of those of us who are much newer to our positions. Baroness Ashlin has graciously opened her home and pantry to meet our considerable needs, yet you have hardly permitted her to speak. If it were not for Sir Abbas, her capable trade warden, the East would be left almost wholly out the dialogue."

"We have heard from the East enough to last us a lifetime," Ralin countered, sloppily draining his mug. "And what we *have* heard sounds to me like half-veiled threats and betrayal—echoes of the not so distant past. I am sure the rest of you barons agree—Ashlin, although not a chore to look at, is lucky to be at this table at all."

"I would watch what comes out of your mouth, and the tone you use to deliver it," Sir Abbas warned the intoxicated baron of the West. As he stood to show his seriousness, Chrystan saw Sir Glenmore, his counterpart in the West, do the same.

"Enough of this wearisome posturing!" Tooras yelled, with a strength belying his years. "I have sat through such contentious meetings far too many times. You are out of line, Baron," he said, boring his eyes into Ralin. The use of only his title was a sign of disrespect, as all in the room were aware. "I shall no longer tolerate your behavior or your drinking. To an extent, they are connected. As for you wardens, with your hands upon your swords and menace in your eyes. You shall take your seats for the remainder of this meeting." Looking at Ralin with a softer expression, Tooras added, "Your father, Baron Vellom, was a man of strong opinions, and a shrewd negotiator who understood the value of the oil his fields produced. Yet he also knew that one cannot eat oil, nor use it to construct a house or wagon. The baronies must work in conjunction, despite the chaos that certain men's egos have caused. I say this to you now… what is past is past. We each have our reasons for shame—I stand here owning mine. Will you do the same?"

Ralin made no sound, which his counterparts took as a yes.

Satisfied with the silence, Tooras continued. "The Spring Tournament is but a month away. I need not remind you that High Lord Petror shall attend, and it will have little to do with the games. He shall expect a full accounting of the agreements made between the baronies so the Elves can prepare their proposals to present at the Annual Trade meetings. We must either be united, or do our damnedest to appear so. I would much prefer the former."

"Thank you, Baron Tooras," Chrystan said, as the pair of serving maids helped the elderly man to his chair. "Words of reason and of wisdom. The baronies must work together. I know that you wish this as well, Baron Ralin, as do we all."

You play your new role well, Ralin thought, giving Chrystan—and the rest—his most disarming smile. *Although you also underestimate the boy whose father ran him. And the man who likes his mead.*

That is why I will win.

CHAPTER FOUR

"Missing? What do you mean the Stone of the Ruenai is *missing*?" Kiegan Hefflar, warden of the waters and therefore the most powerful person in the room, except perhaps for Carra the sea-shaman, who did not think of herself in such terms, slammed his fist into his oak and teakwood desk, which dominated his office in the Admiralty building. "Are you not charged with keeping it safe, Carra? Is that not your primary responsibility?"

All eyes—those of the grand admiral, the Tribunal of the Seas, and the rest of the Grand Admiralty—turned toward the sea-shaman, although, as she noted, none of them dared to glare at her with the ferocity of the warden.

In none of their memories could they recall anyone raising their voice to the Keeper of the Stone.

Although, they silently acknowledged, it had never before gone missing.

"Warden Hefflar," Carra cautiously began. The effort she was making to keep her notably lyrical voice at an even pitch was palpable to all in attendance. "The Stone of the Ruenai is kept—as you know—as you *all* know," she continued, pausing only to look into every pair of eyes looking into hers, "in a special chamber in the Inner Temple. A few in this room have communed with it... And, as you are also all aware, the Keeper only removes it when a new class of captains has graduated from the Admiralty-Mast, and, prior to today, it had been three years since the last Conferring of the Captaincy. I sleep in the Inner Temple. I take my meals in the Inner Temple. I leave only to bathe each week in the sea and to oversee the thrice-daily offerings to Vael, Xaer, and Braen, or for the rare meeting such as this, here in the Admiralty complex. The Stone must have been taken during one of those times I was absent."

"Dare I ask if it was one of the Ruen-Eret?" Warden Hefflar asked. "They appear to be the logical suspects, given the circumstances you describe."

"To what point and purpose would one do so?" Carra asked in turn, placing her hands upon the desk and leaning inward to meet the warden's stare. "They have forsaken a broader education, husbands, and offspring to serve the Ruenai. No one forced them to take the oath. We meet their basic needs. The citizens of Eret treat them with respect and hold them in high esteem. Your accusation makes no sense."

Aldemere's Dilemma

Warden Hefflar frowned. "It was not an *accusation*, Carra—merely a *question*. As to motivation, it could be as simple as a matter of money. A greater sense of power. You seem to forget that some do leave behind their agreed-to life of chastity and service to marry, although I know that it is rare. There is not one amongst them above material aims. Not to mention their... carnal... vulnerabilities." The warden shook his head, as he would in the presence of a disappointing child. "You ought to be less naïve."

"Perhaps it is you who are being naïve. Any one of *you* have more to gain. The shippers, the timber barons—you could use the Stone as leverage. You have chosen to accumulate wealth as your direct benefit from the boons granted to each and every one of you through the generosity of the Ruenai."

"Proceed with care now, Carra," Janzalon Waelsbun cautioned. "Insulting the Admiralty will not improve the situation."

Carra lowered her head and laughed. "It is not only the Admiralty to whom I refer, Tribune Waelsbun. For it might have been one of you judges. Or you, Grand Admiral, or you, Mister Undersecretary," she said, meeting the wide-eyed expressions of Athes and Hathom. "The Ungerfils are a powerful family—and with Thaker now the captain of the *Salt-Serpent*, and there being some question of his worthiness for the—"

"How dare you!" This came from Janzalon. "The Ungerfils have been wardens, captains, and admirals in good standing for more than three hundred years! Next, you shall suggest it was a Waelsbun! Do not point your finger when the error was your own. You deflect the warden's questions as tarred planks deflect the water. You are the Keeper of the Stone. And, lest anyone forget... the thirty-second."

Those last three words sent the room into silence.

Including Ettana, the first Keeper of the Stone, who had pleaded with the Ruenai to restore the Eretians' skill and safety upon the seas more than twelve hundred years before, there had been thirty-two appointed sea-shamans. There was a long-known prophecy—its origins unclear, but its legitimacy regarded by most as unquestionable nonetheless—that the thirty-third Keeper of the Stone would use its knowledge to betray the Ruenai and usher in an end to Eretian dominion of the seas.

"It is childish nonsense," one of the timber barons muttered. "Do not make matters worse by speaking of it here."

"What about you, Carra-shaman?" Athes Ungerfil asked. "Do you believe the prophecy is nonsense?"

Looking her questioner in the eye, Carra replied, "I do not, Grand Admiral Ungerfil. It is my duty—my sole purpose—to carry out the rites of water, wood, and wind, and the prophecy is part of those rites. All in this room would be wise to assume that whomever stole the Stone did so precisely *because* of the prophecy. What do you know of our allies and enemies and their recent activities?"

"We know it is not the Dwarves," Hathom Ungerfil reported. "Our trade agreements are fair and our relationship strong. We have two ships ready to sail weighted down with timber and they will return from Mettlec just as full with the tools, winches, and finely crafted metals made by the Dwarves that we need to maintain our fleet. Not to mention that the Dwarves abhor magic of any kind. If they know about the Stone, I have never heard them mention it."

"It is not the warrior-agent from the once-great lands north of the Topmost Mountains—the one who came to see us not many months ago," Tribune Kaelhul added. "The Tribunal and the warden were with him every waking moment. Furthermore, as an added precaution, no mention was made of the Stone, as is our practice with outsiders—especially with Humans."

"Besides which," Warden Hefflar said, "we trust this man implicitly, as the Admiralty historically has with all who bear his family name."

Carra nodded to the tribune and warden in confirmation. "Although he visited the Vessel, we did not mention the Inner Temple, and he asked none of the Ruen-Eret what lay behind the doors. I agree—his honor is not in question."

"Then we are saying it was the Mellyans," Grand Admiral Ungerfil uttered, the only one present able to find the courage to articulate what most of the Ereti in the room knew must be the truth. "It is perfectly in scale with the ambitions of their leader."

"But the Stone of the Ruenai would be of zero practical use to them," Tribune Mastmin argued. "We have nearly a dozen admirals and captains who know the ways of the Stone, who have gone through the rites and recited the prayers that it contains and who have made the journey to the spirit realm to be instructed and blessed by the Ruenai. The Mellyans could not hope to best these sailors upon the seas, even if they could build a comparable fleet of ships. So what would they gain by obtaining it?"

"A valid point, Tribune Mastmin," Carra answered. "Unless they are also aware of and accept the truth of the prophecy."

"The Lyseans had prophecies of their own," Tribune Kaelhul offered. "Perhaps the Mellyans believe in them as well."

Aldemere's Dilemma

As the din of speculation began to grow amongst the group, Warden Hefflar cleared his throat to sharpen their focus. "As chilling a thought as that may be, let us consider more practical matters. As to the speculation that the Mellyans are building a fleet, let us not forget the disappearance of Millet Ronng, which we discovered not long after the Mellyan ambassador departed. Millet's shipwrighting skills are unsurpassed. If he is building them a fleet, and the cliffprince has the Stone—"

"But no one can interpret its runes but me," Carra answered, caution filling her voice. "And we are speaking too freely of things of which only conferred captains should have knowledge. No offense meant to those of you not privy to these things—but the Ruenai decreed such secrecy for a reason."

Indeed, it was the runes upon the Stone—the practices and prayers the Ruenai had transcribed upon it in the days of Ettana-shaman, which only the Keeper of the Stone, the sea-shaman, could read—that gave the Ereti their prowess on the seas. That and the ritualistic communion with the gods maintained through the dream journeying undertaken and offerings made by the half a dozen Ruen-Eret.

Rituals the details of which only the Ruen-Eret and the sea-shaman were aware.

"The Stone must be tracked down and returned to the Inner Temple at the earliest possible opportunity," Warden Hefflar said with a tone of undeniable authority. "All of Mynoweth is in danger should the cliffprince build and launch a fleet. And should the prophecy be true…"

"There is a more immediate matter to which we must attend," Tribune Waelsbun responded. "We cannot sail against a fleet or make war upon the seas, provoked or not, unless the Ruenai agree. Am I painting an accurate picture, Carra-shaman?"

"You are," the shamaness confirmed. "I will beseech the Ruenai this very evening, but until they favor me with an answer you must not outfit your ships with the implements of war. The consequences would be as grave—or graver—than before Ettana's time."

"We will drown like hog-tied sailors in a tide pool if something is not done!" Warden Hefflar shouted. "Surely there is something we can do while we are waiting for the gods to answer!"

"I have a place to start," Janzalon Waelsbun answered. "If the Mellyans were told about the Stone, I know who it was who did the telling. Nakret Wilsbern."

"I pray that you are wrong," Athes Ungerfil replied, his voice low and full of fear, "or this is all my doing."

"You saved your ship, your crew, and your cargo," Hathom said, approaching his father. "Nakret's arm was a reasonable price to pay."

The incident of which they were speaking had occurred three decades earlier, during an unexpected and brutal late-January storm while the *Salt-Serpent* was delivering timber to the western ports of Mettlec. As they rode the weather out, Athes, then the *Salt-Serpent*'s captain, gave the order, once the sails had been secured, for all hands but Nakret—who was serving as his navigator—to confine themselves below-decks. With Nakret at the helm, Athes prayed the prayers Carra's predecessor had taught him when he had graduated from the Admiralty-Mast and learned the words carved upon the Stone of the Ruenai, journeying to their realm to learn the secrets of the sea that no one could teach him in the classroom or upon the deck of a ship. When a spar broke loose and threatened to tear the ship apart, Nakret rushed to secure it, while Athes took the wheel.

Nakret had almost completed tying off the spar when a rogue wave crashed over the portside bulwark, pushing the spar tight against the mast and catching Nakret's arm between them.

"We were headed for a shoal," Athes told the group, reliving those dire minutes as he had done a thousand times before, including at his conduct hearing when he had returned to Llafen Eret. "I could not abandon the helm, no matter how loud or persistent Nakret's screams for me to do so. Because I held the wheel, we reached the harbor in Mettlec with every sailor safe. The Dwarven doctors did what they could, but Nakret's arm could not be saved."

"Navigator Wilsbern was decorated as a hero for tying off the spar," Janzalon added. "Given a good pension and offered a position with the teaching staff at Admiralty-Mast, he foolishly turned it down, choosing instead to live at the docks weaving sails and mending nets. He traded his medals for liquor and lived in a shanty not fit for the storing of fresh-killed fish."

"And he harbored a hatred for me," Athes resumed. "When he suddenly disappeared—What? Six years ago, I believe it was—it was assumed he had fallen into the sea in a drunken stupor."

"I never thought that to be true," Janzalon replied. "He was born of the sea, and had spent most of his life in her arms. Drunk or not, she would not claim him so quietly as that. I believe he is alive, and I am fully determined to find him."

"If you mean to do this, I shall go as well," Athes declared.

"I will not allow it," Warden Hefflar replied. "Your place is here, training our newest set of officers as best you can without the benefit of the rituals of the Stone and readying the fleet for what is to come."

"But if it is my doing—"

"Let me go then, Father," Hathom volunteered. "I too am an Ungerfil. It is a matter of family honor, and I am not needed here as desperately as you and my brother."

"Under these trying circumstances, I cannot but agree," Athes said with a bow to his son. "If Warden Hefflar will allow it and grant his blessing to the task."

"The blessing is not mine to give," the warden replied, turning to the sea-shaman. "What say you, Carra-shaman, thirty-second and rightful Keeper of the Stone. Do you give your blessing to this task?"

"I am but a servant in the Vessel who serves the will of the Ruenai," Carra answered. "I have much to ask of Vael, Xaer, and Braen. I shall take my leave that I may undertake the rites."

The room fell silent as she headed for the door. Before she opened it, she added, "Three is the number of the Ruenai, of water, wood, and wind. Should the god and goddesses grant their blessing to this journey to find the sail-weaver, they shall need a third."

"Then I know whom it shall be," Janzalon Waelsbun answered. "It shall be a Dwarf."

The fire in the Hall of Books and Ancestries was nearly burned to ash by the time Frederick—prompted by dozens of questions and requests for clarification by Talorous and Laurianna—had once more told his tale, including Lyseum's fall at the hands of Mellya and the suspension of trade by the Eretians and Dwarves when the Mellyans took control.

After stoking his pipe with a series of short breaths while inserting an almond in Nigredo's eager beak, Talorous leaned back in his chair and, letting out a long stream of blue-grey smoke, considered all that he had heard.

Also in attendance were the three knights—Peecwyl, Linead, and Aldemere—and Elde, who had been unwaveringly silent over the past ninety minutes.

"Master Talorous," prompted Peecwyl, eager to break the silence and hear a fresh assessment. "Do you believe what this wanderer has told us?"

Nodding almost imperceptibly while keeping his eyes turned skyward, Talorous whispered around the curved stem of his pipe, "And I am willing to wager Jester Elde does as well."

"That I do," Elde confirmed, without hesitation. "There are things the jesters of Glittereye are told as they ascend. Things concerning our lineage—about those from whom we descend. Things about which our predecessors swear us to secrecy—and with ample reason. All that I have heard this night falls in line with what I was told the night my father died. The night I donned the motley and took my place as jester."

"Your words are much appreciated, Elde the Jester," Frederick said, surprise and relief intertwining in a dance across his brow and down into his eyes. "I did not know what is now known or not about my people this side of the Topmost Mountains. I am confident you understand the gravity of what is occurring for me to reveal myself as I have. And that is why you have spoken about things that you ordinarily never would, until it is time for Aldemere to take your place."

"Let us not speak of that which is countless years away," Aldemere said from his spot away from the rest.

"I am sorry to have mentioned it," Frederick answered.

Aldemere approached him. "Tell us what to do, Frederick of the North, and we shall do it."

Placing his hand upon his student's arm, Talorous said with the gentle but firm tone Aldemere knew so well from a thousand times before, "You forget yourself, Captainguard. We have not yet told the king all that we have heard and, unless he decides to ride to meet what is still a rather shadowy foe, your focus and authority lie solely in the security of this castle and its occupants." Motioning to Linead and Elde he added, "It is on the both of you that we must by law and necessity rely."

"Might I say a few things more, before you take me before the king?" Frederick asked.

"No one said you shall see the king!" Peecwyl exclaimed, standing. "Your story will be told on your behalf. We might have heard some truth, but you have been foggy on your motives. And, as Master Talorous observed, about this still rather shadowy foe."

Looking to Elde, Frederick asked, exasperated, "Is this true? I shall not be permitted to speak directly to the king?"

Aldemere's Dilemma

"I am sorry, but it is," the jester replied. "It was not so long ago that a handful of those closest to the king sought to end his life, so we cannot take the chance. What more must you tell us before I take my leave to counsel His Majesty?"

Shaking his head in disappointment but keeping a level voice, Frederick answered, "It is the Forest of Tombal, beyond the barony to the east, which is the primary point of concern. The cliffprince cannot hope to sail the ships he has commissioned without something of great power hidden in the forest. I believe he will seek further allies there amidst its secretive inhabitants."

"You are speaking of the Greybaer, are you not?" Laurianna asked, crossing the room and pulling a torn and dust-heavy scroll from the bottom of a pile. "I was told of them by my grandfather when I was barely walking. It was our special bedtime story— dressed up in the storyteller's love for tall tales and hard-to-reckon happenings. Nonetheless, it contained a resonant truth absent in made-up tales. I have always believed the magical Greybaer are real."

"Sounds like more of his delusional myth-making to me," Peecwyl countered, moving to the door. "If this kingdom is in danger—and I know in my gut that it is—you had best quit living in the world of fairytale and ready for the realness of war."

Heading for the door as soon as Peecwyl had exited, Linead bowed to the others to take his leave. "My skeptical friend and I shall continue to talk this through, I assure you," he said. "Men who engage in war have difficulty with diplomacy in times of peace. But if things go as we fear, he will be indispensable to our defense."

After Linead had left, Aldemere sat beside Laurianna. "May I have that scroll?" he asked, extending his hand. "A little nighttime reading, if for nothing else." After she gave it over, he turned to Talorous. "It will be like when I read about the mountains and the desert before Kal-Gadras and I left for Vaelsport, Teacher."

Smiling at his son's conniving ways, Elde said, standing, "I will confer with the king without delay. What is it you are requesting of him, Frederick?"

"No more than a handful of trustworthy men to accompany me to the Forest of Tombal. Seasoned in combat and able to navigate amongst the shadows and the trees."

"Only a handful?" Aldemere asked, turning his attention from the scroll. "We have had reports of strange faces in the eastern forests for weeks now. As a result, I have sent two of my lieutenants to

Eerbell with the barony trade representatives. Are you sure a full company is not a more prudent choice?"

"Strange faces in the eastern forests…" Frederick said, knitting his brows in thought. "They must be Mellyan spies. Or worse… As to your question, Captainguard, a handful will be sufficient. Provided they are the *correct* handful."

"Very well," Elde replied. "I shall take your request to the king."

Joining the jester at the door, Talorous and Laurianna took their leave so that Aldemere and Frederick could continue their conversation in private.

Adding more wood to the fire, and shifting the coals until the pieces were ablaze, Aldemere sat himself across from their fascinating visitor. As the fire brightened the room, he noticed dozens of small scars and other signs of prolonged travel, combat, and adventure upon Frederick's calloused hands, muscular forearms, and bearded, longhaired visage. He noticed the tarnished buckles and well-worn leather of his jerkin and the pinched and gathered places along his shirtsleeves where someone—most likely the warrior himself—had hastily repaired numerous tears and holes.

"I feel as though there is more you wish to tell me," Aldemere started. "I wish to hear it all."

"And you shall. In time," Frederick answered, placing his hand over the captainguard's own. "But now is not that moment. Know this, Aldemere—the blood that bubbles through your veins is powerful—and ancient. And the dreams you have had of black-horsed warriors riding in the rain—"

"How could you possibly know that?"

Aldemere had not thought of those dreams since he had first had them in the dragon's cave on Mount Lyse and again when a blow knocked him unconscious defending the castle gates from Garamin and his rebels.

"I have also had them," Frederick answered, smiling. "As have several others. Men of great achievement and greater heart. However, the trap that these dreams set—the lure of wealth and power—be it by words or by the knife and sword—is equally as great, and should one follow that lure, madness is the price. We must remain ever vigilant against the darkness." Releasing Aldemere's hand, he said, "You have reading to do, and I have my own company and counsel to keep while the good king considers my request. May I find a place among the knights and squires in the Great Hall?"

Aldemere's Dilemma

"They shall each of them be better for having you amongst them," Aldemere answered, carefully rolling the Greybaer scroll and tucking it in his belt. "I shall fetch you at first light."

"Welcome, honored guests," Nadrim said with a smile, extending his arms in a gesture that allowed the three chieftains approaching his throne to see his two knives and the broadsword he had added to his belt just before they entered. "I trust your journey was uneventful?"

The tallest of the chieftains—also the broadest-shouldered and visibly scarred—grunted in reply.

"Moktar Caveraider," Nadrim said, stepping forward off his dais with his arms still open wide, "I did not mean to insult you by using a fancy word. By uneventful I meant, 'you no kill humans'?"

"Not yet." Moktar shrugged. *"Kill them very soon."*

"Yes, indeed, you shall," Nadrim answered, contorting his face into a facsimile of concern. "Not being able to raid has been hard on your tribe, I know. Hard for yours as well, Kull of the Krags and especially for yours, Bokk Riverskab—I know your... *kind*... thirst for blood and lust for shanks of flesh."

Kull only nodded, while Bokk—whose tribe were cannibals—produced a lopsided grin revealing rotted, sharpened teeth. As he darted his tongue in and out of his mouth, producing ropes of dark green drool, Nadrim motioned for them to sit.

"When we raiding the mines?" Moktar asked, barely fitting in his chair. "Caveraiders have a hunger. *Axes* have a hunger."

More nodding and drooling from Kull and Bokk.

Hiding his disdain behind a toothy grin, Nadrim pulled his sword from its sheath, resting it on the arms of his chair as he sat back his seat.

They did not even flinch, he noted. *How foolish their lack of fear.*

Running his fingers along the cold steel length of the blade, Nadrim lay his thumb upon its tip, until it drew a drop of blood. "It shall be soon. I promise. First, you shall take the town of Vaelsport. I shall gift you boats as you leave Amdar—better boats than yours. You shall use them to attack. It is rightfully yours, Vaelsport, despite the Eretians naming it for one of their gods. It was the land of your ancestors—the females who birthed those who birthed you and those before you—before it was invaded and corrupted. Now, just a few generations after Ereti seed was spilled inside their wombs—they think they are better than you."

"Blood not ours," answered Moktar, an understanding gleam in his eye.

You are less of an imbecile than your companions, Nadrim thought, *or your dull-minded father, the chieftain you replaced. You shall also be the first whose head I take for my wall when you have fulfilled your purpose.*

"That is right," said the cliffprince. "The Ereti poisoned it, and they now control those lands. I shall end the Ereti. Then you shall rule in Vaelsport, or whatever you choose to call it."

"Break their bones, bathe in blood, taste their hearts, eat their eyes," Bokk chanted, once more showing his sharpened teeth and tongue.

"Drink from their skulls if you wish," Nadrim added, "but you shall follow my instructions until they are carried out. You will slaughter the males, but leave the babies and women alive. Mate with them if you must, but leave them to their work. Bring the boys to me. This is of great importance—there is an ore the Eretians mine. Bring back every bit of that ore that you can. Is this understood?"

Satisfied with their guttural groans and nods, Nadrim continued. "Split your forces. Vaelsport is unarmed, their males unskilled in the art of war. I shall need your best fighters for what I have planned for the Humans in the Centerlands. You will oversee the preparations for those raids, Moktar. Send your most trusted warrior to Vaelsport with the forces these two lead."

"Cen-ten-lants is what?" Kull asked, a blank look in his eyes, although Moktar nodded, understanding perfectly well.

"The places of the miners and the cities south of the mountains," Nadrim answered, his patience growing thin. "*Cen-ter-lands*. Where the enemy Humans dwell. One in particular. The one who led the forces that destroyed your predecessors." Moktar and Bokk's eyes were now as blank as Kull's. "The chieftains before you," Nadrim corrected himself. "The ones I *used to* deal with. The ones I told to fight the Humans in *all* of the villages and mines in the north. You ate well last year—those of you that lived—did you not? Maybe you are grateful that they killed the chieftains you replaced, but you will kill them nonetheless. And when this Human rides to save them, you will bring him broken but living to me."

Realizing by their stares that he had lost them a dozen multisyllabic words ago, Nadrim dismissed the chieftains after requesting they leave their largest, strongest warriors to learn to work the oars of the ships that lay in port awaiting their savage crews.

77   *Aldemere's Dilemma*

Once they were alone, Calrain asked, "Why not send a few of your army officers with them, to be sure it is done as you ask?"

"*Brother*," Nadrim said in such a way that it sounded like an insult, "the way I have asked those brutes to do it is the only way they are *capable* of doing it. Let them think I trust them. That I *need* them. I cannot believe I sent you to the Eretians as my ambassador... Your mind is as crippled as your body, Crickback."

"Perhaps so, Brother," Calrain replied, digging his nails into his palm to keep his voice from breaking, "but would even one of your most senior officers have brought you the gift of the shipbuilder?"

"Most likely so," Nadrim answered, standing and sheathing his sword. "And the Stone of the Ruenai as well, which is why I originally sent you."

Sticking out his arm for his brother's help in rising from his chair, although he cursed himself as he did so, Calrain found himself grateful that Nadrim gave the requested aid without resorting to a taunt.

"Perhaps the Stone is nothing but a myth," he said, straightening his cloak in lieu of his back. "You have only the word of a one-armed Eretian sailweaver that such a thing exists. A shamed and bitter specimen who would say anything for attention..."

"And who would know the intentions of dissembling men such as him better than you, Brother Crickback?" Nadrim answered. "And if it were not for the level of torture suffered by the shipbuilder until he died, I would put credence in your assessment. He had no reason to lie about not knowing where it was as we took out his teeth—one every half an hour—like pins from a plank. The Stone exists—and I shall find it. Having the ore from the Tirili range with which to fashion our rudders in the Ereti tradition shall help to further level the waters. Now, on to other matters. My agents tell me that the barons of Glittereye are nearly two weeks into their trade negotiations in the eastern forests, in the unfortified dwelling of a *woman*."

"Garamin's aunt?" Calrain asked, grinning. "Ironic, Brother, is it not?"

"*Hardly*." Nadrim discarded any pretense of masking his disdain for the monster who stood before him. A monster his father had cared for more than him. "Dylwyn and his nobles have not an ounce of imagination. They think it poignant, no doubt. Healing and forgiveness and all such useless drivel."

"What are you planning for them?" Calrain asked.

Nadrim leaned in close. "My... *agents*... have been scouting the site for weeks. They shall soon descend upon it, now that time has passed and everyone is relaxed. They will take a few of the barons for ransom and savagely kill the rest. First will be the Baroness Ashlin, in payment for her nephew's failures. Two of the barons are old and should be grateful to die before they are pissing their britches and coughing chunks of lung. The one from the north— once he is dead, the mine leadership will be in transition as his brother ascends to the vacancy I am creating. And that will be the time I send Moktar and the rest to make their attacks upon the north."

"Who will your *agents* take hostage?" asked Calrain, annoyed at the genuine interest he had in his brother's latest plan.

"A former knight, named Chrystan, now a baron near the castle and the other a *would-be* knight. The son of Vellom, who had not the fortitude to follow his hatred into Garamin's company and contribute to our cause. Their flesh is worth some coin. If it turns out it is not, the Adjudicator will happily feast upon their necks.

"My wineskin will not last much longer. The ink from the tattoo is already beginning to fade. I will soon have need for a new one."

No matter how meticulous and precise the Ereti think they are, they will never do things with precision enough to please a Dwarf, Gadrun Grundling thought, suppressing a grunt of impatience as the dockhands worked to finish loading lumber into three of the nine Eretian cargo ships anchored in the slips arrayed before him. He had watched in silent dismay as the crew of the *Sea-Sprite* had scrambled to fix the damage done from a minor squall that had taken them unaware while their sails were all unfurled.

He had resisted the urge to call them out for the obvious imbeciles they were.

However, Gadrun had kept quiet. There were larger considerations at hand, and it was on those that he must focus.

One day, though, he thought, *I shall make them all swim in the truth.*

"Nearly finished with the loading, Timber Master," the lead stevedore shouted. "I hope you could keep up your count. Our loaders move quickly, do they not?"

Quickly? Yes they do—and sloppily as well.

"Is the dunnage properly placed?" Gadrun asked, hiding his chagrin beneath his thick, braided beard as he checked the ships for listing. "All *appears* to be in order..."

"I have never known a Dwarven eye to miss even the slightest pull to port," Gadrun heard from somewhere just behind him. False

79   *Aldemere's Dilemma*

flattery was another Eretian trait he had come to dislike in his eight years as Dwarven Timber Master in Llafen Eret.

"Janzalon Waelsbun," Gadrun said with a good-natured grunt, turning to face the speaker. "I would know that officious voice of yours anywhere. Have you come to check the manifests? I assure you they are in order."

Should there be any doubt, Gadrun thrust them forward as the tribune approached, letting them go as they touched the sleeve of the Eretian's sea-blue robes.

"There is no need for such formalities, good master Grundling," Janzalon replied, pressing the thick stack of number-filled parchments to his chest before they blew out to sea. "I have an urgent—and rather delicate—matter to discuss with you. This is my colleague, the undersecretary to the warden of the waters, Hathom—"

"—Ungerfil. Of course," the Dwarf replied, moving Hathom several inches to the left with the force of a good-natured slap to the shoulder. "I know your father well. Now that your brother is a full-fledged captain, I am sure we will learn to get along as I always have with the admiral. Which provokes in me a question, Tribune," Gadrun said, pointing to two ships anchored away from the others. "There sit the *Salt-Serpent* and the *Sea-Sprite*. The two finest ships in the Eretian fleet. Yet they hold no lumber. I hear they are bound for Vaelsport. One would think this would be an opportune time for two newly conferred captains to pay their respects to the royal family of Mettlec."

All too used to Dwarven directness after dealing with Gadrun Grundling and others like him over the course of several decades, Janzalon easily overlooked what many might see as an unforgivable breach of protocol in questioning an Eretian on a decision regarding the fleet.

"We are sending them to Vaelsport a few days hence, Gadrun. We have stocked their ships with provisions. They will return with Tirili ore. *The Sea-Star*, *Storm-Spear*, and *Sea-Snake* are well crewed and captained, loaded with fine timber, and capable of meeting your needs."

"I do not question that," Gadrun answered, taking back the manifests and shoving them into his satchel. "I have made many a pleasant trip back and forth on the *Sea-Star*, as I shall again tomorrow. It is just that…"

Hesitation, Janzalon noted. *Not a usual or preferable Dwarven trait.*

"Just that what?" the tribune asked, as gently as he felt his position allowed.

"Given that the king's son Stanchion was last seen in Llafen Eret when he disappeared some time ago, it might help to keep the winches greased if we would see the flagship anchored in our ports every now and again."

Janzalon clenched his teeth at this ill-timed posturing on the part of the Dwarves. "Has Buttress Pilon, king of Mettlec, conveyed as much to you?"

"I am not the ambassador to Eret, Tribune," Gadrun answered.

"Although, since the king has failed to send a replacement since his son took his wordless leave…"

"I am the closest thing. Yes. Yes, Janzalon. He has. You know what it would mean—strained relations between the Ereti and the Dwarves," Gadrun said, any vestige of pretense finally melting away.

Dwarven interactions away from the mountains, mines, and forges of Mettlec had always been brief and fraught with tension. Their origin stories were viciously guarded secrets, as were the names and rituals associated with their creator god, Boldac.

When the Ereti had first been gifted their ships, they were met on the southwest shores of Mettlec by barred gates and locked doors and the glinting tips of arrows arrayed on the turrets rising from the U-shaped Dwarven fortifications, which had their closed ends shaped to the shoreline.

The Ereti were wise enough to take their primitive implements of warmaking and turn for fairer winds and easier prey.

"We have always respected Mettlec and its kings," Janzalon said, with as much earnestness as he could muster.

"As well you should," Gadrun answered, straightening his back and tilting his head upward to look the two Eretians in the eyes. "For twelve thousand years we have mined the mountains and forged from metal the finest tools, swords, and axes. Swords that once hung from the belts and spilled the blood of Mynoweth's greatest warriors. We were trading and warring with Humans millennia before you first left your meager farmsteads and ventured out to sea. And now you stand before me and posture about friendship while you harbor the son of our king!"

"If he is here, he goes unknown!" Hathom shouted, weary of holding his tongue. "If he stowed away on one of our ships returning from Mettlec that indicates to me a family matter for which our country cannot be blamed."

Aldemere's Dilemma

"Well, well, well," Gadrun said with a laugh. "An Eretian with a backbone. Rarer than an ice floe in August, I have to tell you true. I have always admired the Ungerfils. As I said, I consider your father a friend. The way he saved his ship… He showed a stouter heart than any *Human* ever has."

In the earliest days of Lyseum, thousands of years before, the Dwarves and Humans had been uneasy trading partners, often going to war for months at a time over the tiniest of perceived slights. As time progressed, they each developed larger, more complex fortifications, at which the Dwarves particularly excelled. It was the need for timber after denuding their own forests that had led the Dwarves to agree at last to trading with the Ereti. A single stronghold required the wood of eight thousand trees. There were hundreds of such fortresses between the southwest and southeast shores of Mettlec—the largest and best-manned ringing Port Alum in the west, the only port where the Dwarves permitted Eretian ships to anchor.

And, unknown to either the Eretians or Lyseans—*the Mellyans*, Gadrun reminded himself—they were now arrayed around the northern cape as well.

Further complicating the necessity for trade were the vast marshes that surrounded each stronghold, which left even less land for planting along the coasts.

"Perhaps we can help each other," Janzalon said, extending his hand in peace. "Have you heard of Nakret Wilsbern?"

The Dwarf nodded, for the moment ignoring the tribune's gesture. "Athes's navigator when the *Salt-Serpent* went afoul. Lost his arm. And, no doubt, his pride, which is always the larger matter. What of him?"

Hathom was the one who answered. "We have been tasked with finding him. Will you join us?"

A Dwarven belly laugh is an invasive, derisive thing, and more than a few heads turned up and down the docks when Gadrun's was unleashed. "Tracking lost and bitter Eretians is the kind of thing best suited for trained dogs and your own meagre race. Why do you ask this of me?"

Janzalon now spoke. "I have more reasons than I now have time to share…"

"*Secrets*," Gadrun whispered, spitting on the dock as he did so. "You are no better than the Humans, Tribune."

"It is the Humans who are at the heart of what we ask," Janzalon answered, ignoring the Dwarf's latest show of disrespect. "I believe they are holding Stanchion Pilon. In Mellya."

Although he had heard this from Janzalon on their walk from the Admiralty building to the dock, Hathom had not known if or when the tribune would share it with the Dwarf.

"What are you hiding, Waelsbun?" The tone in Gadrun's voice was equal parts curiosity and incredulity. "I thought you broke off contact with the Mellyans when we did."

It was King Affram, Buttress Pilon's grandfather, who had ceased trade with the Mellyans when they had first seized the lands of Lyseum and declared themselves a military state.

"We did," Janzalon answered, "although they later sent the brother of their self-declared cliffprince to us as an ambassador near the time King Buttress claims that his wayward son went missing."

"So you believe the prince is in Mellya…"

"Along with our most capable shipwright," Hathom answered.

"Millet Ronng," Gadrun said. Seeing the look of surprise on the two nearly hairless faces before him, he added, "It was not exactly a secret—and it is my responsibility to know the happenings that affect our trade agreements."

"It cannot be a coincidence," Hathom whispered, mostly to himself.

"On that we do agree," Gadrun Grundling said, releasing another head-turning laugh. "Where are we going and when do we leave?"

Sitting alone in the Hall of Books and Ancestries, the candles burned to nubs and the sun about to rise, King Dylwyn of Glittereye ran his hand over the open book before him. Beside it sat his crown. How familiar it all seemed, how recent, although it had been nearly three years ago that he had been sitting in this very spot, reading this very tome—the First Book of Ancestry—when Sir Laurel had brought him the news that Baron Vellom had been poisoned in his bed. Little had he known what the colossal cost would be to stem the avalanche of violence and treachery that act had set into motion—no less than Laurel's life and the near ruin of the kingdom over which his grandfather had been first to rule.

"Manthes Fragenoar," Dylwyn whispered, closing the book with a reverence no one but he could understand, "still your secrets burn me. Is this cliffprince the regent of which you spoke the night you fell to your death? Or is he the usurper about whom this stranger Frederick warns us? If I go to war, who will be the foe?"

Aldemere's Dilemma

As always, only silence.

Then, at the door, a gentle knock.

It was Elde, with whom he had recently spent several hours in careful conversation before taking leave to clear and focus his mind for the decisions he must make.

"Are they assembled as instructed?" he asked the faithful jester, placing his crown upon his head.

"They are, Sire," Elde replied, watching as the crown laid its unnatural weight upon the king's neck and shoulders, bending his frame and making the wrinkles in his face slightly more pronounced. "If you will forgive me for saying so, we have never allowed any but the barons to sit in the Six Seats. Your request to bring the seventh from the corner… Talorous has asked the same questions of me as I now ask of you… I know this is no ill-considered whim or hastily made choice, but I cannot figure the why."

"Nor have I, fully," the king replied, pulling his cloak tighter around him and placing the First Book of Ancestry back upon the shelf. "Although I know it is the only thing to do. Let us not keep them waiting—their doubt shall grow as the empty seconds pass."

Taking a key from a chain around his neck, Dylwyn turned the lock in a slim door between two tall shelves on the northern wall. The mechanism groaned from lack of use but the key did its job. Although they rarely had reason to use it, the door that Dylwyn opened led directly into the Council Room.

The king was pleased. His attendants had followed his instructions to the letter, placing his own chair and the Seventh Seat—once reserved for Manthes Fragenoar and long-ago banished to a distant, dusty corner—directly opposite one another a dozen feet apart, while to the left of the king's seat they had positioned three chairs and two more opposite to those. Flanking the Seventh Seat, which was at the moment empty, were Laurianna and Peecwyl, looking noticeably uncomfortable in such unaccustomed surroundings.

"Elde," King Dylwyn said, approaching his chair, "you shall sit to my right." Talorous had already claimed the seat beside it.

In the three chairs opposite the jester and the scholar were seated Linead, Frederick, and Aldemere, with Linead closest to the king, as dictated by his rank. They stood as the king took his seat.

"Welcome to Glittereye, Frederick of the North," Dylwyn said, with a nod of the head.

"It is an honor to stand before you, King Dylwyn of Glittereye," Frederick answered, bowing deeply and holding the position several seconds longer than necessary. "I appreciate the haste with which you have agreed to see me. Time is still our ally, although soon it will be our enemy's."

"The need for us to take action is well understood," answered Dylwyn. "Although the matter of precisely who our enemy is and what such an enemy might want from this kingdom are still to be deciphered." As the three men to his left took their seats, the king instructed, "Frederick, please—take that chair over there."

He was pointing to the Seventh Seat.

Ignoring the whispered sounds of wonder and surprise that came from almost everyone in the room—only Talorous remained silent—the king continued, "And fair Laurianna, whom we never see enough of, please do take a seat between these two honorable knights of the realm."

As soon as Frederick and Laurianna had done what the king had asked, Dylwyn turned his attention to the final attendee still without a chair.

"Sir Peecwyl, trusted warrior of Glittereye. Chief Knight of the Central Barony. I beg of you to choose a chair and sit amongst us. The ones on the west wall are those used by the Elves when they have occasion to visit. I heartily recommend one of those."

To Aldemere's surprise, Peecwyl did as the king instructed without hesitation, question, or protest. Talking with Linead hours later, he learned that the knight-marshal had half expected the stubborn knight to refuse a chair and stand for the duration of the meeting, as had the captainguard.

"I shall be brief," Dylwyn began, looking around the room. "I know I am breaking tradition by conducting our meeting here, for you are not barons and the Seventh Seat has remained empty for decades, but it is clear to me, hearing all that I have on Frederick's behalf from Jester Elde, that many of our traditions and habits will soon be rendered old and obsolete. A long-unspoken-of world is beckoning to us... make no mistake. The mountains and seas will no longer be the barriers that we once perceived them to be. They will barely be boundaries if what I believe shall happen occurs. This is why I have seated you as I have, and why I have asked Laurianna to join us. Talorous has spoken to me of the bond you have begun to form with Brother Farvon—the young and forward-thinking keeper of the scrolls in the Seers' temple. What is your assessment of his value toward our goal of repairing our relations with the Seven Lords, gentle scholar?"

Aldemere's Dilemma

Without hesitation, Laurianna replied, "He is, not unlike myself, just young enough to calculate recent events and their causations and correlations with future probabilities differently than most of you sitting in this room."

Do not be shy, Aldemere thought, impressed with her straightforwardness. *I never am.*

"It is the same sense of history coupled to new ideas that is most clearly manifest in Sir Aldemere, Sire. His amalgamation of the jester and the knight has saved the kingdom on more than one occasion, as you are well aware. Brother Farvon possesses a different, but equally potent, power."

King Dylwyn, judging by the range of motion and speed of his nod, readily agreed. "Very well, then, Laurianna. I am hereby commissioning a new book, which yourself and Brother Farvon will author, detailing the relationship of the rulers of Glittereye and the Seven Lord Seers. Is it best that you undertake this project there or here?"

"Sire, I—"

Aldemere was amazed at the change in confidence he was seeing in Talorous's prized protégé. Moments ago, she had been stone.

Now she was soup.

"Perhaps you will want to confer further with Master Talorous?" Dylwyn asked, acknowledging the scholar's change in demeanor.

"No, Sire," Laurianna answered, summoning strength into her shoulders, which quickly returned to square. "No further time is needed. I think it best to work in the temple library. It will ease the Seers' minds and lessen their inevitable suspicion about why I, a woman, and one of Talorous's closest companions, am all of a sudden engaged in this project with their fellow brother."

Enjoying the game he understood Laurianna to be playing, Dylwyn asked with a smile, "And what suspicions might they have?"

"That this book is but a ruse—a pretext—for my and Farvon's ideas to conjoin and bring new fruit. Fruit that might be all too bitter when it is time for the brothers to taste it."

"Then I suggest you write a brilliant book while you are facilitating our real intentions," Dylwyn answered, although the smile was gone. "You shall take the First Book of Ancestry with you. I look forward to seeing you when you and Farvon come back to the castle to ask Talorous and the others from the Council of Elders and me what you need to know to continue what will no doubt be an already well-begun book. Say nothing of this part of the plan when you are there.

Let it be a surprise. Expect a messenger hawk in a month's time. You shall leave immediately, yes?"

Rising from her seat, Laurianna replied, "Just as soon as I fetch the book and my owl, Beazor, and have the stable boys prep a horse, my King."

"The horse already awaits you," Dylwyn answered, "as does an escort of two hand-picked knights dressed as farmers with a wagon full of supplies Dictus recently requested. You are far too valuable to our plan for me to permit you to travel alone. May the Deities bless your endeavor, gentle scholar."

Laurianna was out the door and down the hall before Aldemere—or anyone else, he wagered—could fully fathom what had just occurred.

Even Talorous looked like a calf caught in the candlelight.

"As to larger matters," Dylwyn continued, ignoring the puzzled looks of his audience, "if, as Frederick says—and we have no reason to doubt him—the eastern forest is once more the seat of peril—and the mysterious Forest of Tombal beyond it—we should send several companies there under Linead's command with all due haste. The barons—and baroness—would be easy targets if someone meant them ill."

"You must not send so many," Frederick said, shaking his head. "As I expressed to Elde the Jester, a much smaller incursion is needed. Such a sizable force as you are suggesting—no matter how well intentioned—will not only unsettle the Greybaer—it will alert the cliffprince to the fact we know his intentions. Any advantage we might now have—and I assure you, it is slim—will be lost."

"What of our barons?" Elde enquired.

"I have heard nothing through my network of any intention to attack your barons," Frederick answered. "Nadrim's spies are in the east solely for the Greybaer. Of this, I am fully confident."

"And what do we know of these Greybaer?" Dylwyn asked, looking at Talorous.

"Sire, if I might offer an answer," Aldemere interrupted, quickly ceasing his talk as Talorous caught his eye with a fierce glare and a severe motion of his arm.

"Only what is recorded by a scribe of unknown origin on a single scroll," Talorous answered. "They are described as taller than we Humans, with heads said to resemble those of the forest lions that once roamed the south and east in the times before the Unity Wars, when many a clan chief wore their pelts and flowing manes as a symbol of enlightenment and strength. As to the Greybaer, the author believed their worship of the natural world parallels that of the Elves. And they are further said to possess the ability to harness the forces of the forest to achieve miraculous things."

"Such as what?" Dylwyn asked, regretting the untold hours he had spent pouring over Manthes's at the expense of the other volumes and scrolls kept in the room next door.

Talorous shook his head. "The scroll does not elaborate. As I said, Sire, we do not know either its origins or its accuracy."

"All it says is true," Frederick offered, anxious to stop the endless counsel and finally take some action. "I have lived at times with the Greybaer. I have a handful of companions presently protecting them. Working with them to watch over the sacred acres of Tombal until I can organize a larger plan and deliver the help they require. Sire, please—I beg of you, although I beg of no man—ready your armies, yes, but as quietly as you can. The cliffprince may have spies within your ranks, as he has managed to have in the past. Your preparations must seem, Sir Linead, as nothing more than drills. Organize melees in lieu of your annual Spring Tournament. As for me, I must return to Tombal as soon as you will allow me to leave—with a handful of well-trained men, as I asked of Elde the Jester... And someone must go north, so we can acquire firsthand reports of exactly what it is the cliffprince is planning."

"Why not do that yourself?" Peecwyl asked. "You profess to have been there. We can send word to Sir Connal—Sir Linead specifically selected him to be chief knight in the east because of the unwavering loyalty of he and his kin to those lands—and he can send an emissary to the Greybaer. Perhaps Baroness Ashlin would be sufficiently nonthreatening to soothe your nervous allies..."

"I cannot go north again," Frederick explained. "The cliffprince knows my face—as do the members of the Shadow Knife— Nadrim's secret enforcers—and the officers of his army. It has to be a stranger. It has to be Sir Aldemere."

Instead of the din of protestation those words would normally elicit, those assembled met Aldemere's ears and eyes with an unsettling silence and zero looks of surprise.

How he wished it would be as it was.

"So be it," Dylwyn agreed, with an unsettling absence of emotion. "What else do you require?"

Sinking to one knee and touching the floor before him, Frederick answered, "For the time being, Dylwyn King, only that you trust me, for my asking has just begun."

CHAPTER FIVE

Sir Eric wrinkled his nose at the smells from the kitchen just behind him. Used to eating simple soldier's food and sleeping on a pallet and an inch of straw, the past two weeks had subjected the young knight to more exotic smells, soft surfaces, and meaningless council etiquette than he wanted to remember.

Not even as a boy, being the father of a soldier and then a page and squire, had he been allowed to sleep on a proper bed, or indulge in foods drowned in rich, fattening sauces or anything considered a "sweet." His mother had tried to sneak him some on occasion, but fear of his father and a tongue that no longer liked the taste of anything more than a simple stew or roasted chicken breast kept him from accepting.

Adjusting his stance slightly to relieve a cramp in his calf, Eric silently cursed his comrade Lan, whose insistence on reporting what he had heard about strangers in the Eastern Forest from his friends in the local garrison had been stirring in Eric nothing but bouts of second-guessing. After all, their commanding officers made reports of their own, and they should have been the ones to make it known to Aldemere. To make matters worse, in the midst of this day in, day out, mind numbing, muscle-weakening boredom, their volunteering as extra security seemed no less than a presumptuous mistake. He would much rather be back at the castle—riding patrol, training, and trading dirty jokes and comments about the serving maids with his comrades.

Even when taking into account the almost daily outbursts that erupted amongst the barons and trade wardens the first ten days—that never came to anything at all beyond some posturing and grumbles—Eric knew that this escort assignment better suited Lan. The quiet, the routine, the fabricated civilities… they were exactly what his unambitious friend had bargained for, but Eric was more like his father. Sir Prima, Chief Knight of the Western Barony, was respected and feared, and had been chosen by Baron Ralin for that very reason over dozens of other knights who had also sworn loyalty to Baron Vellom's son in the wake of his father's murder.

My future is all but assured, Eric thought, suppressing a smile, *as long as I can keep the timidity and lack of ambition of lesser knights like Lan from pulling me into the horse-waste.*

There had been one positive in the past two weeks. Eric had listened closely to the trade meeting proceedings, especially noting the forceful way Baron Ralin led the discussions in the direction he wished them to go. Although Chrystan had managed to rein him in after he overplayed his hand several days earlier—resulting in the last four days of relative cooperation and peace—Eric was confident that Ralin was merely recalculating, and the Western Barony would emerge from the meetings considerably greater in strength. Lan was less than pleased with having to take the exterior watch day after day, but Eric had made it clear that he needed to be close to the action.

To extend his education even further, he had broken bread twice daily with the trade wardens, who were also knights, so they ate at a table far removed from the barons. Sir Glenmore, warden of the west, was more than happy to sit beside Eric and share with him the most recent session's highlights. Although theirs were, on paper, parallel positions, Glenmore was wise enough to understand that doing right by Eric meant doing right by his father, which could only bring him benefit.

"I saw you put your hand on your sword when Abbas and I had our bit of tension," Glenmore revealed at their most recent meal, referring to the evening of Ralin's final outburst. "It is good to know where you stand."

I stand with those who help me reach my goals, Eric had thought. *At present, that means Baron Ralin.*

Blinking his eyes several times as a pair of serving maids carried hot bowls of heavily spiced soup past him from the kitchen for the barons' midday meal, Eric willed them to refocus as the attendants shuffled past. He smiled at several of the serving girls—especially the buxom brunette who had met him in the apple orchard the past several nights after all had gone to bed—and glared at a few of the young men who had chosen the peeling of potatoes over service to their king.

Several minutes later, as the kitchen staff were serving the soup to the barons and baroness, Eric felt his body embrace the tension that occurred a split second before it went into action at the sight of five tall men emerging from the kitchen with trays of their own. Trays that they kept covered, unlike the preceding serving staff.

Now on high alert, Eric quickly processed two more, intimately related, bits of information: They were too old to be servers, and they were not dressed in the white leggings and tunics of the chefs.

Trained as he was to react on his instincts with a minimum of thought—apologies were preferable to burials—Eric drew his sword and yelled so all could hear, "Arms at the ready, my knights! Unknowns in our midst!"

His suspicions were confirmed when the kitchen staff instinctively dropped their trays, following them onto the floor in a single collapsing mass, which left the five strangers exposed in their deceit.

Pushing aside the pride that surged inside him at the sight of swords unsheathing around the room in the hands of the trade wardens and handful of knights guarding the room from the eastern garrison, Eric widened his stance, and prepared to engage with the enemy.

As the knights arrayed around the room began their approach, one of the five intruders removed the cover from his tray, revealing a scaled down version of a crossbow. Without a shield, Eric was defenseless as the assassin fired a feathered bolt into the center of his throat. As his mouth filled with blood, and he felt himself collapsing, Eric watched as his assailant's companions made the same swift move for crossbows of their own, taking down three barony knights and the trade warden from the northern barony, Sir Ovit, with identical wounds to the throat.

At least I gave them a warning, Eric thought, feeling the blood running fast around his fingers in hot, relentless rivulets as he tried to plug his wound. *I will die a hero's death*.

As the battle around him raged, that is quickly what befell the only son of Sir Prima of the West.

"No ships must leave our port for Vaelsport or the Kingdom of Mettlec. This is what the goddesses and god decree," Carra reported, closing the door to the Inner Temple and facing the four Eretians who had been waiting four worrisome days for her to emerge from the Vessel's sanctum sanctorum.

Although they were, each of them, unhappy with this news—and each for his own particular reasons—not one of them—not Warden Hefflar, Grand Admiral Ungerfil, Tribune Waelsbun, nor Ambassador Waelsbun—dared to be outright defiant.

"Are you absolutely certain this is the will of the Ruenai?" the ambassador asked, in the diplomatic tone his station demanded. "The messages you receive through these secretive rituals of yours must sometimes be—"

"In this particular case, they are undeniably clear," Carra answered, knowing the question was the best the four males could muster under the circumstances and allowing them to have it. "At no time in my tenure as sea-shaman have they been clearer. I have seen many things that I am not yet ready to speak of, but as to what I have told you, the message was exact. No loaded cargo ships nor the singled-masted ones are to depart Llafen-Eret until the Ruenai allow it."

In addition to the nine-ship fleet of merchant vessels, the Eretian Admiralty maintained the seven single-masted vessels that their ancestors had first built under the guidance of the Ruenai. They had named these sleek and speedy ships for the seven stars by which Eretian navigators sailed.

"Has there been an answer about fitting the ships for war?" the grand admiral enquired, hopeful that this might be the explanation for keeping the ships in port.

Carra shook her head. "Not as yet. We cannot undertake such important beseechments as the request to prepare for war as easily as the rites we have recently enacted. The Ruen-Eret and I are preparing a more complicated set of rituals within the Inner Temple, to which I must shortly return."

Frustration now laced the faces arrayed before her, but Carra heard not a single word of argument. The sea-shaman said a silent prayer of gratitude for the respect this quartet of powerful males was showing the Ruenai and, by extension, to her. It was encouraging that they seemed to remember that it was the ancient ancestors of families like the Waelsbuns and Ungerfils who had gone to sea as would-be conquerors to lands whose names they had either long forgotten or had never bothered to learn. Therefore, they were in large part responsible for all that befell their people when the Ruenai decreed "No more!" For this reason, not even newly commissioned captains had permission to view the only completed map of Mynoweth that Carra knew to exist.

The sea-shamans had kept it with the Stone. It had gone missing as well.

Although no one knew that but her.

"If there is nothing more to share, we will leave you to your rituals," Warden Hefflar said, standing as a cue to the others. "We will send a runner each morning and early each evening, as we have done the past four days. When there is something for you to share, we will answer the summons with haste." Turning to his colleagues, he added, "Let us away. There are ships to be unloaded and crews to disappoint. It is most inauspicious to have newly conferred captains unable to take charge of their vessels."

As they started to exit, Carra reached for the sea-blue sleeve of Tribune Waelsbun's robe, indicating her wish to have him stay. If the others were anything more than passing curious when they noticed, none of them let it show.

The sea-shaman sat beside the reseated tribune, although she waited to speak until the others had departed through the Vessel's aft-most doors.

"When were you planning to start your search for Nakret Wilsbern, Tribune?" she asked. "And will the Dwarf accompany you as requested?"

"We planned to leave tomorrow—meaning, the day after you summoned us," Janzalon answered. "And, yes—Gadrun Grundling has agreed to come along."

"Very well then. You must leave at dawn," Carra said, leaning in close so her words could be a whisper. "I have had a vision during my communing with the Ruenai. Nakret Wilsbern is in Mellya, but not for very much longer. Therefore, your destination is not that dangerous land, but a forest further south. *Directly* south."

"Does Nakret have the Stone?" Janzalon enquired, a trace of guarded hope strengthening his voice.

"The Ruenai have not spoken to me of the Stone," Carra answered, placing her hand upon the tribune's in a gesture of support. "Which can only be taken to mean one of two things—they do not know, or they will not say."

Wanting to slam his fist into the pew in frustration and curse the games of the gods, Janzalon refrained. He instead found himself grateful for the warmth of the sea-shaman's hand as it lay gently upon his own. Speaking out against the Ruenai in the spot where their essence dwelled was like setting fire to your ship for light to read a map.

"Did they speak the forest's name? Or reveal the route that we should take?"

Carra nodded yes. "If you sail southeast, past Xaen's Point, and turn south well before the scouting towers of Boldac's Blade in the far south of Mettlec, and make a course to the west of the Islands of Kirr, you will sail well away from Mellya. We do not know if they have ships, and if so, how far from land they can venture. Just below the Ambir Mountains, there the forest lies. There are beings that live there who are in grave danger. Great-headed, with long shaggy hair and an animal-like countenance, they are capable of feats of power comparable to the Ruen-Eret."

Aldemere's Dilemma

Janzalon shook his head. "If we are to travel by sea, but none of our ships may sail…"

Carra also shook her head. "I did not say they said *no* ships. Only those scheduled for Vaelsport and Mettlec, and the single-masted. That leaves the *Spear-Shaft* or the *Sea-Sword*. You are welcome to take your pick."

A question often asked by Eretian children—and Dwarves like Gadrun Grundling—was why the Ruenai permitted ships that sailed in peace to carry warlike names. The answer was achingly simple—ships must not change names, or else they are ever cursed.

"I would be content with either," Janzalon said, doing his best to process all he had heard. "But the *Sea-Sword* is captained by a Skarling, and—although I would not say this to an Ungerfil—no finer family has ever sailed the seas."

"Then the *Sea-Sword* it shall be," Carra agreed with a reassuring smile.

The Ruenai had said as much, although she saw no point in letting the tribune know.

Since Carra was a child, the previous sea-shaman had made it known that the Ruenai favored the Skarlings above all the other families. Former sea-shamans had called upon them now and again in times of greatest trouble. Now, their capable descendent, Captain Billec Skarling, would be asked to answer the call.

"You have much to do, Tribune Waelsbun," Carra said, removing her hand from his. "I know Eretian ships are always rigged and at the ready. The voyage will take a little more than a week, and the Ruenai will be of help with calm seas and steady winds. It is once you reach the forest that the hardships shall begin."

"What am I to tell the Admiralty?"

"Tell them only that it is the Ruenai's will that you sail, and that I will explain it to their satisfaction when the time is right."

Janzalon nodded, but said nothing and turned for the exit. He was already starting to catalog the dangers and trials ahead.

Opening the door to the Inner Temple and breathing in the incense from the censors the priestesses kept filled as part of the offerings they were making to the Ruenai in preparation for the spirit-journey she was soon to undertake, Carra cast a quick glance back as the tribune left the Vessel.

What was to come would test each and every one of them—each according to the tasks the gods had chosen to give them. As for Carra's mission—to journey to the realms where the souls of the Ruenai dwelled—its price might be her life.

Aldemere reined Poet, his pure-white Elven horse, to a hard stop a mile from Eerbell at the sight of a dozen mounted knights in a tight defensive formation. He recognized the red and black diagonal stripes upon the foremost shield as the coat of arms of Sir Connar, Chief Knight of the Eastern Barony.

Acquainted with most of the knights in Aldemere's party—including Sir Linead, who had chosen Connar for his position at the conclusion of the Rebellion—Connar saluted in the way of subordinate knights, touching his right fist to the opposite shoulder and then bringing his hand back across his body and forward, palm out.

Returning the first part of the salute in unison, as was expected by their higher rank, Aldemere and Linead brought their horses forward while the other six knights in their party, and Frederick, remained in place. They had not sent advanced word of their planned arrival, sensitive to the possible presence of spies in the Eastern Barony.

Leaving the asking of questions to Linead, his right as Connar's commander, Aldemere hung back a few feet as they rode closer, allowing the knight-marshal, who sat proudly upon Titan, the black forest charger that once belonged to the former captainguard, Sir Laurel, to reach Sir Connar first.

"The barons' trade meeting was attacked yesterday at midday," Connar reported. "Five assassins, dressed as servers, entered the meeting hall from the kitchen, drawing miniature—but deadly—crossbows from beneath their covered trays. All were subdued. We have kept one of them alive for questioning. He has a nasty wound to the abdomen, courtesy of a trade warden's blade, but shall survive a few more days, should you wish to question him, but he has yet to utter a word. Did not even moan when the doctor stitched him up. We sent a messenger hawk to the castle. You no doubt crossed beneath it."

Linead, after commending Sir Connar for his brevity and thoroughness, turned toward Frederick, whom Aldemere had positioned in the center of Linead's six most trusted lieutenants. Although they had returned the northerner's weapons to him the previous day when they departed Castle Silveth, Linead had made it clear to his men to keep a constant watch over their mysterious traveling companion.

"You told the king you were confident Eerbell was safe!" he hissed, immediately relaxing his tensed-up shoulders as Titan

95   *Aldemere's Dilemma*

grunted in frustration as his rider's hands tightened unconsciously around the reins. "If Sir Peecwyl were here, I would order him to thrash you where you sit."

"I understand your anger. I truly thought it was," Frederick answered, silently cursing himself for this inexcusable miscalculation at a time he could ill afford it. "Have you suffered any casualties?" he asked Connar, already knowing the answer and bracing himself for Linead's further derision.

"Five," Connar replied, looking with distrust and disdain upon the unidentified rider, who bore no coat of arms and certainly was no knight. "Three of my men were killed in the assassins' initial strike. And Sir Orvit, trade warden of the north, was fatally wounded by a knife as he fought to bring one of them down." Looking at Aldemere and sitting up even straighter in his saddle, he added, "And one your lieutenants, Captainguard Aldemere." His voice nearly breaking, he whispered, "Sir Prima's son. Sir Eric."

"The Deities have mercy," Linead whispered, giving Frederick a look filled with hate.

"What of the barons?" Aldemere asked, as an alternative to dwelling on the news he had just received. "Are any of them injured?"

"All of them are healthy and well," Connar reported. "Their protection was our first priority. I have patrols riding the perimeter in all directions and a hefty contingent guarding the barons within Eerbell, although they are anxious to return to their baronies. Sir Ralin is particularly agitated—even more so than he has been."

"I will talk with Baron Ralin," Aldemere said, shaking his head at the thought of what his friend had been saying to the others throughout the past two weeks.

"Then let us ride with haste," Linead ordered, anxious to question the sole surviving assassin.

A considerable show of force met their gaze as they arrived at Eerbell minutes later, just as Connar had promised.

Aldemere winced as the familiar, nauseating smell of burning flesh entered his nostrils.

"Who is being burned?" he asked, dismounting.

"The four deceased assassins, Captainguard," Connar replied. "Back behind the stables, in a clearing in the woods. Doused them with oil and set them alight. It is not a proper funeral pyre, of course…"

"Understood," Aldemere said, glad that Connar had denied the cowards proper passage to the place where the Deities dwelled.

Turning to Linead, he asked, "Do you want assistance in questioning the lone survivor?"

Drawing a misericord from his belt and dismounting, the knight-marshal shook his head. "It is best if I go it alone. I would not want anyone to see what I am planning to do to this gutless river monster." Taking Connar by the arm he demanded, "Show me where he is."

"If you do not mind," Frederick said, not daring to dismount, "I would like to go with you. I could be of help—provided there is no chance that you will permit the bastard to live. He may know my face, and the one who hired him must not be told that I am here."

Linead adjusted his grip on the misericord. "I can assure you that he shall not know another sunset. Although he shall not see your face. Sir Corvit sent a hawk back to Peecwyl vouching for your story, but given what has happened, and your inability to conceive of it, I have no more reason to trust you." He turned the point of the knife in Frederick's direction. "Perhaps you were part of it, leading us into a trap. If that is the case, and this poxy whoreson knows it, I do not want you near enough to silence him before he can speak the truth."

Frederick clenched his fists in frustration. "I knew nothing of this attack!" he protested, his tone turning ugly and bitter. "It may serve only to condemn me further, but if you check the assassin's lower left leg, you will almost certainly see the tattoo of a three-taloned falcon. It is Nadrim's crest. And if the image is there, I can assure you that whatever details you seek from him, he will take to his grave no matter the pain you inflict, as he has sworn and been trained to uphold."

"We shall see," answered Linead, turning toward the entrance to Eerbell. Before he entered the door Connar was holding ajar, he yelled back, "Take Frederick to the stables, men, and confiscate his weapons. Be sure he does not leave."

Watching Linead disappear through the darkened doorway, as if he were entering a cave, the contents and events of which would change his soul forever, Aldemere fought the urge to both prevent Linead from doing what he intended and to offer some words of comfort to help ease Frederick's guilt. He also found himself having his own sense of guilt with which he must first contend—a sharp feeling in his gut that increased in intensity as Lan entered his field of vision.

"May I have a word, Sir?" his distraught lieutenant asked, as Linead's men rode for the stables with Frederick.

Aldemere's Dilemma

"As many as you need," Aldemere said, taking Poet's reins and walking him toward a water trough positioned several feet away. "But know you hold no blame. This is not your fault."

His face reddening as his grey eyes filled with tears, Lan dropped his head in shame. "I should have been beside him. We were comrades, like you lectured. I should have had his back."

"So then, make your report—why did you fail in your duty?"

It was a question Sir Laurel would have asked.

"Eric was annoyed with me. He thought we were wasting our time. He insisted on being inside, so he could learn all he could from the trade wardens, and the barons' negotiations. And he did not want me around, so I kept the watch out here."

Aldemere placed his hand on Lan's shoulder, lifting his subordinate's chin to force him to meet his gaze. "The attack could just as easily have come from somewhere out here... From the forest. Then I would be talking to Eric instead of you. That is the hardest truth I can offer. Your father, Sir Laurel, Sir Orvit—each was a fierce, capable fighter, experienced in the ways of battle. When the Deities deem it our time, we can only proceed with swords drawn, eyes open, and the enemy before us."

Lan nodded, rubbing his eyes with the heels of his hands. "It was Eric who saw what they were. He managed to warn the room before he took a bolt to the throat. Baron Chrystan told me that. He saved a lot of lives."

"If that is true, and I would not dare to question the baron's accounting, then Eric died the best death for which a knight could hope. His father shall at least have that, as shall we. You must know that he is nothing like these assassins. There was no honor in their attack. Secretive and stealthy. No one will mourn them, Lan. That is the difference that provides us with some comfort." Acknowledging the acrid black smoke rising from just beyond the stables, Aldemere whispered, "They deserve to burn. And you, my lieutenant, deserve to live. But you must find your strength. The members of the King's Guard will be counting on you to have a clear head and unwavering resolve as this coming storm descends. Upon my return, I shall make a full report. In the meantime, upon *your* return, you must tell any who will listen that Eric died defending those who could not defend themselves and, given the chance, you shall do the same."

"Aye, Sir," Lan replied, saluting. "I shall take you to Baron Ralin. He saw your colors through the door and sent me out to retrieve you."

While Aldemere was talking with Lan, Linead had taken the opportunity to comfort Baron Ciloto. The loss of Sir Orvit, his long-time friend and trade warden, had broken the old man's heart.

Excusing himself as quickly as he could, Linead followed Connar into the room where the wounded assassin lay.

Half an hour had passed before Linead learned for himself that Frederick's second statement was true—the assassin would not talk, no matter how many times or how deeply the misericord entered his flesh. Not even the knight-marshal's boot pressed into his bandaged abdomen elicited even the slightest sound from the reticent warrior. As to the tattoo—it was right where Frederick had said it would be.

Which proved only that Frederick knew far more than he was thus far willing to share.

"I have no more patience for this," Linead whispered, sheathing his knife before he could act upon his deep desire to draw it across the assassin's pulsing jugular vein. "There shall be no more visits from the doctor," he instructed Connar. "And he is only to have half a bowl of salted broth. Although I doubt he shall drink it. If he is not dead by morning, I shall give you further orders before I leave for the garrison."

Exiting the room and making his way to Eerbell's central hall, Linead spotted Aldemere approaching Ralin.

"I would like to join you, if I may," he asked, crossing the room to meet them.

"Sir Linead," Ralin said, clapping him on the shoulder and indicating that he and Aldemere should sit. "I had not expected to see you here. The same for you, old friend. We could have used you yesterday, to be sure."

"We have come on urgent business," Aldemere answered, relieved to see no mead nor ale in sight and Ralin's temper in check. "Which we shall discuss with you in time. Any guess as to their aim?"

"Their *aim*?" Ralin asked. "Deadly. However, if you are enquiring as to their *purpose*, it seemed to be nothing more than to inflict as much death as quickly as possible before they were subdued. None intended to leave here alive. Sir Eric prevented a slaughter," he said, patting Aldemere on the forearm. "And he paid the ultimate price."

"I am well aware of his actions. Will you take his body back to Spiltrow?"

"In the morning, if you will let me. We made quite a bit of progress the last several days. There is no more to say, and ever so much to be done."

Standing abruptly, Linead said, "We will gather together tonight. As Aldemere suggested, we have much to tell, and I have questions still to ask."

"Very well," Ralin replied, sensing that considerably more than the recent attack was fueling the tension in Linead's voice. "What of the one still alive? At least, until you met with him…"

If Aldemere did not know better—and he was no longer sure that he did—he would have been tempted to lay a wager that there was more than a little wish for murder in the western baron's voice.

"He remains just as I found him," Linead answered, not pleased that Ralin had brought it up. "More or less. If you will both excuse me," he added, offering a half-hearted salute as he unsheathed his misericord, "I have some business in the stables. I shall see you both tonight."

Watching Linead walk away, Ralin motioned for Aldemere to sit even closer beside him. "I am glad that you are here. I have been an ass, and you always set me straight. I have no trouble pushing when things need to be pushed, but now is not the time for drunken behavior and being a stone in the soup." He removed a pitcher and two cups from the adjoining table. Seeing Aldemere's jaw muscles tighten, he assured him, filling both of the cups, "It is only apple cider—fresh and unfermented, from Baroness Ashlin's orchards." Handing a cup to Aldemere and raising his own, Ralin said, "I am bringing Prima his son, draped on the back of a wagon. The West is at your service, and the service of the king, no matter what you need."

Draining the cup in a single swallow, he watched Aldemere do the same.

Fifty miles north of the Mellyan capital of Amdar, amidst an impenetrable network of waterfalls and moss-slickened ledges, stood the formidable fortress of Ravinscliff. Designed by Nadrim's grandfather, Ravin, during his years as first chief administrator, Ravinscliff was built by hundreds of slaves, mostly drawn from the families of his Lysean enemies. Few of them survived to see it completed. Although most of them died from exhaustion, or by falling from the scaffolding erected in the cloud-hidden heights, the first chief administrator had ordered several dozen executed. This was especially true of the architects, foremen, and others that knew the secrets of Ravincliff's complex warren of rooms and fortifications. Until the time when thousands of additional slaves had built and fortified Amdar, the impregnable mountain fortress served as Ravin's center of power.

Having spent most of his childhood at Ravinscliff, Nadrim had laid claim to it—along with the title of cliffprince—as his preferred stronghold to lay his plans, construct his plots, and deal with his own enemies as brutally as had his grandfather.

And so it was that he had ridden with all due haste the previous day when a messenger falcon had delivered word regarding the outspoken remarks being made by a local lord on the north-central shore of Mellya who did not agree with Nadrim's intent to go to war. Members of the Shadow Knife—the Damonessas' secret security unit and extensive network of spies, formed in the months before Lyseum was undone—had overheard his criticisms, loudly explicated over pints at the local tavern.

As Nadrim entered the Interrogation Room at Ravinscliff, he felt his heart pick up its pace and his skin flush red with blood at the sight of various instruments of information extraction set out in gleaming order atop a long, rectangular table. Beside the table was a vertical slab of oak fitted out with an array of straps and chains and two large, geared wheels to change its height and angles. For the further discomfort of Nadrim's chosen guests was an oak and iron chair with half-inch spikes in the seat, buckled leather restraints on the arms and along its bottom, and a wire and iron mechanism in which to affix its occupant's head.

In a far more comfortable chair, carved and cushioned, with an ottoman to match, sat Astrin Callenhor, the lord whose ill-considered words had brought Nadrim to this room.

He does not look afraid, Nadrim thought. *What an unexpected delight this shall be.*

"Have the household staff offered you wine and some nibbles?" Nadrim asked, running his fingers along the edge of the table of tools as he made his way to the closed double doors on the far side of the room.

"In abundance and with insistence," Lord Callenhor replied, undaunted by Nadrim's little playroom. He had not attained his position by being soft, nor did he have a history of backing down in situations such as this, when the bruised ego of a bully like Nadrim needed soothing in the form of childish games. "But I am not daft enough to ingest anything offered in such a place as this."

Opening the double doors and breathing in the thin, crisp mountain air, Nadrim peeked out over the high, narrow balcony to the jagged rocks and churning waters below.

"I know you think this room is frivolous and silly," he said, walking toward the lord. "All this show of strength. All this threat of violence. I can see that I misjudged you. You are a man of stouter heart, of truer resolve, than most who sit in that chair. I cannot tell you how many times I have had to have that cushion replaced. The sight and smell of a man's solid and liquid filth is impossible to remove."

"I know your dogs have made reports," Lord Callenhor replied, pushing the image just described from his mind. "I stand by what I said."

Nadrim whistled in admiration. "I really must tell you, Lord Callenhor—Astrin—I am duly, duly impressed. I could use your iron nerves in my Ministry. Why are you not a leading member? It seems with guts and insights like yours, you would not waste yourself by being lord of an arid, piss-swamp acreage that would not be missed a day were it to fall into the sea."

Callenhor rolled his eyes and shifted in his chair. "You know well enough why that is. Your father made the offer, when you were still a boy, but I was unwilling to lose my testes for the privilege."

Nadrim whistled again, even louder and longer. The entertainment value of such a fool as this was precious merriment indeed.

The requirement of castration for all who held a chair in the five-member Ministry was another of his grandfather's enviable ideas. Given the treachery of certain Lysean ministers—himself foremost amongst them—Ravin Damonessa had ensured that none of *his* ministers would sire sons who might join with their fathers in rising up against him.

It was also a fact that a man without his testicles was no longer much of a man and was easier to control.

Considering what he had learned about and taken advantage of as the likes of Garamin and Ralin angled for power in Glittereye— despite the admittedly bold maneuvers of the son of its puppet king's personal clown—Nadrim had acknowledged his grandfather's genius and extended the policy to include the four generals who commanded his imperial army.

"Correct me if I am wrong," Nadrim said with a smile, dragging a chair across the floor and placing it arm to arm with his guest's, "but you have no living children, so your aging pair of testes and the greying sack that holds them, which you thought to be so precious, have kept you from achieving greatness."

"True enough, Prince Nadrim," Callenhor replied, not altering his position as his host situated himself in his chair, "and yet it is a comfort to know they are there. To feel the weight of them, as it were."

"I suppose," Nadrim said, noticing the poor condition of the lord's doublet now that they were in close proximity and finding himself suddenly weary of talk. "Though the things you have said—the reason why you are here—relate to Ministry-level matters about which low-level lords like yourself have no right to speak. Therefore, it seems to me that you want the best of those positions. That, my grey-balled friend, is simply not allowed."

Callenhor dropped his jowls as confusion filled his head. "Your father set no boundaries, so I was not aware—"

"Oh, my little lord, I fully beg to differ."

Nadrim's voice had become as cold as the breeze that blew through the open doors. "Do I seem to you a man who would let the middlings speak? *Opinions* are dangerous things, Lord Callenhor. Some say that *opinions* are full of virtue—that they aid in the exchange of ideas, usher in improvements, and, most incredulously, that they increase the health and wealth of those who think we serve them, and not the other way around. I know that you know better, as did my sainted father—of whom you should never speak again if you desire to die still feeling the weight of your testes. Yes, yes, dear Astrin, you certainly do know better. Yet you not only *offer* your *opinions*—unsolicited and ill-considered—you shout them to your puss-laden peasants and their lazy, lard-loving overseers in very public places."

"I meant you no offense, My Cliffprince," Callenhor said, his voice and stature diminishing in tandem. "I only wanted to verbalize what many of us think."

Nadrim sat erect, all of a sudden intrigued. "Are you offering to give me *names*?" he asked, his voice now full of mirth. "Are we going to barter and bargain? *Dickering*, the puss-laden peasants call it, do they not? You would know better than I... Very well then, Astrid! I start the bidding at three. Three names and you shall leave this room alive, still feeling the weight of your testes."

Regardless of the outcome, Nadrim knew he would not soon forget the sight of every bit of color draining from Callenhor's frightened, snow-white face.

"I am an honest man," the flustered lord replied.

"Oh, again, I beg to differ. You made me say that again. And I so dislike the drudgery of being required to repeat myself..."

Nadrim was then up and out of his chair, bringing his hands together twice as he stomped his foot on the floor. Within seconds, two large men entered the room, grabbing Callenhor by the arms. Behind them entered a third, dressed, as were they, in the black and grey uniform of the Shadow Knife.

"Well done, Captain Nagelbrau," Nadrim shouted, applauding. "You take the 'shadow' seriously. What about the 'knife'?"

The word had barely hit the air before Lord Callenhor felt a blade against his throat and another pressing into the soft, sagging skin of his belly.

"You talk of honesty, Lord Astrin," Nadrim hissed, approaching the open doors. "And yet you have some secrets. Let us bring them into the light." Nagelbrau, acting on his cue, nodded his head and the two men holding Callenhor dragged him to the doors.

"I do not know what you mean!" the lord protested, although he made no move to resist. "I have only spoken my mind, openly and honestly."

"But you hid your *daughter*," Nadrim countered, grabbing his guest by his sweat-stained collar and throwing him hard against the iron railing of the balcony. Callenhor gasped, as his forehead hit a sharpened edge of scrollwork. "Is that not correct? It seems she did not die of fever three years ago, as you so tearily and seemingly earnestly reported. *No*. In truth, she is nineteen, with cornsilk hair and a body for bearing children. At least, that is what Captain Nagelbrau reports, and I know him to be thorough when he does an investigation."

Despite the blood running into his eyes and the piercing pain in his skull, despite the two knives and now Nagelbrau's sword all pointed menacingly at his body, Lord Callenhor made a grab for Nadrim, who took hold of both his wrists and shoved him up against the railing with force enough to bruise the skin of his back.

"Tell me she is alive," Astrin Callenhor whispered, weeping in his despair.

"That, you shall die not knowing," Nadrim said with a sneer, pushing him over the rail and watching with glee as the rocks and then the sea took the liar's life away.

After watching Aldemere's eastern-bound party disappear into the early-morning mists beyond the castle, Elde descended the Watch Tower steps into the castle courtyard as the guards closed the twin oaken barriers of the gatehouse, followed seamlessly by the lowering of the exterior portcullis. As the three gates reached the ground with a reassuring thud, two other guards raised the interior portcullis and the interior gate that allowed entry into the castle proper. Elde felt a surge of pride at this intricate display of cooperation and coordination, which Aldemere had instituted daily drills to perfect.

Passing the armory, with its oaken door secured by a triple lock, designed by the castle's senior blacksmith to Aldemere's specifications, Elde reached into his pocket and ran his thumb over the notches in the key his son had left in his care the previous night. Should the armory need to be opened, it would take the key that Elde now held, plus those kept by the Sergeant at Arms on duty, and Sir Peecwyl, all inserted into the lock and turned at the exact same time.

It was another of the blood-earned lessons from Garamin's failed rebellion. Never again would they allow a single person to access the store of weapons the castle held, no matter his rank or presumed level of loyalty.

Making the long walk down Silveth's central hallway, Elde slowed as he reached the closed doors of the throne room. Two members of the King's Guard, halberds held tightly across their bodies, blocked his path.

According to a policy that he himself had penned, one of the guards nervously asked him to identify himself and his business. Offering a slight bow, he answered, "I am Elde the Jester. I have been summoned by the king and request your permission to enter."

Entering the throne room after praising the guards for their adherence to what some of the barons and lesser nobles had called an outright insult when asked to do the same—and suggesting they dispense with their embarrassment in the future—Elde found the king awaiting him in a pair of simple peasant's pants and a homespun, earth-colored tunic. His purple velvet cloak hung haphazardly over the back of the throne, with his crown perched precariously upon it.

"I hope those are not your greeting-the-nobles clothes," Dylwyn said as Elde approached. "You might need to have them laundered after we are finished."

"Are we riding somewhere, Sire?"

"We are barely leaving the room, but six feet of distance can make a world of difference," the king replied, a twinkle in his eye. "I know you have been overly loyal in your silence as to the matter of my invitation for our recent guest to occupy the Sixth Seat in the council's meeting chamber. I have decided to show you something that shall provide an answer to the question you have so graciously refrained from asking." Removing a large rug from behind the dais that elevated his throne, the king removed a key from around his neck that Elde had never seen and turned it in a lock embedded in the floor.

"Given me a hand with this," Dylwyn requested, lifting into a vertical position two metal rings spaced three feet apart. "If we each take one, this process will be easier."

Although both men were more than passing fit despite their advancing age, the lifting of what Elde could now see was a thick oaken hatch proved a considerable challenge. Looking down into the exposed rough-framed opening as they moved the hatch upward and out of their way, he noticed a ladder. "Sire, I had no idea…"

"Up until this moment, no living person did but me," Dylwyn answered, wiping the sweat from his upper lip and forehead with the sleeve of his homespun tunic. "I had heard it whispered when Alde was a boy that he would get what he wanted from one of the kitchen maids—Pensy, I believe—by offering to show her the box behind my throne. After a series of worrisome nights I realized this was not what he had meant."

"Sire," Elde enquired, scanning the floor behind the dais, "I do not see the box about which my son had spoken."

"Because it is *invisible*!" the king said with a laugh. "Existing only in an adventurous boy's imagination for just such a purpose as he chose so craftily to use it! He has always been a trickster."

"Do not remind me of it, Sire," Elde replied, finding himself anxiously awaiting a descent down the ladder and wishing to avoid the much longer descent into the uncomfortable memories of Aldemere's nefarious, at time reckless, past behavior. Motioning to the opening, he asked, "What is this meant to hide?"

"A repository of sorts," Dylwyn said, taking two torches from the nearby wall and lighting them both with steel and flint from a pouch that hung from his belt. Handing one to Elde, he added, "It is easier to show you than describe it."

Seven rungs later, they stood in a small enclosure. Elde had to stoop slightly to keep from scraping his head on the rough-timbered ceiling.

Arrayed around the room, which a man his height could barely lay across in either direction, he saw an assortment of books, scrolls, bags, jewels in open chests, and dozens of items of exquisite craftsmanship, most of which he knew were not the work of Eastern Barony artisans. Scanning the room in wonder, he noticed the king standing beside a tall, thin object covered with a dun-colored, course-weave blanket.

"Everything in this chamber represents the past," Dylwyn began, a tone of reverence, provocative and profound, lending power to his words. Placing his hand upon the blanket, he continued. "Treasures from the times of the earliest travelers to the Centerlands. Those sea dragons carved in gold over there—they came here with Laurel's people when they crossed the Warwitch Sea. I often wanted to show them to our fallen captainguard, and almost did on one or two occasions, but the secrecy to which my father swore me prevented me from doing so. It is something I now regret..." Clearing his throat and tightening his grip on the blanket, Dylwyn paused for a moment in memory of his protector and friend, a gesture in which Elde instinctively joined. After several seconds had passed, Dylwyn continued. "Some of this was amassed as tribute to the chieftains of old—blood riches, the most of it—and the books and scrolls around us are all in languages long ago silenced and forgotten, including that bag there, which contains the scrolls from which Manthes Fragenoar created the First Book of Ancestry. Manthes knew nothing of the valuables that my grandfather had hidden in another location until such a time as the castle's builders readied this secret space, although my father told me that the mad scribe was very much aware of the books and scrolls our people had gathered from around the world. He just never knew *where* they were. And this," he said, tilting his head toward the object beneath the blanket, "was to hang in the Hall of Books and Ancestries when the volumes and scrolls scattered around the kingdom—as well as those still hidden there—were to fill the shelves of that room, presided over by Manthes. For reasons of which I need not remind you, none of that ever happened. But now that Frederick has made himself known to us..."

Dylwyn pulled the blanket away, revealing a painted portrait, the angular facial features of which Elde immediately recognized.

"If this is Manthes Fragenoar," Elde remarked, approaching the image of the King's Inscriber to obtain a better look at the eyes, "then Frederick—"

"Is his descendent," Dylwyn affirmed. "His great-grandson, I would imagine. He no doubt has his reasons for holding back this information, and I trust that they are good ones." Placing the blanket

Aldemere's Dilemma

back over the portrait and grasping the ladder, he said, as he ascended, "But I thought that you should know."

Laurianna did her best to concentrate on the scroll she was reading as Dictus passed the library window for the fifth time that day, a ritual undertaken many times daily by either him or Vitus—or both— since she had arrived at the Seers' Temple a few days before.

As the Elder Seer passed out of view, Laurianna stole a stealthy glance toward Farvon, positioned at the far end of the table, but he was fully absorbed in studying the First Book of Ancestry.

Dictus and Vitus had been visually unsettled at the female scholar's appearance at the Temple. They of course insisted on reading whatever Laurianna and Farvon might produce after hearing the details of the king's command.

Then Vitus saw "the book of the great blasphemer!" sticking out from Laurianna's travel bag.

Without the fear of Talorous's rebuke to temper him, as it had several weeks ago, Dictus did not stay his comrade's tongue as the chief incantor railed against the book's validity, and the insanity of its author.

Laurianna stood as silent and still as the five statues of the Deities arrayed in a semi-circle just ahead of her in the atrium, stroking her owl Beazor's head to keep her calm. When Vitus had exhausted his supply of hateful words, she stoically replied, "The king accepts this history as accurate, and so we shall employ it as a source. One of many, to be sure—but it must not be ignored."

Although the first day passed without further incident or remark— if one were to discount the laying out of the seating arrangements and the commencing of the window-watching as impotent attempts at authority by two aging, bitter men—Laurianna was not prepared for the news that she would be sleeping in a sectioned-off corner of the hayloft.

"I trust you understand," Dictus explained as they sat for the evening meal, "it has, since the time of the Inscriber, always been thought to be best that those in service to the Deities and those in service to the kingdom's rulers and their armies not intermix unless forced by the utmost necessity. Our meeting with Talorous last month met this criterion—although barely so—which is why you and your teacher slept at the far end of the dormitory. This book project of the king's, upon careful consideration, does not. That owl of yours certainly will be in its element."

Biting on a bit of bread to still her tongue, Laurianna nodded in acquiescence. She noticed the heads of all the other Seers, save Vitus's, dropping in embarrassment.

She toiled in silence that first interminable week, day after day, until an incident one morning with a few errant cows pulled Vitus and Dictus away.

Placing her quill upon the table and flexing her cramping hand, she spoke to Farvon for the first time unsupervised since she had arrived.

"You do know why I am here, do you not, Brother Farvon?"

Swallowing and nodding with equal vigor, the young Seer did not look up from his book.

Leaning into the table, Laurianna said as quietly as she could while still maintaining the imposed distance between them, "In three weeks' time, the king will send us a message, instructing us to travel to the castle together to present what we have written thus far, and to consult with the Academic Council in order to further our task."

"They will never permit me to come along, King Dylwyn's order or not," Farvon replied, still not looking up.

"It is no matter," Laurianna answered, gathering a group of scattered scrolls from her section of the table and bringing them to the shelf just behind Farvon. As she took her time replacing them, she continued. "Whomever comes with us—and I am guessing it will be Vitus—will not be allowed to attend the meetings of the Academic Council. My banishment to the hayloft will be ample precedent for that. And, should he insist, several favorable mentions of Manthes Fragenoar early on should drive him from the room."

Returning to her seat as the voices of the senior Lord Seers grew near, she added, "Until that time, fill all the pages you can, and do not lose your faith in the importance of our work."

Arrayed around the room on specially constructed stands and hanging upon the walls of the Inner Temple of the Ruenai, scrimshawed bones and giant skulls of sea creatures sacrificed to Vael, Xaen, and Braen over the centuries served as a reminder to Carra sea-shaman just who she was and to what she had devoted her life. These immense denizens of the sea—fought with and brought back to Llafen Eret from the far-off shores of places bearing names no living Eretian but Carra had ever known or uttered—were a source of comfort while also suppressing any trace in her of ego. Making a circuit around the room, she whispered the names of their homelands: "Questelleland, Francescia, Nove Ilhas, Kyramm-Zer,

Aldemere's Dilemma

Presidus, Malthos, Bounting…" Names she had learned from her predecessor, Xerra, when she first entered the Inner Temple after the sea-shaman had chosen her from amongst the Ruen-Eret to be the thirty-second Keeper of the Stone.

Standing before the open doors of the inner sanctum, where the Stone and map of Mynoweth that contained the names of the lands she had just recited had until recently resided, Carra felt her heart begin to beat a little faster.

The map was as terrible a potential weapon as the Stone, and yet she had told no one it was gone.

It was a suffocating burden to bear.

Shaking her head to clear it of these troublesome thoughts and taking in a deep draught of air to slow the pounding in her chest, the sea-shaman took a sitting position with her back to the central altar so that the Inner Temple statues of Xaer and Braen stood to her right and left and Vael's was straight ahead. Closing her eyes, she allowed the pungent scent of incense and spices to fill her nose as the staccato beat coming from the drums played by the six Ruen-Eret positioned around the room took hold of her mind and heart and began to pull her essence from its moorings deep within her corporeal body.

"Water, wood, and wind," she repeatedly whispered, as she conjured an image in her mind of an open sea and single-masted sloop, its sails unfurled, propelled by a steady breeze. Feeling a long pair of ivory-white wings emerging from the center of her essence, Carra nodded her head three times, and the drums grew louder, their tempo increasing as her shaman-spirit, winged and soaring in the form of a silver-breasted albatross, left behind her body, the Temple, and the Vessel.

Higher and farther she flew, searching for the dreamboat she had conjured while her essence had remained within the Eretian citizen known as Carra.

Adjusting to the more vibrant colors and greater clarity with which she experienced the world through the piercing gaze of the albatross, Carra-spirit saw in the distance the gently rocking boat on a glassy sapphire sea. As she approached it, she spied a small green bag rolling along the keel at the bottom of the craft. Landing on a thwart, she folded her wings and felt her Carra-body envelope her essence once more, although she knew this was all a vision— her body was still in the Temple.

After securing the bag in her dress, she retrieved two oars from along the portside bulwark and slipped them into the locks, rowing for the tiny island that was steadily materializing on the foggy horizon ahead of her. "Water, wood, and wind," she chanted, in a synchronized rhythm with the oars. The sleek-shaped little craft glided almost effortlessly upon the water, drawing ever closer to the island.

After what would have been several hours in the world from which she had journeyed, Carra-spirit saw three statues on the near shore of the island, which were identical to those in the Inner Temple and the courtyard of the Vessel, although these were made of glinting gold instead of wood.

Increasing the tempo of her chant and with it the speed of the sloop, Carra-spirit watched as the sun began to set behind the island.

Once it was dark, she knew in her soul the Trio would appear.

Landing the boat upon the sandy beach and securing the oars where she had found them, the sea-shaman pulled the small green bag from her dress, gathered an armful of driftwood, and entered the triangle formed by the three golden statues. Opening the bag, she found within it flint and a striking-stone, a bundle of sage, and a small metal bowl. Setting the driftwood alight as the last light faded from the sky, Carra-spirit went to the water's edge and filled the bowl with the ice-cold, crystal-blue water. Returning to the fire, she held the sage to the flame until it began to smoke.

Circling the fire three times while holding the smoking sage and water bowl above her head, Carra said, as she passed each statue, the name of the element with which each of the deities was associated: "water" for Vael, "wood" for Xaer, and "wind" for Braen.

Placing the sage into the now-blazing flames and pouring the water on the rocks that ringed the fire, which caused them to steam and crack, the sea-shaman placed the empty bowl back into the bag, and the bag within her dress.

Sitting cross-legged with the statue of Vael directly in front of her and Xaer and Braen to her right and left, Carra-spirit closed her eyes and concentrated on the sounds of the temple as they reached her from across sea. Started as a whisper, the chanting of "Water, wood, and wind" by the six Ruen-Eret would continue until the conjuring ceremony was complete and Carra's essence had returned to her body, where it remained in a sitting position in the Inner Temple.

Not one of the six priestesses missed a beat, despite the amazement they had felt watching Carra's body undertake the rituals of water, wood, and wind. Once Carra's essence had soared upward and out of the Temple, her body, far from lifeless—which is what each of the six had expected—began to glow with a subtle but steady heat.

Joining her sisters in their chant, Carra-spirit felt the heat of the fire intensify. Were she in her corporeal body, it would have begun to redden and eventually blister. Shouting "Water, wood, and wind!" as the sea began to churn and the wind began to blow with a force that shook the trees behind her, Carra-spirit felt her eyelids open against her will.

There before her, where the golden statues had stood, were the Ruenai—Vael, Xaen, and Braen. Standing and bowing before them, Carra-spirit felt her soul begin to glow as she heard their words as they formed them through the movement of the water, wood, and wind.

Beautiful as the Trio were, the things of which they spoke filled Carra with abject fear.

While high above it all, the Ambir Dragon listened, its tail a swirl of stars, as it moved across the sky.

PART TWO

CHAPTER ONE

Affixing in its woven loop the last of the wooden toggles on the rough-weave vest that Ashlin had provided for him the previous night, Aldemere looked with an intricate mix of sadness and relief upon the accoutrements and vestments of his station and rank, now piled upon the floor in the room he had shared with Linead and Ralin.

Pulling on a battered pair of thin-soled boots, also borrowed, Aldemere found himself thinking about his departure from the castle the morning before, and the look upon Anastasia's face as he rode away.

Their parting had been different from when he had journeyed to the northern mountains as a novice knight, or later to Mount Lyse, or with Kal-Gadras to find the Ambir Dragon. There had been no talk this time of his staying. There had been no discussion about their coming child, or the fact that Aldemere was called upon all too often in times of crisis. They were steadily growing into their relationship, and both of them knew the price that they must pay, both together and individually.

Still, the look on Anastasia's face—a mix of loneliness and love—had remained just beneath the surface of Aldemere's thoughts. Now, however, as he stood on the threshold of yet another new adventure, that look was suddenly more insistent, filling his heart and head with feelings the captainguard could ill afford to feel.

He therefore willed them away, focusing his mind on the events of the previous night.

The dinner with the barons had been amicable, filled with blessed agreement. As was always the case, and as Ralin had already articulated in his own particular way, the news of an outside enemy made their petty squabbles over the details of their trade agreements seem like the fading steam from a cooling pool of water. They pledged the aid of their baronies and professed their intention to get to work as soon as they were home.

Baroness Ashlin was already overseeing preparations in the East, taking Sir Connar aside after the meeting adjourned to begin devising plans for Eerbell's further fortification.

Aldemere, Linead, and Ralin, excusing themselves from the table, where the other barons remained, headed to the stables to talk over plans with Frederick.

The northman's mood was understandably dark, angry as he was over Linead's insistence on what amounted to de facto imprisonment, although he was able to keep his anger in check as they discussed details for their departure the following morning.

"You and I shall proceed southeast," Frederick said to Aldemere as he ate the meager meal of apples, cheese, and bread Linead had allowed him. "And hire a barge at the confluence of the rivers Mirra and Skillen. It is a journey of no more than ten hours from there to where we shall go our separate ways. You shall ride a few hours north to the Stathl Pass with one of Linead's knights, who will return to us with Poet far outside of Mellya, and within hours pickets shall stop you before you reach the border. When you tell them you are a hunter trying to feed his family, they shall—no doubt with invectives and fists—inform *you* that such practices are against the mandates of the cliffprince and take you into custody. It is at that moment that your spying, your gathering of crucial information, shall begin."

"And you shall be going exactly where with my men while Aldemere's subjected to a beating and taken to prison in Amdar?" Linead enquired, taking the plate from beneath Frederick's hands although he had not yet finished his meal.

"To the Forest of Tombal, further to the east," the northerner replied, resisting an urge to ask for the rest of the food. "That is, if you still agree to their accompanying me on my mission."

"I more than agree to it," Linead answered, scooping up the slices of apple from the plate and feeding them to Titan, who stood in the stall behind him. "I *insist* upon it."

An hour later, while the knights prepared their horses and Ralin his own and Eric's, Baron Chrystan joined them.

"I am missing my days in the field," he said, addressing Linead, his former chief lieutenant. "It would be good to be amongst you at such a time as this, although I shall not interfere."

"It is an honor to have you amongst us, Sir Chrystan," Linead answered, making a full salute. "Do not fear about interfering—I welcome your expertise as we face what is to come."

Chrystan returned the salute. "Know that you have whatever you shall need in my capacity as baron, although it seems that we know so little of the enemy that it is difficult to prepare."

"That is why I am going north to Mellya," Aldemere offered, as he checked the straps and buckles on Poet's saddle and reins for at least the dozenth time. "I shall find out what they want of us, their numbers, their strengths and weaknesses. You shall have the knowledge required to mount a defense."

"I know you shall do your best. Let us pray that is enough."

Chrystan's ominous words had stayed with Aldemere throughout the night—as he finished in the stables, settled into his lodgings, and struggled with falling asleep. He felt a trust in Frederick—it was more an intense connection—that was not logical given the stranger's persistent secrecy, miscalculation of the threat to Eerbell, and the brief time of their acquaintance. The captainguard feared that Linead and Peecwyl assumed he was falling prey to Frederick's clever flattery, but he knew himself well enough to know that this was not the case. Frederick had warned them of a threat. But then again, the pieces of the puzzle he had cast into the air before them were too widely strewn to visualize the picture when they landed.

Aldemere knew all too well from his time in the mountains that such a pile of unknowns often led to a grisly death for far too many men.

Placing his belongings, including his Clausmer and garter, in a burlap sack, which he was sending home with Lan, Aldemere rolled the sleeves of the scratchy, uncomfortable workshirt he wore beneath the vest and repositioned his toes in the poorly made boots that completed his new disguise. Pulling his shoulder-length hair from its black-ribboned ponytail and running his hands through its curls to muss it, he grabbed his swordbelt, cloak, and the sack with the Clausmer and garter and made his way to the stables.

"May I have a second, Sir?" Aldemere heard from behind him. Without turning, he knew that it was Lan.

"You recognized me in these clothes?" Aldemere asked, disappointed. "Even with my hair untied and all ajumble?"

"I did, Sir," Lan answered, unsure how else to respond. "I would know your confident, practiced way of walking anywhere. It could only be a senior knight's—and why would any other amongst us be dressed in work clothes such as those? And carrying such a recognizable sword as Crow Feather? Was I not supposed to know it was you?"

"My way of walking..." Aldemere replied, pondering Lan's response. "I suppose I could alter it, but why should the hunter Tun—that is the name I have given myself—not be as proud as a knight to be able to feed his family with nothing but a bow. Which reminds me... I need one. And a quiver full of arrows. But not military made. Something a hunter would use..."

Aldemere's Dilemma

"I can be of no help with that," Lan confessed, "at least not at the moment. But before I attempt to find them, I wish to make a request, if I am not exceeding my rank."

Forcing himself to focus on the man before him rather than the two new problems he needed promptly to solve, Aldemere answered, more impatiently than he wanted, "If it is not too thorny a matter."

Despite his urge to tell his superior to forget he had asked for his time, Lan knew he must press on. "I would like to go with you to Mellya. I do not want Eric's death to go avenged by someone else, even if that someone is you. If my sword is to be of service in his honor, I need to be beside you, and have a chance to confront the gutless bastards responsible for his murder."

Aldemere's demeanor suddenly brightened, despite the weight on his shoulders, at what he was hearing from Lan. "At long last," he exclaimed, grasping his lieutenant by the shoulders, "you are showing me some heart! Your father is smiling, Lan, as is Eric—I assure you. I am genuinely pleased to hear this!"

"So you are accepting my request?"

"I certainly am not," answered Aldemere, the joy on his face increasing. "My decision to send you back to Castle Silveth is proving to be wiser than when I initially made it." Enjoying the look of befuddlement on his young lieutenant's face, he continued. "You shall ride escort for the barons and see your fallen comrade's body halfway home. These were reasons enough for my decision before our meeting here this morning. Now I am going further. You shall act in my stead as captainguard while I remain in the north. Also... I need you to bring this sack to Anastasia. I trust no one else to do it."

Making no move to take the sack Aldemere held before him, Lan shook his head and sighed. "I should not be in charge," he whispered. "There are four lieutenants considerably senior to me. Any one of them is better suited and has more than earned the right."

"If you are talking about age and time of service," Aldemere answered, taking Lan's hand, placing the topknot of the sack within it, and gently folding his fingers around it, "they are senior to *me* as well. For that matter, so are you. Although, Lan, you have something that they lack—a personal reason to lead and to fight. I myself draw upon it daily. I think of Sir Laurel with every decision I make, every task King Dylwyn commands of me to complete. I think of your father, and those we lost in the north. If you think of Eric as you lead—not dwelling on your misplaced guilt, but on what he did, and how he died—there can be no better choice for a leader in my absence. Get me a quill and some parchment, so I can write the order. And please, Lan… find me a hunter's bow and a quiver stocked with arrows."

Signing his name to the order fifteen minutes later, Aldemere rolled the document into a tube and secured it with the ribbon that usually held his hair. Handing it up to Lan, who was horsed and ready to depart, he said, "Trust in yourself as I do. Oh… and one more thing. Take this to my father. It should be kept in his care until I return to claim it."

Lan's cheeks began to redden as he took the sword Crow Feather and secured it silently to his saddle.

Aldemere turned to Ralin and Chrystan, who stood by their horses at the head of the party traveling west. "Take good care, my friends. You are in the best of hands, accompanied as you are by Captainguard Lan and, should the enemy choose to make a move between here and Castle Silveth, I know your swords are eager and at the ready."

If either baron had any doubts or was even the least bit surprised at the announcement of Lan's temporary promotion, neither chose to show it.

Moving to the wagon just behind them to check the fastenings securing the canvas that covered Eric's shrouded corpse, Ralin answered, "May the Deities keep you safe, Sir Aldemere, as you ride for the north again." Satisfied that the body would not move on the journey back to Spiltrow, the baron of the west mounted his horse and gave his childhood friend a salute.

After Ralin's party had departed, Aldemere turned his attention to Linead, who was also ready to ride. "Are you still bound for the eastern garrison?"

"I am. I am giving myself three days to design and implement a fortification plan and drill the soldiers there. Connar will begin to fortify Eerbell and oversee the continued preparations of the garrison when I go. Once I arrive in Silveth, I shall send out hawks to all the chief knights and coordinate the armies from there." Leaning down and lowering his voice, he added, "I have instructed Frederick's escort to take his life without hesitation should they suspect him of any treachery. I wanted you to know that."

"Your candor is appreciated," Aldemere said, saluting. "I pray it is a needless precaution."

Aldemere's Dilemma

"As do I," Linead answered, although he did not return the salute. "I would rather be proven wrong than face the ramifications if I am right. Take care of yourself, Sir Aldemere."

Before Linead rode away, Aldemere took hold of Titan's reins. "What of the assassin? Did he make it through the night? Or did he... *succumb*... to his wounds."

Shaking his head, Linead replied, "If you are asking if I killed him while you slept, I considered it, but I would not stoop to soil my principles over one such as he. He died around daybreak. Connar will see that his body is burned, like the others."

Letting go of the reins, Aldemere stepped back as Linead clicked his tongue and Titan took off at a trot.

As Frederick's party approached, Aldemere climbed upon Poet, turning the Elven horse toward the south.

Silbern Skarling, newly appointed first officer of the *Salt-Serpent*, watched with apprehension as the flame of a just-lit candle at the altar of the Vessel of the Ruenai flickered several times, nearly going out before catching just enough of a breeze to burn with its intended smokeless strength. Whispering a silent prayer of gratitude to Braen, the goddess of the wind, Silbern took a pinch of sage from a nearby bowl with one hand and another of salt from a different bowl with the other, releasing them simultaneously into the ceremonial waters at the center of the altar. Rubbing his hands together, he ensured that he was wasting not a single speck of either.

We need all the blessings we can muster, he thought, sitting himself with a relieved exhalation of breath in the Vessel's forward-most portside pew.

The news that they would not be sailing for Vaelsport as planned had been difficult for the *Salt-Serpent*'s trio of officers to process, as it was for the noncommissioned officers and most of the rest of the crew. The entirety of the fleet was noticeably abuzz with constant postulation as to what their future might hold if the Admiralty waited too long to lift the order.

A ship too long in port is a ship that is dying of rot.

Few of them knew the reasoning behind the unexpected command, and Silbern himself would have been left in the dark were he not as close as he was with his captain, Thaker Ungerfil. It was clear from the first officer's parlays with the junior officers of the *Sea-Sprite* that their captain, Dorrin Waelsbun, had said nothing of the crisis to them.

On the contrary—he had forbidden them even to speculate.

While being privy to secret information had its appreciable charms and allure, what increasingly felt like more than his share of secrets were becoming Silbern's to bear. He shook his head in wonder at how he had come to know them. As a boy, he had never been overly ambitious, although the family into which he was born would settle for nothing less than rigorous study, excellent marks, and acceptance into the Admiralty-Mast as a future officer (preferably a captain) in the fleet.

As it turned out, Silbern loved the challenges that came with his difficult, fated path. Although studying—and particularly retaining—the rigorous course material never came easy to Silbern, he pushed himself consistently beyond anyone's expectation—even the half a dozen highly accomplished Skarlings who had invested themselves in his progress as if it were their own.

Making the most of the external and internal pressures as the months and years progressed, the future first officer consistently distinguished himself as one of the standouts in his class.

His cousin Billec, seventeen years his senior, and for the past eight years the captain of the *Sea-Sword*, had been slow to understand—and even slower to accept—Silbern's decision to serve as first officer under Thaker Ungerfil. After all, the Admiralty had offered him a ship of his own.

Secrets, Silbern thought, staring at the Inner Temple doors just in front of where he sat. *Their danger is that they drive us to do increasingly illogical things.*

Seeking to focus his attention elsewhere, Silbern directed his thoughts toward the rune-filled relic that had been (until recently) kept beyond those doors. He had never understood the reliance of the Eretian fleet on the rituals surrounding the Stone. The presence of the Ruenai all around them was clear—when he made his offerings, as was his daily duty as first officer of the *Salt-Serpent*, he believed in the efficacy of what he was doing—the prayers he prayed, the symbols and their meanings, with every ounce of his soul. It was harder to believe, however, that the rituals tied to the Stone could enhance the ability of a sailor to master the open seas, if he was determined to do so without them. Furthermore, although the rituals that the newly conferred captains underwent by means of the Stone were a mystery to him and to his classmates, he could hazard a guess or two as to what they were actually about, and the possibilities were most unsettling. Relying on mysticism when they had committed themselves to studying so long, so diligently to

Aldemere's Dilemma

understand the ways that their ships behaved; how to convince a crew to work as a disciplined, coordinated unit; and how to stay alive despite the perils of the sea... Well, considering the depth of that commitment, the very idea that the complement of Eretian officers would somehow be less effective without the rituals of the Stone...

That was a notion that would not and could not come easily to a mind like Silbern Skarling's.

He knew all too well that the Ereti believed it to be the price they had paid to the Ruenai for abusing their favor thousands of years before, when Vael, Xaer, and Braen had given them the magnificent design that became the single-masted Eretian ship. Prior to that time, the Ereti were a primitive population living—just barely—from what the rocky terrain provided.

The years that followed the punishment, when the Ruenai forbade the Ereti to leave the land, were ones of relentless hardship and pain.

Ettana, the savior of their race and original Keeper of the Stone, which had been given to her during a journey she had taken to the realm of the Ruenai, had watched as its myriad carvings appeared over time, as she fasted, prayed, and supplicated herself to the will of the god and goddesses.

Twelve centuries later, Carra sea-shaman was the one who held their lives in her hands.

With the assistance of the Ruen-Eret.

One of which now emerged from the Inner Temple as Silbern stood to depart.

"Have you a minute or two for me?" she asked, pushing him gently backward and onto the pew. "Or will the deeply demanding Vael once again have his way?"

"The Ruenai always get their way, Nomma," Silbern replied, finding himself affixed as always by the priestess' shining emerald eyes, "but if you are asking if I must immediately return to the *Salt-Serpent*, then the answer is no. I have checked and rechecked her innards and rigging until I could draw them with both eyes closed, down to the knots in the wood. But if anyone finds us together..."

"I know it is wrong to be here, just the two of us," Nomma whispered, placing her hands upon Silbern Skarling's face, "but I could not help myself."

"Are your rituals complete?" the officer asked, determined not to give in to the insistent impulses surging mercilessly through his body.

"They are," Nomma answered, twirling one of Silbern's trio of beard braids around a slender milk-white finger, "but Carra has not yet sent word to the Admiralty. Her journey was deep and far, and there is much for her to consider. Please say nothing to anyone—not even Captain Thaker."

"I certainly shall not," answered Silbern, taking Nomma's hand from his face and sitting taller in the pew. "He does not know of our meetings. I assure you, no one does. I am making sure of it. You are a virgin of the Ruen-Eret, and I am an officer in the Eretian fleet. What we have forged between us is dangerous. You know it to be true. If any of the others, or Carra-shaman, were to emerge and see us like this..."

"They are sleeping," she said, entwining the fingers of her hand with his. "The rituals were exhausting. I was also asleep, but sensed that you were here." Feeling Silbern's arm and torso tense, she asked, "Is my sensing you a surprise? You and I are now connected. It is the way of things with a priestess and the one who possesses her essence."

Before he could manage an answer, Silbern felt Nomma's lips pressing gently upon his own, their warmth and softness dispelling whatever words he thought he was going to say.

Secrets, he thought, giving fully into the kiss. *How many must I bear?*

As exhausted as he was from his journey home from Ferrukkla—which had been blessedly devoid of dragons and aided by a strong and favorable wind—Kal-Gadras left Lethir-na in the care of the senior stablehand and rushed to his mother's chambers.

The sight of her filled him with fear.

It was not what he had expected.

Far from recovered, Nemmerle lay upon her bed, just as frail and ill as when he had departed.

"Is the thing accomplished?" Petror enquired, from his familiar position on the far side of the bed. Beside him was Izmen, who was stoppering a bottle half filled with a thick, azure liquid.

"It is," Kal-Gadras replied, kneeling beside the bed and taking his mother's hand. Although her fingers were icy cold, he noticed large beads of sweat on her brow. "So how is it that Marlooq-Hir has not been cured?"

"Did you think it would be so simple, my son?" Nemmerle whispered, without opening her eyes. "Sickness such as mine does not strike and suddenly dissipate, like rainstorms in the spring. The darkness that works inside of me took root over the past many years and will take its time in departing. You must have faith, Kal-Gadras, in the deed that you have done."

"But you look worse than when I left!" Kal-Gadras shouted. A piercing look from High Lord Petror made him immediately regret his childish loss of control. Taking a cloth from the bedstand and dabbing his mother's forehead, he whispered, "I am sorry, Mother. I am tired from my journey and was not expecting to see you like this."

"I warned you about the witch," Izmen muttered, stabbing a bony, split-nailed finger across the expanse of the bed. "But you were too proud and stubborn to listen. Now she has what she wants. Why would she bother to help us?"

Kal-Gadras shook his head. "It is not you, nor me, Caecaelev has promised to help. Your selfish cynicism has no value in this crisis. It is a wonder Lord Petror has not banished you to some forgotten corner of the forest, you jealous, bitter wizard. It seems your impotent concoctions have done my mother more harm than good."

Raising his hand to signal an end to the simmering confrontation before Izmen brought it to a boil, Petror said, "It is clear that you are wearied from your ordeal, Kal-Gadras. I can see how your time with the Firegem has depleted you. Perhaps it is best if you go to your chambers to rest. We can talk again tomorrow, if you are feeling more yourself."

"With my deepest respect and admiration, High Lord Petror," Kal-Gadras responded, placing the cloth on the bedstand and rising to his full, imposing height. "I have things I need to share with you, and when that burden is lifted, I promise to do as you ask." Pointing to Izmen, he added, "He need not remain here for what I have to say."

Nemmerle, struggling into a sitting position on the bed, took Kal-Gadras's hands firmly in both of her own. She felt her pain diminish at the sight of his stiff and coiled muscles releasing their tension one by one as her still potent energy caused a slowing of his heart. "Yet Izmen *is* here, my son. Here he shall remain. Do not be so impetuous. I fear that some of Aldemere's less than admirable traits are mixing with your own. The Human way of emotion is not for an Elf to embrace. Izmen is an elder amongst us—and you shall speak to him with love."

Suppressing an embarrassed smile at the thought that he was beginning to show some of his best friend's *less than admirable traits*, Kal-Gadras looked into his mother's intensely focused eyes.

"We are going to war, Mother. Just as you told me we would. Beyond the northern mountains, there has risen a ruthless tyrant. A man who has already done much to unbalance the energies of Mynoweth. His sigil and seal is a three-taloned falcon. This is what Caecaelev told me. He was the one who set the Long Winter into motion by meddling in the affairs of Glittereye and Marlooq Fer. Speaking of, is there any word from Aldemere or the king?" This he directed at Petror, who indicated there was not.

"I am certain it shall come—and soon. When the time arrives, I shall journey north with you to slay him, High Lord Petror, in the vanguard of our armies. Provided my mother has fully recovered."

Nemmerle closed her eyes and smiled, her head sinking into the thick, silken pillows arrayed like ramparts around her. "You must lessen your impatience, Kal-Gadras. My recovery and your riding to meet this enemy, whom I have seen in my darkest nightmares—all will come to pass as Marlooq-Fer decrees. We each must play our role. It cannot be otherwise. Now leave me to my recovery—the three of you."

Kissing the crown of his mother's head and following Petror and Izmen down the hall and into a nearby room, the shelves of which were crammed with books, scrolls, and maps like the ones in the Hall of Books and Ancestries at Castle Silveth, Kal-Gadras closed the door. "I was accosted by a dragon as I crossed the Sea of Silence. His name was Borrenax and he was old and empty of fight. The Firegem forced him to challenge me. I had no choice but to kill him, although the deed was sad and devoid of honor."

"There was nothing else to do," Petror replied, lighting a burner of incense and wafting the smoke toward his nose. "The Firegem is a dangerous piece of magic, and it is well that you are rid of it. Was it difficult to do?"

Kal-Gadras lowered his head, and Petror had his answer.

"What of Abyr-Goon-Draad?" Izmen enquired. "Did you encounter him as well?"

"He was with me on the island," Kal-Gadras answered, stepping up to the burner of incense and taking in a noseful of pungent smoke. His newly knotted muscles immediately began to relax. "If it were not for his guidance, I would not have reached Caecaelev, or had the strength to give her back her eyes."

Petror eased himself into a chair and nodded. "It is an encouraging omen that he did so." Producing an intricately carved churchwarden from his cloak and filling it full of tobacco from a nearby jar, he added, "Our archers and riders are well prepared for what assuredly will come. I have kept them at the ready since the end of Garamin's rebellion. We will defend our northern borders. I shall not allow the war to come to Marlooq-Fer. That must be our plan. Should Dylwyn need fortified numbers, you shall lead the warriors we can spare."

Kal-Gadras shook his head. "Caecaelev said no land would be safe from the war. This enemy will come by sea as well as by horse and on foot. We have never had to defend the southern shore. And if they take the rivers…"

"Our Lord of the South Shore must ensure that does not happen," Izmen said, his voice full of mocking accusation. "You want to help the Humans—always the Humans first. You may *act* like a Human, but you are unquestionably an Elf. *This* is your home, Kal-Gadras. Your duty is to defend it."

"You need not remind me of my duty, you broken, bitter old goat," Kal-Gadras answered, crossing the space between them with fire in his eyes.

"Keep going with that tone," Izmen answered, standing his ground and raising his fists. "Your pride shall be your folly. And all of us shall suffer, and the mighty forests burn!" Pulling his tattered hood over his unruly head of hair, the venomous old Elf took his wordless leave.

"This feud with your former instructor," Petror whispered, slowly exhaling a plume of blue-grey smoke. "What is it about?"

"Nothing I care to speak of," Kal-Gadras muttered, wishing he had not been so openly hostile to Izmen when he had first returned. As his mother observed, such things were the way of Humans. He was an Elf, and bore the Mark of Gal-Rashand, the first of their race. As close as he and Aldemere had become, they could not walk the other's path.

If they tried and failed, Izmen's warning would come true.

Although it would not be just the forests, but the whole of the world that burned.

Securing Poet's bridal to one of the rails of the barge that was taking Frederick, himself, Linead's six knights, and their horses across the River Skillen, just north of where it met the River of Alliance, Aldemere thought back to his journey by sea with Kal-Gadras the previous year to seek the Ambir Dragon. The motion of the barge—so much subtler and more plodding than their little Eretian craft—combined with the briny smell of the water, flooded his mind with memories, and pulled his thoughts to where Kal-Gadras was and what he might be enduring. Aldemere had dreamed no more of his friend since the vision of the fall several weeks before, and because he had experienced no wounds or unexplained pains, he felt in his heart that the Lord of the South Shore had somehow survived his ordeal.

Returning his focus to his own imminent mission, Aldemere noticed the tight circular formation Linead's men were keeping around Frederick, each with his hand either on or near his sword, maintaining an icy silence that had begun before they reached the barge.

Why he was not intervening in this unreasonable state of affairs had been puzzling Aldemere since they had ridden out of Eerbell. If he had to guess, he would say he was exhibiting an oddly Elven restraint.

As the barge drew close to the river's eastern bank, Frederick turned and addressed him. "Once we are across, we shall head slightly south and ride for Stathl Pass. It will fascinate you, Aldemere—thousands of enslaved Lyseans created it by chipping away at the mountain by order of Nadrim's great-grandfather, Rogen Damonessa. Many gave their lives to see his vision manifest. We will not make the pass by nightfall, camping instead roughly twenty miles away."

"We shall camp where *I* decide." Sir Lesster, the knight Sir Linead had put in charge of Frederick in his absence, clapped a gloved hand on his prisoner's shoulder, grasping it tight. "After we have crossed, we shall ride twenty miles more and *that is* where we shall camp. That shall leave us a ride of another *forty* miles to Stathl Pass, which shall place us well shy of any trap you might have laid. Perhaps we shall decamp at first light, or maybe I shall send Sir Tagen and Sir Faxx to scout it for us first, just to be doubly sure." The two knights at whom he had pointed nodded in acknowledgment and, much to Aldemere's chagrin, the latter of them slammed his fist into his open hand for emphasis.

After Sir Lesster had settled the bill with the bargeman, including a few extra coins for him to maintain his silence concerning his most recent fare, the party remounted and rode for nearly an hour before Aldemere took up position next to Sir Lesster and motioned for him to ease his pace so that they might converse.

Letting the rest of the riders get fifteen feet ahead—and noticing how Sir Tagen quickly and efficiently filled the gap left by Sir Lesster so Frederick was once more encircled—Aldemere said, "I understand what Linead expects of you, and I also understand why,

Aldemere's Dilemma

but is this relentless show of force and distrust not going a bit too far?"

Looking straight ahead, Lesster answered, "I have my orders, as you claim to understand. To be blunt, we are not in the castle, and the king is not amongst us, so you have no authority over my men and me. If you want to ride ahead, and leave us to our business, I would find it welcome."

Welcome, eh? Aldemere thought. *Then that is the last thing I shall do.* Increasing Poet's pace to catch up with the others, Aldemere said aloud, "What is to happen to him when I have left for the north? A bit of a session of rough-him-up?"

Stopping his horse, forcing Aldemere to do the same and circle back, Lesster was seething as they again came face to face. "I have not an ounce of care for him *or* for you, *Captainguard.* I fought in the north, same as you did, and I listened to Garamin's agents make their offers in the shadows of the castle, but I do not traffic with *traitors.* If this man we are watching *is* one, we shall deal with him in the same way we did Miv and the rest of the turncoat knights. It shall be even easier, because I never fought beside him. I did not watch cannibals tear out the necks of my comrades with their teeth or stand fast with the king when he was about to lose his country, to piss away my honor on a *bit of a session of rough-him-up.* So sleep easy, jester… *knight.* What happens is up to him."

As Lesster rode for his comrades, who were now nearly half a mile ahead, Aldemere kept his distance. He had much about which to think. It was clear that old resentments against him and his path to the knighthood had not died off with Garamin.

If the Mellyans knew of the fractures that still ran through the kingdom, would they bother to wage a war of ships and swords and arrows? If they knew of Ralin's drinking, or the prejudices against Baroness Ashlin, or the constant posturing amongst the five baronies when it came to matters of trade and access to the ear of the king, would it not be easier to let Glittereye destroy *itself*, as it nearly had the previous year?

Such were the questions Aldemere was asking when, several hours later, he unrolled his bedding and settled in to a night of troubled sleep.

As he listened to the report from the head of the Shadow Knife, Helkirk Nagelbrau, regarding the failed assassination and kidnapping of the barons of Glittereye, Nadrim wished for nothing more than to be back in the interrogation room at Ravinscliff so he could extract two of his chief spy's teeth for each of his excuses.

Now he would have to improvise.

Fingers were quicker than teeth.

He could move the upcoming torture session to the small room elsewhere in the castle he kept for such delicious purposes, but the head of the Shadow Knife had been in there too many times to witness and assist. The uniqueness of Nadrim questioning him in the throne room gave the whole event the flair the cliffprince craved.

He had returned to Amdar in a celebratory mood. News of Astrin Callenhor's death was spreading to the various regions of Mellya like fire through sun-scorched grass, and his fleet of Ereti-patterned vessels would soon be set to sail.

Then word had come through Crickback—had he detected a smile of satisfaction on his brother's face? Because that would also have to be dealt with—that Nagelbrau was waiting for an audience with "less than the best of news."

His brother's flair for understatement only made the details all the more painful to swallow because Nadrim knew, somewhere in the fortress—in some dingy kitchen corner amongst the rats and refuse—good old brother Crickback was laughing at his expense.

"Explain to me why I should refrain from killing you outright," Nadrim taunted, tossing his sword within the narrow floor-space that lay between him and the entertainingly unflinching head of the Shadow Knife.

"Say the word and I will fall upon my sword, My Cliffprince," Nagelbrau answered, sinking to his knees. "Or, if you so prefer—I shall fall upon yours."

Nadrim grunted in derision and sat back in his chair. "Because I have no faith that you would not make a mess of your sacrificial suicide, not to mention my floor, let us shelve your offer for now." Taking a pull of wine from his Garamin skinbag, the cliffprince ran his middle finger over the fading falcon tattoo. "Perhaps they buried your men's bodies without looking at their legs," he said aloud. "After all, if they were like me, and were inclined to strip them bare and hang them from their city's outer walls as a warning and deterrent, I might consider a different approach to taking over their kingdom." He paused a second in thought. "You have received no report of survivors?"

Nagelbrau shook his head. "I only know the attack has failed because no message has been sent of their return to Stathl Pass, which was the arrangement we had made. My senior lieutenants were to meet them there with wagons. As you know, My Cliffprince, we do not permit assassins to enter Amdar. I would not be overly concerned about what they might have said. Their masters train them to end their lives if an enemy takes them prisoner, and none would speak of you even if they were tortured. You know the pledge, My Cliffprince."

The training of assassins was a craft the northern people had perfected over many generations, beginning with the earliest Lysean cities. It had been the philosophy of the first of the Mountain Regents that the quiet removal of a single foe through the actions of an assassin was always preferable to skirmishes, battles, and war. Over time, the assassins had grown into an elite class of skilled, devout, and fearless shadow-killers, chosen at an early age from the elite Lysean families and trained in secret locations.

When Lyseum had been undone at the hands of Nadrim's great-grandfather, he had appointed the Shadow Knife as guardians of the traditions and training methods established by the Lysean assassins.

He had put the initial group of Mellyan selectees to efficient, effective use.

One of their earliest tasks was to put their Lysean enemies to a slow and painful death.

"What I am not understanding, Helkirk," Nadrim said, leaving his seat and taking up his sword, "is how a few household knights and a meeting-room full of *bureaucrats* could overpower your assassins? They *are*, essentially, *your* recruits, *your* trainees, *your* assassins— are they not? This… well, this is vital to how the rest of our time together unfolds, so pay very close attention. Answer this absurdly simple question to my utmost satisfaction, and you shall leave this room with all the fingers with which you were born."

Sheathing his sword, Nadrim pulled a fat-bladed dagger from his belt. "Make an excuse or fail to satisfy me with your answers, and I shall own the pinkie finger of your incompetent writing hand. That is just for starters, Captain Nagelbrau. By way of warning, let me say I have already cleared a spot for your pinkie—and potentially *all* of its companions—upon my bedside table."

Half an hour and three digits—two pinkies and his right index finger—later, the barely conscious head of the Shadow Knife was carried from the room, his hands hastily wrapped in linen by a practiced in-house surgeon and Nadrim no closer to understanding how the mission had failed.

"Let it not be said, Helkirk," he shouted after the moaning man on the fast-departing litter, "that I am not a generous cliffprince. After all, although you only have seven fingers remaining, I am more than content to have you continue as the leader of the Shadow Knife."

He was almost certain he heard a "Thank you for that, My Cliffprince," as the nervous-looking guards closed the throne room doors.

Carra gazed at the small metal bowl she had somehow managed to bring back with her from the journey to the Ruenai, half expecting to see ocean scenes begin to graft themselves upon it, as the runes of the Stone once had. As far as she knew, there was no precedent in the meticulous records of the former Keepers for a material object crossing the boundary between the home of the Ruenai and the Temple, with the exception of the Stone itself, given to Ettana at the time of the Beseechment, as Eretian historians called it.

Outside the Inner Temple, she could hear the voices of Grand Admiral Ungerfil and Warden Hefflar as they drew closer to its still-locked doors. Their impatience was palpable through the thick wood and its wide iron banding. Her recovery from the spirit journey had taken several days, and she was sure that the departure of the *Sea-Sword*, carrying as it did Tribune Waelsbun, Undersecretary Ungerfil, and the Dwarf Gadrun Grundling for an undisclosed location, had further provoked their moods.

Concealing the bowl in an inner pocket of her sea-green ceremonial robes, Carra took a deep, cleansing breath, whispered "Water, wood, and wind," and opened the sanctum doors with a reassuring smile.

Taking their seats in the rearmost pew on the starboard side of the Vessel were not only the grand admiral and warden, but also Ambassador Waelsbun and the two remaining tribunes, Ammon Mastmin and Sorva Kaelhul.

None of the five so much as nodded hello.

Water, wood, and wind, Carra silently prayed. *May you Ruenai grant me the strength to do your sacred will.*

Broadening her smile, she said aloud, "I am sorry for the wait, my friends. It was unavoidable, although I shall not waste your time laying out the reasons. The decision to delay was not one I made with ease. I am sure that you have questions, all of which I wish to answer. Warden Hefflar?"

An essential element of the training of the sea-shaman was the delicate and, of course, subtle manipulation of interactions with the

Admiralty, in order to manage their aggressive masculine impulses. Carra had placed the power she had taken with the delay in contacting them back into their hands by offering to answer their questions rather than talking *at* them, and more importantly, giving the first opportunity to do so to the most powerful amongst the five.

"Thank you, sea-shaman," Warden Hefflar answered, the rigid set of his face almost imperceptibly softening. "We mean you no offense by expressing our frustration. We do not dare to question the no doubt complicated rituals required to speak with the Ruenai, nor the physical toll they must take." He paused for a moment to gauge whether Carra was accepting the peace offering he was so clumsily attempting to give her.

His mentor had likewise trained *him* in the navigation of sandbars along diplomacy's often-treacherous shoreline, especially with regard to the Keeper of the Stone.

"Have they given you an answer?" the warden asked, satisfied that Carra had accepted his gesture.

"They have," she replied. "War will be upon us, and the Ruenai, who love the Ereti and acknowledge the Admiralty's loyalty, will allow the ships of the fleet to be outfitted with the implements of war." Anticipating the question that the delegation would ask, she added, confident that doing so would not erase the progress made thus far, "Preparations can begin when the Admiralty is ready."

Raising his voice above the overlapping comments of his fellows, Tribune Kaelhul enquired, "What of the matter of the *Sea-Sword*? She sailed three days ago. Tribune Waelsbun told us nothing of where she was going. He left that *courtesy* to you."

"The Ruenai have willed it," Carra answered. "I do not know when, or by what means, but the one-armed sailweaver will not be in Mellya much longer. And your fellow tribune, and his companions, are sailing south to the place where he is headed."

The reference to Nakret Wilsbern sent the five members of the Admiralty into renewed chatter amongst themselves. Carra waited patiently for further questions to emerge.

Instead, it was a statement. A bitter one at that.

"I should have been told." Grand Admiral Ungerfil's face was a deep shade of red, verging on purple, as he turned to address her. "The ships that comprise our fleet are my responsibility. I should have had the opportunity to confer with the *Sea-Sword*'s captain. Eretian ships have not sailed southward for more than a thousand years. Without the magic of the Stone to ensure a successful voyage…"

"It would have made no difference," Carra replied. "Billec Skarling is your most experienced captain, chosen by the Ruenai. Yes—the Stone is missing. Therefore, the fleet must survive on the skill of its captains. If we are to be punished for losing the Stone, I do not believe it shall come until later, when the outside danger has passed."

"Then perhaps it is all for the best," Warden Hefflar observed, forgetting for a moment in whose temple it was that he sat. "Do not misunderstand me—we need the Ruenai. Without them and the magic held in the Stone, we are but ordinary sailors. Tribune Waelsbun, Undersecretary Ungerfil, and the crew of the *Sea-Sword* are putting themselves at considerable risk to find and return the Stone. The goddesses and god have willed it, and I wish it with all my heart. But Athes is right—a ship of the fleet making sail without conference with the grand admiral is highly irregular and makes all of us—if I can speak for you all—more than a cleat's-length uncomfortable."

Carra watched the heads of the others bob up and down like buoys in a storm.

If she did not change tack, she would lose any chance of directing them any further, and she had considerably more to tell them.

As for the debate about the function of the Stone, the fleet's dependency upon it, and the necessity of the rituals of the Ruen-Eret, men such as these had navigated the crests and troughs of these questions for as long as she could remember, and no doubt long before. Grateful as the members of the Admiralty were, the prideful males that held its positions of power also harbored more than a little resentment at their reliance on the Ruenai and their representatives in the Vessel.

Near to giving up, Carra then remembered the bowl.

"Respected members of the Admiralty," she said, motioning with her hands to get them quiet, "there is something I must show you. The manner in which I obtained it, as far as I know, is unheard of since the time in which Ettana-shaman returned with the Stone from the realm of the Ruenai. Perhaps it will prove to you how serious our situation is and how much Vael, Xaer, and Braen wish to assist us."

Withdrawing the bowl from her robes, Carra held it before the five now-silent males. Although they could not know what the object truly was, all had their eyes upon it.

"When I undertook my spirit journey, I was given several items by the Ruenai to use in the summoning ritual at the sacred place of

Aldemere's Dilemma

meeting. One of those items, this bowl, came back with me. I do not yet know how I am to use it, although in time I know it shall be revealed."

Reaching toward it, although not bold enough to touch it, Ambassador Waelsbun whispered, "Perhaps runes shall appear upon it... Perhaps the bowl is a surrogate for the Stone."

Deciding not to acknowledge the fact that she had thought the same, Carra instead replied, after returning the bowl to a pocket within her robes, "It is not for us to know. At least at present. I have let you see it only as a reminder of the power and mystery of the Ruenai, lest any of us forget in this troubled, dangerous time that we cannot survive this without them."

"Speaking of, let us return to the central subject of the preparations for war," a calmer, better-colored Athes Ungerfil suggested. "As welcome as the Ruenai's permission may be, we have no weapons with which to outfit our ships. The Ruenai destroyed them when our forebears angered them with their reckless warmaking, as all of you are aware. We have bladed weapons, grappling hooks—but nothing to defend a ship at a distance. The old scrolls in the Admiralty archives have drawings of such devices, but we would require the aid of the Dwarves for the metalwork and casting. It would take months to produce what we need, and that is only if our distrustful trading partners would agree to grant us such assistance..."

The grand admiral's observations sent his fellows into a cacophony of murmurs, which Carra silenced with her hands before they could rise to a din.

"The weapons were not destroyed," she said, motioning to the males to keep silent as their mouths began to move. "The people were only led to believe that they were, to avoid any further temptation. The Ruenai see far into the future and knew the day would come when we would require such infernal tools of destruction, which you all must agree to use solely for defense."

"Well," Warden Hefflar said, rising from his seat, "where are these infernal tools of destruction, as you call them?"

Carra pointed to a spot before his feet. "You are standing on them, Warden."

The mid-afternoon sun was warming the backs of Aldemere's party of riders as the mountains began to loom in the shrinking distance before them. Although the jester-knight had managed to keep his nerves in check throughout the day, now that Stathl Pass was nearing he could feel his guts begin to churn. Memories of his time in the Topmost Mountains fighting the nomads were dueling for dominion with those of his adventure upon Mount Lyse and his battle with the two-headed dragon, Diette and Simnac.

Almost against his will, he found himself scanning the sky, but he detected no presence of dragons.

"We shall ride together for just a few more miles," Sir Lesster informed him, "at which point you and Sir Tagen shall proceed northward for Stathl Pass. Have you any issue with that?"

Aldemere shook his head, wishing for a Caveraider or a dragon with which to duel instead of a fellow member of the king's army. "Although," he said, summoning his strongest tone and looking Lesster directly in the eyes, "before we do so, I would like a word with Frederick—without you breathing down our throats."

Looking to the sky in consideration of the request and then spitting a mass of greenish phlegm onto the ground between their horses, Linead's first lieutenant answered, "I shall give you a handful of minutes. Any less, you would accuse me of not trusting you, and *everyone* must trust the heroic Captainguard Aldemere."

Garamin may be dead, Aldemere thought, reining Poet away, *but his prejudices haunt us like spectres.*

Fifteen minutes later, Lesster, riding well ahead with his men, Frederick still amongst them, leaned over and whispered gruffly to the northerner, who stopped his mount as the other knights rode on, reining their horses beneath a stand of peach trees half a mile away.

"Linead's enforcer ceaselessly surprises me," Frederick said with a laugh as Aldemere approached. "I would never have guessed he would permit us to speak."

Aldemere answered with a laugh of his own, tinged though it was with concern. "He is a man who despises complexity. Which makes him an ideal lieutenant. Therefore, were he to push me any harder—or treat you any rougher, though nothing would please him more—he would be forced to rely on one of two potential outcomes—that I was afraid enough not to report his actions to Linead, or even worse, the king, or that I did not come home from Mellya. I doubt he puts hope in either. And very rightly so."

"I am glad to hear you believe you shall return," Frederick replied, placing his hand on Aldemere's forearm. "You shall need even greater belief in yourself once you are taken prisoner. Mellya is a place such as you have never seen. The nomads are nothing compared to the warriors trained from the time they are boys in

Aldemere's Dilemma

Amdar. Their organization and efficiency, because they focus upon the making of war to the exclusion of all else, far surpass the current capabilities of Glittereye. And the numbers of men and older boys who fill out the ranks of its highly trained foot soldiers are vast."

"Then what chance will we have against them?" Aldemere asked, surprising himself by verbalizing the question.

"Your reports will be crucial to our victory," Frederick answered. "Concentrate on your mission, and you will not succumb to doubt."

"I understand the concept," Aldemere answered, shifting in his saddle as Lesster and Tagen turned their horses toward them. "But I do not yet grasp how I shall gather enough information to be of any use to our cause from behind the iron doors of a ruthless dictator's prison."

Aldemere watched the northerner's jaw tense as he brought his horse in closer. He could see a shadow settling in Frederick's eyes. "Because there is something else. Something I have been waiting to tell you until our final moments together. You are going to Amdar, not just as a spy, but also as a rescuer. Within the cells, you will find a prisoner called Simon. A Greybaer. He is of great importance to his people. A combination of your teacher Talorous, the Seven Lord Seers, and Hir Marlooq. The Mellyans took him for leverage. The Greybaer are lost without him. I shall use your rescue mission as a sign of good faith when I meet them. It shall smooth the way for an alliance between the Greybaer and Glittereye in the battles that are to come. They have little reason to trust Humans, as you can imagine. If my instincts are correct, you will find another there as well. A Dwarven prince called Stanchion Pilon."

"So I am to be weaponless, alone, and tasked with these two very important missions," Aldemere answered, filled with equal parts trepidation and exhilaration. "I am utterly unsure how I shall accomplish all that you ask."

His eyes twinkling with mischief, Frederick said, "Because I am giving you this." He pulled a glove from inside his saddlebag. "But first, I will show you *this*." He pulled a knife from his belt. "It comes apart like so." He rapidly but clearly removed the sharp, thin blade from its wooden handle, and, turning it around, slid it back inside so only a bit of the tang was showing. He then handed both the glove and the knife to Aldemere. "You will need to sew these into the leg of your pants. Here is some needle and thread." As he handed the items over, he leaned in until their foreheads nearly touched, as the two knights were nearly upon them. "No matter what, that glove must not be discovered. It is the key to your success. Without it, my plan for you will fail, and you will assuredly die."

Placing the glove, which was made of a fabric similar to Elven-weave, between his vest and shirt so Lesster would not see it, Aldemere quickly, quietly asked, "What does it do?"

"It is called the Slaaver's Hand," Frederick said, in an equally rapid whisper. "An invention of the Elves. Where I got it is no matter. As to what it is for... Next time you are alone, slip it on and you shall see."

"Your time for talking is up," Lesster informed them with a scowl as he brought his horse to a halt inches from where they sat. "Tagen is ready to ride to the pass, Captainguard," he said to Aldemere, who had slipped the disassembled knife into a pocket of his vest unnoticed. Then, to Frederick he said, "You shall continue on with us."

"And here I thought it was *you* continuing on with *me*," Frederick replied, turning his horse toward the waiting riders. "But however you shall have it, as long as we get on to Tombal." Turning around and winking at Aldemere, he said, "Safe travels, jester-knight. I know you will not let us down."

Touching the mysterious glove with the tips of his fingers, Aldemere nodded to Tagen, who barely nodded back, as they prodded their horses into a gallop toward the mountain and Stathl Pass.

Izmen caught up to Kal-Gadras just as the Lord of the South Shore reached the entrance to the stables. Cursing the length of the young Elf's stride, the elder Elf doubled over from what he determined to be an unnecessary and cruel exertion—his former student knew well enough his once-respected teacher had been following just behind.

"You are holding something back," Izmen wheezed through chipped and tea-stained teeth.

"If you are referring to Caecaelev," Kal-Gadras answered, retrieving a brush and bucket and heading for the stall where Hir was kept, "I told my mother and High Lord Petror everything of consequence she chose to share with me."

"Ah-ha!" Izmen whispered, still unable to stand erect. "You choose your words with care, in the manner your teacher taught you. What did the blind witch say that was *not* of consequence to *them*—but could be to one such as *me*?"

Aldemere's Dilemma

Filling the bucket with water from a barrel, Kal-Gadras shook his head. "It would not do any good to talk of this at present. Were you not listening to me before? We will soon be going to war. Mother has known it for months. She tried to warn me… I shared what I could with Aldemere the night before his wedding. Now is not the moment for playing victim to regret."

Izmen, his ears moving perceptibly backward in response to his agitation, straightened his spine and grasped Kal-Gadras's arm, causing the water to spill from the bucket.

"You should watch what you say to me, my human-loving lord. Do not think for a second that a mark upon your neck or riding the master's horse make you more of an Elf than me! I too bested the Water-Asp, and I can take a dog like you with nary a weapon in hand."

Pulling his arm from Izmen's admittedly solid grip, Kal-Gadras glared at his former mentor. "Neither the Mark nor any task I have accomplished makes me superior to you. No—it is your hatred of the Humans and your utter betrayal of your own that makes you reprehensible. Now, leave me to my duties. I shall not ask you again."

Hearing the hate in Kal-Gadras's voice, Izmen retreated several feet, creating a physical distance to match the one so apparent in their relationship. Once a hair-thin crack, it was now a gaping chasm.

"The sightless conjurer told you, did she not?" the old Elf asked with a scowl. "I had known in my heart that she would."

Rubbing Hir between the ears as he drank from the bucket his master had just refilled, Kal-Gadras replied, "It was not hard to puzzle out. It is why you tried to stop me from going in the first place, is it not? You started the story that day—Caecaelev only completed it."

"Rotting corpses stacked in a pretty row!" Izmen shouted, spitting on the ground. "She could not *wait* to paint me as the villain, and vindicate herself—and no doubt her mother as well! Curse the evil father who sent his girl away. Did she tell you how they treated her? How they *mocked*, distrusted, and *abused* her? I sent them away to protect them. The Humans were at war, and Petror—and your mother—they did not always trust and welcome the Humans as they seem to as of late. I loved them both, Kal-Gadras, but I had no other choice…"

"So that is what it was," Kal-Gadras asked with a sneer. "Country over family? Race over child? Is that how you rationalized their banishment? How you lived with the knowledge that your own flesh and blood had *blinded* herself?"

"You would think that the shape of one's ears or the number of deities one worships would be of no consequence for two souls so in love," Izmen quietly replied, looking at the ground. "But, for us, the consequences were grave. She was a dairy maiden who lived on a farmstead across the River Mirra. I still remember the day I first gazed upon her face. She was filling a bucket for her cows, as you just did for Hir. I was gathering herbs on the Elven side of the river— and as the sun shimmered upon the water, how like a dream she seemed.

"Then she smiled—just for an instant—and maybe not at me— but that was all it took.

"We did not mix with Humans then. Our parents taught us from birth to distrust their every action. They were only interested in war and the endless spilling of blood. They were dirty and given to lying. Only High Lord Petror and a few of his advisors—my father included—ever spoke with them, and then only to ensure that they would remain on their side of the river and keep their arrows out of our forests. I knew what it would mean, my wanting to get to know her, but I could not remove the imprint of her smile from my heart. More and more often, I would sneak away from my studies—or devise botanical experiments using plants only found in that blessed spot beside the river. It took us weeks to speak, months to touch, a year before we finally found the opportunity to consummate our love. When she told me she was with child, my heart leapt high with pride. I promised to tell my father before the sun had set."

"But you did not keep your promise," Kal-Gadras whispered, no malice in his voice.

"I intended to—I swear it! Trust in nothing if not that. The deities were clearly displeased. They must have been, because, that very evening, as I entered our dwelling to share my joyous news, my father received a report that a half-mad chieftain had ordered the slaughter of an Elven patrol not a mile up the river. No one knew the reason why. No one cared to ask—though I knew in my heart the cause!

"My father rallied his supporters and demanded of Petror and your mother an immediate answer in blood. Petror convinced them to settle for the chieftain's head and the hands of those who had loosed their arrows in the ambush, but my father's heart was filled with hatred for the Humans evermore."

Aldemere's Dilemma

"Everyone knew when your daughter was born that she was of Human and Elven blood," Kal-Gadras replied, all trace of sympathy gone. "That poor woman—a woman you say you loved—going it all alone."

Falling to the ground, Izmen sobbed, his shoulders rising and falling with the intensity of the truth. "I know what you must think. What was I to do? I felt my heart begin to harden as I received word of how those in her village treated her. The things they did to my daughter... Yet I worked with the Humans in time. I helped to forge the Alliance after the Unity Wars were over—I know that you never knew that. I worked carefully, with proxies, behind the scenes, so as not to anger my father and those that shared his mind. Let me tell you, there were many. My heart and my mind were never in accord. They beat each other bloody every hour of my life."

"And when she took her eyes out," Kal-Gadras replied, standing over his crumpled former tutor with folded arms and a hard and heartless look, "did you go to see her then?"

Izmen, choking on his sobs, barely managed a nod. "I did more than just go to my daughter. I brought her to Ferrukkla. I thought of staying with her, of abandoning my life amongst the Elves, but she... she... she looked too much like her mother."

Kal-Gadras fashioned and dismissed a dozen responses as Izmen lay sobbing in the puddle of earth and filth where the water had spilled from the bucket, but as a storm began to rage, he silently removed his cloak and placed it over Izmen's, threadbare and soaked as it was.

He then attended to Hir.

CHAPTER TWO

Janzalon Waelsbun stood in the bow of the *Sea-Sword*, reveling in the feel of the salty spray upon his face, and the sea air in his nose. Running his hand through his long, unbraided beard, he collected tiny bits of salt between his fingers. Gazing up and back at the taut array of sails driving them steadily onward, he thanked the Ruenai with a soundless "Water, wood, and wind" and Carra for enabling them to enjoy what had thus far been an uneventful voyage.

"You, sir, look like one who has missed the open water somethin' fierce."

Captain Billec Skarling, an unusually stocky and muscular specimen by all Eretian standards, joined the tribune in the bow, a highly polished astrolabe of his grandfather's design and Dwarven construction in his weathered, calloused hands.

"In truth, it seems I have," Janzalon answered. "I was not supposed to be a land-locked administrator. I was bred and schooled for the sea."

"I sense a story comin' on," Captain Skarling said with a smile. "Just the thing ta keep the ship a-clippin'. An' ye have a captive audience. I need ta take some readin's."

Realizing that it had been far too long since he had spoken of his past, Janzalon leaned against the bulwark and began to unspool his narrative. "I was the navigator of the *Sea-Spear* for barely a year when I was reassigned to clerk for Sorgan Hefflar, the tribune I would succeed half a decade later. My brother Pashter had been appointed ambassador to Mettlec a few years earlier, and, when our father died, it was determined that one of us needed to remain on land. As much as I loved the sea and sails, I was destined for legalities, treaties, and contracts—diplomatic and administrative are how I have made my mark. I did not realize how much I missed this 'til we were out on the open sea."

Billec belly-laughed. "'Tis an easy thing ta love, wit' fine weather an' a fine wind such as this one, Tribune Waelsbun. The *Sea-Sword* is a capable craft wit' a well-traveled, tightly knit crew seein' ta her needs, extractin' her potential, but we must not take the credit fer the impressive amount a' water we have traversed. Not a month an' a half ago, we were breakin' ice floes durin' our initial post-winter trips ta the lush lands a' the Dwarves. I would be heartily grateful fer a contrary wind or a bit o' rough seas lest my seamen get ta slackin'. Chatter is we are headin' fer certain war, an' if that truly be the case, knife-sharp fer me sailors is the order a' the day."

Janzalon shook his head. The spreading of rumors amongst the members of a crew while at sea—or in port, or at the pub, or anywhere they gathered—was something with which he was all too familiar and certainly had not missed. "If we are," he said, shielding his eyes with his hand as the sun burst forth with renewed vigor from behind a dark grey cloud, igniting the water with a blanket of diamond blazes, "I have no official orders. The Ruenai will decide."

Tucking a hunk of dried tobacco in his cheek, Billec began adjusting the rete and rule of the astrolabe, his rough hands gliding over the instrument in a delicate, practiced dance. "Another four days should get us where we are goin', Tribune, if the winds stay as fair as they have been an' presently are. 'Tis a shame we had not the time ta explore the Islands a' Kirr as we passed 'em. A bevy a' me ancestors cataloged the flora an' fauna on half a dozen of 'em in ages long ago."

"I know their drawings well, Captain Skarling," Janzalon said, glad to be sailing away from any talk of war. "I studied, duplicated, and was tested upon them at Admiralty-Mast when I was a lowly first-year cadet. Perhaps when this is behind us, we can arrange an excursion, you and I, to finish what they started."

"I would be more'n grateful fer that," Billec said, making several notations in a salt-chafed leather logbook. "Nary a sign a' stormin' in the skies. The Ruenai are blessin' this voyage, their Stone gone missin' or not. I have a solid feelin' yer mission is important, Tribune Waelsbun. Mayhap ta do wit' the Stone?"

"This had *better* be important, for all the trouble it is causing."

The two Eretians turned in perfect synch at the unpleasant sound of their Dwarven guest's deep and surly voice. Gadrun Grundling had been in a foul and fighting mood since they had put Llafen Eret behind them.

Spitting a steaming stream of tobacco over the portside bulwark, Billec refrained from eye contact with their grouchy new companion. "I am sorry the *Sea-Sword* is not ta yer likin', Lord Grundlin'. Given more notice, I woulda had the bilge darkened down so ye would think ye were in the guts of a mountain. I would guess the smell is the same..."

"Stow your titles and your sass in your sea-bag, Skarling," the Dwarf barked back with a scowl. "I am not a lord—and never has a Grundling seen the silly need to call himself as such. And before you talk of our mountains, you had best remember that that piece you hold in your hands, and all the metal that makes this boat a boat—from the nails to the cleats to the anchor—come from the *guts* of those mountains!"

"Do not be talkin' disrespectful a' the *Sea-Sword*," Billec warned, looking his adversary in the eyes, "an' I will not do it 'bout yer mountains. She is not a *boat*—she be a damned impressive *ship*!"

"It is not about your *ship*," Gadrun Grundling bellowed. "It is as fine as any other and a far sight better than some. It is this Dwarf-damned southern weather. It does not suit our blood. Boldac made the Dwarves to thrive in the damp and the dark. I am itchy and sick from this heat!"

"Gadrun," Janzalon said, placing his hand firmly on the Dwarf's sweaty, salt-sheened shoulder. "Hathom and I caught a fine open-water whitefish this morning. He is dressing it below decks as we speak. Some oil and fire-spice and a side of stewed vegetables will make it a memorable feast. Fit for the sea-gods, you might say. Perhaps a meal and a quarter-cask of mead will help to temper your mood."

"Mayhap it will," the Dwarf replied, removing Janzalon's hand from his shoulder, although not unkindly. "Lead the way, my friend."

Turning to Billec, intent upon his astrolabe, Janzalon enquired, "Would you care to join us, Captain? There is more than enough for four and your company would be welcome. I regaled you with my story—I would welcome hearing yours."

Making more notations in his logbook, Billec looked at the gruff visage of the Dwarf and said, "Thank ye *both* fer the offer, but I will be dinin' wit' senior staff. I am sure ye understand. Me story will keep, Tribune, until it begs ta be told. If yer still sober at the bells, join me fer evenin' inspection."

As Billec turned his attention back to his navigation, Janzalon wondered what he had been thinking when he had suggested Grundling should be their third. Then again, he reminded himself, as far as Dwarven moods, Gadrun's was not so bad.

Aside from the awkward, painful, and often messy navigation of his chamber pot, the cause of greatest frustration and embarrassment for Calrain Damonessa when it came to daily activities was the simple act—for almost everyone but him—of putting on his clothes.

Undressing was far easier than dressing. After undoing the rows of simplified clasps on his clothes designed by a sympathetic seamstress—whom Nadrim later punished for her kindness, although he claimed the infraction was centered on uneven seams

Aldemere's Dilemma

on a custom leather bodkin—Calrain could count on gravity to do the rest. *Dressing*, however... Dressing was complex, and a biting source of shame.

Nadrim had, some months before, delivered a stack of threadbare, dingy nightshirts to his brother from the ward where the eldest men of Mellya—those who could no longer raise a sword, pound a nail, or plant a row—were "attended to" as their bodies and minds marched persistently onward into oblivion and finally death.

"I cannot bear to see you in such writhing swirls of pain, poor brother," Nadrim had said, although his body language and ash-grey eyes delivered a message wholly opposite.

Although Nadrim was two years older, Calrain's brother had always been the smaller and dimmer of the two, and their parents, Philod and Trina, had known it.

Everyone had known it.

They also recognized early on in Nadrim a pronounced mean streak, tendency toward jealously, and fascination with the dark practices of information extraction, manipulation, and power seeking practiced by the boys' grandfather and great-grandfather, Ravin and Rogen.

Calrain had enjoyed his parents' attention and favoritism as the boys grew out of childhood, even though he knew that their relationship with their younger, favored son was at the expense of keeping Nadrim from slipping ever more toward a permanent home in the darkness of his heart.

It was in Calrain's fifteenth year that the pain in his joints began. A minor annoyance at first, the family physicians had passed it off as a normal teenage growth spurt, and the result of the intense routine of running, climbing, and body strengthening he would put himself through for several hours a day. Within months, however, his once straight, strong back had begun curving to the left just below his shoulder blades and then, further down, back to the right.

The chief physician and his selfishly inquisitive staff poked and prodded him with their knives and all manner of exploratory instruments, taking his blood and giving him vials of foul-smelling, worse tasting potions to swallow, but nothing they did stopped the twisting of his torso or eased the at times scream-inducing pain.

Trina, whose heart had been broken in equal measure with her favored child's body, had died in his twenty-first year. Shortly after, Calrain had begun losing feeling in his right foot and most of his fingers—which had once been skilled enough to carve intricate figures from wood and to pluck complex melodies of his own creation from the harp, the lute, and the lyre.

Within months, those once beautifully shaped and dexterous fingers had curved like the talons of the falcons Nadrim had taken to training in the aviary tower, with which Calrain's brother—the self-proclaimed cliffprince—so deeply, forebodingly identified.

His brother, who had stood in the shadows of the sickroom smiling triumphantly as the physicians humiliated him with their implements of hooked and sharpened iron. His brother, who had pulled his hair and covered him in blows in their shared room as they lay in the dark of the night. His brother, who had shed not a tear when their mother, and then their father, had died.

Triumphant Cliffprince Nadrim, he of the three-taloned falcon, who, after their parents' bodies were burned, forced Calrain to sleep in the same small room they had shared for all the years their parents had loved him best. A room where Nadrim had ordered mirrored glass the height and width of a man hung from each of the walls and in the corners where the walls met the ceiling so that Calrain could see his broken body no matter where he looked. A broken, brutalized body replicated and further distorted up to a dozen times depending on the angle from which he was looking.

Although the oversized dressing gowns with an open front Nadrim had offered would have solved the problem of dressing himself in a heartbeat, Calrain refused to stoop to going about his daily business clothed in the trappings of a dying old man in the death wards. His body may be broken, scarred, and barely of any service, but his mind was sharper than ever.

It had to be, just to survive.

Wincing in pain as he dragged a pant leg over his angled lower leg and bulging, misshapen knee, Calrain leaned back against the bed from his position on the floor and rested a moment before fastening the clasps at his crotch.

Pants, he thought, his breath catching in his throat as he clenched his teeth and willed away at least a portion of the pain. *The mere act of wearing them is a victory most profound.*

Thrusting his forearm into the strap affixed to his headboard and hoisting himself up with an enviable arm strength conditioned from three decades of such humiliating daily activity, Calrain gazed upon himself in the mirror directly in front of him. Countless nights had he thought of smashing the mirrors, although he knew without a doubt that there would be new ones installed as soon as Nadrim's spies made their daily report.

Aldemere's Dilemma

He would not let his brother know how much the mirrors upset him.

Letting gravity pull him forward, Calrain concentrated on his eyes, a sedate shade of green, as his mother's had been. He had become a master of hiding the hate in those eyes, but as they bore into the mirror, he let his hatred rage.

He, and not his brother, was the rightful heir to Mellya, in his mind and in his heart, and one history-making day in the not too distant future, his brother would pay in blood for every hair he had pulled, every blow he had landed, and every tear he had not shed.

First, however, Calrain would see him humiliated to a degree only a monstrosity like himself could truly understand.

Aldemere was exercising all of his will not to take the Slaaver's Hand—which he had surreptitiously removed from the inside of his vest and placed inside his saddlebag while he and Sir Tagen had stopped to eat and relieve themselves before entering Stathl Pass—and slip it on.

His curiosity concerning what it could do was nearly getting the best of him.

Tagen, however, who had barely muttered a word in their hours alone together, had been watching him without fail since they had parted company with Frederick and the others.

Now the mysterious glove would have to wait a little longer. It was time to enter Stathl Pass.

Gazing at the steep walls of reddish-rock that rose dauntingly upwards on either side of the pass, Aldemere noticed that the opening was only wide enough for four horses or two decent-sized wagons to fit across at once, which he realized was the point. Even taking into account its narrowness, it was no small feat that a crew had removed the large amounts of rock from the mountain necessary to create it.

The Mellyans have had their minds on invading the eastern forests for a very, very long time, Aldemere thought, scanning the walls of the Pass for any shadows that would indicate an indentation where an archer or scout might hide. Shifting over to his strategist's mind, Aldemere realized that Nadrim could lead a fair-sized army across the River Wythe. Aldemere himself would cross it in just over three days—although considerably farther west of the bridge that Frederick, in one of their rare moments alone, had told him the Mellyans had built there—and march unseen across the expanse of empty landscape to the mountain that rose before him as the exit of the pass drew near.

"This is as far as I go," Tagen said, without emotion. "Give me your horse's reins."

Ignoring Tagen's disrespect, Aldemere climbed from the saddle, moving to Poet's head to take his muzzle in his hands. "Well, trusted friend, it is time to send you back."

Although continuing on to the southern bank of the River Wythe on horseback would get him to Mellya considerably quicker than covering the distance on foot, Aldemere—with Lesster and Frederick's consent—had decided the latter option was unquestionably the wiser of the two. Aldemere doubted the Mellyans had ever seen an Elven horse, although, regardless of such inexperience, Poet was too magnificent a creature for them to believe he belonged to a poor and lowly hunter desperate to feed his family.

Besides, knowing he was going to surrender, Aldemere did not want to risk the Mellyans harming or misusing his beloved pure-white horse.

Poet dropped his head in acknowledgment of their parting, and Aldemere returned the gesture with half an apple from a burlap shoulder sack he had unslung from his pommel. Unfastening from his saddle the bow and quiver that Lan had found for him at Eerbell, he handed Poet's reins to Tagen.

"He is an Elven horse," Aldemere said, despite the fact that everyone in Glittereye knew of Poet's pedigree, "so there is no need to be rough. He will follow where you go without the slightest hesitation."

"You need not worry for your friend," Tagen said, saluting his fellow knight. "Good luck to you, Sir Aldemere."

"To you, Sir Tagen, as well," the captainguard answered, returning the salute.

After watching Tagen re-enter Stathl Pass, Aldemere turned his attention northward. He had sixty-five miles of hopefully unoccupied terrain to cover, and his destination was not getting any closer as he stood like a statue lamenting his separation from Poet, Crow Feather, and his pregnant wife left to wait for him at home.

"Get walking," he said aloud.

In an instant, he did just that.

"Boldac's beard and biscuits! You best be careful and kind regarding that steel before you, Axsen—it is for the prince's sword!"

Aldemere's Dilemma

Eggard Starforge shook his remarkable head of uncombed crimson hair in frustration before banging his hammer three times against the anvil upon which the steel in question lay, both to emphasize his statement and as a less messy alternative to hitting his young apprentice upon the head with it. Looking around him at the hive-like activity in the forge of which he was master, Eggard felt a sudden urge to kick over a stand of swords, but just before contact, he refrained. After all, just hours earlier, a half dozen metalsmiths had righted and reorganized several such stands after a visit by the prince he had mentioned and his clumsy, rambunctious brother.

The entire mess had begun several moonrises ago, when the elaborate metalsmithing operation Eggard and his ancestors had overseen for the last four thousand years had still been operating at its normally brisk but ordered and organized pace. Crafting weapons, mining tools, and parts and pieces for various sailing vessels, the Dwarves of Sur Mountain Forge were capable of exquisite artistry while maintaining a pace that no non-Dwarven craftsman could ever hope to match.

However, the flurry of activity of which Eggard now tried to make sense and order was giving his belt-pinched innards an insistent, biting twist.

A pair of the king's heralds had delivered orders a few days earlier that all production of maritime pieces—aside from the fashioning of seven iron prows for which they were given unusually exacting measurements—was to cease. The forges were to be devoted solely to the making of swords, spear- and arrowheads, battle-axes, and armor, both chain mail and plate. The heralds would soon be issuing similar orders to the other three Mountain Forges, as they already had to the one at Mount Mettlec itself, home of King Buttress Pilon and his gaggle of advisors.

"It is damned odd," Eggard had replied to the heralds upon hearing the order, a surly, sour pair who had demanded food and drink and several wenches to serve them. "The Eretian ships are due to arrive within days. We have orders to make ready for shipping."

After their meal, during which they had persistently harassed the wenches, the heralds had departed without a word—not even so much as a thank you—and Eggard had set about putting King Buttress's orders into action.

Then two of the king's three sons, Dramel and Affram the Second, had arrived.

"We hear you have questions, Starforge," Dramel—the older of the two, but younger than the king's missing heir, Stanchion—had said, training his eyes on the impressive array of weapons on racks, in barrels, and on tables throughout the forge.

Eggard, who was not so fond of the monarchy—although it was not personal to the Pilons, with whom he had always gotten on, but more of a general dislike of authority, especially in the running of his forge—shook his head. "Just talking aloud, princes," he had replied, cleaning his oily hands on a rag hanging from his apron. "You run the country and I run the forge—that is the way it has been since my ancestor Daggarmill made swords for the far-flung rulers of Mynoweth. It is not my place to ask."

"Our father, the king, says otherwise," Affram the Second, named for his great-grandfather, answered, choosing a broadsword from a rack and testing its balance with a series of slashes and thrusts that came all too close to trimming Eggard's unkempt beard.

"He does?" Eggard asked, standing his ground despite a wish to, at the minimum, shift his weight back and away from the sharp and shining blade repeatedly coming his way. "I find that to be a surprise."

Discarding the sword—and *not* where he had found it, Eggard noted—in favor of a piked, double-bladed battle-axe, Affram moved off to a section of the room with more space for him to test it. As he walked away, Dramel put up his hands in frustration. "Forgive my little brother—he is full to the brim with energy at the recent news of war. Not yet made a captain, and he fancies himself a general."

"So it is to be war for Mettlec then," Eggard answered, stroking his beard. "And with whom shall we dance, might I ask?"

Dramel came closer in order to lower his voice. "The Mellyans, most likely, although the full extent of what we must face is not completely clear. Word has come from Llafen Eret that their gods have granted them permission to outfit their ships for war. Speaking of—the prows the heralds ordered you to forge… What is their status?"

Eggard motioned for the prince to sit on a nearby bench. "It takes time to make the required mold, but my most experienced forgers have been working with little sleep. They shall be ready within a week."

"Excellent, Master Starforge," Dramel replied, making himself comfortable on the bench. "My father shall be very pleased to hear it."

Aldemere's Dilemma

Hiding a smile, Eggard asked, "Can I get you a mug of mead, Prince Dramel? And a lovely wench or two to serve it?" He was covering for the fact that he had many questions to ask, although he did not want to annoy the prince by asking them all at once. "I may have some dried, salted meat hidden somewhere around here as well."

Dramel waived off Eggard's offer of hospitality. "The mention of wenches can only mean that father's heralds took advantage of you—and of them. I shall make note of that, Master Starforge. It shall not happen again."

I hope this Dwarf will one day be king, Eggard thought, *and I am alive to see it.*

"We have very little time," continued Dramel, his tone weighty and full of confidence. "Affram and I must bring this news to the other forgemasters as quickly as we can. Father made sure we came to see you first, since you are the most talented and loyal of all."

"I am honored," Eggard said with a bow. "And should you see any weapons that suit you, good Prince Dramel, it would be my pleasure to have you take them—with my compliments, of course."

"That was part of the reason I was so pleased to come to you first," the prince replied, rising from the bench. "I have axes and spears aplenty from my grandfather Joist's collection, but I have not a sword that is worth its name. My father gave Joist's to Stanchion—his right as the eldest son. I do not know if we will ever see it again. You know the one of which I speak…"

"Indeed, indeed I do," answered Eggard, his voice climbing in pitch in anticipation of what Dramel was about to ask. "Hawkclaw. One of Daggarmill's greatest creations. A work of art, as I recall. I have heard it said that King Joist's enemies were so mesmerized by its shine, they would walk right up to him and impale themselves upon it."

"I do not know about that," Dramel replied with a smile. "But if you could make me such a sword, I would be forever grateful."

Eggard's eyes were blazing like red-hot coals. "I am no Daggarmill Starforge, my Prince. I have no claim to creating Star-blade, the lost sword of Questelleland, nor of Crow Feather, also lost to the mists, but I swear to do my best. I have an exquisite mother of pearl for the hilt—or perhaps you would rather precious stones? If you have them brought to me, I can inlay them in the pommel and the guard. I shall have our most skilled engraver carve the names of the kings of Mettlec deep into its blade. That is, if that is what you would like... The stories this sword will tell to all who gaze upon it... To those who witness its wrath..."

Dramel placed his hand upon Eggard's arm to halt the swordmaker's revelry. "I require none of that. I shall never be the king. I just need a dependable sword."

Eggard bowed again, truly confused at the prince's words, but too moved by his simple but stately manner to ask for clarification. With Stanchion gone missing after a pair of public, all-but-physical fights with Dramel and their father over trade policies during a visit by the malformed Mellyan ambassador, almost everyone assumed that Dramel was now next in line for the throne.

"It shall be just as you request, my Prince," Eggard answered, bowing yet again. "I will set my personal apprentice upon selection of the steel, although I shall do all of the most essential work myself."

Hearing a crash of wood and metal from the area Affram had entered, the two Dwarves turned to see the younger prince, his face a mask of embarrassment behind his not yet grown-in beard, come quickly towards them as half a dozen metalsmiths left their hammers, anvils, and fires to right the racks that Affram had knocked to the ground.

"I had best get my brother out of your way while you still have a forge to run," Dramel said, his own face flushing red. "I will make sure he does not lift that axe again until we are outside. Oh and... thank you for the sword. The day I return to claim it will be a memorable one indeed."

Since the princes had taken their leave, Eggard had been making sketches of possible pommels and crossguards and putting his apprentice, Axsen, to work on the initial hammering and folding of the three feet of steel that would ultimately be the blade of the prince's battle sword.

A sword whose name had already spoken itself deep into Eggard's mind.

"I am sorry to disappoint you, Forgemaster," Axsen replied to Eggard's criticism. "I lost my focus for just a second. I swear I barely blinked."

"Aye, apprentice," answered Eggard, tightening the straps of his apron in anticipation of the first of many sleepless nights, "and only a half-second's lapse is often the difference between a shattered blade and the making of a king."

Melak Caveraider was already feasting on a swath of fresh, salty blood from his blade, and his three dozen ships had yet to arrive in Vaelsport.

Moktar had repeated Nadrim's wishes to his second in command for what seemed like hours the morning after he and the other chieftains had returned to the Unsettled Wilderness—not that the Caveraiders referred to it by that name; to them it was "our walk-world"—with the eighteen Mellyan boats with which to make the raid. Single-masted vessels, twenty-five feet in length and nearly eight abeam, they could each hold fifteen warriors. Not that such mathematics, simple as they were, were a possibility for Melak's undersized brain. For him, it was the uncomplicated matter of looking into the boats and picturing wild-eyed, blood-hungry Caveraiders lined up with weapons within them.

Melak could also use his vision to imagine how the boats now in their possession would make their prospects beyond raids to the northern mines and fighting with the other tribes much broader than they had ever been before.

The boats had departed two days later, the nomads' own black-tarred badgerskin ropes replacing the less reliable ones the Mellyans had provided. They had coiled the latter in piles at the aft of each of the boats. They would work just fine for tying up their captives.

Heeding the instructions Nadrim had provided, Moktar had remained behind to organize the three clans for the coming raids on the northmen's mining operations, while Melak Caveraider, Kull of the Krags, and Bokk Riverskab took six boats each (again, it was more of a visual parsing of resources than an actual counting) and had chosen their crews for the journey.

Never leaving sight of the shoreline, the eighteen boats remained under oar in a steady rain, their sails used as covers to keep the stinging precipitation off their crews. The swing of a sword by a warrior standing in the bow kept the rhythm of the rowers steady, brisk, and coordinated. As day followed day, bringing them ever closer to Vaelsport, the easy cooperation and calm behavior of the three tribes began to shift to a simmering agitation as their furs and horsehide armor grew damper and more uncomfortable due to the incessant, biting rain. Once their bellies began to ache from the combination of raw fish and seawater that was their only source of sustenance, their minds first turned to violence.

It was on the sixth day, still another three days from Vaelsport, that the first expression of those violent thoughts occurred. It was over in seconds—one Krag stabbed another in the throat with a sliver of iron when the first stepped on his bench-mate's foot one too many times as they rowed. The Krags on either side of him tossed the bleeding body overboard before the winged sea scavengers circling above could descend upon it, and the crew of Krags resumed their rowing without so much as a grunt.

Melak had watched, however, as the Riverskabs quivered their lips as the pooled blood from the discarded body began to spread around them. A few hours later, as the sun began to shine for the first time in days, and the leaders ordered the rowers to hoist their sails when the wind began to blow, Kull's boat made a beeline for Melak's.

"My boat first," Kull barked out, pointing to a spot in the water a boat-length ahead. "I lead. You boy of Moktar. Do as Kull command." The posturing chieftain's crew nodded in agreement, as what passed for laughter amongst the Krags erupted in cacophonous spurts up and down the oar lines.

"You, Kull," Melak said, "weak and pissed on by me. *This* boat must now first." Raising his hand to indicate his crew should cease their rowing, Melak jumped the bulwark while pulling his axe from its sheath on his back, landing in Kull's craft as it continued to move past his own.

Before Kull had time to react, his head was floating in a rain barrel in the aft of the vessel, cut cleanly from his thick-muscled neck by Melak's axe in a single, brutal stroke.

"My boats each now first!" Melak shouted to Kull's former oarsmen, and then to the rest of the boats around him as he ran his finger along his axe blade, licking it clean with a rough and knobby tongue. "Row and no speaking," he ordered, making no move to leave the headless chieftain's boat. As the Krags took up their oars and Melak's former boatmen did the same, all that they heard was the creaking of the planks, the straining of the ropes, and the movement of the sea.

I am must be first, Melak thought.

The notion made him smile.

Finding sleep to be impossible, no matter how many remedies and techniques he employed, Elde the Jester slipped into his leggings and a heavy, fur-lined robe and walked quietly out the door without waking his sleeping wife. Pleased to find the passageway empty, he proceeded to the room where the castle's artisans worked.

Aldemere's Dilemma

Searching the worktables full of half-sewn dolls, puzzle boxes, and implements designed for carving wood and tooling leather, he pushed aside paint pots and bundles of brushes until he found the thing he sought—the model horse he had been working on when he and Aldmere had been speaking about the challenges of fatherhood. When he had completed it some days later, he had brought it to the castle's toymaker with a request that he use it as a model for making similar horses for the children of those who kept the castle's many occupants clothed, fed, and protected. Pleased to see that the toymaker had already prepared the templates, Elde lit a trio of candles, opened a jar of the purest white paint he could find, and selected a brand new sable-haired brush.

He would paint the horse he had carved like Poet, exacting in every detail. The miniature had to be perfect—Elde intended to present it to his grandchild on the day the baby was born. Then he would sit beside his son and speak of easier days.

As he dipped the brush in the paint, he heard a rustle of robes in the doorway.

"I am sorry to bother you, Jester. I thought I would be alone."

Setting the brush on the open paint pot at the sound of an old friend's voice, Elde turned with a smile and said, "It is no bother at all, Talorous. Come in and have a seat. Would you like to paint a pony?"

Waving away the suggestion, Talorous leaned his hickory walking stick against the nearest workbench, took a deep but rattling breath, and settled onto a stool. Rubbing his ashen cheeks, he closed his tired eyes.

"Are you alright?" enquired Elde, his concern in full bloom as he saw in the light from the candles the deep lines of worry and fatigue on the scholar's wizened face.

"That is a question," Talorous replied with a lyrical bit of laughter, "that neither one of us has the stamina for me to answer at this ungodly hour of night. So instead, I shall tell you this—the burdens of this kingdom fall on far too few of our shoulders. Things are not going well, my friend. I have heard conspiratorial whispers in the hallways regarding the attack on the barons. Do not think for a second that there is a single soul in this cramped and crowded castle who is not aware that Aldemere is off again on some vague and dangerous mission. We write this narrative far too often, praying the end will remain unchanged. That, of course, is nonsense. The narrative *has to* change. How else are we to grow?" He reached into his cloak and produced a briar pipe. "Do you mind if I indulge?"

"Please do," the jester replied. "My sitting here painting a horse in the middle of the night betrays as false anything I might say to assure you that those of us shouldering the weight are handling the task with confidence, so let us talk plainly, you and me. This stranger who came to the castle, who led Aldemere and Linead east. I know you know who he is, Talorous. And about the family from which he comes."

Taking a long, strong pull on his pipe, Talorous nodded his grey-haired head. With a thick, sweet-smelling smoke carrying his words aloft like a whisper, he said, "I would say he is a Fragenoar. Perhaps by marriage or adoption, although I believe his lineage is more direct. One thing more. He has arrived at the time he is needed."

"There are things I know as well… things my father told me," Elde replied, carefully choosing his words. "Things that Aldmere, according to family tradition, should not have knowledge of until his time of ascension as jester. Although I am thinking of breaking my vows and telling him the truth."

"At last—the crux of the issue," Talorous replied with a nod, producing an oiled pouch from his pocket and refilling his briar pipe. "You want to do right by your child. No one could judge you for that, but consider this, Jester Elde—the days of Glittereye's imposed isolation are behind us. The luxury of this kingdom merely being barons and Seers shuffling for power and bending the ear of whomever is on the throne with their petty egos and over-inflated pride is now a thing of the past. You know this better than I do. This kingdom is still a child. Her enemies are ancient. Ambitious. We must not trifle with the Mellyans. They excel at devastation. There are also others—maybe allies, maybe not, depending on how we proceed. We must not trifle with them either. Our world has changed forever, and this kingdom might not survive the changes still to come. Does Dylwyn see this, Elde? I honestly do not know. In the end, it is no matter—we are old—myself by far the oldest of us all. It is nearly time for others to take our place."

Releasing a weary sigh, Talorous, with the mouthpiece of his pipe, tapped lightly on the horse that Elde was holding. "*That* is a fine piece of carving."

Pleased enough with the compliment, but unable to produce a smile, Elde simply nodded in acknowledgment. He then felt a flash of insight. "So that is the reason Laurianna was sent to the Seers… She is your chosen successor?"

Aldemere's Dilemma

Talorous put his thumb in his pipe to extinguish the dying ashes and placed it back in his cloak. "Come now, Elde... It is not at all like you to ask questions to which you already know the answers," he said, grasping his walking staff and sliding off the stool.

He suddenly felt so frail.

Although he saw what Talorous felt, Elde resisted the urge to reach out and steady the aged scholar as he found an agreeable posture, with his back relaxed and his weight more comfortably distributed by bending his elbows so he could space his hands along the upper expanse of the stick. As Talorous turned for the door, Elde wiped the paint from the brush and placed it where he had found it. He then returned the lid to the pot of paint he had opened and, placing the horse in his pocket, grasped Talorous by the elbow, saying, "I shall walk you to your rooms. There is more I would like to say, and the walking will be of help in ordering my thoughts."

"I warmly welcome your company," Master Talorous replied. "Nigredo gets upset if I wander the castle at night. Seeing I am with a friend will calm that bristly old bird."

Without Poet's quiet companionship, Aldemere was lost. The Elven horse had served him well throughout his training for the knighthood, and during the campaigns and difficult missions he had been tasked with ever since, and to not have him along on this latest and strangest adventure seemed an ill omen the captainguard could not ignore.

After making his camp on the third day of his walk within a dense grove of sycamore trees just after the sun had settled below the horizon, Aldemere studied the star-filled sky, thinking of Anastasia and the child growing within her, as he had the two nights prior, while he settled into sleep.

At first light, with a girding intake of breath, Aldemere slung the quiver and then the bow across his back and tightened the laces on his boots. If everything went as planned, a border patrol would cross his path sometime during the morning and take him into custody.

Wishing he knew more than what Frederick had managed to tell him about the foe he was about to face, Aldemere made his way further north toward the River Wythe, which marked the southern boundary of Mellya, keeping a relaxed but steady pace. He might just need an extra reserve of strength to withstand any brutalities the patrol might choose to inflict upon him.

Adjusting his gait to hide the weight of the dismantled dagger and the Slaaver's Hand, both of which he had sewn inside his leggings the previous night, he tried his best not to think about all he had left behind.

He had only been walking a couple of hours when a border patrol of half a dozen men on horses emerged from the tree line just in front of him.

"Halt," the headsman said, dismounting. "What business have you in Mellya?"

"I was in the forests to the southwest, hunting with men I had met while seeking work on the river near Mirra Pass after winter had finally broken," Aldemere replied, showing the right amount of fear for a commoner. "The snows and frigid temperatures were hard on my growing brood. I had no choice but to leave them in a desperate search for meat. I was tracking a good-sized woodhart when I noticed the others had vanished. Not sure where I should go, I headed north, toward the river, with the hope of having better luck with fish than I had with catching deer."

"Place your quiver and bow on the ground," the headman commanded, stepping closer and drawing his sword.

"Happily," Aldemere answered, doing exactly as commanded. "I do not wish for any trouble. Either for you or for me."

"An intelligent choice," the headman answered, picking up the quiver and bow and sheathing his sword. "You would mostly likely meet with very ugly ends." Considering the stranger before him, he added, "Alright, then. You will have to come with us."

Aldemere buried a smile. "If that is what you command, I will readily comply. Perhaps there is work for an able-bodied man in the place where we are headed."

"Perhaps," the headman answered, signaling for two of his men to see to his prisoner. "Or, depending on what is made of your story, you might wind up in a cell. Or, then again, a grave."

After the two patrolmen had situated Aldemere on one of the soldier's horses, his hands bound loosely in front of him so he was able to grasp the pommel, the headman gave the order for the company to proceed.

Traveling southeast along the river, they crossed the well-guarded bridge that Frederick had mentioned, and turned their horses north. The headman mumbled something about a superior officer and the danger of spies to the bridgemen but otherwise kept his silence. As they traveled, Aldemere took the opportunity to study the patrol's armor, weapons, and saddlery. Well-constructed from

Aldemere's Dilemma

dense leather and tempered metals, Aldemere could see that the Mellyans were of a martial mind, confirming what Frederick had said. They rode in a tight formation similar to those employed by the Armies of Glittereye, and their gazes and reflexes were as sharp as were those of the kingdom's most capable knights.

As they approached an outpost comprising a few hundred soldiers several hours later, Aldemere looked with a practiced eye on the efficient, extensive preparations happening before him, both outside the walls and through the opening gates.

One need not be a soldier to see they were prepping for war.

CHAPTER THREE

Attuned as he was to the vibrations at work in the air through his skill at hunting and tracking, Frederick Fragenoar immediately felt a jolt of energy deep inside his body as he, Lesster, and the rest of their company crossed in the late afternoon into Tombal from the Forest of the Black Light. The subtle vibrations crackling in the air around him brightened his mood and relaxed the shoulders of his traveling companions—not that they were aware enough to know it.

Although they still rode in a tight circle around him, and took turns at times of rest to guard him, Linead's knights had been as good as their word, denying him neither water, food, nor a sound night's sleep—and none had laid their hands upon him, or even threatened to do so.

Mixing understanding with patience, Frederick had managed to find some peace in the past few days, focusing his thoughts on Aldemere's journey north and into the hands of the Mellyans, and his own responsibilities now that he was in Tombal.

Finding courage in necessity, he addressed Sir Lesster as they stopped to make camp for the night. "Tomorrow morning, it is my intention to lure out the Greybaer so we can make a start to our council. In order to do that, I must hunt their favorite food—the fleetdeer. One would be enough. Two, even better. Seeing that I am most likely the best shot amongst us, and they are smaller and quicker than the woodharts you hunt in Glittereye, I respectfully request that you lend me a bow and some arrows at the rising of the sun."

After running his hand through his thick mass of bootblack beard half a dozen times, as he considered Frederick's request, Lesster pointed to one of his men. "Sir Allan here has won many a sack of coin at the barony tournaments for his skill in the archery lists. He will accompany you on the hunt. And Faxx will go as well, keeping twenty paces behind, should you attempt to play us false while Sirs Brogan and Kiegan and I protect our position here."

"However it has to be," Frederick replied, bowing low to the ground.

"I thought you were friends with these creatures?" Faxx enquired, removing a dozen stones from the ground before unrolling and spreading his blanket. "Why then must you lure them?"

"They have suffered much this year," answered Frederick, selecting a moss-covered tree against which to lay his tired back.

     Aldemere's Dilemma

"One of the leaders amongst them, a magician named Simon whom they refer to as a Keymage, was kidnapped by men from Mellya not far from where we sit. So the effort that we make to bring them dressed and ready fleetdeer will prove our honest intentions."

Satisfied with the northman's answer, Lesster ordered Sir Brogan to stand first watch while the rest of the party slept. Comfortable and content beneath the moss-covered tree, Frederick closed his eyes and thought of the following day's reunion with his trusted fellow northmen.

The following morning, as the rays of the sun began to peek through the dense canopy of the treetops, Frederick and Allan checked the fletching on their arrows and tested the strings of their bows before setting off on the hunt. Faxx, following Lesster's orders, followed far enough behind that he would not spoil their task, although never so far away that he could not kill the northerner if Frederick gave him the smallest reason.

Within an hour, the two hunters had spotted a female fleetdeer. Seeing Allan draw his bow, Frederick allowed him to claim the prize. Forty minutes later, the trio of men were returning to camp with the pair of fleetdeer for which they had hoped, the second being a fair-sized eight-point male felled by Frederick with a shot between its shoulders.

"Once we have cleaned and skinned them, we will place the meat upon that flat rock over there, between the two tall oaks," Frederick explained, sharpening a knife Lesster had loaned him on a leather strop from his saddle. "As for us, we shall hide within that thick stand of pine to our right. It would be best if one of you takes charge of the horses, hiding them past that hill just beyond it. The Greybaer have a keen sense of smell."

"You are asking a lot of me, Northerner," Lesster replied, his hawklike eyes tracking each movement Frederick made with the knife. "But I shall agree to your plan. Brogan—you will see to the horses when the time comes."

Pleased with their progress so far, Frederick, careful not to appear too confident or in command, asked, "Sir Allan—do you know how to field dress a woodhart?"

"I have not done so since my youth," the capable bowman replied, embarrassed to admit it in front of his fellow knights.

"It will come back to you quickly enough," answered Frederick, encouragement in his voice. "A hunter should always prepare the prey whose life he has taken, and not leave it to anyone else. As you can see, the fleetdeer is a smaller breed than your woodhart, but the vitals are arranged the same. Take your knife like this"—he held his own over the breastbone of the buck—"and make the incision like so." Allan watched as the blade slid smoothly to the crotch of Frederick's fleetdeer. He then did the same with his own.

"Well done," Frederick said. "Continue to do as I do, and we shall soon be finished."

Proving to be as skilled with the knife as he was with the bow, Allan gutted and skinned the fleetdeer as quickly and flawlessly as his mentor.

Once they had buried the organs and packed away the deerskins on the backs of their saddles, the knights placed the meat on the rock Frederick had selected and hid themselves in the stand of pine as Brogan led their horses to the rear of the hill behind them.

"No tricks," Lesster whispered, grasping Frederick firmly around the forearm. "I am starting to think I can trust you and disappointment and feeling the fool have a sharp and focused effect on brawlers such as myself."

"I assure you, Sir Lester—I intend nothing but to lure the Greybaer," Frederick replied, showing neither fear nor force. "We must await them without further sound."

Not an hour's time had passed when the knights detected a slight rustling in the woods behind the oaks where they had positioned the meat. They were soon watching in wonder as a tall, impressively built being emerged from the trees, its broad snout twitching as it neared the offered meal. Lesster, as he would any potential adversary, quickly sized the creature up. Dressed in unadorned robes the color of winter holly and displaying no weaponry, the Greybaer stood over six feet in height, with an impressive width to its shoulders and bulk to its arms and legs. It had a full head of shoulder-length hair and a face like that of a barn cat, with yellow, oblong eyes sitting just above the wide, flat snout they had observed it twitching moments before.

"I have never seen such a thing in my life," Lesster whispered, his voice full of awe. "And look over there! Two more have just emerged..."

Lesster's men tensed as the newly arrived Greybaer joined the first as he examined the slabs of meat. While one wore identical robes to the first, matching him exactly in height, the other's robes had adornments of leaves, sticks, and herbs. Upon his golden-haired head, he wore a delicately woven crown of holly branches and bundles of goldenrod. He also stood four inches taller.

"That is Gidon," Frederick whispered. "He is their leader—what the Greybaer call a Regencymage, a cross between a king and one of your Seers. He is the one we are here to talk with."

Staying put as Gidon approached the meat, the Humans watched as the Regencymage motioned for his two companions to take a step back, their snouts anxiously twitching and their tongues moving back and forth over their powerful teeth and jaws as they agonizingly obeyed. Surveying the nearby ground, the rock, and the two oaks for signs of a trap, Gidon extended what looked to Lesster like a combination of a Human hand and a cat's paw and lifted one of the hunks of meat, which he passed to the Greybaer who had first emerged from the woods. He then repeated the task, giving a second piece to the other. The rest of the meat he gathered into his long and powerful arms.

As the trio turned away, heading for the tree line, Frederick rose and, motioning for Lesster and the others to remain where they were, exited the stand of pine, his arms open wide to show he was unarmed.

"Regencymage," he called, falling to one knee and placing his hands on the mossy ground before him, "I have returned to you as promised."

"At last you have come back to Tombal, Mountain Traveler," Gidon said in a voice both sonorous and kind. "I knew without a doubt who had left us this fine feast! It is the reason I dared to take it. Rise up fast and embrace me."

"I am honored to do so, my friend," Frederick said with a smile. Although the northerner was nearly as tall as the Greybaer, Lesster watched again in wonder as Gidon placed the deer meat back upon the rock and took the northerner into his arms, where he seemed to disappear.

"Is all here peaceful and well?" Frederick enquired, once Gidon had released him. "I have heard nothing from Christoph and Martin."

Pulling a fist-sized chunk from one of the slabs of meat, Gidon passed it under his snout, nodded his approval, and devoured it with a growl. "They are both well, and of great help to me and the others. They will be happy to see you after so many months apart. All has been quiet, Mountain Traveler. Too quiet, even for us Greybaer. We have heard nothing of Simon since the Falcon's warriors took him away. Have you heard word of his location, or more importantly, of his health?"

Frederick felt his heart grow heavy as he shook his head in reply.

During the summer of the previous year, ten months past, a group of Nadrim's assassins had entered the Forest of Tombal. Using their considerable skill in tracking, they were quick to find the well-hidden lair of a Greybaer and his family. As the men held their blades to the throats of his wife and three small children, the frightened husband revealed to them the location of the one they had come to kidnap.

The one called Simon Keymage.

"I should have been here, protecting him," Frederick said, lowering his head in shame.

Gidon's immense paw lifted the northerner's chin so they were once again eye-to-eye. "I know where you were, and the importance of your mission, Mountain Traveler. I also know your love for Simon Keymage runs as deeply as my own. One man cannot save this troubled, ailing world. Even one as capable as yourself. Have you heard whispering on the wind as to what the Falcon plans?"

"I have," Frederick answered, "and I promise to tell you all of it, although I confess, I am not alone. I bring a handful more of my kind, all trained and loyal warriors. They will help us to prepare for the war that is to come."

Spreading his arms wide and looking directly at the spot where the knights were still in hiding, Gidon let loose a great mirthful laugh and said, "I was wondering when you would mention them." He then shouted so the hidden knights could hear, "Come forth, our friends, and we shall all make feast upon this generous gift you have brought! Welcome to the Forest of Tombal! And please, by all means, invite the one with the horses, waiting behind the hill."

Since returning to Castle Silveth with Aldemere's orders pronouncing him temporary captainguard and his most precious belongings in hand, Sir Lan had found himself most at ease when he was making morning and evening rounds to the guardposts that his mentor had ordered constructed at the northern and southern points of the Major and Minor Sentinels. If the other members of the King's Guard were talking about him, his promotion, and the details of Eric's death—and he knew in his heart that they were—it was best not to be around it.

Most mornings, like the one that had just broken so brilliantly upon the land, Peecwyl joined him on Arrow, his seasoned slate-grey courser.

"Our preparations are proceeding well," the veteran knight reported, as they left the southern guardpost of the Minor Sentinel

Aldemere's Dilemma

and rode north on its eastern edge. "Your leadership of the King's Guard has thus far been impressive. It has left me free to concentrate on the drilling of the knights beneath my command here in the Central Barony. My counterparts in the other four baronies are engaged in similar martial work. We learned a great deal during the Nomad War and in squashing the Rebellion. Sir Linead shall be well pleased upon his return. Sir Aldemere shall be as well, and that is largely thanks to you."

Lan nodded at the compliments. "I have no intention of ever again letting a knight of the kingdom down."

Peecwyl whistled low and shook his helmeted head. "That is a promise impossible to keep. Do not waste your energy on proclamations such as that." Pausing for a moment of needed consideration, Peecwyl subconsciously fingered the deep, jagged scar trailing several inches below his eyepatch. Having made a decision, he said, "I have something to share with you, Lan. It arrived by hawk from Spiltrow a little after midnight."

As Peecwyl pulled a scroll from his belt, Lan forcefully shook his head. "If it is from Spiltrow, I would guess it concerns Sir Eric. I am not sure that I should know what it says."

Peecwyl laughed dismissively, as Lan knew was his way. "It does, and you should. Which is why, as a senior officer as well as… well… if not a friend, then as someone interested in seeing you through a difficult time… I choose to share with you its message." As he unrolled the missive and opened his mouth to read it, the two knights felt their eyes drawn toward a bright flash of light from the northern guardpost as a rider came charging toward them.

"This must unfortunately wait until later," Peecwyl muttered, handing the scroll to Lan and drawing forth his sword. "Read it in a quiet moment, and return it to me after."

"A single rider is approaching from the east," the guardsman yelled, reining his horse up fast. "He bears Sir Linead's shield."

"The four foxes," Peecwyl replied. "There is no reason to believe it is anyone but Linead—he was due to arrive any day—but swords nonetheless at the ready. With the fire signal sent from the guardpost, we shall have reinforcements arriving from the castle just as he draws near."

Several minutes later, as Sir Linead appeared over a gentle rise in the landscape, twenty well-armed knights met and surrounded their leader.

"I am pleased to see the system of signals and protocols Aldemere and I devised is working as it should," the knight-marshal observed, reining Titan just shy of a wall of swords and shields. "It is good to be back home."

"You are no more pleased than I am," Peecwyl replied, sheathing his sword and saluting. "You men are free to go," he said, motioning the knights from the castle and those from the guardpost northward. Only Lan remained. Turning to the knight-marshal, Peecwyl enquired, "What news do you bring from the east?"

"Sir Connar and I made our inspection of the eastern garrison and the various outposts in the Forests of Everrain and the Black Light and found them to be in battle-ready order, as I see that things are here. Connar has further fortified Eerbell. Aldemere should be near or inside Mellya, and Lesster and his men should be in Tombal with the *northerner*."

"Corvit assures me he is a valuable ally, Linead," Peecwyl offered, urging Arrow into a trot. "We have no choice now but to trust him."

"I received your message from Corvit," Linead answered. Then, with his jaw visibly clenched, he added, "I do not question our comrade's judgment, although you did not see the bodies in Eerbell as I did. The northerner assured us..." Grasping Titan's reins until his knuckles were white, Linead let the rest of it go unspoken.

"I saw Sir Eric's corpse," Peecwyl replied. "Our comrade Prima's only son. So do not think I do not know the pain that you are feeling. I have also watched Lan here punish himself relentlessly since his return. I say it is time to stop. For the good of the kingdom, I ask you to put aside your distrust and try to find some faith that Frederick is exactly what many of us believe him to be."

In lieu of a vocal reply, Linead galloped away.

Captain Thaker Ungerfil watched through one of the brass porthole windows in the Admiralty conference room as a busy network of winches, cranes, and stevedores loaded the ugly implements of maritime war onto his ship, the *Salt-Serpent*, as well as onto the seven other three-masted ships in the harbor. He had last stood in this spot on the day he received his commission. So much had changed in far too short a time. His life, so carefully planned since his birth, was one that Thaker was barely able to recognize.

"It is quite a sight, is it not?" asked Dorrin Waelsbun, captain of the *Sea-Sprite*, a broad smile on his face and an unsettling gleam in his eye.

Thaker was not surprised that their opinions on the current situation were at opposite ends of a vast, unnavigable sea.

165   *Aldemere's Dilemma*

Word of the Ruenai's decision to grant the Ereti their request to equip their fleet for war and the disclosure of the hidden weaponry beneath the floor of the Vessel had split the fleet captains directly down the middle. Those who shared Dorrin's enthusiasm were the captains of the *Storm-Spear*, the *Sea-Star*, and the *Spear-Shaft*, while the captains of the *Sea-Seeker, Storm-Star*, and *Sea-Snake* had been much more unsettled and circumspect, in line with Thaker's position.

No doubt, he thought, *the captain of the* Sea-Sword, *Billec Skarling, is thrilled at the news as well.*

The assembled captains broke from their knots of conversation at the anticipation of the arrival of Thaker's father, Grand Admiral Athes Ungerfil, as well as Warden Hefflar and whomever else amongst the Admiralty wished to attend the scheduled briefing. As he watched them take seats around the room, which a pair of stewards had hastily reconfigured to accommodate the rare occurrence of a meeting such as this, Thaker began to regret his father's decision to exclude first officers and navigators. With his older brother Hathom on a ship heading somewhere to the south, he would welcome Silbern, with all of his wisdom and wit, standing here beside him.

Deciding it was best to let Dorrin's remark go unanswered, Thaker was grateful to see the half dozen members of the Admiralty and tribunes Mastmin and Kaelhul filing into the room, along with Ambassador Pashter Waelsbun and Carra.

When everyone had found a seat, Grand Admiral Ungerfil called the briefing to order.

"I am proud of you all," he began, addressing the eight captains sitting before him. "Conversion of our merchant ships into vessels of war is proceeding ahead of schedule. Your crews are showing no signs of inefficiency or unruliness under what are brand new procedures for us all. It is clear you have conveyed to them the seriousness of our situation. Carra sea-shaman continues to commune with the Ruenai, with the assistance of the Ruen-Eret, and we pray that their blessings will be upon us as we venture into the dark and dangerous waters that imminently await us.

"I know you must have questions," he continued, after sipping from a glass of water placed on a shelf inside his podium, "but I ask that you hold them until the conclusion of my talk. Once you have received your orders, know that I, and the entire Admiralty, wish you to speak freely regarding any concerns that you may have, which is why I have limited this briefing to only the eight of you captains.

"The preparation of your ships will be completed within days. The harpoons, deck-secured catapults, and other machinery we are installing are easy enough to operate with practice, and your first officers will be primarily responsible for the assigning of offensive and defensive crews and their training, which will be brief and full of trial and error, as we have no surviving documents to guide us. The catapults will be capable of launching iron projectiles as well as incendiary devices that one can activate before release. You can all appreciate the dangers of working with fire at sea, so you will also designate and train water brigades. Crews will outfit your ships with extra rain barrels solely for the purpose.

"As to the plan of deployment." Athes paused as the eight officers, who had been sitting in rapt silence throughout his presentation, now rolled forward in their seats like waves approaching the shoreline. "The *Salt-Serpent* and *Sea-Sprite* will go east to Mettlec as soon as they are fully outfitted. Ambassador Waelsbun will accompany you. It is our hope that our allies in Mettlec can further provide the means of making war. Carra has reason to believe that they can.

"The *Sea-Star* and *Storm-Star* will sail tomorrow for Vaelsport, your sole objective being the Tirili ore operation. Should the Mellyans be building ships—we are all but certain they are—we cannot allow them access to the ore to craft their rudders. Upon arrival, you shall gather all available tonnage and return immediately to Llafen Eret. Warden Hefflar shall provide you with documents ordering the cessation of all mining in the Tirili Range until the crisis has passed. You shall see to it that all of the equipment is disabled. The other four ships shall sail the coasts of Eret, as patrol and first defense, should we be attacked."

"Forgive the interruption, Grand Admiral Ungerfil." All heads turned to Capstan Mastmin, captain of the *Storm-Spear.* "That is a lot of coast to cover for less than half a dozen ships, prepped for war or not."

Athes nodded. "Which is why our seven single-masted ships will be put into service as well." Letting the anticipated buzz amongst the captains rise to a peak and then dissipate, Athes sipped again from the glass behind his podium.

The seven ships of which he spoke were amongst the oldest in Mynoweth. Each eighty feet in length, and twenty feet abeam, able to hold fifty oars and plenty of cargo, their ancestors had named them for the seven stars by which the Ereti navigated: *Skor, Keipr,*

Nygla, Snaeldr, Kjolr, Tresaumr, and *Innvior.* All of the first- and second-year Admiralty cadets trained upon these ships.

The Admiralty had never used any of the seven for war.

To subject the cadets to the dangers of war at sea in these single-masted ships brought home to everyone in attendance how perilous was their position.

"Custom-crafted iron prows are being forged by the Dwarves as I speak. Dorrin... Thaker... they are part of the cargo you will be bringing back from Mettlec."

"Who will provide the crews for the single-masters?" The question came from Sterrin Wilsbern, captain of the *Sea-Snake.* "None of us can spare a soul."

"I will captain the *Innvior,*" Athes replied, this time without pausing when a buzz began in the room. "And other members of the Admiralty with captaining experience will take command of the others. As to crew, they will be a mix of second- and third-year cadets, as they are familiar with the ships and far enough along in their training to see the plan to success. They will patrol the Rivers Fen and Tere, and, if needed, can protect the coast in open water. Are there any other questions?"

After a few moments' silence, as it became clear that everyone present knew what was at hand and what role they each must play, Athes motioned for all in the room to stand.

"Water, wood, and wind," he intoned. The room began to pulse with the energy of resolve as the assembly made its reply.

As the patrol whose custody he had been in for the past two days finally rode into Amdar, Aldemere stifled a groan as his stiff legs, which their commander had ordered his men to tie tightly to his saddle as the party approached the city, began to ache.

They had made half a dozen stops at various guardposts and garrisons like the one they had reached within hours of taking him captive, where the process of questioning to which their commanders subjected Aldemere was always the same.

"What do you want in Mellya?" a brusque commander would ask, his breath smelling of whatever he had last consumed, after which Aldemere would once again relate his story, the details of which he had created, memorized, and rehearsed on his solitary ride to the river. He knew well enough that even the slightest deviation would catch the attention of the headman who had captured him, and things would go ever more poorly from that moment to the hour of his increasingly inevitable death.

It was clear that Mellya bred its men for war and little else. He had seen little in the way of artisanship as they had made the journey to Amdar. Clothing and the instruments of daily living were all unadorned and utilitarian in design. The signs that hung from inns and shops had only the essential information, plainly carved and devoid of illustrations, and the buildings themselves showed no evidence of originality or individualism.

Then there were the people. Stiff and joyless in their work. Nothing like the farmers and artisans that Aldemere so enjoyed visiting on his travels throughout the baronies. Even the children— the few that he could see—were hard-muscled and far more serious than parents and teachers should ever ask their children to be. He saw not one doll, nor a wooden horse nor puzzle. Even the smallest amongst them were working beside the adults, carrying bundles and boxes or organizing piles of goods. Most of the boys wore wooden swords, which they would pull from their simple leather belts in order to try to defend themselves when a passing soldier would attack them without warning.

All eyes turned away as Aldemere passed, as if they knew something about what atrocities were bound to befall this unfortunate stranger brought amongst them.

Entering the city through the metal-banded and iron-studded doors of Amdar's southern entrance, Aldemere made a quick, efficient survey of Mellya's capital city. Down the main thoroughfare, which ended in a fortress, forbidding and impressive, long columns of soldiers marched in lockstep, eyes forward, weapons shining and at the ready.

As the patrolmen halted and dismounted, two mounted officers approached.

"What is this you bring us, Sergeant Straith?" the older of the two men asked.

"A trespassing hunter, sir," Straith replied, straightening his back in deference to his superior. "Separated from his party three days ago while seeking food to feed his family beside the River Wythe."

"And why is he here with you?" Straith's superior asked, looking Aldemere over as though he were a sack of cornmeal on its way to sale at market.

"No one seemed to know what else to do with him, sir. So I have brought him to you."

"I see," the commander replied, fingering the knife that lay at a slant behind his belt buckle. Then, to Aldemere, he said, "My name is Captain Purloch. The security of this city is my sole concern. I have little use for strangers."

Acting as though the captain's words were a signal, the men of the patrol and the new arrivals drew their swords in unison.

"If you are a hunter, where are your quiver and bow?"

Determined to execute the next part of his plan as quickly as possible, Aldemere answered, "I have no quiver, for I am not afraid and no bow because I have nothing with which to tie it."

Edging his horse closer and withdrawing and holding his knife so that the blade was inches from the stranger's neck, Captain Purloch whispered, "Have you a name, *friend*, or shall I call you *fool*?"

Suppressing his normally harsh response to that long-hated word amongst the jesters of Glittereye, Aldemere forced a grin. "My name is Tun, and I have done nothing to be so close to so many sharp and shining blades."

"Just being here is plenty," Purloch answered, keeping his blade pointed at Aldemere's throat. "Straith."

"Yes, Captain Purloch?"

"If this man is a hunter, why do I not see a quiver and bow amongst you?"

"He had one when we met him," Straith mumbled, shifting nervously in his saddle. "We took it from him and... well, sir, I traded it at a guardpost for half a barrel of ale."

"Was it smooth and intoxicating, Sergeant?" Purloch asked, clenching his jaw. "I truly hope it was, for the lashes it has earned you."

Knowing enough not to answer, Straith sat in silence, awaiting further orders.

"Take our new arrival... *Tun*... to the prison for... safe keeping," Purloch ordered, putting his knife away. "I must go and see the cliffprince. We are expecting a group of hirelings from the wilderness later today. Further reinforcements as the ships are nearing completion. As for you," he said, training his eyes once more on Aldemere, "I would keep my clown's mouth shut. Your fellow peasants may find you charming, but you shall find the people of Amdar are more likely to smash your smile than share it."

"Duly noted," Aldemere replied. *Your remark, that is—and your alliance with my enemies, the nomads.*

"It had better be," Purloch answered, reining his horse away. "I shall deal more thoroughly with you as soon as I am free."

Watching the captain ride away, Aldemere whispered, as Straith grabbed his arm, "Until then, I shall not be."

The princess Anastasia was growing weary of the endless stream of questions the castle's inhabitants were asking her day and night as she went about her business.

"You are starting to show that you are with child," her mother began one morning after watching Anastasia's increasingly rude behavior and enduring another barrage of her complaints about people's unreasonable interest in her pregnancy. "A child is a blessing no matter who may be its parents, but this child that you carry... Born of the love of the heir to the throne and one of the kingdom's most beloved knights. One would wonder if they did *not* ask after the child and its father at every opportunity."

"It is a private matter," Anastasia answered, blowing her bangs from her eyes in frustration.

Laughing quietly, Queen Cecile replied, "You must no longer be so naïve about your circumstances, Anastasia. There is nothing private with families such as Aldemere's and ours. Eyes are watching, ears are listening, always. Although it may be inconvenient at times, it is as it should be—treachery and oppression come of secrecy. Of privacy. You are the daughter of the king—this pregnancy belongs to us all. This child you carry shall one day be a king or a queen."

"That is fair enough, Mother... I suppose," Anastasia said with a scowl, "but I have other things to consider, and I am certainly entitled to do so." She grabbed a tangle of linen bandages from the box from which she had been working and began to roll them as she spoke. "Being the heir to Glittereye, a fact of which you so needlessly reminded me, I want to be known as a woman who was willing to lead at the brink of the war—not one who hid behind her pregnancy, as you and Glenna midwife are demanding that I do!"

Selecting a bright red thread from the table beside her for the tapestry on which she was working—a family tree of the lines of chieftains, kings, and jesters that would hang over the newborn's crib—the queen, on the first try, passed the thread through the tiny eye of a three-inch needle. "You are reminding me of the impatient, tomboyish girl you were when Aldemere first began to court you. Next, you shall be donning your old britches and pulling out your bows! You have nothing to prove to anyone, my child. Neither does your husband, although, to talk to his mother, it is clear that Aldemere is as intent on proving himself as you are. You have half a year before your son or daughter arrives—then nurturing your child must be your priority. Stop being heroes and prepare to be parents!"

Aldemere's Dilemma

Anastasia had spent as much time as she could in isolation since her mother had uttered those words, struggling with their weight. Admittedly, she was jealous of the squires with whom she had grown up who now were full-fledged knights. The maidens of the castle seemed to want nothing more than to marry a knight of rank with fair prospects for land and a home with many rooms. They all talked about how lucky she was—that is, until the next time Aldemere left on a mission at her father's behest. Then they could scarcely look her in the eyes. She could not understand them. She still wanted to saddle her bay mare, Saffire—named for the striking color of the horse's eyes—and ride off to battle with the boys.

If the castle's inhabitants had been reluctant prior to her pregnancy to have Anastasia do anything resembling work, Glenna Gravenal's pronouncements had now made it almost impossible for her to do any more than roll bandages and stuff feathers into pillows.

"May I take that box from you, Princess Anastasia?" Sir Gadwin of the King's Guard asked her one morning, as she neared the infirmary door.

"Does it *look* like I need your assistance, sir knight?" she asked, turning her torso so the box was out of reach of his eager, grasping hands.

"You do not at all, my lady," Gadwin answered, wishing he had passed her with a silent salute, or stayed in the Watch Tower instead of seeking a remedy for an unsettled stomach.

Anastasia bit down on her sarcasm—she found herself moodier than usual as of late and always hungry for chocolate and pickled pork knuckles—and simply said, "Then continue on your way."

Filling her days to keep from thinking of Aldemere, with and for whom she found herself both angry and constantly pining, was not working as she had intended. He had left her with a cold resolve meant to spare her pain, but it had caused her nothing but. When Sir Lan had returned from the east with the sack bearing Aldemere's Clausmer and Garter, she had willed herself not to open it, placing it instead on the rack in their room where he kept some of the clothes he had worn as a squire.

She retrieved it an hour later.

Fingering the Clausmer on its long leather thong—the symbol of his unified path of the jester and the knight—as it hung beneath her dress, she recalled the first time Aldemere had placed it in her care, the night before he left to vanquish the dragons Diette and Simnac.

"Come back to me now, as you have before, my love," she whispered, placing her free hand on the curve of her growing belly. "I am unsettled when you are gone."

She then made her way to the infirmary, taking stock of its supplies, the concentration required to keep from losing count and having to start again a welcome bulwark against the heaviness in her heart.

Kal-Gadras had been scanning the skies from the overlook outside his mother's bedroom when a hawk from Glittereye alit upon a ledge. The Elf had been waiting for nearly a day for the raptor to arrive, although there had been no indication that it would beyond his own intuition. As he put out his arm to provide the brown and red messenger bird with a proper perch, he felt a surge of promise as he eyed the ink-filled scroll tethered to its leg.

He had been home for barely a week. His mother's illness was at last abating, as she had assured him that it would, although he found himself in short supply of patience for the process. Adding to the stress and strain of his worry for Nemmerle was his conflict with Izmen, who had holed up in his library tower following their altercation in the stables. Kal-Gadras felt he was on the verge of lashing out in a manner unacceptable for an Elf, much less the son of their spiritual mother and the Lord of the South Shore of Marlooq Fer.

Not to mention, he reminded himself, putting his hand to his neck, *the bearer of the Mark of Gal-Rashand, slayer of the dragon Rilvax and all-father to the Elves*.

Kal-Gadras had never before questioned the responsibilities into which he had been born. He accepted them with humility. Self-doubt was all too human a trait upon which to waste a moment of his time. Since his return from Ferrukkla, however, he had been grappling with a feeling that he had only known through his experience of the energy that pulsed through the personal stories of his best friend, Aldemere. Their connection was growing stronger every day, and the insights Kal-Gadras was gleaning would have been more than welcome at any other time, although, under the circumstances, he wished the complex human feelings would diminish, if not disappear completely.

Detaching the scroll from the leg of the hawk, Kal-Gadras stretched his arm to an overhanging branch of a lemon tree, upon which the majestic raptor settled.

Aldemere's Dilemma

As he began to unroll the tiny piece of parchment, Kal-Gadras heard the sounds of footsteps upon the stairs leading to the overlook, and within seconds, High Lord Petror was by his side.

"I heard the hawk approaching," he explained. "What news from Castle Silveth?"

Kal-Gadras read him the message, which Elde the Jester had written and signed, detailing all that had happened in recent weeks.

"A Fragenoar has emerged," Petror whispered, moving to the edge of the overlook and sinking into thought.

"I know that to be an old and respected name from the past," Kal-Gadras replied, sooner than either he or Petror would have liked. "A name from the height of the rule of the Lyseans, is it not?"

"It is," Petror replied, taking the scroll from Kal-Gadras and scanning through its text. "The Mellyans are a threat such as we have never seen. Not all of the families of Lyseum were interested in doing what was best for the people. There were struggles, at times between brother and brother, often between the ruling families, that gave rise to a class of trained assassins and treacherous spies, who were the instruments of secret deals and maneuvers for control. Those who were ultimately victorious have created a military state that now threatens the Centerlands as well as the eastern forests. They care for nothing more than the amassing of power through chaos, fear, and death. We must do all we can to protect our borders." Glancing down at the scroll, he added, "If they have ships, as is speculated here, they will approach from just past Tombal, which will most likely be subdued and used to stage their armies, so it is equally likely that they shall land on our southeastern shore fully supplied and eager to invade."

"Then I shall ride south with all due haste and fortify our defenses, as is my duty as lord of that shore."

"Who is acting in your stead?" Petror asked, surprising Kal-Gadras with the question.

"My cousin, Nal-Koyyan," he answered. "He underwent the Passage less than a year after my own encounter with an asp. He has never failed to ably steward the affairs of the South Shore in my absence."

The Passage to which Kal-Gadras was referring was the rite of adulthood for all Elven males of noble birth. A competition against the formidable water asp, as it left the sea to lay its eggs upon the shore. Several of his friends from childhood had succumbed to the asp's poisonous, quick-acting bite.

"Then leave him to do just that. We must move inland the horses of Ahkete-Val and ring the valley with guards. I will send word to Nal-Koyyan to look to those tasks immediately. I shall then ready a battalion to take north and send a second east, to the River Skillen."

"And what of me, my lord?" Kal-Gadras enquired. "Shall I ride to Glittereye?"

Petror shook his head. "I see no need of that. Linead and his knights are making their preparations. You shall take five of our best archers and sail for the Forest of Tombal. You must remind their Regencymage of the ancient alliance shared between our races, and offer your help in protecting the Greybaer from whatever Mellya is planning. They possess powers that would be catastrophic to our chances of victory should they be turned for ill. You must also make alliance with the descendent of the Fragenoars. It will serve to bring you closer to Aldemere. The message does not say if he will return to Silveth when his spying is complete or if he shall join with those in Tombal, but I am guessing it is the latter. We can split the eastern battalion in two should the need arise. Send word if Tombal is threatened beyond what you can handle, and I shall see it done."

Kal-Gadras, alive with renewed purpose at hearing Petror's orders, slapped the ancient Elf on his powerful upper arms and said, "As soon as I say goodbye to mother and choose my handful of bowmen, we shall ride for the ship. Thank you for this, my lord!"

As the younger Elf pulled back the curtain of palm fronds that led to his mother's chambers, Petror stood in renewed contemplation regarding Kal-Gadras's very human gesture and overly emotional response.

He did not know how much more like Aldemere Kal-Gadras could become before he would be of little use to his country and its cause.

Sir Corvit, Chief Knight of the Northern Barony of Glittereye and veteran of the Nomad Wars, felt a commander's pride.

The feeling was one that surprised him.

Watching the three hundred knights under his command make their final preparations for the attack that was to come, Corvit thought back to the depths to which he had fallen when an inexperienced knight called Aldemere had ridden in full armor astride an Elven horse into his dilapidated, diseased, and undisciplined border camp in the northern mountains eighteen months before. He thought of the comrades they had lost in the months of desperate fighting that followed as they withstood onslaught after onslaught from the savage nomadic tribes. He

Aldemere's Dilemma

thought about the price, both physical and mental, that the cosmic butcher had finally named for defeating them, through targeted assassination of their chieftains.

Now he and his men would have the element of surprise, and therefore the advantage, as the nomads so often had before.

Corvit had been in council with the northern baron's brother, Milani, who ran the ambir mines that were the economic backbone of the barony when he had received a message from a falcon that had flown in from the east.

The earth-colored scroll, so unlike the sand-colored parchment produced in the eastern barony, contained a script that Corvit also did not recognize. In a scrawl hard to read and looking like that of an elderly, trembling hand—or that of a man in a great and pressing hurry—the sender had alerted Corvit to an attack upon Vaelsport, to come by sea in a joint operation by the three nomadic tribes.

The timely arrival of the missive would give Corvit ample opportunity to gather a force of riders and head west to Firoth Pass, the only land passage to the Vaelsportians, which necessitated the crossing of the one hundred and twenty miles of scorching sun and arid wasteland that lay between the pass and Vaelsport—the Desert of Wylt Ccen.

First, though, he must meet with the baron.

Excusing himself from his talk with Milani with a vague explanation of "pressing matters," Corvit had ridden with all haste to Cabral, where Baron Ciloto had arrived only days before after the difficult and deadly trade meetings at Eerbell in the east.

Steeling himself for yet another argument with the aged baron regarding priorities and the safety and security of the wealthy mine owners—of which Ciloto was the wealthiest—Corvit removed his helmet, shook the dust from his boots, straightened his sash, and willed into being his most disarming smile.

If only the jester-knight could see me now, he thought, *dressed like a soldier instead of a savage*, taking the stairs into the receiving room of Ciloto's sizable home two at a time.

Aldemere—with a combination of his authority as commander of the northern forces and good old-fashioned threat and coercion—had forced the baron into providing adequate supplies to the men and horses who kept the mining operations running by keeping the barbarian tribes at bay. When Corvit's promotion to Chief Knight of the Northern Barony became official after one too many northern winters had prodded his predecessor into retirement, Ciloto had surprised him by endorsing his appointment. Perhaps it was simply a matter of Corvit being a familiar sparring partner, one with whom Ciloto had learned to get his way more often than not, but the reason did not matter—Corvit now had final say with regard to northern martial matters.

He knew beyond a doubt what it was he had to do.

Making his way past Ciloto's two secretaries with a brusque "I need to see him *now*," Corvit reapplied his smile and entered the baron's office.

"Sir Corvit," Ciloto said, clearly displeased at the sight of his unexpected, unannounced visitor, "I am on my way to a garden concert. I am surprised you are done with my brother so soon. I know he had a great deal on his mind, and many recommendations on how you should be allotting your forces and focusing your daily patrols. We have been more than lucky with the lack of raids this spring, but I know it will not last. As you know, it never does… Thus my having to feed you…"

"It is the nomads of whom I am here to speak, Baron Ciloto," Corvit replied, silently wondering what a "garden concert" was and why anyone would wish to attend one. "I have received a warning via falcon that they are sailing to annihilate Vaelsport." He passed the piece of parchment to the baron over his expensive teakwood desk. Ciloto barely glanced at it before tossing it back at the knight.

"How can you begin to make out what it says?" he asked, pushing in his chair and donning the gold-trimmed brocade coat that hung from it. "My youngest grandchild writes more neatly. It is no matter—Vaelsport is of no concern. It is an Eretian colony, and from what I understand, its inhabitants are wholly mad. So let them deal with their own."

Had an Eretian sent the unsigned message? Corvit wondered, pushing the question from his mind for later contemplation. He was about to engage his foe.

"I do not know if the Ereti are in pursuit, or even know of the attack. *I* am now aware of it, however—as are you. I must therefore take a squadron—"

"To do what?" Ciloto came around his desk with a speed belying his age and usual pace. "It could be a diversion, designed to draw you away. Perhaps a new chieftain—one whose brain is less pickled than that of his predecessor—wrote the message. It would explain its illegibility. You must remember that the other barons and I were nearly the victims of a well-coordinated assassination attempt at Eerbell. So forgive me if I am disinclined to lose the full strength of

177   *Aldemere's Dilemma*

my protection so that you can ride in search of glory in a place whose fate—bloody or otherwise—concerns me not in the least."

Digging his fingertips into the palms of his hands to keep from losing his temper, Corvit said, in a measured tone, "It will matter most greatly to you if the nomads overtake Vaelsport, cross the desert, and then march on the mines from the south while their comrades attack from the north. What if they decide to continue south, raiding the oil fields and glass workshops in the western barony? How would he take it if Baron Ralin were to find out you had the knowledge, time, and opportunity to stop them at Vaelsport and chose not to? He is a fiercer fighter than many a knight I have known."

Corvit was counting on Ciloto's well-known dislike of the young baron—which he knew was based mostly on fear of his unpredictability and ugly temper—to force him into approving Corvit's plan.

"Very well," the baron answered, after a moment's contemplation. "You shall take no more than three hundred knights and only that many horses. The other seven hundred shall remain for future allocation as my brother and I decide. If you can agree to those terms, you may leave for Vaelsport as soon as your force is assembled."

Shaking hands with the baron even as he formulated the instructions he would give to his lieutenants to prevent Ciloto and Milani from taking wholesale advantage of them in his absence, Corvit readied himself for revenge.

It was now only hours away, as he stood upon a cliff at the shoreline in Vaelsport, his men arrayed around Seafarer's Pass in tight formations. Several hundred male Vaelsportians under the supervision of dismounted knights were hiding high up in the mountains, ready with all manner of projectiles, including torches soaked in oil that they would light and toss into the nomads' ships as they approached.

Enjoying his pride and satisfaction for a moment more before stuffing them down inside his gut, Corvit raised a vision glass to his eye, training it just beyond the Gap, adjusting its focus until he could see, just upon the horizon, eighteen ships full of the bloodthirsty nomads, heading toward them fast.

"Come to Corvit now, you bastards," he whispered, "and see what surprises I have planned."

With his arms pinned behind him by a pair of malodorous guards, each of whom had far broader shoulders and more than a head's height on their prisoner, Aldemere fought to keep his balance as they shoved him through the prison entrance, which opened onto a steep set of stairs that led downward to two rows of tiny, ill-kempt cells. As the pair of jailers pushed Aldemere roughly down the passageway, he spotted what had to be a Greybaer huddled in the corner of a straw-filled cell. His feline face and great mane of hair were as majestic as Talorous had described. In the cell across the aisle, he noticed a small figure devoid of hair except for above his eyes and on his chin.

An Eretian, he thought. *How curious…*

As the Eretian stepped into the weak light of the prison to get a better look at the new arrival, Aldemere saw he was missing an arm.

Stopping him with a jerk of his elbow at the far end of the prison, the guard to Aldemere's right pulled a thick ring of keys from his belt and unlocked a cell already occupied by a rough-looking Human and another being the likes of which Aldemere had never seen.

Standing the height of a boy ready for the squirehood, although his face was weathered and aged like that of a Human in his sixties, the being had a white-grey beard hanging over his heavy, rounded waist and thick waves of hair cascading over his shoulders, except where it hung in thin woven braids in front of his ears. His short arms and legs rippled and bulged beneath his sand-colored tunic and white fitted pants.

This was without a doubt a Dwarf, such as Frederick had described.

As the guard slammed and locked the cell door and headed for the stairs, the man stood nose to nose with Aldemere. "Take that corner there and stay quiet and still unless you desire a pummeling!"

Needing time to think, Aldemere did as the man demanded. As he passed the sneering Dwarf on his way to the spot assigned to him by the Human, he thought back to his first night in the Great Hall, when he first became a squire.

How little progress I have made, he thought, fighting not to smile.

After an hour of silence, a female child of maybe ten arrived, dressed in an apron and bonnet. Without a word, she served a thin, foul-smelling soup in rough-hewn wooden bowls at each of the cells, which she pushed beneath the lowest horizontal bar, their unappealing contents slopping over the sides, while a snarling guard kept his poleaxe at the ready.

Aldemere's Dilemma

"Eat," the Dwarf mumbled, pushing the single bowl delivered to their cell toward Aldemere with his foot.

"I am fine for now," Aldemere answered. "But I hope that you enjoy."

"What have you done to earn a dung-filled corner in the infamous dungeon of Amdar?" the Dwarf enquired, lifting the bowl to his mouth and drinking deeply, before setting it on the ground and pulling chunks of whatever had been floating in it from his beard and swallowing them down with a groan.

Grasping the bowl in a pair of chapped and shaking hands, the other Human slurped down the dregs the Dwarf had left behind.

"I was arrested by a patrol while hunting near the river to feed my wife and children."

"It is a fool who hunts illegally in Mellyan lands, Human—especially in times like these. If your family was starving when you left them, they are certainly dead by now."

"Although I am touched by your concern, my family will be fine," Aldemere replied, turning away from the Dwarf to signal an end to their exchange.

Throughout his first night in the prison, Aldemere sat silently in his corner and watched as a guard arrived hourly to count heads and check the locks. Every fourth time, he noted a different face.

How kind of you, my friends. Keep to your routine so I am able to exploit it.

CHAPTER FOUR

Situated deep within the rockface of Mount Mettlec sits the throne room and council chambers of its country's line of kings. Since the time of Boldac the Creator, when he formed the five mountains of Mettlec with five blows of his fabled forge-hammer and bestowed upon the Dwarves the gifts of mining and metalworking, the fires that illuminate the mountains' vast system of tunnels and chambers had cast their light upon the faces of those with the family name of Pilon.

Over the 8,000 years of its existence, Mettlec had known no other kings but these. One hundred and eighty Pilons had lived and died—some of old age, some in battle, and some at the hands of ambitious relations—wearing the iron and agate crown that now sat squarely just above the browline of Buttress Pilon, who had assumed the throne ninety-three years before, following the quick, natural death of his father, Joist.

Swallowing a deep pull of mead from an ancient dragon horn the length of his arm, the winged owner of which an ancestor called Alum the Cold had slain, Buttress pulled a clump of honey from his grey and grizzled beard and stared daggers at his advisors, collectively called the Trinity Council. A set of identical two-hundred-plus-year-old triplets named Gorvin, Purug, and Stelcore Thorburn, they had come to their positions midway through the reign of Affram the First in the year 884.

At present, the three wizened old Dwarves wished they were somewhere else.

"I have not had an answer from you," Buttress barked, letting out a resonant belch to emphasize his disdain, "and it is making me woolly and weary. My heralds are spreading my orders throughout Mettlec, my sons ride from mountain to mountain, ensuring the forgemasters comply, producing an unprecedented amount of weapons, and yet here you stand in a triple dose of silence. The Ereti are on their way to receive those weapons. This we have agreed to, for Boldac has willed that we war on these Human vermin for once and for all and be done with them for good."

Stepping gingerly forward, Gorvin, who had exited his mother's womb a full three minutes before his brothers and so held the designated title of spokesperson for the Council, said, "Then your question is all the more a mystery, our king."

Smoothing down his bushy brow with a honey-covered thumb, a piece of which he had lost in a forge accident as a young apprentice, Buttress ran his tongue along the backs of his upper teeth and considered Gorvin's point.

"Fine then," he said, taking another pull from the half-full dragon's horn. "I shall rephrase. Despite the fact that we have already helped the Ereti, and intend to do so even more for at least the foreseeable future, do we help them in the end?"

Such questions, which the kings of Mettlec asked as a matter of habit, were the reason why it took a council of three to parse through the queries almost daily made to them.

The three Thorburns placed their heads in a huddle and conferred.

After several minutes of whispers, groans, and headshakes, Gorvin said, holding tight to his brothers as if their combined mass might prove equal to that of the lone figure upon the throne before them, "It is impossible to say. They would, one would think, abide by the wishes of their gods, the Ruenai, and go back to peaceful sailing when the coming war is over, but should they find that they like the taste of pirating sampled so long ago by their forebears, perhaps they will not listen to their gods."

"Why anyone would choose to listen to the council of a threesome endlessly vexes me," Buttress muttered, poking his index finger into the depression of his thumb. "But please do keep on talking."

"The enigma of their intention, Sire," Gorvin continued, "is that some of their most important leaders took Gadrun Grundling with them when they journeyed to the south."

"They say he is with them should they be fortunate enough to locate Prince Stanchion," offered Purug, born second of the three. "That tells us there is trust. Or, perhaps, he is a hostage and the whole thing is nothing but a lie. Where did they sail south *to*? *That* they did not say."

"Boldac's burning beard!" Buttress shouted, signaling a steward for more mead lest he use the horn to impale the three quivering figures arrayed in a line before him. "Why can I not get an answer that keeps the tip of the iron orange for more than half a minute?"

"We know so very little of the Ereti," said Stelcore, born twelve minutes after Purug and the tallest of the three. "This is where the difficulty lies, our king. Do forgive, but Stanchion, sent to Eret as an ambassador by Our Highness, after your grandfather and father saw no need at all for such a position, told us nothing, and then he… he… well…"

"Disappeared." This one word, spoken by all three Thorburns at once, brought Buttress from his chair.

"Do not tell me things I already know!" he bellowed, spilling mead down the front of his triple-link mailcoat and onto the tips of his boots. "I have had enough of you. *All* of you. Therefore," he now approached them with unsteady steps, "*you* shall serve as the new ambassadors to Eret. You shall sail back with the ships coming to us and you will oversee, advise, and report to me with precision and clarity any riffraffery or untoward action you observe. Am I clear?"

"Sire," Gorvin said, the look of surprise on his face replicated to the smallest detail on those of his brothers, "we have not been out of Mount Mettlec in our lives. Here it was we were conceived, birthed, bred to be advisors, appointed so, and where we have executed our office as best as we are able."

"Iron oxidizes, yes?" the king replied, after staring at them for a moment.

"Yes, Sire. Yes, indeed, it does."

"And so it proves that nothing stays the same. You will do this thing I ask of you as a way of cleansing the rust that rims the iron of our little ring of camaraderie, yes?"

The three brothers replied with a unified affirmation, although the substance of their individual thoughts was as different from one another's as one could imagine.

For Gorvin, it was fear.

For Purug, fear as well, although mixed with the slightest anticipation.

For Stelcore, it was a chance to get away from both the king and, if he could find the opportunity, from his two brothers, with whom, outside of their identical features, he had nothing at all in common.

Stelcore was more like Stanchion, whom he hoped Gadrun Grundling would find, so he could sort a way to join him in whatever he was doing.

Laurianna was trying her best to settle comfortably into the straw-covered pallet in the hayloft behind the Temple of the Seers when she heard a rustling too small and delicate to be a horse and too big to be a pig.

Pulling her hairpin from the bun the Seers insisted she wear and grasping it tightly as a weapon, Laurianna rolled to face the ladder that led to the loft. Raising her arm in readiness for an attack, she opened her eyes to see whom it was that was so unstealthily approaching her.

Hearing a creak as the unknown man placed his weight on the ladder's bottom-most rung, Laurianna took a deep breath and readied herself to drive the hairpin into the eye of whomever it was intruding upon her modest, makeshift chambers.

Stifling an urge to quell an itch where several strands of hay were irritating her ankle, Laurianna thought back to the morning. As she had placed her foot upon the cistern and hiked the hem of her dress to wash her leg, she had noticed Vitus staring a little too long as she completed her morning wash. He had not turned away in red-faced embarrassment as she looked at him, as other Seers had done on prior mornings. On the contrary—he lingered a little longer before going about his business.

He may have even smiled.

Try anything at all, and you shall never smile at the sight of my legs or me again, Laurianna silently warned, aiming the tip of the hairpin at the spot where she expected the top of a red, wrinkled, tonsured head to appear.

She barely halted the hairpin's arc at the sight, not of Vitus, but the hooded head of another, far more pleasant-looking Seer.

"You nearly lost an eye," she whispered, falling back with a heavy exhalation of breath. "You, Brother Farvon, should not be here."

Although I am glad that you are, she thought, utterly unsure if it was relief that it was not Dictus she was facing or the fact that it was Farvon in such private, unsanctioned proximity that was causing her face to flush.

"I know that well enough," Farvon replied, ascending another rung and leaning into the loft so their noses nearly touched. "But I really had no choice."

"Is that so?" Laurianna asked, rotating her shoulder so that her sleeping gown slipped just enough to show a bit of her neck and collarbone. "Am I truly worth such a risk?"

Farvon raised a brow. "Well, not *you* perhaps, per se… but what I have to tell you. I am not sure we are safe here for two more weeks as we planned. Dictus and Vitus spent several hours this evening looking over our work, and they profess to see in it not a modicum of sense. They are anxious to get me back to my primary duties, which they say I am neglecting. In truth, Laurianna, their assessments are more than fair."

Raising the neckline of her gown and pulling up her blanket until it touched her bottom lip, Laurianna attempted to will away her disappointment and force her mind to find a solution.

Then Beazor, her owl, whistled, from his perch at the peak of the rafters.

Laurianna thanked her wise old friend. Turning to Farvon, she said, "I shall get word to Castle Silveth. Vitus's insistence that Beazor stay at all times in the barn gives us the opportunity for him to fly to the castle and back under cover of darkness without detection. Once I have made the king aware of this inopportune shift in our circumstances, he shall no doubt summon us to Silveth under some inventive pretext with little delay. I have observed what I have needed to of Vitus and Dictus. You shall tell the king the rest. Answer what he asks, Farvon, as best as you can… That is, if you still wish to go through with this plan, and accompany me to Silveth."

Placing two of his delicate fingers upon Laurianna's cheek, Farvon whispered, "I wish for nothing more. Send Beazor as soon as you can."

Leaning forward until their lips touched, Laurianna felt a stirring in her stomach. After lingering for a moment, she pulled herself away. "Do what they want come morning. I can stall for a day under the guise of needing to go through an unread stack of scrolls before making my return. Show just enough resistance to maintain a reasonable air of disappointment in not continuing our project."

Visibly stunned from the unexpected kiss, Farvon answered, "And if they accuse me of impure thoughts?"

Laurianna hid a smile. "Then confess and repent on the spot— but only to a point. Now, get back to your bed before those two old cassowaries discover you are missing. I shall pen a message and send Beazor on his way. Do not despair—we shall soon be free of their wicked machinations."

"My soul requires vengeance, Baron Ralin. When will word arrive?"

The Night Guardians, the twin moons of Mynoweth, had risen and set twice since the burial of Sir Prima's murdered son, Eric, and the chief knight of the Western Barony had been prowling like a half-starved wolf who had caught the scent of blood from unseen prey since placing the final stone upon his child's burial cairn.

"There are forces at work to the north and to the east," Ralin replied, resisting the urge to refill the empty cup before him. "Information is being mined through Aldemere and the northman. When the king has made his plan, after careful consultation with

Elde and Sir Linead, we shall know our role. Do not think for a moment that they are ignoring or dismissing your grief."

"Listen to yourself," Prima growled, slamming his gloved fist upon the table with enough force to rattle and nearly tip the empty cup. "You once stood tall for your rights, for your father's legacy, as I had hoped my son would one day stand tall for mine. Now, I am standing tall for his. Do not make me stand alone, Baron, I beg of you."

Knights should never beg, Ralin thought, looking around the great hall of Spiltrow, his family's ancestral home, at the vast collection of stuffed and mounted heads, rare tapestries, and ornaments that were the evidence of his ancestors'—and most of all his father's—capabilities, ambition, and wealth.

He found himself embarrassed to be sitting in the midst of such reminders.

That is the truth of it, father, he thought, swallowing Prima's words in lieu of another draft of ale. *You died because you stood up for the king and this kingdom in the face of Garamin and Filgrith's rebellion. You fought for a peaceful and prosperous collection of baronies. So why do I sit here doing nothing?*

Ralin had once shared his father's ambition, and he knew in his heart that he could lead and protect the people of the West—a set of skills that his father's premature death—his *murder*—had robbed him of ever seeing.

"I know the pain you suffer," Ralin said, glad that Prima had rattled the tempting cup just out of reach of his trembling fingers. "It was an assassin who infiltrated these walls and ended my father's life. An equally cowardly act to the one that ended Eric's."

"And you broke all manner of rules and rode to avenge him!" Prima said, placing his hands upon the table and leaning over Ralin, who shrunk back in his chair. "It is why I accepted your offer to be chief knight in the west, although it meant leaving my offspring alone at Silveth. My *only* offspring, baron. My Eric... My *son*... whom *I* must avenge—not Sir Aldemere, and not some nameless stranger from the north. Your confidence in them is admirable, but misplaced. As was my trust in you."

"I am still the man to whom you swore allegiance," Ralin whispered, although he did not have enough faith in the truth of his words to meet Prima's furious, grieving gaze. A gaze that had locked itself on the empty cup as he had spoken. Although he had never uttered a single word of concern, Ralin knew that Prima was aware of and troubled by Ralin's increasing fondness for drink.

Ralin thought back to what he had said to Aldemere the night they spoke at Eerbell. He had had every intention of keeping away from the spirits. Upon his return to Spiltrow, however… The look on Prima's face as he uncovered Eric's body in the back of the wagon… His heart-rending sobs… The baron had retreated to his rooms, opened a quarter cask of ale, and had done very little in the way of refraining since that night.

"If you must put the horns of the woodhart back upon your helm, if that is what it will take for you to remember who you are, then let us choose one from these walls, draw our swords, and make quick and purposeful work of it." Prima stepped back, placing his hand upon the pommel of his sword, to show that he was serious.

"There is no need of that," Ralin said, relieved that Prima's heated breath was no longer upon his brow.

"Then prove it," Prima retorted, shaking his head. "I am willing to wait no more than a week. Then I shall take any and all horsemen, knights or not, willing to avenge my son and ride for Silveth, where I shall make my case for immediate action and then proceed to meet these northern bastards and force them into a fight."

"I appreciate the time you have granted me to spur the king to action," Ralin replied, wishing to end their conversation and rid himself of Prima without seeming too abrupt. A quarter cask of newly delivered ale was awaiting him in the larder, a few rooms away. "I shall not see you hung for treason, which would be your fate the minute you entered Silveth. The waning trust the other barons already have in me would meet its death the moment you did so. Eric died doing his duty as a knight of the realm. I urge you not to forget that." Pushing back his chair and standing, he added, "See to the men in your charge, then go and comfort your wife. I hear she has not left her bed since the burial."

"Very well then, Baron," Prima said, the mention of his wife softening his stance. "I shall keep a watch for messenger hawks. Pray that word arrives before the week is out."

Barely able to restrain himself until Prima had departed and the door had closed behind him, Ralin, rather than wasting the time it would take to retrieve and tap the quarter cask of ale, pulled a half-empty bottle of corn whiskey from the sideboard and, removing the cork with a noticeably trembling hand, drained it in a single desperate swallow. Feeling his nerves settle and his mind begin to cloud, he said a silent prayer that Aldemere would once more be the hero Ralin was unable to be.

On his second morning as a prisoner in Amdar, just as the sun was rising over the horizon and its welcome rays were drifting into his cell, Aldemere felt a kick in the ribs as a new guard hauled him to his feet and out into the street. As his eyes adjusted to the light, another, even gruffer guard whom Aldemere also did not recognize seized him at the elbow. Confident he knew where they were taking him, Aldemere refrained from speech, which appeared to suit to a tee the simple-minded duo.

Entering a heavily fortified building in the center of the city, the guards led him up two flights of stairs to Captain Purloch's headquarters.

"Ah... our unsuccessful *hunter*—do come in," Purloch said, producing a dangerous, disingenuous smile as he signed several sheets of paper, which he handed to an aide. "I am done with my morning reports and ready to give you my attention. I hope a night in our dungeon has cooled your witty tongue. Or perhaps it was the soup that has stilled it?"

Aldemere got as close to the captain's desk as the pair of guards permitted. "Your cells are certainly drafty enough to cool the warmest of tongues. As for the food—I was not inclined to eat."

Purloch laughed. "Brains trumping hunger... that is rather impressive. You know, of course, that hunting on the border of Mellya is an offense punishable by death—either beheading or the noose, depending on my whim. You do know that... correct?"

Aldemere sat in silence.

He did not. Why had Frederick failed to mention it?

"You seem surprised," Purloch said, pouring a mug of ale. "It seems strange to me that a Mellyan would not know that—it is the first thing a commoner learns if one wishes to survive to adulthood." Draining his mug and wiping the foam from his lips with the back of his hand, the captain continued. "No matter—ignorance is not an excuse. I have sent a search party to collect your friends, to save you the sadness of dying alone. Of course, should they *not* be found, sadness shall be damned. Your head will meet the street by the midpoint of the evening."

Coming around the desk, he put his hand on Aldemere's shoulder. "You do not appear to be handicapped in any way... You have the body of a soldier. How is it you are not serving in our army?"

Aldemere put his hand to his head. "Fell as a boy. From a tree. I have difficulty remembering things. Never could remember a drill from start to stop. It is what you take as my wit. It is really just befuddlement. When it comes to the laws, however… I am well aware. I am. It is just that I forget. It is hard for one such as myself to find steady, good-paying work… Seeing as I cannot remember the steps to complete a task… But I have little ones at home…"

Purloch stared at his prisoner for almost a minute, trying to decide whether he should believe the young man's tale. "Have you ever seen a Mellyan beheading? You do not forget such a sight. Come to the window with me, Tun."

Looking down on the public square, Aldemere saw a two-tiered platform with a wooden hand wheel attached to its far side and a thick pair of well-braced uprights some two feet apart set through its middle. A crowd was beginning to gather as a prison wagon approached. Two more of Mellya's grim and grizzled soldiers yanked a prisoner from the back of the wagon as it stopped and threw him to the ground.

"You recognize him, Tun?" Purloch asked, putting his arm around Aldemere's shoulder. "Of course you do. You shared a cell last night."

Aldemere saw the man who had so brusquely assigned him his corner, his face now badly bruised and swollen around the eyes and mouth.

"He must have fallen on his way up the stairs," Purloch said with a grin, squeezing Aldemere's shoulder. "Accidents are bound to happen in such poorly lit accommodations. I have been meaning to request more torches, but there is always so much to do. So much poaching … and other forms of criminality… to punish."

"Is that what he did? Snatch a rabbit to feed his family, as I was trying to do?"

"As a matter of fact, that is *exactly* what he did. So nice that you two talked."

"We did not." Aldemere watched with interest as the soldiers secured the condemned man's ankles to the uprights with lengths of rope as he stood on the lower platform. A guard tied his hands behind his back as a second joined two pieces of wood with half moons cut from their sides around his neck to keep it still. These he locked into place between the uprights, which Aldemere followed upward past the second platform with his eye as the sun escaped from the embrace of a skyblanket and reflected off a wide blade set in two tracks near the top of the uprights.

"Magnificent, is it not?" Purloch asked with a disturbing breathlessness as he tracked his prisoner's gaze.

Aldemere's Dilemma

That is not quite the word that comes to mind, Aldemere thought as he noticed two ropes attached to the top corners of the blade, which then snaked through pulleys at the top of either upright and down to the hand wheel, which a muscular figure in a coal-black hood held in his immense, leather-gloved hands.

The crowd, which had grown in size and intensity as Aldemere surveyed the death-rig, was beginning to cheer as the hooded executioner quarter-turned the wheel so that the blade pulled tight to the pulleys before placing his hand on a locking lever that Aldemere had failed to notice before.

So that is how it works…

"I await your signal," the executioner shouted upward, his eyes trained on an area several feet to the right of the room where Aldemere and Purloch stood. Tilting his head out the window and turning to his right, Aldemere saw a balcony, upon which stood a crowned figure dressed like a warrior in silver, black, and scarlet. Upon his tabard was a crest containing a three-taloned falcon holding a sword, lance, and vivid stream of fire.

So… This is Nadrim, the cliffprince of Mellya, Aldemere thought, recalling Frederick's description.

Nadrim slowly raised his arm, the crowd's excitement rising in perfect synch with their leader's movement.

Enjoying the tension a bit longer than would any sane and civil man, Nadrim clenched his fist. Acknowledging the signal with a nod, the hooded executioner released the locking lever, sending the blade along its tracks toward the poor poacher's neck.

Aldemere felt his own fingers clenching into a fist as the crowd's cheers swelled to a wild crescendo as the blade cut cleanly through muscle and bone. The severed head, its eyes still flickering with unmistakable fear, spilled from its former ally and rolled to the platform's edge, where a laughing child pushed it back toward the poacher's feet.

What kind of country have I found?

Aldemere was witnessing a level of spectacle and brutality unlike anything he had ever seen or imagined.

May the Deities protect us from war with these terrible devils.

"So then, Tun," whispered Purloch, his breath hot and smoke-tinged in his prisoner's ear, "are you ready to tell me what you were *really* doing, or would you rather meet the Adjudicator? Our executioner gets the clothing of the beheaded. I think he would be very fond of your tunic, and quite anxious to get his bloodied hands upon it."

"I told you," Aldemere said, fighting the urge to pull the knife that he had hidden in his boot. "*Hunting.*"

Purloch laughed silently and motioned to the guards. "Take our friend *Tun* back to his cell. And bring him his recently deceased cellmate's head and hands to keep him company while he contemplates the weight of his lies."

"Boldac's blistering brow! I have never been so happy to see a shore!" Gadrun Grundling bellowed, as a bosun's mate lowered the longboat that held him, Hathom Ungerfil, Janzalon Waelsbun, and the first officer of the *Sea-Sword*, Eglin Bront, for their short journey to the southern shore of the Forest of Tombal.

"Look at all those trees," Gadrun continued, scanning the densely forested land where it began forty feet from the shoreline. "I might be able to engineer a deal for timber rights with these Greybaer. The forts we could build with just a fraction of those forests…" He rubbed his fat fingers together until the boat hit the water, causing him to fall back and over a bench.

"Do not forget why it is we have come all this way, Gadrun," Hathom said, offering an outstretched hand, which the proud, cursing Dwarf predictably refused. Beyond the point of frustration with their non-Eretian traveling companion, Hathom added, "While your business acumen is laudable, you are only here so you can help us find the prince, who will hopefully lead us to Nakret Sailweaver."

"Aye… and then the Stone. You need not remind me why I was tossed into the bargain," Gadrun growled, climbing onto the bench over which he had fallen. Letting out a grunt of relief to be sitting, he said, "I know no Dwarf is truly worthy of sharing a plank's worth of space on a fancy Eretian ship."

Looking for an opportunity to change the trajectory of the conversation, Eglin Bront handed an oar to each of his companions and, grasping his own, used it to push off from the side of the *Sea-Sword*. Dipping his oar into the water, he cleared his throat to secure everyone's attention. "It is my responsibility as commander of this landing party to keep each and every one of you safe, which means I will not stand for any arguing nor even off-subject banter when it might impede our survival and the success of this endeavor. Now is one of those times. Tribune, Undersecretary, you know the laws of the sea. Tell this Dwarf I am in command of this expedition."

"You need not bother," Gadrun muttered, placing his oar into its lock and then into the water. "It is clear I am outnumbered. But mark

Aldemere's Dilemma

this well, *Commander* Bront… I do not give a sea-green stream of snot for the Eretian laws of the sea, nor the gods who imposed them, nor slaves like you who enforce them. We have no weapons, no armor, in a place we know nothing about. So just how is it that you plan on keeping us safe?"

Reaching behind him while keeping one hand on his oar and his eyes facing forward, Bront pulled a canvas tarp away from a bulge in the stern. "With these," he replied.

Glancing back from his position next to the first officer, Gadrun saw several axes, machetes, and three ceremonial officers' swords in their scabbards, which looked like no one had worn them, or even pulled them free, for ages. "A wonderful array of makeshift tools and stage props," the Dwarf observed with a laugh. "I will wager I am the only one with the skill and stomach to use them. Perhaps *I* should be in charge."

A silence fell over the boat as Eglin settled the tarp wordlessly over the weapons. The foursome rowed in a tight, cooperative rhythm, rapidly closing the distance to the shore. As the boat's keel made grinding contact with the sandy bottom, they raised and stored the oars and jumped the sides, guiding the nose of the boat securely onto the beach.

"Tide is going out," Janzalon observed, leaning on the bulwark to catch his breath. "The boat will be fine where it is. What are your orders, First Officer Bront?"

Scanning the shoreline and peering into the forest, Bront shook his head and pointed to the darkening sky. "We have little left in the way of daylight, which was Captain Skarling's plan. We need to gather wood and organize a camp. My orders are to await contact by the Greybaer, so we may be camped in this spot for several days."

"That is the plan?" Gadrun asked, throwing back the tarp and selecting a machete and an axe, the heft of which he tested with a quick and efficient series of motions. "Sit by the fire like school chums and let *them* come to *us*, perhaps fully armed and cloaked by the cover of night? What have I agreed to?"

"Your regret at our agreement is of zero importance to me," Janzalon said, removing the axe from Gadrun's grip with an equally impressive flurry of movements that left both the Dwarf and the other Eretian wide-eyed with surprise. "Since you have that machete, what say you gather the wood while we three tent the tarp in case of nasty weather?"

Walking away in silence, Gadrun Grundling counted the myriad ways he planned to pay Stanchion Pilon back for all the trouble he had caused when at last they located the missing heir to the royal throne of Mettlec.

As Janzalon Waelsbun partially disarmed Gadrun Grundling on the south shore of the Forest of Tombal, his brother, Pashter, ambassador to Mettlec, was preparing himself to face an entire country of ill-tempered Dwarves.

Pashter stood on the deck of the *Sea-Sprite*, just to the left of his nephew, Dorrin, who was her captain, as they watched his crew at work. A few hundred yards behind them, the crew of the *Salt-Serpent* were making identical preparations as the two ships readied to dock at Port Alum, located at the midpoint of the western coast of Mettlec.

"It appears our friends have more than doubled the warriors upon the ramparts of their forts since the last time I was here," Pashter observed, his jaw tightening as he noticed a mass of mounted cavalry waiting at the docks to receive them.

He also noticed a trio of Dwarves in identical attire with similar features standing closely together, nervously gesturing toward the approaching ships and talking back and forth.

"King Buttress sent his Trinity Council to meet us," Pashter whispered to his nephew. "I have never known them to leave Mount Mettlec. What I am seeing unsettles me. We must be cautious and alert—follow my lead and do not speak without careful consideration of how it might be taken."

"Should we sink the anchor, uncle?" Dorrin asked. "Give you time to ponder the meaning of what the Dwarves are indicating with all of this?"

Chuckling softly, Pashter placed his hand on his nephew's shoulder. "You spend so much time learning the art of sailing, the Admiralty Mast teaches you nothing of diplomacy, and yet they are almost as identical as those three robed Dwarves in fretful conference upon the docks. Both at times require navigation of rocky shoals and stormy seas. We will proceed into port, Captain, as if nothing is amiss. King Buttress is attempting to rattle our nerves, to assert his dominance ahead of the coming parlay. Ignore the bait and we are back on an even keel."

"Give me a ship over a diplomatic post, even in the throes of winter," Dorrin answered, a picture of calm in the midst of the

Aldemere's Dilemma

carefully coordinated dance of rope, sail, and sailor undulating around him.

"You sound like your father, before he was called to service on the Tribunal. Listen to me, Dorrin. Do not let them take you from your ship. Too few Waelsbuns now sail the seas, and it is clear it is what you were born to do. Your father carries regret the way stevedores carry barrels. I wish a smoother tide for you."

Before Dorrin could reply, the *Salt-Serpent* took position alongside the *Sea-Sprite*. Her captain, Thaker Ungerfil, called across her starboard gunwale, "That looks to be quite the unwelcoming party situated before us. Perhaps they were expecting someone else, or, even worse, they knew who was coming and were not at all pleased by the news."

Raising his brows at his nephew with a mischievous smile, Pashter called back to Thaker, "I have seen it worse. The threesome in front are the closest the Dwarves have to a diplomatic corps. They are a welcome sight. We will proceed to port as planned, Captain Ungerfil."

"The art of lying, even to your allies, is an interesting one, Uncle Pashter," Dorrin observed, making a notation in his logbook. "I do not ever care to learn it."

"Do not underestimate the power of the bluff, nephew," Pashter answered. "All ship captains should carry it in their seabag of options. I have a feeling you shall see the sense in my words before all of this is done."

On the deck of the *Salt-Serpent*, First Officer Silbern Skarling was shaking his head. "I think he is playing a game with them, Thaker. Whatever welcoming might look like amongst the mountain race, it is not at all like this."

"Such maneuvers are not our concern," Thaker replied, scanning the activity on the deck and along the lengths of the masts as his crew prepared the *Salt-Serpent* for docking.

"As first officer, security *is* my concern," Silbern answered, straightening his shoulders. "Especially once we have landed."

"Fair enough," Thaker replied, "although I will need you for other things at first. Once we have docked, you shall see to the exchange of cargo." He pulled a folded piece of parchment from his jacket pocket and handed it to Silbern. "This is a manifest for all we are due to receive. It is important we get everything the Admiralty is expecting. As for you, Corbit," he said, turning his attention to his navigator, who was standing at the wheel, "you shall keep ship and crew at the ready, should we need to depart in a hurry."

"And you my friend," Silbern said with a smile, "I suppose you shall be dining with the Dwarven king and court?"

"Would that make you jealous, Silbern?" Thaker asked, with a smile of his own.

His first officer again shook his head. "Not in the least. My ancestors, Altear and Fromm, had many a supper with the Dwarves beneath their mountain. I have read the details in their logbooks. Lively language all throughout and no compliments to the chefs. I am content to see to my duties out here in the open sky, where Eretian sailors belong."

Taking note of his longtime friend's dislike of the Dwarves, Thaker said, "I would want no one else in charge while Dorrin and I are under the mountain with the ambassador. I shall let you read all that I experience in my logbook on the morrow." Then, to the crew, he shouted, "It is time to bring our lady, the *Salt-Serpent*, into port! Let us show those newbies on the *Sea-Sprite* how it is done!"

Aldemere blinked his eyes several times in an attempt to adjust to his new surroundings. The light, as dim as it was—the space he was in was lit by only a pair of braziers—was more than he had seen in several hours.

The girl in the bonnet and apron had not yet served what passed for dinner in the cells when Purloch had entered and ordered three guards to secure Aldemere's hands behind his back and place a hood, similar to the one the executioner had worn, over his head. Yanking him roughly to his feet, they had drag-walked him along the stone corridor that split the two rows of cells and out into the mud and up and down several flights of stairs. He had heard at least half a dozen doors open and close around him—some wood, some a combination of wood and metal, all sturdy and thick from the groan of the hinges that moved them and the heavy thud as they were slammed shut and, in most cases, locked.

Scanning his surroundings with the quick eyes of a warrior accustomed to battle, Aldemere found himself in a small room filled with a variety of devices and tools that he deduced some man or men of peculiar tastes and questionable morals had designed to pull forth confessions from anyone they thought was harboring secrets.

As his eyes continued to adjust and focus, a figure he recognized from the morning's execution appeared through a door to his left and quickly stood before him.

Nadrim was smiling, although his visage was that of a snake.

"Welcome to my workshop," he said, lifting Aldemere's chin with a leather-gloved hand, similar to the executioner's. "I have a much bigger, more elaborate one elsewhere, but it is reserved for *very special* guests, and you, Tun—you are just an incompetent hunter, are you not? Too damaged to serve in our army, too weak to feed your family..." Nadrim pressed his fingers into Aldemere's lower jaw until his captive winced.

"Your timing... Your arrival," Nadrim continued, holding the pressure as he spoke. "Your... *story*. I find them rather curious." Squeezing Aldemere's jaw three times in rhythm with the final word before releasing his grip and grasping a pair of pliers from the table beside him, Nadrim ran his tongue around the circumference of his mouth. Raising the pliers so they glimmered in the light, he said, "When you fell as a boy—from a tree, I believe—and hit your head and were therefore unable to remember the infantry drills, which of our military physicians gave you the stay from service? I need a name, so I can consult with him, obtain the proper documents, rectify this obvious misunderstanding, and send you back to your family. They must be delirious with worry."

"I do not recall. My memory, as I have said..."

Aldemere tried not to flinch as Nadrim pressed the cold metal pliers against his trembling lower lip.

"Is faulty, yes... So I heard from Captain Purloch. That is truly unfortunate. No answer to my question means I shall have to take a tooth."

Aldemere shook his head. Struggling to speak with the pliers upon his lip, he managed to mutter, "I beg you for mercy, my prince."

"Do you? Am I?" Nadrim asked, dragging the pliers downward so they separated Aldemere's lip from his teeth. "Your prince, I mean... Because you do not look, speak, or act like any Mellyan I have ever known. *Tun*. Your teeth... They are so white, so straight and well maintained for a commoner. That is just another reason why I find everything you say so very hard to believe. Complete and utter honesty? I think you are a spy. Perhaps from Glittereye, or working with some remnant of what was once the Lysean nuisance. I mean *resistance*. Or is it both?" Placing the pliers on top of one of Aldemere's lower teeth, Nadrim asked again, "Give me a name, or I shall own this tooth. And I shall keep on taking them for every minute that passes without the identity of the physician being recalled."

"Cliffprince Nadrim. I am sorry to interrupt."

Aldemere swallowed hard as Nadrim removed the pliers from his mouth.

"What could possibly be so important, Purloch, that you dare to come to me here?"

Nadrim sounded to Aldemere like a half-starved beast whose keeper had suddenly whisked away his prey.

Not that Nadrim had a keeper. He clearly was in charge.

"Moktar Caveraider insists upon an audience. The raiding parties were met in force at Vaelsport. Well-armed knights, supported by the locals. A total rout. He is threatening to take his forces and return to the wilderness to engage in raids on the north."

This report was given nearly in monotone without pause or breath, as if Purloch feared that any opportunity for Nadrim to interrupt would lead to the captain's immediate death.

Moktar. Aldemere knew the name. They had been on opposite sides of the field of battle on more than one occasion when Aldemere served in the northern mountains.

"Shall I send him in?" Purloch managed to ask, his voice strained and full of fear.

Nadrim stared at the pliers, menacing and silent.

Knights in Vaelsport… Aldemere cursed his current predicament even more knowing that things were moving rapidly and he knew almost nothing of the details. There was something else…

If Moktar were to recognize him…

"Do not allow him entry into my workshop, Purloch," Nadrim finally spat, tossing the pliers onto the table. "You are well aware of my policy—once they cross the threshold, no one leaves this room with all the parts with which they entered. I am not yet ready to take the Caveraider's life. I shall talk with him in the war chamber."

"And what of the prisoner?" Purloch asked.

Nadrim fingered one of his daggers. "Take him back to his cell." Turning to Tun/Aldemere, he said, "Consider one of your teeth on account—whether or not you remember the name. I shall once again have you as my guest here just as soon as I am free from this unexpected interruption."

Feeling the hood descending over the back of his head, Aldemere took one last look at Nadrim as the cliffprince turned away.

I look forward to settling our accounts, he thought. *Although it will take more than a tooth or two to see me satisfied, my friend.*

He was then in darkness again.

Aldemere's Dilemma

Crossing the King's Bridge and making his way to the rear gatehouse at Castle Silveth, Brother Farvon gazed up at the worn, weathered stones and realized how much he had missed spending time here.

He had barely turned seven—the age when local knights and members of the King's Guard chose many of Farvon's friends to be their pages—when his mother and father, at the behest of Dictus and Vitus—had agreed to have their son train in the Chapel of the Trying Soul as apprentice to a monk. His parents held the fervent hope that Farvon would one day, when he reached adulthood, become one of the Seven Lord Seers.

In other words, they prayed that one of the Seers would die, thereby opening up a spot for their son.

If such (mis)fortune did not occur, or if the promise Farvon had shown with reading and writing failed to progress to the point where the Seers deemed him extraordinary enough to consider for a position in their temple, he would live out the remainder of his days within the walls of the Chapel. His duties would include assisting with and eventually presiding over minor festival days, Naming Ceremonies, weddings, funerals, and the like, or, if he proved to be lackluster in his duties, his superiors would assign him to a barony chapel or as spiritual administrator to a mining or logging settlement.

Secretly preferring to live out his days in the Chapel of the Trying Soul, near to the people and landscape he had known and loved all his life, first and foremost his physician father, now deceased, and his mother—who had moved south to be with her sister shortly after the funeral—Farvon worked hard and excelled at his studies. His father's private library, as rare as such a thing was, was rarer still due to its size and wide-ranging contents. Having no estate to maintain since his family lived in the castle, his father had focused all of his spare time and accumulated wealth into the pursuit and acquisition of books, maps, and scrolls. He had also, as part of the negotiations of which Farvon was the object, acquired copies, often illuminated, of many of the scrolls and texts, copied by the Seers, of which Farvon was now the custodian.

It was not until he had been working with Laurianna at the Temple that Farvon had learned just what a prize Vitus and Dictus had considered him as a boy of barely seven.

"The Council of Elders, and most especially Talorous," Laurianna began one morning as they prepared a batch of ink for the coming day's work, "had made the request to tutor you themselves, but Dictus and Vitus had used your father's love of his library as shrewdly as Manthes Fragenoar had manipulated the king into banishing them."

Unbeknownst to the two budding lovers, Dictus's exact words to Farvon's father on the day the Seers had forced his decision had been, "The boy can come under our tutelage at the Temple, or you can get your manuscripts directly from the scholars you choose to favor over us." The two connivers knew well enough that the Council frowned upon private collections, as the holdings in the Hall of Books and Ancestries were open to all who wished to avail themselves of its carefully curated collection.

So it was that Farvon began service to the Seers within the castle. Two and a half months past his seventeenth birthday, however, Farvon received word that the Temple's Keeper of the Scrolls, Pylus, had passed on to his greater reward and the remaining Seers had unanimously chosen Farvon to be his replacement.

Since his transfer to the Temple that day, Farvon had only been allowed to return to Silveth once or twice a year, and always in the company—although Farvon thought the word *custody* more appropriate—of Dictus and Vitus, who had adopted a false-fatherly attitude toward the newest Seer as their means of maintaining control. Perhaps it had been the initial look of disappointment and pain on the seven-year-old's face when his father had told him of his fate—a look they had seen again ten years later as they escorted him from the Chapel—that prompted their relentless grip on his life.

It was with Dictus and Vitus that Farvon now entered the castle. Laurianna was walking just far enough ahead that he could not smell the essence of orange that she brushed into her hair each morning, as he could in the back of the wagon in which the four of them had arrived. During the journey to Silveth he had to watch for hours as his two guardians rubbed their fat, robed thighs against Laurianna's shapely, delicate legs as the trio shared the bench at the front.

Dictus and Vitus had been less than understanding when word had arrived by messenger hawk that Farvon and Laurianna should gather the work they had thus far completed and all materials from the Temple library that they would require to fulfill the king's request and return immediately to Castle Silveth.

"This is most improper," Dictus had growled at dinner two evenings prior as Vitus read him the missive. Laying the pinkie-sized scroll upon the table, Vitus responded, with a snarl of his own, "The king does not deign to give us a reason for his pressing need

Aldemere's Dilemma

for Farven and the girl to present their work to the Council of Elders. He says only that he apologizes for any hardship and appreciates our cooperation and understanding."

"I *do not* understand it," Dictus answered, slamming his spoon into his bowl of soup with enough force for the runny, spice-flecked broth to spill over the rim and soak the offending scroll, "nor do I appreciate it or *wish to* cooperate! This is Talorous's doing. He will not get away with it! I would like nothing more than to deny the king his request."

"But you of course cannot," Brother Ayron whispered.

"And being that that is the case," Vitus added, "and we must abide by his rules, we will accompany our two scholars to the castle and personally explain this inconvenience. This ill-timed and suspicious irregularity. This breach of accepted protocol."

That is what they had done. Neither Laurianna nor Farvon had tried to argue. On the contrary, and according to their loft-hatched plan, they feigned surprise and even confusion at the sudden change in Dylwyn's plans. They then gathered their things in silence, including Beazor, who had secretly returned half a day before the hawk.

Farvon could not help but feel his heavy heart begin to lift at the sight of Talorous, as he rounded a corner to greet them. He could feel Dictus's energy sharpen as the old monk caught sight of Nigredo perched proudly upon the scholar's shoulder.

"Ah," Talorous said, pushing a handful of dried peas past his lips, and talking around them as he chewed, "Dictus and Vitus. This is a most unexpected addition to the joy I am feeling at my reunion with Laurianna. Farvon—it is good of you to come. I have your bed in the scholars' quarters prepared. Laurianna will show you the way."

Following Talorous's protégé, Farvon gripped his bags a little tighter as Dictus hissed in his ear, "Do not get too comfortable, my son—you will not be staying long."

If Talorous heard the taunt, he chose to keep it to himself.

"Affram! I swear by Boldac's unborn babes that I will use that axe to maim you if you do not put it away!"

Why his father, King Buttress Pilon, had insisted that Prince Dramel's younger brother accompany him on his tour of the mountain forges in the south, east, north, and west of Mettlec he did not know—unless it was to get the overly energetic handful of a Dwarf out of his father's hair and into his own.

What of Stanchion, Father? Dramel thought, pointing his horse to the nearest of the three hidden entrances to the complex of rooms and tunnels deep beneath Mount Mettlec. *Did you send him away as well, because his ideas were different from yours?*

Dramel remembered the day of the quarrel as though it was the one just passed and not two years before. He and Stanchion had been meeting with the Mellyan ambassador, Calrain Damonessa. Their father had tasked them with the initial negotiations. The Mellyans wished to secure Dwarven-forged weapons, other metalworks, and even requested a blade that they could insert in a contraption whose sole purpose was to remove the heads from the necks of those who disagreed with the cliffprince.

The king had made it clear—the Dwarves were more than happy to provide the finest iron tools for farming, building, and logging and silver utensils for the nobility and all manner of household items for everyone else. They would even produce both plate and chain-link armor, for they were for defense, but they would not aide the Mellyans in their blatant preparations for war, no matter whom they were targeting or how much coin was in the boxes and bags the ambassador had brought.

Up until the moment before the official start of the meeting, Stanchion professed alignment with their adamant father's wishes. He and Dramel were in full agreement on presenting a united front.

Thinking back on what happened next, Dramel recalled the beads of ice-cold sweat that had formed on his neck and back when Stanchion, before they could even take a seat after greeting the oddly formed ambassador, offered him a tour of the forges.

"What are you doing, brother?" Dramel had asked, motioning Stanchion away from the ambassador. "Father said nothing about showing this stranger what we can do—what our techniques and stockpiles consist of."

Stanchion shook his head. "The idea is solely mine. We will show him the array and number of weapons we have amassed for our country's defense. As an initial offering, we will suggest some simple swords and spears that they might buy—enough to put us in good stead with him and his war-hungry brother—and he will leave knowing that we are a country not to be menaced."

"Your plan holds no logic," Dramel answered, watching from the corner of his eye as Calrain Damonessa grew impatient at having to wait. "You know nothing of the weapons they already possess! Perhaps it is they who seek to lure *us*. Perhaps he is more a spy than a diplomat, and you shall be handing them exactly what they want… You know what they did to Lyseum."

"A land of scholars and farmers," Stanchion replied, shaking his fist in Dramel's face. "We are the mighty of Mettlec. We have defended our shores from all manner of enemies—and no one has ever come close to entering our mountain fortresses after landing on our shores. Let us show him why. You have to trust me, Dramel! Perhaps we can make an alliance with them. Better an ally than an enemy—you know this to be true."

Dramel had gone along, watching Calrain's pain-contorted face turn to one of deeply shadowed thought even as the blistering blue and white fires of the forges illuminated its features. Even worse, as the younger prince had feared, the exposure of their workshops and weapons did not have Stanchion's hoped-for effect on their guest.

The ambassador made it clear that the Mellyans wanted more than swords and spears. They wanted the weapons, only developed in recent months by the Dwarven alchemists, which employed what Calrain had heard a loose-lipped guard outside his rooms refer to as "powder and shot" the previous night as he was going to sleep.

Dramel's heart sank as Stanchion clumsily denied that the Dwarves had developed anything that matched that description.

Later in the evening, when King Buttress had heard what Stanchion had done, he called his eldest son forth and gave him a berating in front of the assembled court that echoed through the halls of Mount Mettlec like a soulless winter wind.

It was the next morning, after the Mellyan ambassador had left, empty-handed and unleashing a stream of threats, that it had fallen to Dramel to tell the king that Stanchion was also gone, as was the family sword Hawkclaw.

It was unclear from the look upon the king's face and his ensuing silence which of the two he was more upset to lose.

Guiding his horse along a series of ledges beginning at the bottom of the mountain to a well-masked opening thirty feet up from where had he started, which led into the heart of Mount Mettlec, Dramel blew a small horn that hung from his saddle. The deep, almost inaudible sound quickly drew a group of heavily armored lookouts stationed near an iron gate just within the well-shadowed entranceway.

"It is Prince Dramel and Prince Affram," a grizzled sergeant declared, signaling an unseen guardsman to open the gate from his position inside the mountain.

"Welcome home, princes," the sergeant said with a bow. "Prince Dramel—your father has been most impatiently awaiting your return. Ambassador Waelsbun of the Ereti has arrived with a pair of ships. He and the king are deep in conversation with the Trinity Council. I have been tasked with taking you to the throne room without delay."

"I will take care of our horses, brother," Affram said, taking the reins of Dramel's horse without dismounting from his own. "Then I would like to practice with my axe."

"Then go and do so," Dramel answered, wishing that Stanchion was not missing and he were as free as their younger brother to find some excuse not to immerse himself in the swirling pool of politics and posturing into which he was now being forced to wade.

At least, if we do see battle, I shall have a proper sword, he thought, although even his anticipation of such a weapon as Eggard Starforge was crafting proved to do little to quell his concerns.

Kal-Gadras found what he was seeing almost impossible to believe.

As his single-masted ship approached the beach just past the terminus of the River Skillen, where it joins the Sea of Silence, he watched as a small boat was nosed onto the shore by four figures wading onto the sand—three Eretians and, could it be?—a Dwarf.

"Throw the anchor," he whispered to his crew. "These trees will block their view until we are ready to be seen. It appears they are preparing to make camp for the night." He watched as the Dwarf, a thick-bladed, inelegant weapon clutched in his hand, stomped toward the tree line while the three Eretians removed a tarp from the back of their boat.

Kal-Gadras watched with fascination as the Dwarf gathered wood while the Eretians staked the tarp so it served as a makeshift tent. Within an hour, a roaring fire was set, a simple dinner was prepared, and the foursome was sitting with steaming bowls in hand, making small talk as they ate.

Stretching his legs, Kal-Gadras said to the five archers comprising his crew, "After their meal has made them sleepy, we will approach them with lanterns lit and bows tucked out of sight. I see no long-range weapons beside them. Any indication of trouble, we shall draw and, if necessary, shoot to wound—weapon hands only. The Eretians prefer peace and diplomacy, but the Dwarf is not to be trusted."

Although he much preferred cooperation to conflict and coercion, Kal-Gadras was having trouble making sense of three Eretians and a Dwarf having journeyed so far south.

Aldemere's Dilemma

Before another hour had passed, the foursome around the fire began, one by one, to lean back against the boat or lie beneath their blankets in the tent. As they settled into sleep, Kal-Gadras raised the anchor, and the six Elves rowed quietly for the shore. As their boat lost cover from the tree line, Kal-Gadras lit the lamps at the bow and stern and, raising his hands in the air, shouted, "Ahoy! We wish to bring our ship near to shore and join you. Do you grant us permission?"

One of the Eretians, dressed in an officer's uniform, stood at the sound of the intruding voice and, motioning to the others to remain where they were and keep quiet, yelled back, "We might be persuaded to do so if you identify yourselves. I want to see your shipmates' hands as well."

Kal-Gadras nodded to his companions to do as the Eretian instructed, confident that, with an arrow nocked in each of the bows across their laps, they could fire off a well-aimed shot before the Eretian officer could blink.

"I am Kal-Gadras, son of Nemmerle. I am Lord of the South Shore in the Elven land of Marlöoq Fer. I am here to seek council with the Greybaer and to offer aide to the human Frederick Fragenoar, whom I believe is now amongst them."

"I am Eglin Bront, First Officer of the Eretian vessel *Sea-Sword*. We know of no such Human, although we too seek council with the Greybaer. We believe an Eretian and a Dwarf are being held captive in these forests and we are here to bring them home."

Kal-Gadras focused his eyes on their lips to make out the conversation between the uniformed Eretian and one of the others, dressed in the robes of a judge, who had stood up and engaged him.

"You may approach," the first officer called, after the other had his say. "Keep your hands upon your oars and then in the air as you slowly wade to shore."

Waving his arms in acquiescence, Kal-Gadras took a seat, placed his hands upon an oar, and whispered to his crew, "I shall go ashore alone. Remain at the ready should our parlay take a turn."

Less than ten minutes later, Kal-Gadras stepped onto the shore twenty feet from the fire, where the one called Bront and the one dressed as a judge came to meet him.

Each of them carried an axe.

"You know Frederick Fragenoar?" the one in the robes enquired.

"I know *of* him—and his family—by reputation. Our allies in the Centerlands of Glittereye assured us he would be here."

Before the Eretian could reply, the threesome turned in unison toward the sound of half a dozen bodies approaching through the tree line.

"Two separate parties, and both of them searching for me?" a tall Human shouted, emerging with a laugh from behind an ancient oak. Although he wore a sword, he made no move to draw it. Nor did the five knights arrayed in an arc around him. Kal-Gadras noticed that one of them wore a quiver and a bow, as did the one whom had spoken and laughed, whom he assumed to be Frederick Fragenoar. "I think introductions are in order," the Human said with a smile, leading his party closer. "And I hope that all of you will continue to play as nicely as you have been and leave your weapons where they are."

Fifteen minutes later, Kal-Gadras, cleared to bring his band of archers ashore after the three factions exchanged identifications and explanations to everyone's satisfaction, stood beside Frederick who motioned for all of them to sit around the fire, leaving their weapons aside. This last request was met with resistance by the one Kal-Gadras took to be the leader of the knights—Sir Lesster—and by the Dwarf Gadrun Grundling, but Frederick held his ground until both of them complied.

"Aldemere speaks of you both highly and fondly, friend Kal-Gadras," Frederick said, pulling pieces of dried meat from a pouch and offering them around the circle. "It is an honor to have you here amongst us. I believe the Greybaer, whom I shall take you and one Eretian to meet tomorrow, will find your arrival a positive omen. Such things are important to the Greybaer, as you will learn." Turning to Janzalon, he said, "I have seen no signs of Eretian nor Dwarf anywhere in this forest. If the Ruenai say they will be here, perhaps they have yet to arrive."

"But where, pray tell, would they be?" Hathom asked, sinking his teeth into the tough fleetdeer jerky and twisting it back and forth several times before putting it aside. "And how would you guess they would get here from wherever it is that they are?"

"Time will answer your enquiries," Frederick replied, eyeing the discarded jerky with a scowl. "Let us enjoy the fire and the images made by the stars and get a good night's rest. Your both arriving at nearly the same instant tells me that the peace we have all enjoyed is coming rapidly to an end through the will of our common enemy, although there are larger forces aligning to aid us in our rising up against him."

Watching the self-assured Human lean back on his foraging bag and focus on a cluster of brilliant stars high above the horizon, Kal-Gadras found himself missing Aldemere, and wondering at the energy and playful language a conversation between he and Frederick must produce.

I pray it will not be much longer until I know, he thought, weariness overtaking his will as he settled into sleep.

Aldemere kicked at the damp and odor-filled straw on the floor of his cell—which had not been changed since his arrival—and thought about the complexities of his predicament. There was of course his imprisonment, and the brutal execution Purloch had forced him to witness. There was also the growing problem of Purloch and the cliffprince knowing he was not a hunter named Tun, which had nearly led to the removal of one of his teeth. He was also navigating the fact that at least one occupant of the city, Moktar Caveraider, knew *exactly* who he was.

Yet, none of those things, as troublesome as they were, unsettled Aldemere half as much as the contemptuous stare he had been receiving the last several hours from the Dwarf with whom he shared the cell.

"Have I wronged you in some way of which I am unaware?" he asked the surly figure, when the tension grew too great to endure an instant longer.

"Humans have wronged my race since they crawled from the swamp that birthed them—you are just one more in an endless, unlikeable line," the Dwarf barked back, kicking the burlap sack with the poacher's head and hands into the corner closest to Aldemere. "I pray to Father Boldac that you end up just like he did!"

Aldemere forced a smile. "I hope for exactly the opposite." Crossing the cell to get away from the growing stench of the sack, he rubbed his legs, which the cold stones of the cell were causing to ache. Intent on a different tack, he asked, "What brought you to Mellya? I thought your king suspended trade with the Mellyans a hundred years ago."

"How is it, Human, that you know this fact of Dwarven history?" his cellmate enquired, his steel grey, piercing eyes almost imperceptibly softening. "Are you one of the few remaining offspring to come from a Lysean family? If so, I would keep that fact a secret. As for me, I left my home in Mettlec nearly two years ago by stowing away on a Mellyan transport ship after a disagreement with my father and brother. Being skilled in mining, as all Dwarves are—

although I far more than most—I was appointed to the position of Vein Boss. Over time, I realized the folly of our family's quarrel and wished to return to my home. Prince Nadrim, however, had no intention of losing such a valuable asset, so he forcefully denied my request and sent me back."

"So how did you wind up here?" Aldemere asked, astonished at the Dwarf's willingness to share his story after so much incessant silence.

"Not long after my return to the mines, my team found a rich deposit of gold. I took some—just enough to secure my passage home on the first ship out of Mellya. My next opportunity to return to Amdar I met with an Eretian—a one-armed sailor who was in the process of betraying his country—and gave him some gold as well. He was supposed to get us a suitably sized boat and guide me in sailing it home. On the night we were to leave I was met, not with the boat he had promised, but by a dozen of Purloch's ruffians."

"He betrayed you. The one-armed Eretian, I mean."

"I am damned near impressed with you, Human," the Dwarf responded. "You are sharper of mind than most that I have met. I should have seen it coming. Any sack of skin that would betray his country would have no trouble betraying a stranger."

"This one-armed Eretian," Aldemere said, hoping to gain an ally in this fierce and formidable Dwarf, "is in a cell not far from the stairs."

After staring into Aldemere's eyes, as if searching out his character as he would a vein of gold, the Dwarf stood up and smiled. "I believe I can trust you, Human. My name is Stanchion Pilon, eldest and ablest son of the sovereign king of Mettlec."

"I am Tun," Aldemere answered, thanking the Deities for his excellent fortune. "I am a hunter."

"Well, Tun—I am guessing you were Purloch's guest for the offing of our cellmate."

Aldemere nodded. "I have no intention of following in his footsteps. The cliffprince nearly tortured me. I have less than zero interest in staying around any longer than I need to. Listen to me, Stanchion Pilon. I can see to our escape, if you are willing to help."

Aldemere's Dilemma

CHAPTER FIVE

Carra-shaman, thirty-second Keeper of the Stone and high priestess of the Ruen-Eret, watched closely as the six priestesses under her care and supervision completed their morning rituals at the central altar of the Vessel, bowed to their mistress, and filed through the doorway that led to the Inner Temple.

All, she noticed, but one.

Closing the door behind her fellow priestesses, Nomma, the youngest of the six, turned, saying to Carra in a whisper as she neared, "If you will allow it, I request a moment with you in private."

Nodding her approval, Carra motioned for Nomma to join her on the foremost pew on the port side of the Vessel.

"Have you heard anything from the Admiralty about the progress of the *Salt-Serpent*?"

"I have not," answered Carra, taking Nomma's delicate hands into her own. "But I can intuit the reason why you ask, because I know it is the same reason why Silbern Skarling refused the captaincy of the *Sea-Sprite*. You two have fallen in love."

"Is it so obvious?" asked Nomma, her voice alight with fear. "We have done our best to be discreet. If Silbern was to learn we are discovered…"

"There is no reason for him to know, or for you to be afraid," Carra answered, smiling kindly as a mother might at her teenage daughter under similar circumstances, were she pleased with the match. "It is far from common knowledge. In fact, I may be the only one who knows. The Ruenai see all that there is to see and, since my journey to meet them, I can see nearly all of it, as they do. Your secret is and shall remain forever honored and safe with me."

"Thank you, Carra-shaman."

"But Nomma… you must understand," Carra continued, her grip on the priestess's hands growing stronger along with her tone. "This is not the time for the Ruen-Eret to be weakened by such all-consuming distractions as love. Not love like the one you feel for a male newly tasked with taking the lives of others. You must respect your vows and remain devoted solely to the will of the Ruenai until this crisis has passed."

Nomma pulled her hands from Carra's to wipe away the tears that were spilling from her eyes. "I understand, Carra-shaman. I do. It has affected my concentration during meditation, I ashamedly admit it, but I am committed to my vows and the fulfillment of my

Aldemere's Dilemma

duties. Perhaps more so now than ever. If you feel as though I have been unsatisfactory in any way, then please tell me and I shall try to—"

"I would have said so," Carra answered, standing. "I am pleased that you have confided in me. Say nothing to your sisters. There are soon to be heroes everywhere amongst us—such is the way of war—and I cannot bear to lose anyone other than you to these daring young men seen as saviors. Yours shall be hard enough a loss, if indeed you are destined to leave. I need you for now, Priestess Nomma. Completely and without distraction. As do the Ruenai, and your fellow priestesses. Those five most of all."

Throwing her arms around Carra, Nomma squeezed hard and whispered, "Thank you" before running for the Inner Temple door to join her fellow priestesses as they began their meditations.

Reaching into her robe after Nomma had departed, Carra pulled forth the metal bowl she had brought back with her from her journey to the Ruenai. It had produced no runes as she had hoped, but had provided something else.

Several days before, while cleaning the bowl after the morning ceremony, Carra had looked down into the half inch of water she had poured into it from the pool that stood between the pews in the center of the Vessel, and a series of images appeared. Try though she might, she could not make sense of them. It was as though she was watching a play through a blowing curtain in a room with a flickering light.

Glancing behind her to make certain she was alone, Carra made her way to the pool, and, filling the bowl to the rim, whispered, "Water, wood, and wind. Help me to see what I must, sacred Ruenai." Gazing into the bowl, Carra held her breath as a scene she had witnessed in snippets and flashes began to unfold before her in brilliant and breathtaking detail. A scene that suddenly made sense since Nomma had confessed.

Turning away from the vision, Carra began to pray.

Sir Corvit sheathed his blood-drenched sword as his well-disciplined division of knights rounded up the few stragglers from the nomadic tribes still foolish enough to fight.

Looking down from his position on a cliff above Seafarer's Pass, Corvit smiled as he counted six ships aflame and, with ten remaining that could still be sailed, he calculated that two had already sunk below the surface of the foaming, red-tinged water.

The well-coordinated attack on the approaching ships had taken the nomads by surprise. Of the less than three hundred would-be conquerors, only half had made it to shore, and those had little defense when they landed against the three hundred knights and two hundred Vaelsportian males entrenched on the high ground, each of whom had a personal reason for vanquishing their foe. For the knights, it was revenge for their slaughtered comrades during the war in the northern mountains, and for the Vaelportians, it was the commitment to protect their families, their homes, and their town.

As Corvit descended, one of his lieutenants, Sir Verrin, approached. Offering a weary salute, which Corvit did not return, his subordinate reported, "We have captured the leader of the Krags, a one-legged bastard called Towk. Had to put him in chains. Nearly severed one of my men's fingers with his teeth. We also have the leader of the Caveraiders, who claims to be the general who led the attack. The Riverskab leader is dead."

"What is the name of the Caveraider chieftain?" Corvit asked, pulling his studded leather gloves over his bloodstained hands. "Is it Moktar?" He tightened his fists at the thought of a chance to confront a nomad leader responsible for the deaths of so many men beneath his command.

"Melak. Although he may have mentioned that other name as well. I cannot be certain of that or anything else. I am sorry, sir. I am not schooled in demon's tongue."

"Bring me to this Melak," Corvit replied, feeling his back muscles tense at the opportunity now before him. It would take a considerable amount of restraint not to kill Melak before the knight obtained the information he required.

Minutes later, Corvit found himself smiling at the sight of the barbarian leader secured to one of several poles in the town that the Vaelsportians used to hang, gut, and dry their daily catch. It seemed fitting that this fly-kissed filth was now his sole companion. As Corvit approached, Melak growled and spat.

He knows me. And I him. He is not Moktar, but he will do.

"My man here tells me you led this attack," Corvit began, staring into the eyes of his captive and trying his best to block out images of past battles fought and the memories of the buried dead they evoked. "Who sent you to do it? Moktar?"

"Moktar send. I *do*," Melak hissed.

Grabbing the Caveraider by the throat, Corvit shouted, "And who gave Moktar the ships?" He increased his grip until Melak's eyes

211   *Aldemere's Dilemma*

began to bulge and his pale skin to turn grey and then blue before releasing his grip so his captive could answer.

Melak barely gasped. "Human king."

"It could not have been a king," Corvit answered, resisting the urge to punch Melak in the throat. "There is only one king, and that is Dylwyn of Glittereye. A king who will see you all executed as insurgents before the week is out. If you speak of the Mellyan, you speak of a pretender. One whose days are numbered." Leaning in close, he whispered, "Before you die, Melak, you should know. He has a rat amongst his men. We were *warned* that you were coming."

If the Caveraider understood what Corvit was saying, he did not make it known.

"Lieutenant!" Corvit shouted, deciding it was best to keep Melak alive for the present.

"Yes, Sir Corvit."

"No food or drink for this one till I say. The Krag called Towk—slit his throat. Payment for fallen brothers."

"It shall be an honor, sir."

As Verrin drew his dagger and walked away, Corvit caught sight of Melak's face.

He was smiling.

Corvit knew why.

"Boldac's burning beard!" King Buttress Pilon yelled, slamming his hand on the arm of his chair. "I have heard nothing but excuses since you docked here, Pashter Waelsbun. You call yourself an ambassador… Where were you months ago, when this insanity began?"

Taking a deep breath and calling upon the training that kept him from saying what he thought in situations such as this, Pashter pulled from his mind a new set of words that might succeed in appeasing the Dwarven king where his previous explanations had failed.

"I was needed at home, your highness. Our best shipwright had gone missing, talks with the Mellyans had disintegrated, and we were dealing with a betrayal within our ranks that unfortunately has not yet been resolved. I have come at the earliest available opportunity, I assure you."

"Yes, indeed you have—now that you find yourselves on the brink of war! And because your gods have decided to allow you to use your ships for more than shipping. You are here because you *want* something. Something only we Dwarves can provide."

Before Pashter could respond, one of the triplets that made up the king's Trinity Council stepped forward from their position in the corner.

"My king," Stelcore said with a smile. "Ambassador Waelsbun is here in a diplomatic capacity. Common courtesy dictates that you not be so... *forceful*... in showing your displeasure for his actions, or lack of action, as it were. My king."

Stelcore quickly stepped back into place, where his jaw-locked face was book-ended by the fearful ones of his brothers.

Pashter was now girding himself for the worst, while silently cursing his decision not to have the first officers of the *Salt-Serpent* and *Sea-Sprite* within shouting distance should he need them. As he considered his limited options, Pashter noticed Buttress's middle son, Dramel, stepping from the shadows. Positioning himself between the king, who was rising from his chair with a look of ill intent and Stelcore, who stood defiantly between his brothers even as they urged him to stand behind them, Dramel yelled, "Father! Stelcore is correct in what he says. One wonders at the Eretians sending their ambassador to you at all considering treatment such as this."

"My son," Buttress said, stepping forward to meet him. "I am happy to see you have returned, although I cannot and will not allow you to talk to me like this in front of an Eretian and my advisors. Do not forget your place."

"My place is beside you, Father. Learning, yes, but also advising, and speaking up when you have erred," Dramel whispered back. "So please allow me to do so. I can be of assistance to you here."

A stillness fell over the room as Buttress stroked his beard in thought with one hand as his stroked the hilt of his sword with the other.

After several moments, in a voice filled with pride, he shouted, "Boldac has blessed me, my son!" Throwing his arms around the prince, he added, "You are twice the Dwarf your older brother was."

"You mean *is*, Father. Yes?"

Breaking the embrace and returning to his chair, Buttress muttered, "We can only hope." Then, with a gesture of his plump, bejeweled fingers, he said, "Well, then, Dramel. Have at it. If you want to be king one day, sort this bloody mess out."

Thanking Boldac in silence for the timing of his return, Dramel poured forth to the ambassador and the court his thoughts regarding the war that was to come, including how the Eretian and Dwarves could successfully work together.

Aldemere's Dilemma

Buttress did not interrupt. Not even once.

While his younger brother talked reason and strategy with those assembled in the Mettlec throne room, Stanchion Pilon mentally beat on Tun's plan as he would with a hammer upon a length of red-hot steel. He reluctantly abandoned the exercise as a malformed shadow—an echo of Calrain Damonessa—slowly approached the cell. Struggling to balance a tray with two bowls of the foul-smelling soup using a withered arm ending in a two-fingered hand, the boy to whom the shadow belonged did his best to keep two steps ahead of the most bad tempered of the prison guards amongst a bevy of abusive bastards.

"Where is your cellmate, Dwarf?" the guard enquired, while pulling the boy backward by his threadbare collar with enough force to send the tray and its contents crashing to the floor. Ignoring the mess—and the child's cries of fear and pain—the guard pulled his keys from his belt, unlocking the cell so he could make a closer inspection.

Although it pained him to cower—a nearly impossible action for a Dwarf, no matter it was only pretend—Stanchion stuck to the plan. "Please… do not beat me… I told him not to—that he would make it bad for us *both*—but he managed to dig an escape tunnel using the jawbone of the dead man." He pointed his shaking fingers toward a pile of ruffled hay.

"Step back, Dwarf," the guard ordered, drawing his sword and approaching the pile. As he made the mistake of kneeling down to move the hay rather than first using his sword to impale it, he felt a knife at his throat.

"Move and your life is forfeit."

The voice did not belong to the Dwarf.

Grabbing the boy, who was trying his best to gather the spilled contents of his tray and covering his mouth before he could let out a yell, Stanchion pulled him into the cell.

Within a handful of minutes, the two prisoners had the guard and the child bound and gagged with pre-cut strips of the Dwarf's leather vest.

After apologizing to the boy for the added humiliation, Stanchion asked of his cellmate, "I just have to know—when you disappeared, where were you hiding?"

"I was near the pile," Aldemere replied, producing a delicate-looking glove from his leggings. "Wearing this. It is Elven. It can render its wearer invisible provided you touch nothing else while wearing it. You will need to put it on."

"I most definitely shall not!" Stanchion protested. "It is unnatural—Dwarves want nothing to do with evil Elven *magic.*"

Putting on the guard's hooded cloak and strapping on his sword, Aldemere shook his head. "You honestly have no choice—not if you want to escape. You are far too short to pass for an Amdarian guard. No offense to you or your kind of course."

"Height is overrated, *Human*," Stanchion shot back. "That is why we have ladders and stools." Grasping the Slaaver's Hand, he asked, "Tell me where I shall go should I choose to put this on."

"Only where you wish to," Aldemere assured him. "But no one will see you do it. You will need this knife as well." Aldemere held out the weapon he had been hiding in his leggings until that morning. "Time is short—will you wear the glove or no?"

Storing the knife in his boot, Stanchion closed his eyes while forcing his thick, large-knuckled fingers inside the glove.

"It is not working," Aldemere heard him whine. "I still see me perfectly well."

Stifling a laugh (not wanting to offend any further his overly sensitive ally) and raising the hood of the cloak to cover his face, he answered, "I, however, cannot, nor will anyone else, and that is all that matters."

Exiting the cell and locking the door behind them, Aldemere walked toward the staircase at the end of the prison aisle, where he awaited the relief guard's arrival.

"How goes it, Ral?" the expected guard asked him an hour later.

"Quiet, as always. They are fearful of the Adjudicator."

Eyeing the stairs, Aldemere prayed to the Deities that Stanchion was ahead of him.

"I warn you, Ral—Captain Purloch is in an irritable mood tonight."

"Just give him another hour." As the guard raised a brow in confusion at his response, Aldemere closed the distance between them, striking him on the head with the hilt of his sword. Catching the man as he fell, Aldemere dragged him to the escapees' former cell, where he bound and gagged him like the others.

Several minutes later, mounting the warhorse the relief guard had tied to a post, Aldemere smiled as he felt the considerable weight of the Dwarf settling in behind him. "Glad you could make it up here," he whispered, nudging the horse into a trot, "without the aid of a stool or a ladder."

*****

Aldemere's Dilemma

Sir Linead, knight-marshal of the Combined Armies of Glittereye, had just completed his morning inspections with the Chief Knight of the Central Barony, Sir Peecwyl, and the temporary captainguard, Sir Lan, when, upon his return to the Guard House in the inner courtyard of Castle Silveth, he was summoned by a waiting herald to the Council Room.

Aware that any summons in these tense, prewar times was cause for concern, Linead hurried down the hallway, hastily saluting the knights he passed and surveying the ongoing preparations of the castle. They had learned a great deal about protection and strategy during the months of the Rebellion and the Long Winter, but the potential for a prolonged siege was very real, and Linead was doing all he could to prepare.

Entering the Council Room, the knight-marshal took a moment to look upon its occupants before bowing to the king, who sat in his accustomed chair at the head of a group comprising Elde the Jester, Talorous, Laurianna, and the two eldest Seers, Vitus and Dictus. One chair remained empty, designated, he assumed, for him. Scanning the circle for the Seventh Seat, Linead relaxed his shoulders upon seeing it empty in its corner.

"Sit, Sir Linead, please," said Dylwyn, his voice both thin and weary. "I know there is much for you to do, and we do not wish to keep you unnecessarily long from doing it."

"Thank you, Sire," Linead replied, taking the empty seat in the circle, although he much preferred to stand. "What can I do to be of service to you all?"

Indicating to Elde with a nod that the jester should proceed as leader of the meeting, Dylwyn rose from his chair and began to circle the room.

"There is much in play, as you are well aware," Elde began. "Your preparations of the castle and the surrounding areas have been no less than what we expected. Your coordination with Sir Lan in my son's absence and with Sir Peecwyl is noted as well. They have nothing but praise for you, as does your predecessor, on whom we once so greatly relied for all things martial in the kingdom, Baron Chrystan."

Nodding in appreciation, Linead decided to use his solid standing to risk offense. "Although all men—and knights most especially— enjoy hearing such positive assessments, I must ask, Jester Elde, if that is why you have summoned me, for if it is—"

"It certainly is not," Dictus interrupted, with a rough exhalation of air and a swat at the arms of his chair with his plump, pink hands.

"We need protection at the Temple," he continued. "A company of mounted knights should suffice… for now. They will return with Vitus and me when we leave tomorrow morning. Have them ready by dawn."

Linead held his tongue as he gauged the reactions on the faces of Elde, Talorous, and the king, who happened to be entering his line of sight as the Seer finished speaking.

It was clear that the threesome had already acquiesced.

"Perhaps," Linead began, choosing his words as carefully as he would the ground for an assault upon a field of battle, "it is best to petition Sir Peecwyl for a larger patrol, or perhaps a platoon, as the Temple is in the Central Barony and its protection is—"

"Not so," Vitus interjected. "The Seven Lord Seers merely *live on* a meager amount of acreage in the Central Barony—a mistake made by Paquom in the days of the mad scribe that shall one day be corrected. Our work is for all of Glittereye. Would you ask the king to make due with only one of the kingdom's five armies in such precarious times as these?" Not giving Linead time to answer, Vitus added, "Of course not. So why should we have to ask your subordinate for what is a rather reasonable requisition of knights?"

Because, Linead thought, *you are not a single one of you kings.* Instead, he answered, "I will see it done as you have requested."

"See that you do," Dictus replied, motioning to Vitus that it was time for them to exit. "And see as well that Sir Arans is put in charge, so we know we shall be respected."

Linead considered the knight they had requested as he watched the two schemers depart. Arans had risen through the ranks by means of his father's wealth as a provider of stonemasons and builders to the barons and other powerful nobles. It was common knowledge that Arans's father had made sizable contributions to the Seers, although, considering the poor condition of the Temple, the funds were not for anything related to his area of expertise.

"Sire," Linead began when he knew the Seers were out of earshot, "why was I not warned about their request?"

"Things are moving rapidly," answered Elde, as Dylwyn continued to circle the room. "What you have just agreed to—and your decorum in doing so is noted—was part of a bargain to keep Seer Farvon here at Silveth. Surely a hundred knights and their requested commander, Sir Arans, shall not be deeply missed?"

"They shall not be," Linead responded. "Especially not Sir Arans. However, I cannot adequately defend our barony and this

Aldemere's Dilemma

kingdom—or even this castle—if the men under my command are bargained away. It smells of the sludge that spawned the Rebellion."

Dylwyn ceased his incessant circling as Linead spoke the final word.

"I am well aware," the king replied, taking his seat. "Your honesty, as always, is welcome. There are reminders all around us. We must proceed with caution."

"Of what are you speaking, Sire?" enquired Linead, the tension once more palpable.

"Sir Prima has made it clear to Baron Ralin, whom promptly conveyed it to us, that he demands action within days against those who killed his son." The king was speaking just above a whisper and his voice was dressed with concern. "Although Sir Corvit has successfully vanquished the would-be raiders of Vaelsport, his absence leaves the north vulnerable without its commander and the units that are with him. Perhaps that is what the nomads wished to accomplish with their attack upon the port. Baron Ciloto believes it to be so and therefore requests reinforcements."

Linead looked around the room at those remaining. He had never had much occasion or reason to get to know the members of the Council of Elders, but he knew Talorous by reputation to be wise, fair, and honest and his pupil, Laurianna, to be his equal. He also had nothing but respect for both the jester and the king.

"What would you have me do?" he asked. "If I further fragment the armies to appease Ciloto and to give Prima his chance at vengeance—and it would more probably be a death sentence for him and anyone rash enough to follow him—it would leave the Central Barony grossly under-protected. We all know how difficult taking this castle shall be, although what we do not know is how powerful this ruler of Mellya is, or how expansive are his army and machines of war, but if we trust the northman, we should be prepared for the worst. A long siege will bring misery and death to the people on a scale history shall never forget. Is this Farvon so important? Are you willing to cede your power back to the Seers and the barons and their knights as we sit on the brink of war?"

A contemplative silence filled the room as the council considered Linead's words. After several moments had passed, Talorous said, "I have been told you are as wise as was Sir Laurel. I have now heard it for myself, so I shall tell you the naked truth. Farvon is to remain at Silveth at my urgent request and council. I do regret that we dragged you into the bargain we have made to see it done. I underestimated the audacity of my ... *peers*, Dictus and Vitus. It shall not happen again."

"As to the allotment of resources and the requests of the barons," Elde added on behalf of the king, "you are knight-marshal of Glittereye, with full authority to make such weighty and complex decisions."

Linead nodded and rose from his chair. "Then this is what I shall do. First, as Baron Ciloto may be correct, I shall honor his request for reinforcements. The nomads lack the coordination to acquire boats in such numbers or to conceive of a raid so far from home. Mellya must be behind it. We cannot afford to engage in a prolonged mountain campaign as we did the last time the nomads moved in force upon the mines. Corvit's lieutenants shall coordinate the additional companies until his return. As to Sir Prima, I am overdue to inspect both the western armies and their fortifications. As soon as I reach Spiltrow, I shall share with him our plans and buy us additional time."

With nothing more to say, Linead exited with a bow.

Since arriving earlier in the day at the forest complex comprising the Greybaers' cave and treetop dwellings, Kal-Gadras had felt like he was home. The Greybaers' attunement with nature's peace—as Gidon had so eloquently expressed it—was as strong as that of the Elves, although they did not worship or commune with a god or goddess and they designated no individual amongst them to be its personification or administrator the way Nemmerle was in Marlooq Fer. Unsure of the meaning of such vastly different practices breeding identical results, and feeling ill equipped to explore it, Kal-Gadras focused upon the waves of energy coursing through the natural structures around him, which brought to mind what he had experienced on Ferrukkla when he had entered the purple flames.

Gazing around the gathering in the amphitheatre formed by the crystalline outcroppings into which the Greybaer had led them as the sun began to set, Kal-Gadras guessed that less than half of those present—numbering twenty-one including himself—were aware of what he was sensing. The three Greybaer—the Regencymage Gidon and his companions Payon and Cyrok—recited soft, continuous prayers while they worked at preparing the gathering place for the soon-to-be-started council. As they began to intone a repeated cycle of guttural grunts and whistles, the six knights with which Frederick had traveled from Glittereye and the lone Dwarf seemed to Kal-Gadras subtly agitated by something on

Aldemere's Dilemma

which they could not put their fingers. Of the three Eretians, only the one called Eglin Bront, the ship's first officer, seemed to sense it. Knowing what he did of the Ruenai and the Eretian connection to the energies of the sea, Kal-Gadras guessed that Janzalon and Hathom had been too long on land to remain as attuned as Bront.

Frederick—as well as his fellow rangers, two equally powerful-looking and always alert humans named Christoph and Martin, not only appeared to be aware of the coursing, concentrated energy, but to derive from it strength and pleasure.

As the sky grew dark, Payon and Cyrok lit half a dozen firepits and torches. As they finished, Gidon raised his six foot, three inches of majestic bulk and clapped his hands three times, causing the race-centric pockets of varied conversation to cease.

"I welcome you all to the Forest of Tombal," the Regencymage began, his voice both authoritative and musical, as Nemmerle's could be. "I know that all of you have traveled far and left behind for a time the troubles and trials of your individual lands so that we might come together as one in a binding union to vanquish a cunning and malicious foe."

As if acting on a prearranged cue, Frederick Fragenoar stood and continued the meeting. "It is no small thing for the sacred and solitary Greybaer to welcome you to White Rocks, Tombal's soul of resonance and healing. It is their hope that the energies that flow through these crystalline structures and the trees and grasses of the surrounding forest will provide the clarity and peace needed to make a mutually beneficial accord before we go our separate ways."

Kal-Gadras glanced across the modest amphitheatre at the Dwarf, Gadrun Grundling, who was digging the blade of his axe a little deeper into the loamy earth at his feet but otherwise keeping his tongue and body still.

"Regencymage Gidon. Honored Greybaer. On behalf of the Eretian delegation, I thank you for the generous welcome," Tribune Waelsbun began. "I am empowered by the Grand Admiralty of Eret to not only seek your assistance but to offer you our own."

Gidon moved the muscles of his leonine face in such a way that they formed what Kal-Gadras considered a smile. "We are most grateful, Tribune Waelsbun. I know that your sea-gods, the Ruenai, sent you to seek your lost shipmate in these acres, as well as the missing prince, Stanchion of the Dwarves. We can only wait in patience for them to arrive or reveal themselves if they are here but still in hiding. In the meantime, we shall help you as we can and provide a safe and secure shelter for all those who seek it."

"Speaking of safety and security in these acres," Sir Lesster said, urged on by the collective head nodding of his fellow knights, "how is it that one of your most important citizens, the Keymage called Simon, was allowed to be taken by the Mellyans?"

"For the same reason some of your fellow knights were surprised and killed at the recent trade meetings in Glittereye—Nadrim Damonessa is cunning and cold and shall stop at nothing to control the countries and waters of Mynoweth."

Kal-Gadras watched Lesster's eyes avert to avoid meeting the fiery gaze of the man who had answered him, Christoph Vallens.

"Christoph is correct," Frederick said, placing a hand on his companion's shoulder in a show of solidarity, "although he means no offense, Sir Lesster, to your heroic fallen comrades. Like me, Christoph and Martin come from families ravaged during the Damonessas' rise to power. No one wishes to see Nadrim deposed or dead more than the remnants of the loyal Lysean families. The Mellyans have already invaded the sacred forests of Tombal. Not only was Simon taken, but a force of their men felled trees to take back to the Bay of Philod so that they could be used for building warships."

Kal-Gadras noticed that this news especially unnerved the Eretians.

Frederick continued. "As to the larger matter of the contents of our accord—those sitting here tonight represent the great dominions of Mynoweth. I do not know of a time noted in any of our people's histories when representatives from so many of our countries gathered all at once, and certainly not for such a clear and common purpose. I regret the jester-knight, Sir Aldemere, is not here with us as well, but his mission to Amdar will provide much-needed information on the Mellyans' plans and preparations. And, if your collective deities will it to be so, he shall return to us with something even greater." Pausing to let his mysterious words work their magic, Frederick faced Kal-Gadras. "We have yet to hear from you, Elven Lord of the South Shore, child of Nemmerle and bearer of the Mark of Gal-Rashand. What say you, friend Kal-Gadras?"

Throwing the root on which he was chewing into the firepit beside him, Kal-Gadras stood and bowed low to the group. Extending his arms in peace as he straightened, he said, "I feel the energies at work here in White Rocks and in the Forest of Tombal, and I know they are the same energies that give life to the sacred mother of Marlooq Fer. My mother and her adviser, High Lord Petror, know the dangers of the Mellyan occupation of this forest, both with

221   *Aldemere's Dilemma*

regard to its proximity to the borders of the lands of which the Elves are custodians and the River of Alliance and what it would mean if the cliffprince were to succeed in harnessing these energies. The Elven armies are preparing for the defense of our homes and, if need be, an all-out war, and should you ask, Regencymage, we shall fight within this forest in defense of all your race holds sacred."

"Are there no dissenting voices?" Gidon asked, after bowing in appreciation to Kal-Gadras for all that he was offering. "What of Mettlec, Gadrun Grundling?"

Leaning his axe against a low stone and standing upon the one that served as his seat, the Dwarf eyed the crowd. "I am empowered only to secure the return of King Buttress Pilon's son, Stanchion, whom I was made to understand would be waiting when I got here. Such are the mistaken insights of the various gods to which so many of you supplicate. I am neither a ruler nor an ambassador. I will not sign an accord, nor even pledge our help as a nation. But do not despair, for the Dwarven armies will fight against this foe on our borders until he and his army are vanquished or our country is destroyed."

Waiting until Gadrun had climbed down, regripped his axe, and retaken his seat, Gidon said with a laugh so full of mirth it quickly spread to almost everyone present, "Then we shall happily take your delightful presence amongst us as the happy gift it is."

The lone participant not laughing, Gadrun Grundling, felt his face grow as red as his beard, although it was embarrassment, not anger, that caused it to do so.

"May we all try to make this merriment last while we can," Frederick said, clapping his hands three times to signal the close of the meeting. "This is an unprecedented opportunity for us to be ambassadors of our respective countries and races—whether officially appointed or not. This will be the spirit that binds our accord and assures us victory in the mirthless days to come."

Frederick is correct, friend Aldemere, Kal-Gadras thought, as the attendees stood and intermingled, *you have more than earned the right to see this. I pray you are resting easy in whatever precarious place you find yourself tonight, knowing there is growing hope for Mynoweth and that many of us deeply miss you.*

"I do not understand why we did not ride under cover of night while we had a strong horse and surprise on our side," Stanchion complained, burrowing himself into a damp stack of hay in the stable loft in Amdar. In the stall just below Aldemere and him, he heard their horse devouring an apple. "Staying here even another hour is madness!"

"There is something I need to do," Aldemere answered, slipping the Slaaver's Hand over his own. "I shall return within the hour. I need my knife. You can have the sword."

"Little comfort it gives me," the Dwarf mumbled, making the exchange. "What I would not give for a shirt of mail and a double-bladed battle axe."

Hurrying through the dark, deserted streets toward the dungeon, Aldemere prayed that the prison captains had made no changes to the guard rotation he had so meticulously tracked. If the schedule remained unaltered, he would have another half an hour before anyone discovered or reported their escape.

Unless someone in the kitchens had become curious about the boy.

Pushing the possibility from his mind, Aldemere entered the prison, heading straight for the cell of the Greybaer.

As he unlocked the door, he heard the majestic-looking creature whisper, "You have a strange glow about you, Human."

Aldemere looked toward the Slaaver's Hand, afraid it had fallen off.

It had not.

"You can see me?" he asked, leaving the cell door open behind him.

"That is superb Elven craftsmanship," the Greybaer answered, rising to his impressive height. "You must have truly powerful friends."

"They are your friends as well," Aldemere said with a bow. "I am Sir Aldemere, captainguard of Glittereye. I know your name is Simon. I have been tasked with returning you to Tombal by Frederick of the North."

"Very well, then, Captainguard. I place my safety in your hands."

"Put this on as best you can," Aldemere said, studying the Greybaer's large, pawlike hands as he handed him the glove. "And stay close. Another guard will be along at any moment." Aldemere watched with amazement as the Hand morphed itself to Simon's paw as he slid it on and the Greybaer vanished from view as they exited the cell.

"*Just a moment, guard!* What do you think you are up to letting *him* go?"

Aldemere felt a bony hand grab the back of his cloak with an iron grip. "And where has the big oaf gotten to?"

223   *Aldemere's Dilemma*

The one-armed Eretian.

"I have no time for games," Aldemere hissed. "I shall kill you if I must. Do not raise the alarm."

Keeping his grip on Aldemere's cloak, the one-armed Eretian said, "I am scheduled for execution in the morning. If you take me with you, I will do whatever you say."

Knowing the tied-up guard's relief would arrive at any moment, Aldemere answered, "Come along if you must, but you must not make a sound."

Releasing Aldemere's cloak, the Eretian nodded his agreement.

Noting the prisoner's diminutive stature as he unlocked his cell, Aldemere made a plan. "Get beneath my cloak and stand on the tops of my boots."

Staying close to the sides of the buildings as the sky began to lighten, Aldemere moved as quickly as he could toward the stables. Turning back as he reached them, he saw the morning relief descending into the dungeon.

"The alarm will soon be sounded, Simon," he whispered to the place in which he sensed the Greybaer was standing. "We must climb into the loft." Entering the stables and ascending the ladder, he searched for signs of where the Dwarf might be was hiding.

"Stanchion, where are you at, my friend?"

"I am here, Human." He sounded impossibly far away. "I can tunnel into the hay as well as I can a mountain. Follow my voice and join me." As a bell began to peal, he added, "It sounds as though our escape has been discovered."

Talorous and Laurianna stayed silent as they returned to the suite of rooms where the Council of Elders studied, wrote, and slept. Beazor the owl and Nigredo the raven fluttered their wings on their perches at the sight of their masters, although they quickly settled down when it was clear that no bits of seed, carrot, or corn were in hand.

"I have been respectful and patient, Master Talorous," Laurianna began, lighting several candles and pouring two cups of water in Talorous's private study, "but I am now at a loss. You know I see the promise in having Farvon as an ally, and I have both befriended and encouraged him as you have asked, but to allow the Seers to dictate military policy to keep him here... Is this not working against our original purpose of containing their ambition and *lessening* their power?"

Pulling his pipe from his cloak and taking a sip of the hibiscus-infused water Laurianna insisted he drink, Talorous sank into his chair. Taking a pinch of pungent tobacco from the bowl on the small weathered table beside him and packing it gently into the pipe, he said, "I will not live forever, my girl. I am feeling the truth of it deep inside me. And though you are strong-willed and wise, you are no match for the Seers."

"I do not need a man to help me fight my battles. Especially against a group of pathetic and lecherous schemers!"

"I can see that well enough," Talorous answered, striking a match on the side of the table. "But you do need an ally—a *partner*—who knows the workings of the Temple and just how far Dictus and Vitus are willing to go in their own waning years. Because, I tell you plainly, the distractions they are causing are ill timed and dangerous. Sir Arans is not the harmless nuisance Linead believes him to be. We made that mistake with Garamin. Only Aldemere's intervention prevented Baron Ralin from joining his rebellion, which would have been enough to tip the scales. We must not repeat the past."

Talorous took a single, weak puff on his pipe before placing it on the table and sinking lower in his chair. "You must trust me, Laurianna. I will not see our country saved from those without only to see it defiled by those within."

Seeing Talorous's eyes close and his body press even deeper into the chair as age and fatigue overtook him, Laurianna slipped from the room and into the next, where she found Farvon, his sacks of belongings arrayed around him, awaiting news of his fate.

"A bargain has been struck," she said, closing the door and joining him on the bed. "Your mind has been deemed to be equal in value to that of the swords of a hundred knights, who will leave with those two decrepit schemers in the morning."

Suppressing a smile at the news as well as an urge to press Laurianna back upon his bed, Farvon instead scratched his head of short-cropped hair. "I do not understand the role I am to play."

"Neither did I," Laurianna whispered, taking his hands in her own, "but I am starting to. At least a little. We are part of the future of this kingdom—of Mynoweth herself—to an extent I would not have thought possible even a day ago. We will not only *write* the histories, Farvon—we have been chosen to aid in *creating* them."

Shaking his head, Farvon answered, "I would have been content to preside over the ceremonies in the castle chapel. I never asked for responsibilities such as this. I am more like the Seers than you think, Laurianna—at least the ones devoted to simple service. You must not ask me to be a hero."

225   *Aldemere's Dilemma*

"I did not ask for it, either," Laurianna said, leaning her head of fragrant hair on Farvon's shoulder. "But we shall answer the call, and we shall derive the strength we need by doing it together." Pulling away and standing, she added, sternly, "Now get your things unpacked. The king and Jester Elde have paid dearly for your knowledge and they shall soon summon you to share it."

As the warning bell of Amdar began its insistent, skull-pounding pealing, Nadrim Damonessa counted with forced patience each of the handful of seconds before the heavy, studded door to his sitting room flew open, revealing a sweating, panting officer.

"My lord," Purloch spurted, kneeling before the cliffprince. "I am hesitant to report…"

"Report what, *Captain*?"

"The hunter Tun and his Dwarven cellmate have escaped."

Nadrim bore his hateful gaze into the captain of his guard for a few endless seconds before asking, "Is that all you are hesitant to report?"

Purloch rose, keeping his eyes upon the floor and willing his fingers not to release his helmet and betray the extent of his fear. "They have taken the sailor… and the mage."

"Do you think I am a fool?" Nadrim shouted, rising from his seat and approaching the quaking officer. "The moment the alarm was sounded, I knew that you had failed in the most important of your duties. Make no mistake—although you think yourself a mighty, valiant warrior, you are nothing more to me than the keeper of the dungeon. The keeper of our *prisoners*, which you have let escape."

"Aye, My Cliffprince. I have failed you, and I shall make it right."

"You shall make it *more than* right," Nadrim hissed. "So tell me, Purloch… What have you done thus far to correct your colossal mistake?"

Believing his answer would determine whether he lived or died, Purloch answered, "I have sent my most capable squadron toward the forest to find them."

"Your 'most capable squadron'?" Nadrim raised a brow and smirked. Never had he looked so heartless. "Pardon me for not relaxing—considering that you are my most capable captain yet not worth a horse's feces. Recall this *capable squadron* at once."

Purloch, convinced he had misheard, replied, "My lord?"

"If you force me to repeat myself it shall be while I am removing my sword from your gullet, *Lieutenant* Purloch. Shall I utter the words again?"

"No, my lord. I heard you. I shall make it so."

Nadrim shook his head. "You shall make it so… Without knowing *why* you make it so. As a boon, I shall enlighten you. I doubt the man who calls himself Tun is a hunter… or a father. Tomorrow, I was going to satisfy my suspicions by continuing with the tools in my interrogation room the process you recently interrupted. *If* your men could find this pack of fugitives, which I doubt, I am sure that he would best them. I want to know more about the intruder who dares to defy me. Who dares to take what is mine. For now, we shall let this gaggle be. The Greybaer are weak—their keymage proved to be useless—so let them have their leader. He shall die with the rest of the beasts before our swords are fully sated. We have matters far more urgent to which we must attend.

"I have just returned from the harbor. Our warships are ready to sail. Half the ships I sent to Vaelsport should be returning within days. When Bokk Riverskab and Kull Krag arrive and make their report, I shall finalize my treaty of war with them and Moktar Caveraider. I have held the tribes back from their mountain raids and they are starving and eager for blood. I trust none of them any more than I trust you, but an idiot with a force of armed savages is more useful with proper direction than the best-trained warrior with the most elite of armies. Remember that, *Lieutenant* Purloch."

"Yes, my—

"Cliffprince. Or is it Lord? Or is it Lordly Prince? Save it, *Lieutenant*. Round up your 'men' and have them ready when the chiefs arrive. I want no slip-ups, no mistakes, or I swear I shall take more than your captain's commission."

"I appreciate your patience," Purloch whispered, relieved he was leaving intact.

"Oh, and *Purloch*." His name was a knife in his back. "To prevent them from being a burden, executed the rest of the prisoners. The Adjudicator begs for necks."

After Purloch had nodded his acknowledgment and exited, Nadrim approached a painting hanging on the western wall. It was a portrait of his father, Philod, who had held the title of second chief administrator of Mellya following the death of Nadrim's grandfather, Ravin, for whom his cliff-perched home away from Amdar was named.

"You had a chance to be great," Nadrim whispered to Philod's image. "Though you lacked the stomach and heart. I have them in abundance, just as grandfather did."

It was during Ravin's time, called the Second Great Enlightenment, that the first king of Glittereye had organized the vast central lands of the world called Mynoweth into a kingdom composed of baronies. Ravin, who had garnered considerable power as leader of the mining teams in the eastern Ambir Mountains that kept the forges full of metals during the years of the Unity Wars, resisted central rule on behalf of those he supervised.

So fervently did King Paquom wish for peace that he declared he would permit Ravin and his followers to hold title to the lands east of the unsettled wilderness, across the Mirra River and north of the River Wythe. These comprised roughly half of the lands of the long-forgotten Lyseum, a difficult decision that meant that Paquom was effectively cutting off the soon-to-be-named River of Alliance from the northern and eastern seas.

Ravin named his fiefdom Mellya, ancient Lysean for martial strength, and began to turn the city of Amdar into a stronghold and to forge his followers into an army.

For thirty-six years, Ravin strengthened Amdar, exploiting trade with Mettlec and Eret for the first three, until Buttress Pilon ascended the Dwarven throne and ceased all trade with the increasingly powerful Mellyans, convincing the Ereti to do the same.

Your son, Stanchion, Nadrim thought, fingering his dagger. *I should have killed him, Buttress, for what you did to Mellya. For burning our merchant fleet. For how you laughed at our pain.*

Was it you who sent the assassin who took my grandfather's life?

It was impossible to know. Mellya was full of intrigues and angry, slighted families… the Pavalettis, the Mallenhis, the Fragenoars…

When Philod began his tenure as second chief administrator, he swore to forge a more peaceful path to prosperity. He sought renewed trade agreements with the Ereti, which their northern, sea-loving neighbors quickly, insultingly declined, leaving Mellya, a newborn, hungry hawk, brimming with ambition but too weak to snap its tether.

For the next fifty years, Mellya bristled with frustration, as the baronies of Glittereye prospered, trained armies of their own, and allied with the Elves.

Until Philod finally died.

With a push and a prod from his son.

Before the old man deigned to comply—thinking it was cancer that was killing him and not the steady ingestion of poisonous mushrooms Nadrim mixed with his food—he called his progeny to his bedside. Naming Nadrim third chief administrator and Calrain negotiator of treaties, Philod spoke with his dying breath of the time when Mellya would once again trade peacefully with her neighbors.

The day of Philod's funeral, which Nadrim did not attend, the third chief administrator traveled to Ravinscliff, where he had spent most of his time as a boy. He remained within its walls for a week, summoning in secret those amongst the army and the governing class whom he knew to be as anxious as was he to fulfill Ravin's promise of a rich and mighty Mellya.

They rode as one into Amdar, not with a weak and fearful administrator at their head, as Philod had desired, but the self-proclaimed Cliffprince Nadrim.

Their preparations for war had begun that very day and had steadily increased ever since. Calrain had been all too happy to travel as ambassador to Eret with a small contingent of warriors and servants in ships Nadrim had ordered built based on old paintings of their once fine fleet of Eretian trading vessels. How ridiculous his brother had looked in expensive robes that hung limply on his withered frame and an abundance of jewels that jangled and spun on his fragile fingers and wrists.

"Bring me ships for the waging of war," Nadrim had said with a grin, "and I shall make it so you have rare fabrics and bangles in such abundance that no man will dare to call you malformed or crickbacked again. Your bed will be filled with women and your coffers with silver and gold."

It was certainly a surprise when, four months later, Calrain returned, not with the warships Nadrim had requested, but the chief Eretian shipwright, Millet Ronng.

"They refused to negotiate, brother," Calrain had explained. "They worship the seas, you see, and will not risk their triad of deities' wrath by giving us the means to make war upon the waters. So I brought you the next best thing."

Nadrim had made the best of this turn of events, placing Millet Ronng in charge of the building of his ships—not employing local timber, but the sacred trees of the Forest of Tombal, made magic by the power of the Greybaer. He sent his lumbermen across the River Wythe—guarded at present by a band of cutthroat mercenaries who would succeed in killing the hunter and his companions after Lieutenant Purloch had failed—via a bridge made of stones removed from the Ambir Mountains when his ancestor, Rogen, had ordered Stathl Pass carved out nearly one hundred and forty years before.

Aldemere's Dilemma

Then, one of his most trusted soldiers had sent word of a discontented and newly knighted son of the eastern baron of Glittereye. One whom Nadrim might enlist if the price for betrayal was sufficiently high.

Nadrim offered Silveth itself, and Garamin had agreed. The upstart knight had designs upon the princess Anastasia as well—every king must have his queen—and although Nadrim had offered her as part of the bargain, well... *Cliffkings also required queens.* He had not yet given up on that particular part of his plan, despite her ludicrous marriage to a sword-wielding clown.

The past year had been one of maintaining patience as he watched the thirteen warships slowly take form in the specially constructed docks in the Bay of Philod—the naming of which had been his father's single stab at remembrance. Four ships were ready to sail—save for their rudders, the material for which Nadrim had sent spies to Vaelsport to obtain—and the rest were mere months from completion when Nadrim asked Millet about training Mellya's sailors.

"I only build them, Cliffprince. I know naught of training sailors."

"Then whom amongst you does?" Nadrim had asked, resisting the urge to shove a spike through Millet's face at the point where his eyebrows came together to make a bushy, bright red V.

"The Ereti are born with the ability to sail. We take to the rivers and lakes of Eret as soon as we can walk down a ramp and board a boat without assistance. Our boats are a simple matter to sail—your people handle our vessels well. However, the three-masted ships I have built for you are a complicated matter. The Ruenai do not allow the making of war upon the seas."

Nadrim nodded, and asked Millet a second time when he could begin training Mellya's sailors in the intricate workings of the sails, rigging, and tiller assemblies of the ships within the bay.

Millet again denied that he could do so.

It was with a mix of blinding rage and supreme confidence that Amdar's native boatwrights could complete the unfinished ships that Nadrim began the torture of Millet Ronng. He did his work in secret, for the fair-minded, talented Eretian had been popular amongst the boat-builders. After five days and nights of using his tools on Millet's head, face, and body without success, Nadrim summoned two senior members of the Shadow Knife to operate the room's larger apparatus while Nadrim asked the questions.

Just before he died—and it was well noted by Nadrim just how much he had endured—Millet, who had not said a word no matter the level of pain, finally whispered, as if trading what he had withheld for a single second's peace, "Steal the Stone of the Ruenai. The Stone is how we learn. The Stone is our strength. The Stone is what you require."

"And where can I find this stone?" Nadrim had asked, pouring a few drops of water from a calf's bladder on the dying Eretian's lips as payment for his answer.

"I shall not tell you that."

Nadrim, dropping the calf's bladder and grasping the bloodied, weakened shipwright by the throat, began to apply all of the pent-up pressure he had kept in check during the days of steady torture. "I shall find this stone without you. And, as your countrymen are put to the sword, I shall tell them who betrayed their sacred secret."

Noticing his hands were clenching as the memory unspooled, Nadrim looked upon his father's portrait once again.

"I shall find the Stone of the Ruenai. My ships are at the ready. You wanted no part of the Shadow Knife, but I knew they had their uses. Once I have the Stone—and I shall soon send my spies to find it under cover of the war I am ready to wage—all of Mynoweth shall fall. Piece by piece, I shall seize it by land and sea—Mettlec and Eret, Tombal and Marlooq Fer. Then Glittereye herself. I shall be the Cliffking, with Dylwyn's daughter bearing me sons. Know this, you worthless bastard—the libraries of the countries I shall conquer I shall stock with rewritten histories. Then, in celebration, I shall change the name of your bay, burn your portrait in the square, and piss upon the ashes."

CHAPTER SIX

"You are torturing these… these… *things!*"

Knot Railhull, captain of the *Storm-Star*, who had arrived in Vaelsport a handful of hours earlier, along with the *Sea-Star*, was standing red-faced over Corvit's camp desk in the knight's tiny, sparsely furnished field tent. Beside him stood Captain Kelvan Kaelhul, who showed no signs of being in agreement with his comrade's criticism.

Corvit stared eye to eye with the complaining Eretian captain, although he was sitting and Railhull was standing. "These… *things*, as you rightly call them, attacked this town intending to slaughter its occupants. Your relatives, so I hear. Furthermore… had I not stopped them, what they would be doing to you and your crews this very minute would make what my men are doing to them appear like a game of tickle."

"The Human speaks the truth," Kaelhul whispered to his peer. "If the Tirili ore had fallen into their hands—and it must be the reason they came—then the Mellyans would prove to be all the more formidable upon the seas."

Encouraging this more rational Eretian to elaborate with a subtle motion of his hand, Corvit listened as Kaelhul related the details of what had taken place between the two countries, what the Eretians knew of Mellya's plans, and the Admiralty's decisions regarding the strategic allocation of the Eretian fleet.

"You say too much, Kelvan!" Railhull shouted when his fellow captain had finished. "You enjoy this war-making—I can sense it in your eyes, in your posture—but I say it is a fool's folly that shall see the most of us dead or slaves."

"You are correct, Captain Railhull—war *is* the folly of fools," Corvit interjected, eager to hold this common ground. "It is wise to leave it in the hands of those who have the experience and stomach to wage it with success.ir Put the prisoner's compound from your mind, and finish your mission. I am sure your ships are needed at home."

"That would be convenient, would it not?" Railhull asked with a laugh. "Perhaps we will stay a few days and look after the needs of the Vaelsportians. We are, to an extent, as you mentioned, kin. I have made many a trip to this port. As have you, Kelvan. They do not understand what has happened and the cruelties you are inflicting in the compound."

Aldemere's Dilemma

The compound to which they were referring was a fortified wood and iron fence Corvit had ordered his men to build to hold the eighty-plus nomads still left alive. Melak remained tied to the pole a quarter of a mile beyond it.

"You are starving them," Railhull continued. "The sun beats relentlessly down upon them, while you sit here in the shade."

"To conflate the two as you have—to see them as one and the same—is absurd, Knot," Kaelhul advised. "Sir Corvit saved Vaelsport and, whether he knew it or not, protected the ore."

"I did not," Corvit replied. "My sole focus—why I begged my supervisors to allow me to bring a force here in the first place—was the people, not the product that they mine. I come from the northern mountains of Glittereye. The miners who live and work there suffer a similar existence. One of relentless labor, little comfort, and little thanks from the ruling class." Turning his gaze to Railhull, he said, "Stay if you want. But the rest of your crew does not come ashore, unless it is to get what you came for. Once you have it, however, I shall insist that you hoist your anchors and go."

"How dare you!" Railhull spat back. "We have more of a claim on Vaelsport—"

Rising to his full height, Corvit hissed, "I do not think you heard me. Claims, governments, exploitation of workers—none of that is a knight's concern!"

"What is your plan of action, Sir Corvit?" Kaelhul interjected. "I have no doubt you are also needed at home."

"I am," Corvit said, softening his stance but remaining on his feet. "I have information still to extract from the nomad leader—the one that is lashed to the pole. Once I have it—or he is dead—I shall leave. Though a third of my force shall remain to guard the port."

Kaelhul raised his single, bushy brow and leaned forward in alliance. "That is satisfactory. But, might I ask—what are your plans for the nomads' remaining ships?"

Corvit smiled. He liked this Eretian just as much as he disliked the one standing next to him, who obviously received his commission more recently and so had no choice but to stay silent now that his superior was exercising his authority. "I am open to your suggestions, Captain Kaelhul."

"We shall proceed directly with loading our ships with Tirili ore. We shall take all that is available, so the Mellyans, should they send more barbarians or risk coming on their own, shall not have it for their ships. We shall leave a few dozen of our crew to train the Vaelsportians in using the ships for their defense. It is their right to defend themselves from future attacks. Your men can learn as well, if you wish. Are you amenable to this?"

"I am," Corvit said, saluting the two Eretians, a gesture only Kaelhul returned. "Now," the knight continued, gesturing for his guests to sit, "tell me why it is that this Tirili ore is so important to the sailing of your ships that blood has been shed to obtain it?"

Amidst the clinking, clanging din of hundreds of knights practicing with sword, lance, and shield and the rhythmic hammers of armorers working metal plates in the Western Barony, Sir Linead called upon all of his considerable skills to keep Sir Prima calm.

"Do you think an inspection of the barony's army under the guise of your concern for my seeing justice would sway me from my path?" Prima kept his hands at his sides, although Linead noticed how tightly he clenched them. "As Baron Ralin indicated to the king, I will ride for vengeance with his blessing or without it, but I do not intend to be forestalled another day."

Indicating the knights engaged around them, Linead asked, "Have all of them agreed to committing treason by following you to Mellya? How many will go when I order them to stay, as is my duty and right as knight-marshal? Is your pain so deep you would undertake an act of rebellion when you and Sir Eric fought so fiercely to quell the last one? How is such treasonous behavior honoring your son?"

For a few seconds, Prima stood silent, weighing Linead's words. He had thought of Eric's beliefs, his commitment to the castle every waking moment since the funeral, thinking back to the day, a seeming lifetime ago, when his son had asked his father to secure him the position of page so he could also be a knight. Despite the fact that Linead's assessment of Eric was the same as his own, Prima would not allow the knight-marshal's warnings to sway him.

"It does not matter how many of them shall join me," Prima answered, looking Linead in the eyes. "If necessary, I shall go alone. I shall relinquish my knighthood if that is what it takes. However, I shall not endure another idle moment while Eric's murderers go unpunished. And that is something I know in my heart that my son would understand."

"I do not question your right to justice." It took every ounce of Linead's will to hold his comrade's gaze, so heavy was the pain he witnessed in his eyes. "When I leave here, I ask you to consider the ferocity with which these men—*your* men, Prima—are executing their drills. They will fight for you, and for Eric, until they cannot lift

235   *Aldemere's Dilemma*

their arms. Until they take their final breath. We are putting plans in place. Aldemere is in Mellya as we speak, gathering intelligence. The ranger from the north has gone east with Sir Lesster and others to meet with potential allies. The Elves have pledged to act upon our word. They shall not delay as they did the last time. They know the potential cost. Sir Corvit has repelled a barbarian attack on Vaelsport."

Prima's attention heightened and his gaze sharpened with each sentence Linead spoke. "An attack on Vaelsport... The barbarians crossed the Tirili Range. Why?"

"They went by boat, almost assuredly supplied by the Mellyans."

"Does Corvit need reinforcements? Relief? I can send companies north across the desert within hours."

Linead, for a moment, considered asking Prima to go himself, to give his rage a proper outlet, but if Prima wanted to do so, he would have volunteered.

"We do not expect another attack. Corvit is securing Seafarers' Gap and shall leave a force in place. Your men need to continue their preparations if they are to serve as the vanguard when our armies depart for Mellya."

Shaking his head, Prima asked, "Why did you not tell me all of this in the first place, Linead? Why appeal to my heart instead of my soldier's mind?"

"Because it is your heart that must make this decision. Only then shall I know that you are with us."

Straightening his shoulders, Prima saluted his superior, holding his position until Linead reciprocated. "We will be ready to serve as the vanguard. When we do, we shall be flying Eric's colors so I can plant them on these honorless bastards' graves."

Calrain entered the throne room only minutes before blood began to flow.

Nadrim had reacted with unfathomable calm as his army units unsuccessfully scoured Amdar for the escaped prisoners. Hour after hour, as nervous officers passed before the throne to make their reports, the cliffprince received them with a silent nod and a shooing with a hand that rose only inches from where it rested. A full sun cycle had come and gone without a spark of reaction from his brother.

It was as though the four had simply disappeared, and Nadrim had expected it.

"Perhaps the Greybaer employed some type of magic," Calrain had whispered to his brother at the morning's brief, perfunctory commissioning ceremony, where Purloch (who now wore the stripes of a lieutenant) was further humiliated when his most ambitious—and noncooperative—lieutenant, a bug-eyed mass of a man named Stratten, was promoted to captain in his place. Much to Nadrim's delight, the new captain's first act was to name Purloch warden of the prisons, which, for the time being, meant he would aid the builders and ironworkers in a thorough upgrade of the inner architecture.

As ordered by Nadrim, any prisoners still in the cells—numbering more than twenty—had been executed the day Purloch was demoted and any additional men arrested in the days following were kept in a pen in the public square. For an hour each day, the relentless hoist, release, and chop of the Adjudicator filled the air.

Through all of it, Calrain continued to watch as his brother conducted himself like a man for whom all was going his way.

Something had finally, obviously, and dramatically changed.

"Say again, you mush-headed savage?" Nadrim was asking of the barbarian standing before him, whom Calrain realized was Moktar as he sat beside his brother.

"Never mind," Nadrim said, taking his dagger from its sheath. "I can no longer stand to watch your tongue roll in your head as you try to find the words. Take this knife, Moktar. Take it and kill the one who chose to tell *you*, instead of me, that your supposedly mighty warriors were routed by unmounted knights and cross-bred idiots!" Nadrim banged the hilt of the knife repeatedly upon the chair, until three nervous heralds appeared.

Moktar, eyeing the trio with a look of near compassion, took the knife from Nadrim, but made no move to identify the messenger to whom he had initially spoken.

"Do it, you Caveraider bastard," Nadrim said, "or I shall kill all three myself!"

"There is no need of that, My Cliffprince," said the herald who stood in the middle, who was also clearly the oldest. "It is my responsibility."

"Perhaps so," Nadrim answered, approaching the senior herald. "But you did not *receive* the message, did you?"

Nadrim's sword was out of its sheath and through the herald's gullet within seconds.

"Did you?" Pulling free his sword as he kicked the body backward, Nadrim wheeled upon Moktar. "Which of the two, you moron? Which of these sheep turds told you? Put that knife in his throat!"

For the life of him, Calrain could not figure out why Moktar did not do it. Perhaps it was his way of showing Nadrim exactly whom the barbarian was.

As if in answer, Nadrim sliced off the heads of the two remaining heralds and retrieved his knife roughly from Moktar before returning to his chair.

"These not yours," Moktar said, holding out his hands.

"You think not?" Nadrim coolly answered. "We shall see. It is time for you to raid the northern mines of Glittereye. If your warriors can manage it better than Vaelsport. Before the rest of their knights return."

Moktar's reply was a grunt and a pair of growls, the meaning of which Calrain would spend hours attempting to decipher.

When Moktar had left the room, Calrain moved himself out of his brother's immediate reach—and away from the metallic stench of the blood that soaked the madman's clothes—and, indicating the carnage, whispered, "It appears that someone close to your operations is trying to thwart us, brother, and it is making you irrational."

"Let them continue to try, *Crickback*," Nadrim answered, still holding his dripping sword in one hand and his dagger in the other. "The loss of Tirili ore for our rudders is unfortunate, but my fleet is nonetheless ready to launch, and I have a surprise for our enemies at Silveth. Something their prideful king and his advisors would not think to do themselves, so they will not see it coming." Standing, he added, "Make yourself useful, brother—get someone to clean up the bodies."

Calrain nodded as his brother walked away.

I will clean up your messes, Nadrim. That is what brothers do.

Aldemere and his companions waited deep within the hay throughout the day and well into the night as hundreds of soldiers searched the city. Three separate times they heard men upon the ladder leading to the loft, but they had hidden themselves so well their worst fears went unrealized—no sword came stabbing through their cover.

Once the sounds of the search parties had ceased, Aldemere pushed aside the layers of hay that had kept them hidden, stood with a moan, and helped the one-armed Eretian to his feet.

"Breathe deeply in and out," Simon whispered, following them out of the hay. "It shall relax your knotted muscles."

"What in the fiery halls of Mettlec is *he* doing here?" Stanchion growled as he saw the grinning Eretian.

"He gave me no choice," Aldemere answered, reflexively standing between the two enemies as the hair on Stanchion's powerful forearms began to bristle.

"You are most unwelcome, Eretian," the sneering prince spat out. "You deserve to be in cha—"

Seeing Stanchion's look of sudden confusion, Aldemere looked behind him. The one-armed sailor was no longer there.

The glove.

Aldemere thrust his hand into his boot. The Slaaver's Hand was gone.

As was his knife.

"Ow!"

The voice, filled with pain, came from the foot of the ladder.

Descending to the floor of the stable before Stanchion, who followed close behind, Aldemere grabbed for the spot where last he heard the voice. Feeling the Eretian's iron grip on his wrist he watched as the magic of the Slaaver's Hand failed to sustain through their contact.

"Give me the glove." Aldemere's voice was full of threat. "And the knife."

The Eretian wordlessly complied.

As Aldemere tucked them into his boot, Stanchion brushed passed him and took the Eretian by the throat.

"You traitorous..."

Aldemere placed his hand on the Dwarven prince's shoulder. "Now is not the time. Once we get to safety, you can do with him what you will. The Deities know he deserves it. It is nearly light. They will soon resume their search."

"Very well," Stanchion mumbled, releasing his grip on the gagging, gasping Eretian. "Patience is a Dwarven virtue. But I am not sharing a horse with a traitor!"

"I would not think of asking," Aldemere answered, admiring Stanchion's strength of will. "You shall ride with Simon. As for you, Eretian. You shall ride with me."

"We will never make it out of the city, Human," the Eretian said, shaking his head. "Every exit will be guarded. The clever rotters have removed all of the horses from the stables, if you geniuses have not noticed. We will have to go on foot."

Aldemere's Dilemma

"Not all of the exits," Stanchion said with what passed for a Dwarven smile. "And there will be horses near to where we are going, if Boldac chooses to provide them."

"It sounds like your route will take some risk to navigate," Aldemere said, finding himself drawn to the confidence and determination of the Dwarf.

"Not if you do what I say, and let me lead us through it. Dwarves are used to getting out quiet through cramped, forgotten places. It will be a tight fit for you, I fear, Simon Greybaer."

"You need not worry about me," Simon answered, placing his hefty paw-hand upon Prince Stanchion's muscular shoulder. "I shall manage it just fine."

The Dwarf nodded, cinching his belt two notches tighter. "Then all of you follow me."

The hooded traveler had been journeying for days with only sporadic pauses for rest and a handful of food and a few drops of water.

He had departed from Amdar at night, rowing a boat in a driving rain across the Bay of Philod to where it met the Mirra River. Selecting a shallow embankment, he left the boat behind, knowing an elite member of his unit would retrieve and row it back, not knowing the details of whom had left it or where its occupant had gone. Traveling light, he kept an impressive pace, running along the river banks by night and swimming just beneath the surface of the water in the day, receiving a steady stream of air through two six-inch lengths of reed forming an angle when carved and joined together.

Reaching Mirra Pass hours ahead of schedule, he remained mid-distance between Cabral, which he knew to be heavily fortified following the battle of Vaelsport, and the river, which grew busier with barge and boat traffic the closer it got to Eerbell in the east. The local knights had also fortified Eerbell after his fallen comrades' failed attempt at assassination and kidnapping during the trade conference.

Eerbell, he thought, eating a cold, mirthless meal of wild berries, a handful of nuts, and a strip of rabbit jerky—*I wish I had the time to avenge my fallen cousin*.

The cousin of whom he thought was the last of the assassins to die—suffering in silence all Sir Linead had wrought with his knife and boot—although all the traveler knew was that his cousin had left with four others to serve the Fatherland of Mellya and none of them had returned.

Turning west well north of Eerbell, the traveler, dressed as a laborer from the Centerlands, stopped each day at a farm, where he worked at whatever needed doing, in exchange for a meal and a bed. His story, accent, and mannerisms changed slightly as he made progress toward his intended destination. At first, he was a northern miner who had grown weary of the darkness and wished to work in the light of the fields. As he adopted the accent of the farmers and their habits and methods of labor, he became the disgruntled youngest son of a recently deceased farmer whose older brother had cast him out rather than divide the land between them. Aside from the barest details of his story, he said little and made no trouble. He even refrained from contact with the many farmers' daughters beside which he worked in the fields, or while feeding the chickens and goats.

A lifetime of celibacy and harshly administered self-discipline made it easy to ignore their evening advances and breathy daytime suggestions.

Through the silence and distance he maintained whenever possible, he listened. To the idle gossip, to the knights who stopped for water from the well or a bowl and some bread, and he learned.

He would soon reach Elsmore, home of the baron of the farmlands of Glittereye—a former knight named Chrystan, who had chosen the life of the *politician* over that of the *soldier*. An officer, no less... an inconceivable idea for an Amdarian. A lifelong soldier who came from a long tradition of soldiers, the traveler wondered at the fact that Glittereye had lasted as long as it had with such undisciplined men in its ranks. No one would make such a trade in Mellya—the Damonessas had seen to that. Such things had undone Lyseum, within which the traveler's ancestors had once been a powerful family.

Most of the Lyseum families had adjusted, succumbed, or perished. All but the Fragenoars. The traveler directed almost all of his harbored hatred at this rival family of assassins, politicians, and scholars who had caused so much pain to his own.

It was a Fragenoar named Felzban—older brother of the mad scribe Manthes—who had, in 952, killed Elaric Gamelsin, at the time the highest-ranking general in Amdar and a former lieutenant in the traveler's prestigious unit—the Shadow Knife.

Although a Fragenoar had not technically killed his cousin, Davin Gamelsin, the one named Frederick was responsible just the same, for his betrayal of Mellya and efforts in aiding what soon would be a conquered, kingless kingdom.

For those sins, and those of his family, he would pay with his organs, bile, and blood.

On the morning he awoke just a handful of miles from Elsmore, the Amdarian traveler stretched his body and lifted stones for an hour to keep his muscles strong. After some water and berries for his breakfast, he climbed the tallest tree he could find, gathering needed intelligence. After another hour of exercise, he tracked and killed a small, long-tusked boar in the woods where he had camped—doing so without a weapon.

Just as he would Baron Chrystan.

As he would his primary target, who lived, for now, in Silveth.

Dramel Pilon, second son of the king, looked out on the *Salt-Serpent* and *Sea-Sprite* sitting low in the water at Port Alum, one hundred and twenty miles from Mount Mettlec.

You will sit a little lower before you are under sail, he thought, having made a decision that would either secure his place in history or send him into self-imposed exile with Stanchion.

"Guardsman!" he yelled, signaling to a nearby warrior. "Bring forward four of the big guns, a dozen boxes of powder, and a hundred projectiles."

The guardsman raised a brow. "Pardon my asking, Prince, but are we going to blow those ships out of the water after all the effort to outfit and load them?"

"Certainly not," Dramel answered. "We are going to take them on board."

"Take what on board?" Captain Ungerfil asked, approaching with Captain Waelsbun. "We are nearly at peak capacity."

"The means to not only wage a war but win it," Dramel replied, waving the guardsman away to carry out his orders. "Something our alchemists created for disabling and sinking attacking ships. A means to propel solid iron balls over a distance through use of a concentrated, highly contained explosion. They are designed for the land, but I believe we can also use them, by training some of your crew, by securing them to the deck."

Before the captains could respond, Dramel was book-ended by the advisor Stelcore and the general charged with protecting the port. Behind them were Gorvin and Purug.

"What do you want with the ordnance, Prince Dramel?" the general enquired. "It is needed for our defense."

"Four guns and a few hundred balls shall not be missed here, General," Dramel answered, standing his ground, "but they could be the difference between Mellyan victory and defeat beyond our borders. Do as I command!"

"Does your father approve of this, Prince?" Purug squeaked, wringing his hands and shifting his weight from foot to foot. "I am not certain your authority to work with the Eretians extends as far as you are taking it."

Feeling numerous sets of Eretian and Dwarven eyes boring into his face, as their owners awaited his response, Dramel said, "I shall take responsibility for any coming consequences, Purug. Are the three of you ready to depart?"

Gorvin's face twisted in confusion and fright. "But I am *not* departing. Your father tasked me only with seeing you off. After consultation, he realized I am needed—"

"Like the guns, you shall not be missed. Affram is capable of seeing to father's needs. Ambassador Waelsbun shall remain, so it is only fair that the full council is with me."

"But I do not... I did not bring my personal effects..."

"They are already aboard the *Sea-Sprite*," Dramel said, enjoying the exchange. "General," he continued, shifting his attention and sharpening his tone, "get the guns."

"Will you be sailing on the *Sea-Sprite* as well, Prince Dramel?" Thaker asked, watching the general depart and hoping he would have the opportunity to spend some time getting to know and learning from this refreshingly intelligent and appropriately self-confident Dwarf standing before him.

"I think it prudent to have the council on one ship and me on the other, in case of misfortune," the prince answered. "That is, if you can accommodate me, Captain."

Thaker nodded. "I shall have my first officer see to the arrangements."

"And where should I set *my* belongings, brother?"

Dramel looked up at the rider of the horse that had rapidly approached as he was ordering the general off.

"You should not have come here, Affram. Father needs you beside him."

Climbing from his horse and collecting his armor, bags, and weapons—including his double-bladed battle-axe—Affram smiled. "It was father who sent me." Dropping his belongings with a crash to the ground, he went back to his horse and pulled a four-foot length

Aldemere's Dilemma

of string-tied burlap from the fastenings on his saddle. "And Eggard Starforge requested I bring you this."

Taking the bundle from his brother and laying it gently on the ground, Dramel pulled his knife from its scabbard and sliced through the strings. Unwrapping the burlap, Dramel shielded his eyes as the sun reflected directly into them off the finest length of sharpened, polished steel he had ever beheld or held. Grasping the hilt, he pulled the sword from the burlap and felt its perfect weight and balance in the muscles of his arm.

"Has he given it a name?" Dramel enquired.

Affram shrugged his shoulders. "He said he calls it Storyteller, and you would reckon what that means."

"Storyteller," Dramel whispered, kissing the blade. "I know what it means indeed."

Captain Helkirk Nagelbrau, head of the Mellyan Shadow Knife, had been practicing for two hours a day with sword, knife, and pike instead of his usual hour since Cliffprince Nadrim had taken his two pinkies and right index finger after the failed operation in Glittereye.

Helkirk bore no ill feelings toward Nadrim for what he had done. On the contrary, he admired the man's restraint. Failing to capture the barons had forced alterations to the Mellyan operations. Operations that required years of planning and secret maneuvers. Helkirk knew that the necessary changes to their plans, which his failure as a leader had required, would cost the lives of many fellow warriors and, for that alone, the captain felt a pain deep within that obliterated what he felt as Nadrim removed his fingers.

To lose one's life in the service of the state was a privilege, but waste was waste, and no member of the Shadow Knife or Amdarian army did not know the difference.

Placing two longswords on the weapons rack in his outer room, he wiped the sweat from his scarred and muscled torso. The training of an officer or assassin in the Shadow Knife (Captain Helkirk Nagelbrau was both) was a rigorous, brutal undertaking. Boys aged twelve who passed the initial series of tests—and they were few in number—were taken from their families in the middle of the night by senior members of the Shadow Knife donning masks of dragons and devils. Any father or other males in the home older than the boy, should they dare to prevent the abduction, were beaten. Severely. The abductors had to pull more than half the boys from the arms of their screaming mothers.

Helkirk warned off his own mother with a glare and outstretched hand as the invaders bashed in the door to their simple farmhouse on the night of his abduction.

In an elaborate ritual the following day, after a night passed in pain as their abductors prevented them from sleeping by whipping them with switches any time they closed their eyes, the boys were marked with either a tattoo or hot brand, depending on whom was in charge of the transitional operation. At that point, their officers assigned them a bare patch of floor in their unit's unheated, unadorned barracks.

Thinking back on the rituals he underwent the day after his abduction, Helkirk touched the raised arrowhead that an officer had burned into his left forearm, grateful to have the brand rather than the tattoo of the three-taloned falcon on the leg that Nadrim had insisted upon the past several years.

The rite of passage complete, the boys began their training in weaponry, strength building, stealth, and problem solving. They were toughened up and indoctrinated through daily rituals that had them living for days at a time with only water in extreme conditions and defending themselves from disfigurement and death as veteran members of the unit mercilessly—for an enemy would never show them even a second of mercy—came at them with a variety of deadly weapons. In the first six months, his fellow trainees had stitched up Helkirk numerous times, and he had watched eight of his fellow trainees fall to the sword or some other weapon. Three others died from exposure, while two drowned and two more did not survive falls after slipping from a moss-covered cliff.

Only the worthy served. Only the toughest ascended the ranks. Officers could challenge superiors for their positions, and Helkirk had done so on three separate occasions—culminating in a challenge that resulted in his captaincy. As fierce and ruthless as his predecessor was, Helkirk had used to his advantage a hatred of his superior he had harbored since the night of his abduction. Instinct taking over as the devil-masked officer grabbed a handful of Helkirk's hair, his father had tried to intervene and had been beaten so badly he had fallen into a coma, dying several months later, and leaving Helkirk's mother with no choice but to marry an army sergeant who never took a drink without it resulting in him beating her.

Word was he took up the bottle nearly every night.

Helkirk was waiting to deal with him one evening shortly after his first commission. The sergeant never struck his mother again.

245   *Aldemere's Dilemma*

How could he, with his arms removed at the elbows?

Like any who lived long enough in the ranks of the Shadow Knife, Helkirk felt zero remorse, nor things like cold, heat, or hunger. Unit members could travel on as little as two hours of sleep in a day/night cycle, as one of Helkirk's best assassins, Gregory Gamelsin, was doing as he traveled in Glittereye to fulfill his secret mission.

Helkirk had given himself nearly fully to the rituals, philosophies, and austerities of the Shadow Knife, although there was one area where he steadfastly refused to succumb.

He could not honor an oath of celibacy. Life was too full of willing—and unwilling—beauties for any such nonsense as that.

Moving to an adjoining room, he rubbed a generous portion of spiced oil on his chest and neck and tied his long hair back into a ponytail. Choosing a crimson robe from his maple wardrobe, he slipped it over his shoulders, leaving it unfastened to let the early evening air cool his aching, hard-worked muscles. He then entered a third room, where he kept his "diversion and source of release" as he called her—Deanna Callenhor, the nineteen-year-old daughter of Lord Astrin Callenhor, whom Nadrim had pushed from the balcony at Ravinscliff for being an agitator and insurrectionist.

Lighting half a dozen candles on the wax-stained bedside table, Helkirk approached the narrow mattress upon which Deanna lay. The leather straps that bound her were still buckled and secure.

"How are you today, my lady?" he asked, sinking to his knee and stroking her cornsilk hair with his right hand's two remaining fingers.

He found himself impressed. Deanna did not even flinch.

"I shall have some extra meat and vegetables added to your evening meal," he said, standing, suddenly bored with her lack of response. "We need to maintain your strength. If you carry a son, he shall one day lead the Shadow Knife. And if it be a daughter, we will sell her to some impotent mine boss's whining sow of a wife and have another go."

As he exited the room, he again felt rather impressed.

Despite his despicable taunt, the mother of his spawn was silent as a tomb.

"I am almost impressed, Dwarf," Nakret the Eretian said, as the four escaped prisoners emerged from a quarter-mile tunnel that had taken them under the city's fortified walls and out into the countryside. "How did you know about this passage out of Amdar?"

"Loose talk in the mines where I worked. It was a service entrance for miners and other builders and artisans when the city was first being built," Stanchion replied, looking directly at Aldemere. "The more centralized the Amdarian security became, the less it was used, until it was mostly forgotten. Lucky for us, they left the gate unlocked. A rare lapse in protocol for our stalwart Captain Purloch."

"There is always something overlooked, even amongst the best of leaders," Aldemere answered, recalling his campaigns against the nomads and Garamin's mistakes outside the walls of Silveth. "He shall not allow such oversights again. We would not have had a second chance had we not gotten free of him when we did."

Simon scanned the ground ahead of them. "Where are these horses you thought your god might miraculously provide us?"

"They should be corralled just beyond that hill," Stanchion answered, pointing. "It is where the horsemasters train them when herds are wrangled from the valleys. They might be a rough and rowdy ride, but we have no other choice. I know Tun is a capable rider."

Nakret scratched his hairless head while peering into the Dwarf's formidable, ash-grey eyes. "Who exactly is *Tun*?"

"Tun is me," Aldemere answered, wishing once more that he had left the ill-mannered Eretian in Amdar. He would rather not take the time needed to explain whom he was to Stanchion. Taking a deep breath, he tried to be succinct. "Tun is the name I have used since I was taken prisoner in the south. I have come from Glittereye, where I am the captainguard of the king's security unit. My true name is Aldemere. I was sent here by mutual friends to gather information and rescue both you and Simon."

"By mutual friends, I doubt you mean my father," Stanchion replied, looking Aldemere over with new and softer eyes. "Regardless, I am grateful. But I do not suppose you are tasked with taking me home."

"We are going to Tombal," Aldemere said, finished with explanations. "And now we should see if those horses are in that corral as you have hoped. Purloch and his prince know I am not a hunter named Tun. I think they knew it from the start. I came within a few seconds of parting with some of my teeth. They will not let any of us escape as easily as we have so far found it. I am not sure what they are planning, but our best hope is to get some considerable miles between us."

"What else do you think they know?" Nakret Sailweaver asked.

Aldemere's Dilemma

Aldemere willed himself to be patient. "Given whom I freed, they know why I came to Amdar and also where we are headed. What they *do not* know is if our own forces are waiting to escort us to Tombal, and if so, how large a force it might be. Their preparations are far along, but they are not yet ready to make war upon the world."

"You have put yourself and your people in grave danger, Human," Simon the Greybaer whispered. "Perhaps you should not have come. This is not your fight."

"With all due respect, Simon," Aldemere said, "even if it was not our fight before—and I truly doubt that is true—it became so the minute Amdarian assassins murdered several of our knights. We are wasting time with talk. Let us pray that horses await."

"Just a moment," Stanchion said, selecting a fist-sized rock with a sharp natural edge from the ground and approaching a stout oak several feet away. "There is something I have hidden that I need to retrieve from this tree."

Frederick had been waiting two days to talk in private with Kal-Gadras after the encouraging council at White Rocks. His complement of archers nearly always accompanied the Elven Lord of the South Shore, and when they did not, Frederick had to navigate the still-watchful eyes of Sir Lesster and his band of loyal knights. Although they had shown him more respect since their arrival in Tombal, it was clear that Lesster was taking Linead's orders as seriously as when he had first received them.

In the end, Kal-Gadras had taken the initiative, approaching the northern warrior on a rainy afternoon, as he was hunting for the Greybaer. The legend of the ghostlike stealth of the Elves was in an instant proven true as Frederick, having just drawn back his bow, heard whispered in his ear, "A fern's-width to the left I would say."

Of course, the Elf was right.

"Thank you for that," Frederick said, slinging his bow across his back and pulling his knife to prep the fleetdeer. "My focus is not what it should be with all that has occurred."

"And what is still to come," Kal-Gadras answered, joining Frederick at the spot where the fleetdeer had been felled. "All my life I have heard stories of the great families of Lyseum. It is an honor to meet one of their heirs."

"I too was raised on stories... of the Elves of Marlooq Fer. Tales both light and dark," Frederick replied, setting about his work. "For all peoples and all families are made of both. Mine is no exception.

Few outsiders know the full extent of the reach of the Fragenoars and how large a part they have played in supplying and stirring the ingredients of current circumstances."

Kal-Gadras watched as the knife went deeper than required as Frederick spoke his truth, which was clearly a confession that he had long had the desire to unburden to a suitable confidante.

"It is clear that you carry the burden of generations. Of decisions you did not make and actions you did not take. I know we are far from friends, but you must cast off those weights. It is enough for us to bear our own burdens regarding the way things currently stand, and any legitimate responsibilities each of us has inherited."

"I will carefully consider your advice," Frederick said, hoisting the meat upon his shoulder. "But the lies I have told and the secrets I have kept tie me to the deeds of my ancestors far beyond the fact that their poisonous blood is running through my veins."

Kal-Gadras nodded in understanding. "I see the yoke under which you struggle. And I sense that much of its substance has to do with my old friend Aldemere."

Frederick's face became unreadable. "It has to do with us all, Kal-Gadras. The jester-knight included. If you sought me out in search of details…"

"Not at all," Kal-Gadras answered. "Only to offer companionship in hard and lonely times. I have not known many trustworthy Humans. Aldemere. His father and the king. A handful of knights… Nevertheless, I give my trust to you, Frederick of the North, despite the confessions you have made and the secrets you still keep. That is what I came here to say. Know that you have my trust."

The two warriors walked in silence for several minutes. As they neared the encampment, Frederick said, staring straight ahead. "I pray I do not betray it."

In the first weeks of Chrystan's ascension to leader of the Central Barony, he had two closely connected priorities. The first was to see that the wife and three daughters of his predecessor, Baron Filgrith, were set up in a suitable home holding most of their belongings and that two sentries continually guarded them against those not able to discern between the rebellious deeds of the baron and those of his (mostly) innocent family. Chrystan had also arranged for guards to protect Filgrith's cairn in the cemetery behind the castle, which locals had defaced half a dozen times in half as many months.

The second was to remove all evidence of Filgrith's fortification of Elsmore. Chrystan had overseen the removal of ramparts and

Aldemere's Dilemma

wooden towers and had turned the armory into an Academy where the farmers who were his responsibility could send their children when they could spare them from working in the fields to learn from guest tutors who agreed to travel from the other baronies and Castle Silveth at weekly intervals. The tutors who had met Chrystan's request—with the permission and encouragement of the Council of Elders—covered a wide variety of subjects, from history to science, to building techniques and many popular arts and crafts. One member of the Council, Elder Marsham, was so impressed with the Academy he offered to serve as headmaster. Depending upon whom was lecturing during any given week, one might hear the recitation of lineages, the pop and fizzle of chemical experiments, the scratching of quill on paper, the sawing of wood, or the tones of the lute and pipe. Chrystan believed that a well-rounded child made a productive and happy adult—a lesson he had learned as a page, squire, knight, and as knight-marshal of the Combined Armies of Glittereye. His father's insistence that he continue his academic studies while he was a page and then a squire, although difficult to manage at the time, had given him all he needed to rise through the ranks while acquiring the necessary skills to ascend to the position of baron.

Despite early resistance from a handful of Filgrith's dwindling number of still-loyal underlings, the eight months of Chrystan's time as baron had seen renewed productivity and cooperation amongst the farmers. With the assistance of Sir Peecwyl, chief knight of the Central Barony, Chrystan had brought the incidents of unrest and displays of disloyalty in the first weeks of his transition into steady decline until, with the welcome arrival of spring, they had altogether ceased.

This is what Gregory Gamelsin had learned while working in the fields as he made his way to Elsmore. Through subtle application and weaponization of this knowledge, he intended to interdict himself into the lands surrounding the baron's residence, draw ever nearer to its gates and entry door, and ultimately enter the rooms and life of his target.

He had arrived a quarter of a mile from Elsmore's gates in a wagon full of laborers tasked with doing repair work on the stables and blacksmith shop. He had recognized the son of one of the farmers for whom he had worked gathering men earlier in the day and had requested passage to Elsmore.

"If yer lookin' fer work, my cousin was sick this mornin' an' we're a carpenter short," the farmer's son had said.

"A happy coincidence," Gregory had answered, climbing aboard the wagon. "I am much obliged."

For two days, he worked with the laborers, doing what the supervisors asked, and more, as he had done in the fields, patiently awaiting the time when he had earned enough trust in this surprisingly lax environment to have permission to wander around on his own. When that time came, he knew exactly where to go. He followed the sound of happy children and painfully rendered music to what was now the Academy.

Although the former baron, the fat and ambitious Filgrith, had never met any of the Mellyan agents that nearly succeeded in guiding Garamin to the throne, the Shadow Knife had been well versed in the personalities and histories of those in Glittereye who held positions of power. Looking around, Gregory saw what the reports the Shadow Knife had received since the failed rebellion had indicated. In order for the kingdom to move past the insurrection, its leaders had retreated from any semblance of what Garamin and Filgrith—and that coward in the West, Ralin, who had proven no more pliable than his murdered father—had put into motion with their private armies and fortified castles.

If only the king and his barons knew what they were bringing down upon their heads.

Wiping his hands on a rag from his pocket, Gregory Gamelsin wandered into the Academy just as the six children he had heard were putting their various instruments onto a set of shelves and thanking their instructor for the daily lesson before exiting in a mass of excited, cacophonous chatter.

"Might I help you?" the instructor, a plump woman in her middle fifties, enquired.

"I have heard of the classes conducted for the wee ones, and I would like to humbly but insistently offer my expertise."

The woman shook her head. "All of the instructors are members of the Council of Elders or are otherwise expert staff at Castle Silveth or in a baron's personal service. Are you any of these?"

Hubris, Gregory thought, burying a smile. *It always makes the killing a little more of a joy.* "I am not," he said aloud, "but I am quite skilled in carving and whittling and would be happy to share this skill with anyone wishing to learn." This was, of course, the truth. Gregory's grandfather had developed the skill over years of isolated patrols in the wilderness west of Mellya and had passed it on to his grandchild.

Aldemere's Dilemma

"That sounds like an excellent offer," came a masculine voice from the doorway. "Might you share with us your name?"

Turning around, after shooting a subtle look of victory at the plump, elitist musician, he made a low bow to the well-dressed figure before him. "I am Gregory—a simple farmer and laborer, assigned at present to cutting and shaping roof rafters for the stables. I was given a break and followed the sound of the… the music."

The man returned the bow. "I am Baron Chrystan. Come back after you have finished for the evening and bring a sample or two of your work. Should your pieces prove impressive, I shall arrange for you to stay at Elsmore when your carpentry work is complete. When you are not teaching, I shall pay you for ornament work in the castle."

Gregory again looked toward the woman, who was clenching her jaws at the baron's gracious offer. Winking at her, he said to Chrystan, "But I was told that one had to be in service to a baron or be one of the kingdom's academics in order to teach here."

Chrystan blinked rapidly in remembrance. "I do recall such rules. So let us do things thusly—I shall arrange for the Academy headmaster, Elder Marsham, to be here when you return. If your carving meets approval, you shall first do some ornament work in my employ and, having met that part of the criteria, we shall unleash you on the children."

Gregory bowed a second time as the musician left in a huff. Smiling wide until his jaws began to hurt, he said, "I shall happily do as you ask. Your offer to stay on at the castle would be a gift of the highest value. I shall see you after sunset."

Heading for the stables, Gregory shook his head. *Such a fair and pleasant man*, he thought. *Ending your days shall be my gift to you. You would not be happy nor fulfilled in the world that is soon to come.*

Finishing a long day of preparations with the castle physicians and canning food in the kitchens from the early harvests in the Central Barony, Anastasia entered her chambers with nothing more on her mind than curling up in bed and missing Aldemere for a few tear-filled moments before settling into sleep.

Instead, she found her mother, Queen Cecile, and her mother-in-law, Arianna, awaiting her.

"You are keeping rather late hours these days, my child," the queen said, indicating with a practiced flick of the wrist that her daughter should join them at the table where they sat.

"It keeps my mind and body occupied," Anastasia answered, moving instead to the fireplace and pouring water into the kettle that hung there. "I lift nothing heavy, but the hours exhaust my body to the point that rest comes easy. Glenna Gravenal—"

"Is not at all concerned," Queen Cecile replied, rising, moving swiftly, and returning to the table with her hands on Anastasia's shoulders. "Although I am, and Arianna was nice enough to come with me because she is worried about you as well. Now sit." As she made her command, she gently guided Anastasia into a chair. "I shall see to the kettle."

As her mother walked away, Anastasia looked into Arianna's eyes and found more than sympathy. It was camaraderie.

"I miss my husband, Mother," Anastasia said, launching the first volley in her plotted and planned defense. "As Arianna does her son. Do you know what that is like? I daresay you do not."

If Arianna was already wishing she were somewhere else, she was wishing it all the harder now, and although Anastasia sympathized, she continued. "Father has rarely been away and even rarer has he been in danger, and that is how you prefer it. So do not try to lecture me, or to keep me from coping the best way I know how—the way that will benefit others."

An uncomfortable silence swallowed the air in the room as Cecile took the kettle from the fire and poured its contents into a porcelain bowl on the washstand.

"If I may say something…" Arianna whispered, as Cecile took her seat and Anastasia rose to wash her face.

"By all means," Cecile answered, suddenly unsure as to whose side Arianna was on. "It is why I asked you to come."

"Anastasia is correct. I do miss my son. These past few years I have rarely done otherwise, because, increasingly, from the time Sir Linead first took him from our rooms, I have been without him more than circumstances permit me to be with him. We know virtually nothing of where he is, and what dangers he may be facing. Elde tells me little, mostly because there is much he—and Dylwyn, no doubt—do not know. Why it should always be my son—Anastasia's husband and the father of her child—your grandchild, Cecile—is something for which I have sought answers from the Deities, but I receive no answers. I admire you, Anastasia. You bear a heavy burden, and you bear it with all the dignity and grace of which I often pray I had a tenth."

Anastasia was grateful she had just brought a steaming cloth to her cheeks as Arianna spoke the last of her words so she could blame the redness in her face on the temperature of the water.

"I see it all so clearly now," Cecile quietly replied, staring at her hands in her lap. "I am sorry I have been so blind. Both of you, please, know this. I pray every morning and every evening for Aldemere's safe return and for the avoidance of the war that our husbands, Arianna, are spending so much time behind closed doors trying to prevent. If you will both excuse me," she said, standing and pushing in her chair, "we all could use some sleep. What time shall I meet you in the kitchens tomorrow, my daughter?"

If Anastasia was surprised at her mother's abrupt retreat, she did not let on. "The farmers' children bring in the day's initial harvest just after dawn. We start an hour after. Following the noon meal, I wrap bandages and see to the stocks in the infirmary."

"Then I shall see you in the kitchens an hour after dawn."

"As will I," Arianna offered, joining Cecile at the door. "Unless—"

"You are more than welcome, Arianna," Cecile replied. "My daughter is far kinder to me when her mother-in-law is present."

As her two visitors headed to their rooms, Anastasia closed her door and lay upon her bed. Grasping the Clausmer that lay beneath the bodice of her gown, she held it tight and whispered, "Wherever you are my husband, I love you and pray you are safe. Now hurry back home to Silveth before I murder your troublesome queen."

Much to Aldemere's relief, it appeared as though Boldac had indeed been feeling generous. The horses were where Stanchion had said they would be and, if there had ever been any guards, their superior had called them away or, for some unfathomable reason, they had simply abandoned their posts.

Making matters even easier—a situation Aldemere did not trust— the presence of the Greybaer seemed to have a calming effect on what should have been wild horses. Before Aldmere could choose one for him and Nakret, Simon was hoisting Stanchion—who now possessed a fine-looking sword that he had buried near the tree at the entrance to the mine before his imprisonment—onto an ebony stallion with white and grey speckles.

"Any one will do, Human. Choose and let us be gone!" Nakret hissed, using his remaining arm to prod Aldemere closer to the horses. Eyeing a midnight-colored mare with lean flanks and a well-formed back, he cupped his hands and knelt upon the ground, indicating with his head for Nakret to insert his foot and climb upon the horse.

Without a word, he followed the Eretian onto the horse's back and prodded her into a gallop, Simon following close behind.

What a sight we must make, Aldemere thought, simultaneously cursing under his breath as the Eretian squeezed his mid-section with his arm, which felt like a strap of iron such as the barony coopers employed for binding barrels.

When the four travelers were miles into the woods and beyond the reach of the border patrols, they circumvented rather than fight, Aldemere slowed his majestic mare to a trot. Simon did the same. They had been at a full gallop for nearly an hour and the horses were dressed in a coating of foam and sweat.

After watering the horses and dining on handfuls of berries and nuts picked from nearby bushes, they remounted and headed for the bridge spanning the River Wythe.

Gripping the hilt of his sword, Aldemere prayed that Stanchion's Dwarven god would once again come to their aid.

As the bridge came into view minutes later, he saw that Boldac would not.

"There are soldiers blocking the way," Nakret hissed in his ear. "At least ten of them—well armed. What do you intend to do?"

Stopping his horse and dismounting, Aldemere replied, "I intend for the four of us to cross that bridge. Those are not soldiers. They are hirelings—perhaps pardoned prisoners. They will not fight by the rules of formal engagement. We must be ready for anything." Taking the Slaaver's Hand and knife from his boot, Aldemere tossed the Elven gauntlet to Simon, who slid from his horse and put it on in silence. As the Greybaer faded from view, Aldemere said to Stanchion, "I assume you are skilled with that sword. Once Simon is amongst them, they will scatter, though I doubt that they will flee. The horses are getting tense. We will make them more so and send them into the crowd, disorienting the guards. That should even the odds, if we can get to them quickly enough."

"What about me?" Nakret asked. "I need steel for my defense!"

"We shall have plenty soon enough," Aldemere answered, "or I will be wounded or dead and you can take my knife. Stay behind us for now."

The engagement unfolded much like Aldemere had intended. Nakret proved to be a vicious, unconventional fighter with the sword he grabbed when the first of the clumsy cutthroats fell.

"You work well with sword and dagger, Sir Knight," Stanchion said, standing amongst the dead as Simon appeared beside him. Placing the knife in his boot, Aldemere nodded as Stanchion retrieved two axes, thrusting their handles into his belt. He also took a shield, which he slung upon his back.

"Let me introduce you to Hawkclaw," Dramel announced, holding his sword so it shone in the sunlight. Aldemere thought of Crow Feather. Scanning the field of battle, he selected a bow and two quivers of arrows, while Nakret held fast to his blood-drenched sword.

"See anything you fancy, Simon Greybaer?" Stanchion enquired.

The Keymage shook his mane. Aldemere saw sadness darken the Greybaer's face as he whispered, "I felt the skulls of four of them crushed beneath my hands. I wish to feel no more."

"Your actions are appreciated," Aldemere replied. "You may not believe this, but killing does not come easily nor joyfully to me, although I have had to do more than my share." Scanning the field, he said, "The wild horses have fled. We shall use those two tied to the bridge. I for one will be grateful to have a saddle beneath me and a pair of reins in my hands."

Once they were mounted, Aldemere kicked the bay charger he had chosen into a gallop and said, "We should reach the mountains just about this time tomorrow."

CHAPTER SEVEN

Calrain did his damnedest not to wince or lose his balance as he descended the rough-hewn steps into the passageway of the prison, now lined with empty cells, all in various stages of reconstruction. The soldiers and laborers he passed made no effort to hide their laughter and side-mouthed cruelties. As his accursed luck would have it, the recently demoted, former captain Purloch was standing outside the furthest away of the cells, supervising the installation of new rivets into the iron and oaken framing.

As Calrain limped toward him, he said, "A word with you, Captain, if I may. And a bench and some water would be welcome." Calrain willed his knees to lock and keep him upright as Purloch dismissed the pair of laborers working within the cell. Annoyed at the interruption, he handed his water bladder to his red-faced, out of breath visitor.

"There are no benches here, my lord. Comfort and the cells of Amdar have exactly zero in common. Never shall it be truer, once they are once again ready for prisoners." Rolling a nail keg toward Calrain as he began to slide slowly and awkwardly down the rough-edged, rust-stained wall behind him, Purloch added, "This shall have to suffice."

"Then it shall," replied Calrain, settling his weight onto the barrel's lid as Purloch slid it beneath him. Wiping the sweat from his brow with his sleeve, which was already too wet to be useful, Calrain pulled the cork from the water bladder and took a long, insistent pull.

The water, like the air in the cells around him, was acrid, warm, and stale, but Calrain drank it until his parched and swollen throat began at last to relax.

"You must not call me captain," Purloch said, lowering his voice and turning his body so he was blocking Calrain from view. He did not want the staring soldiers at the other end of the passageway to read their lips as they talked. "A loyal member of the guard, in a momentary lapse, called me captain yesterday and *Captain* Stratten had him whipped."

Calrain pressed the cork into the bladder's gaping mouth with fingers that sang in pain and handed it back to Purloch. "I do not believe that an officer even so ambitious as Carlis Stratten would attempt to have me whipped, although my brother appears far fonder of him than he ever was of you. Or of me."

Aldemere's Dilemma

Purloch clenched his jaw. "Why have you come here, My Lord? Only to tell me what I can already see and hear? Perhaps you are simply gloating! I have helped you as I could, whenever I was able. I never called you Cri—"

"Then refrain from doing so now." Calrain could hear laughter at the other end of the passageway. Turning toward the sound despite his better judgment, he caught a glimpse of a young soldier twisting his hands and back in heartless, angular mimicry. "I do not forget a kindness—rare as they have been since the passing of my parents—and you have shown me plenty, *Lieutenant*. At times at your very peril. Now I wish to return the favor. A chance for your redemption. Your *elevation*, perhaps, depending upon…"

"Upon what?" Purloch asked, growing more impatient. "Tell me what you mean, or leave me to my work before Stratten whips us both."

Pulling himself up using a crossbar from the cell and a ledge on the nearby wall, Calrain leaned into Purloch, as though to keep from falling. "Listen to me," he whispered. "I shall emerge from this war with considerable wealth and power. My brother needs me, and he knows it. Perhaps he shall name me as governor or ambassador to one of the kingdoms our armies shall ultimately conquer. The details are insignificant. Just remember this—wherever I go, I want you by my side. I promise to see it done. You shall be redeemed."

Purloch's look was as cold and hard as the stone and iron to which Calrain's twisted fingers clung. "All because I helped you now and again? I find that hard to fathom."

Calrain nodded. "That is because you are wise. My brother does not see it, but *I* do. I am also rather wise. And *my* wisdom has taught me that a man like you, who has been abused and humiliated, as I have—and by the same persons, no less—shall be a man I can trust when I give him the opportunities I shall give to you. As a means to rebuild and reinforce himself, as you are doing with these cells." Pausing as a bolt of pain shot up his arm, Calrain said, after composing himself, "Do you know what was originally here—before the prison? It was Knorr-Fraga, the ancestral home of the Fragenoars. My ancestor, Feiring, had it razed, turning the subterranean levels into this dungeon, where he transferred many of those who had formerly lived in opulence just above. Do you understand how someone's circumstances can change in the blink of an eye?"

"What must I do?" Purloch enquired, his curiosity piqued.

Releasing his makeshift supports and extending his spine to make his back as straight as he could despite the white-light bursts of pain the effort produced, Calrain replied, "Only what your instincts and wisdom suggest. I shall handle the rest."

Sir Corvit, newly returned to the northern mountains from Vaelsport with two hundred of his knights—primed and eager to continue their fight with the nomads—shook his head in disbelief.

"You will move your camp further south until your army's bloodlust is cooled," sneered Milani, Baron Ciloto's brother, who supervised the amber mines and who had never gotten on with the military. "I can still smell the gore in your hair."

The unpredictability and vacillations of the two brothers over the years of Corvit's time in the mountains had led the war-weary knight to believe that what was actually at work between them was to insist upon the opposite of whatever Corvit advised.

"You do understand whose gore this is, Milani, do you not?" Corvit ran his fingers through his thick tangles of hair, rubbing whatever clung to them between the tips his thumb and middle finger as he spoke. "I have every belief that the three tribes will not stand idle for long in the face of their defeat at Vaelsport. Our period of peace from raids is over. They are going to come here in force. And soon."

Milani, dressed in the expensive attire more suited to a baron than a mine supervisor, laughed so hard that spittle ran down his chin. "I believe exactly the opposite. You have effectively quelled them for now. They have lost all three of their chieftains and all their fiercest warriors. They shall not attack us. Indeed—the loss of their leaders was the very thing that made them give up the last time they attacked these mines."

Corvit pictured the smirk on Milani's face disappearing in a vivid spray of bright red blood extracted by his fist. "Did you not hear all that I have told you? Moktar Caveraider was not amongst them. The Eretians believe that Mellya's ruler ordered the raid and supplied the ships. He shall not suffer in silence such a loss. As I have told you several times, I believe an attack is imminent, if for nothing else, then to sooth their battered egos, or what passes for such in their addled, malformed brains. Do you remember the losses, the horrors, the lot of us endured the last time they made campaign? Yes, we prevailed, but at far too steep a cost."

Corvit could see a cloud of understanding passing over Milani's face. Seizing the opportunity, he pulled a set of drawings from his

Aldemere's Dilemma

saddlebags, spreading them out on a pair of barrels. "We learned a great deal from our previous engagements. I do not expect the nomads to change tactics—such advanced thinking is beyond them. These plans are quick and easy to implement and shall necessitate minimal disruption of your ambir operations. Let me do my duty here, Milani. You do not want our bloodlust to cool. On the contrary—you want those who have returned with me to awaken the warrior's edge in those who remained behind. If you choose to persist in your ill-considered demands, the greater loss of life shall be yours alone to bear. Must I go and see your brother?"

Fingering the gold central button on his tailored, brocaded coat, Milani paused a moment in thought. "You should not. I shall send word to Ciloto regarding what we need to do. I shall fully advocate for it. Until such a time as we hear otherwise, begin your preparations. Under two conditions. No wine or mead for your men, and they are not to enter our camps without permission. Agreed?"

Corvit nodded in lieu of a salute or taking the mine boss's proffered hand in his own.

Once he was alone, he thought, *What I inflicted upon Melak in our final hour together shall seem like benevolence and mercy once I have Moktar to myself.*

He prayed it would be soon.

"It is a sight to behold, is it not?"

Thaker Ungerfil had been making his final rounds, as was his duty as captain of the *Salt-Serpent*, which was sailing under fair winds at full sail midway between Mettlec and Eret, when he came upon Dramel Pilon gazing up at a cloudless, star-filled sky.

The Dwarven prince nodded but kept his gaze upon a bright trio of stars just off the starboard bow.

"Those stars are called Nygla, Kjolr, and Innvior. Our elders teach us their names before we learn our numbers. They are key means of navigation for our fleet."

"They are breathtaking," whispered Dramel, his eyes still fixed upon them.

"That they are," Thaker answered, his voice both solemn and strong. "They have guided many a sailor to safety."

"We are trained to think only of the mountains and ore-filled earth we pile widely and deeply around them," Dramel responded, finally looking away. "It feels as though I am actually seeing the sky for the first time in my life."

Thaker leaned against the bulwark and contemplated the foci of his life in Llafen Eret, which consisted solely of the wish, since he had learned to walk, to leave behind the rocks and dirt of terra firma and sail upon the seas.

The forces that brought he and Dramel together and, by extension, their races and their countries, were far beyond what Thaker knew to be the abilities of the Ruenai or what must also be true of the Dwarven creator god Boldac, but one thing was certainly clear.

Nothing for any of them would ever be the same.

"We shall reach Llafen Eret within the week provided the weather holds," Thaker said, aligning his astrolabe to a star, called Snaeldr, just to the left of the trio, positioned directly ahead. Snaeldr was guiding them home. "You shall be received as a savior by the Grand Admiralty, Prince Dramel. War with Mellya is imminent. They shall wish to strike while we are still searching for our—"

Realizing his near mistake, Thaker abandoned the rest of the sentence.

Dramel, if he noticed, did not ask what Thaker was going to say. Was he aware of the loss of the Stone? Did he think Thaker meant their missing shipwright, Millet Ronng?

"I would like to learn to sail, to command a ship such as this," Dramel said, eyeing the adjustments Thaker was making to the astrolabe. "Mettlec must not keep its citizens land-locked and tunnel-digging, unless they wish to be so and do so. It is time to look upward, into the brilliant, star-laden sky and outward over the seas to other places and ways of living. I have convinced myself that this is the reason why my brother abandoned our family." Twisting his face, he asked, "Are all Eretians forced to be sailors?"

Thaker chuckled and shook his head. "It is a great honor to be chosen for any vocation involving the sea. Carpenters, stevedores, sail-weavers, hull-shapers, rope-makers, and, most importantly, sailors. Yet it is something else again to gain admission to the Admiralty Mast, where we are trained to be officers with the goal of drawing assignments on one of the three-masted ships of the fleet, like the *Salt-Serpent*. Many are disappointed. The Ruenai have blessed us with our knowledge of and prowess upon the seas. To sail is to become closer to Xael, Kaen, and Braen. Our ancestors abused that power, as your histories must also detail. Families such as mine strive to make it right."

"And those who are not fit for the sea?"

Aldemere's Dilemma

"They contribute with the careers and vocations to which they are called and through attending ritual services in our temple, called the Vessel."

"I look forward to seeing such things for myself," Dramel answered, turning his gaze once more to the trio of stars. "Further, I swear to honor and protect the Eretian way of life, Captain Ungerfil. May these stars serve as witnesses to my words."

As the four escapees from the dungeon of Amdar prepared to camp after an uneventful ride—uneventful, that is, if his companions managed to discount Nakret's constant *oohing* and *owching* about his sore and beaten backside—Stanchion suddenly planted his feet and crossed his massive arms.

"Is there a problem?" Aldemere asked, wishing he were already asleep.

"A *pass*? You are asking *me*—a Dwarf—to use a *pass* to cross a mountain? My people *own* the mountains. We go *under* them or *over* them. We do not use a *pass*."

"It is not my intention to cause you embarrassment, Prince Stanchion," Aldemere answered, drawing on every ounce of patience and diplomacy his jester training allowed. "However… these are not Dwarven horses—if such creatures exist. They shall break their legs and therefore lose their lives should we seek an underground route. Besides, we have neither torches, tools, nor time. As for going *over*, the horses shall die of exhaustion before we reach the top. Stathl Pass is our only option. When we are through it, we shall enter the Forest of Tombal, and my mission shall be complete."

Simon gently placed his hand upon the prince's shoulder. "Listen to Sir Aldemere. Sometimes we retain our honor by adjusting how we do things, rather than insisting upon what we know and thereby putting others in danger. I long for a meal of fleetdeer and broadleaf soup whilst sitting amongst my brothers and sisters. Let us get some rest."

In answer, Stanchion twisted a hunk of his ragged beard with enough force to turn his bulbous cheeks a glowing shade of red. After giving the stated points several seconds of his due consideration, he said, "You must never call me prince—it is part of the reason I left my home for foreign lands. I accept your explanation. We shall use the pass."

Realizing in that moment how weary he must be of the Dwarf and the Eretian to be so relieved at Stanchion's effortless change of position, Aldemere wished them all a good night and found himself a thick patch of moss on which to get some rest. He would need it... He intended to run the horses as hard as they could go until they reached the forest.

Although Aldemere had done everything asked of him, it had come at a price. He wished for home, Anastasia's warm embrace, and a few days' rest before heading off again, to face a foe who, the last few nights, had begun to haunt his dreams.

"Carra-shaman. Please come in. I am sorry to bring you from the Vessel at such a time as this."

Carra entered Warden of the Waters Kiegan Hefflar's office, wearing a smile unanchored to her true state of mind. She had been praying for days to the Ruenai with a fervor that the Ruen-Eret were physically and spiritually unable to match. Try though they might to keep pace, they would one by one fall asleep around her as she chanted and supplicated far into the night. She had seen Nomma offering silent thanks to the sky an hour earlier when a runner arrived to summon Carra to the Admiralty.

Nomma. The visions Carra continued to see in the metal bowl of the young priestess accounted for some of the vigor of her prayers. It was not her place to question the Ruenai, although Carra found herself more than once wanting to ask them what it was the visions meant.

"What can I do to serve you, Warden Hefflar?" she asked, with a slight bend of her knees and nod of her head to show she was sincere.

"You can pull up a seat to start," the Warden replied, indicating two cushioned chairs by the office's unused fireplace.

Carra turned quickly for the chairs so Hefflar would not see the surprise on her face. Never once in the dozens of times she had been in this office had he invited her to sit.

The gesture made her nervous.

Placing a chair before the warden's desk, she unobtrusively shifted the bowl in her robes to avoid sitting upon it.

As she sat, Warden Hefflar came around the desk, leaning on its edge.

"I am a bit embarrassed to say this," he said, the red in his cheeks deepening to a shade darker than his eyebrows and beard, "but I do believe the Ruenai are upset with me. Dare I say... immensely displeased."

Resisting the urge to put a comforting hand upon the warden's knee, as she would for one of her priestesses or anyone else who came to her with a crisis of faith or some hidden sin they thought the Ruenai had witnessed, she said, "It would help to have the details, if you are not—"

"Ashamed? Why would I be? My conscience is clean. My wife makes sure of that."

"Then what?" Carra enquired, her curiosity piqued.

"I was out in the harbor yesterday… It was my turn to serve as captain of the single-master *Skor*, as was agreed before Thaker and Dorrin sailed for Mettlec. And… and I nearly capsized her!"

No wonder he is so upset, Carra thought. For an Eretian of Hefflar's station, experience, and reputation, such a mishandling of a ship was a great humiliation.

"Can you guess what might have caused it?" she asked.

The warden's cheeks became fiery red. "We had just raised the sail, and I called to bring her about to catch a bit of wind and see what she would do, when a gust blew up amidships… It had to be the Ruenai, displeased with my being on the water. My crew got her righted before calamity struck, but the looks I received… I dread my next go-round… If I get the chance… If I can convince her crew to trust me…"

Carra closed her eyes and focused on her breath. In her mind's eye, she saw the single-masted ships patrolling the harbor and the triple-masted vessels to the east and west and south. There were dark clouds on the spirit plane above them. The *Skor*'s, however, were the darkest and most foreboding.

Exhaling a forceful breath to send away the vision, Carra opened her eyes and gazed into those of the warden. "I assure you, Warden Hefflar—it is not you. The absence of the Stone is casting a thick and troublesome pall that imperils the fleet in Llafen Eret. Although the Ruenai have allowed the conversion of the ships for the making of war, the energies around them are still in disarray. The Stone is not only a means of instruction; it has energies that govern and manage the waters and winds of Eret. The *Skor* is affected more than are the others. Why? I am not yet sure. I will ask the Ruen-Eret to pray with me tonight for the safety of your ship. This will hopefully prevent any further incidents."

Hefflar found his relief at his own innocence tempered by his concern for the fleet. "Are our other ships in danger? The ones we sent on scattered missions? Have those ships also encountered trouble?"

"I do not sense that they have," Carra answered, standing. "I must return to the Vessel, Warden. Let the Ruen-Eret and me pray upon this matter. In the meantime, my advice is to get back on board *Skor* as soon as you can, for everyone's peace of mind."

"Yes, I shall, Carra-shaman," Hefflar replied, bowing—another first.

Perhaps beyond the clouds, they would find a brighter sun.

"You are nothing but a spoilt *pup*, and your orders are for mongrels!"

Elde the Jester hurried up the Watch Tower steps toward the sound of a voice he had come to know quite well.

"Sir Ambil!" he shouted, turning the corner at the tower's landing to see the venerable old knight with his nose nearly touching Lan's, while several other members of the King's Guard stood in a circle around them, uncertainty tensing their usually confident faces. "What is the cause of your outburst?" Entering the circle, Elde positioned himself between the two knights, reflexively reaching back to place a protective hand upon Lan.

Stepping back and pacing like an agitated beast, Sir Ambil pointed a crooked, deeply scarred finger past Elde's shoulder at the young knight. "This *whelp* is the cause. For over a decade, I have been bell captain, using methods I helped to design. Methods which Sir Laurel—a far greater knight than this *cur* shall ever be—approved. Methods that even your own son, our good jester-knight and captainguard, left virtually intact as he modified the castle's defenses after the Rebellion. But *this* one!"

Removing his hand from Lan's chest, Elde swung his arms forward, creating a barrier with his hands as Sir Ambil took several steps forward toward the target of his wrath.

"*This* one, as you so disrespectfully refer to him, is the appointed captainguard—entrusted with the title by, as you yourself said, our *good* jester-knight. So you shall obey him, or answer for insubordination."

"But his orders are unnecessary," Ambil persisted, although he kept his distance and softened his tone.

Turning to Lan, Elde asked, "What do you wish to modify, Sir Lan, and why?"

"Sir Ambil picks both the tollers and the watchers," Sir Lan began, trying his best to still his shaking hands and voice. "They work in three shifts, these twenty-one men. Day after day, night after night."

"And that is what keeps them sharp!" Ambil interjected.

"That is where we disagree," Lan continued, keeping his eyes on Elde. "Such monotony—such a limited crew of men—puts the castle in peril. All I did was ask him to train three more shifts and allow his present tollers and watchers to accept other tasks, such as armory guards and riding the lake perimeters, once the new rotation begins."

"Why should *my* men—"

"Ah, ah, ah," Elde said, raising his hands a little higher to silence the newly agitated bell captain. "They are the *king's* men, Sir Ambil. They answer to the captainguard. Not to you. You shall carry out Sir Lan's request with due respect and efficiency."

The look the bell captain gave him and Lan as he left the tower landing was one with which Elde was all too familiar from the months before the Rebellion, and it shook him.

Watching through one of the observation windows as Ambil exited the Watch Tower, Elde invited Lan to join him for a walk. Halfway down the stairs, he said, "Aldemere will see the logic in your proposal. I chose not to say that I agreed, for the order must come solely from you. The king may be displeased that I chose to get involved in a dispute amongst the knights, but we cannot afford a break in the ranks. I am proud of you, Lan. Your father would be as well."

Still shaken from the confrontation, Lan managed only a nod.

When they reached the bottom of the stairs, Elde continued. "Sir Prima will be arriving sometime soon, and he shall also be pleased by the actions you are taking. You are becoming everything we had hoped. It is good to see. My son was wise in choosing you to serve as captainguard in his absence."

"Eric would have been even better suited," Lan whispered, straightening his tabard as they exited the tower. "He would not have required your assistance to stand up to Sir Ambil. Although Sir Aldemere stands above us both. It shall be good to have him home."

This time, Elde was the one who could only manage a nod.

High Lord Petror wished that Kal-Gadras could be beside him to witness what his journey of peril to retrieve and return Caecaelev's eyes had done for his mother.

Although her full recovery had taken weeks, Nemmerle now moved with an agility she had not displayed in years. She had a pulsing glow around her that accentuated the whispery lilt of her voice. A glow that far exceeded what she had shown as the representative and manifestation of the Sacred Mother to the Elves of Marlooq Fer.

Despite his nearly three centuries on Mynoweth, the stoic governor-warrior was finding himself grappling with feelings he could not vanquish and was consistently failing to manage whenever she was near. To add to his frustration, he was quite certain, as Nemmerle came toward him in an emerald green gown that accentuated the soft and hard lines of her figure, that she could tell.

"Any word from my son?" she asked, stopping at a table several feet from where Petror stood to rearrange a bouquet of flowers some well-wishing Elf had left at her door.

"None as yet—although that is to be expected," he answered. "There is too much risk of interception by our enemies, and Kal-Gadras would not chance it. We do not know the strength of the enemy's numbers in the eastern forests, but the attack on Baroness Ashlin's home indicates at least some organized presence there. As you are aware, it was the seed-site for Garamin's rebellion."

"I am more than aware, High Lord," Nemmerle replied, the fragrance of the flowers mixing with her own essence and filling the room with a heady scent that required Petror to steady himself against a pillar of oak. "I sense unrest all across Glittereye," she continued. "The air there is thick with thoughts of both rebellion and ambition, just as it was before the Long Winter. Despite the Alliance between my son and the jester-knight Aldemere... Despite the warnings of Ambirgoondrad. It seems, my dear lord, little has changed with the Humans. They are dark-hearted, Petror. Dark-hearted and dangerous."

Watching Nemmerle snap the stem of a bright red orchid for emphasis, Petror felt the spell he had been falling under begin to dispel as he realized that the witch's cure had come with a secret, sinister price.

"Not all of them, friend Nemmerle," he said, approaching the table. "I believe in Elde the Jester, as I do in his son and the king. Although it may have initially unbalanced them, I believe the coming of another Fragenoar to the Centerlands will prove girding when it matters most. Especially one such as Frederick. We must help them to prevail."

"Izmen disagrees."

Ah, Petror thought, *the old mule has come out of his seclusion, and is once more spreading his poison.*

Aldemere's Dilemma

Neither Nemmerle nor Petror knew what had passed between Kal-Gadras and his former teacher after Kal-Gadras's return from Ferrukkla, but it had caused Izmen to retreat into his tower for long lengths of time. When he did emerge, he did little more than scowl and grunt. To a degree even unusual for him.

"You know Izmen's biases," Petror answered, frowning. "Their length and breadth, if not their origins. I beg you to be cautious when listening to his council."

"Cautious I shall be," Nemmerle whispered, lifting the bouquet to her nose and inhaling deeply before removing the flowers from their vase and setting them on the table to begin the arrangement anew. "With his, and yours, and all else's but the Sacred Mother's. On the subject of Glittereye's fate, she has not yet offered her thoughts."

Sensing his dismissal, Petror felt a cold bead of sweat form on the back of his neck.

Whatever the price of the cure, he knew it would be steep.

The two horses Aldemere had chosen after the skirmish at the bridge on the River Wythe had proven to be fleet of foot and tireless, and he and his companions found themselves at Stathl Pass hours earlier than he had planned. Watching the sun begin to set, he urged his horse forward and, much to his relief, Stanchion followed him into the pass without a sarcastic word or show of hesitation.

When they emerged from the other side, they made camp for what they knew would be their last night before entering the Forest of Tombal.

As they prepared to sleep, Aldemere noticed tears in Simon's emerald green, almond-shaped eyes.

"You have missed your home," he whispered. "That is a feeling I know well."

Simon nodded, leaning his considerable bulk against a stout and moss-covered oak. "It has been hundreds of years since I have met an Elf, although we share a deep connection to the land. It was as though I left some of myself behind when the Mellyans forced me from my home. Although we are tens of miles away, I can already feel what I thought I had lost returning to me. Thank you for making this possible."

The next morning, they arose before the sun, packed their meager camp, and rode as hard as their horses could handle. In the early afternoon, as Aldemere and Stanchion led the horses beneath the comforting canopy of Tombal's ancient trees, they began to feel the tension and worries they had been holding fade away. There was a palpable peace in the air. Simon welcomed it with a deep, resounding laugh that seemed to Aldemere to come, not from his lungs, but from his no doubt oversized heart.

"I see that Tombal's majesty is stilling your fretful minds," the Greybaer said as his companions joined him in an audible expression of joy. Even Nakret released a laugh, although it sounded to Aldemere like a rusty pump handle muscled into motion. "Now you understand why Nadrim covets Tombal, and why this forest must be protected."

"Each one's home is the most precious place in the world to him and his people, Greybaer," Stanchion grunted. "Yet I sense a sanctity here I shall vigorously defend."

"Do you also sense the presence of those who daily breathe this air?" Simon asked.

Before any of his companions could answer, a dozen Greybaer filled the forest floor around them, dancing and chanting in delight at the return of their Keymage.

"It is good to see you, friends!" Simon shouted, dismounting and joining them with a spirit and energy that merged with and magnified their own.

"This is a most unnerving display of joy," Nakret muttered, spitting upon the ground.

"Only because you shall not receive the same when your countrymen see you approaching, Nakret the Betrayer," Stanchion hissed, reining his horse toward Aldemere's so that his face was pressed close to the Eretian's.

"You dare to call *me* a betrayer?" Nakret's voice was full of the dark clouds of denial that serve to mask one's secret, deep-seated guilt. "You were fine enough with my betrayal when you needed passage to Mellya!"

"Enough!" Aldemere ordered, staring down the red-faced Dwarf. "We are now the guests of the Greybaer and that is no way for the son of a king to behave."

"Yet your behavior is perfect for a son-in-law of one. Bravo, Sir Knight! Bravo!"

Aldemere turned his gaze toward the dancing crowd of Greybaer for the source of the Human voice, smiling wide as he saw Frederick of the North applauding as he stood amongst Sir Lesster and the other knights of Glittereye, and two others he did not know.

"It is good to see you, my friend," the captainguard said, dismounting.

Aldemere's Dilemma

"And you as well. Your mission looks to have been a success. Quite remarkably, you have also survived the companionship of these two sour souls." Frederick pointed to Stanchion and Nakret, who complied with his assessment by turning their already tense faces into true and proper scowls.

"I had a great deal of help from Simon."

"I have every right to be sour," Stanchion said, climbing nimbly down from the horse as though it were a rocky outcropping five feet from the ground. "This horse is too wide for my legs, I have been subjected to *magic* and the constant prattle of this deceitful Eretian, and I have obviously been lied to."

"How so?" Frederick asked, crouching to meet Stanchion's fiery gaze.

"This Human told me he captained the king's guard," Stanchion answered, gesturing toward Aldemere. "He never told me he was a *prince*."

"Technically, he is not," came another voice from deeper in the crowd, "although he holds more titles than all of us put together."

A voice rich in timbre and pitch, Aldemere knew it well. A voice he deeply missed.

Kal-Gadras, Elven Lord of the South Shore, was in Tombal, and for the first time in weeks, Aldemere allowed himself to believe that, together, they would be able to rally their countries and defeat their ruthless foe.

Leaving Brother Sullus to complete the gathering of carrots, beets, and potatoes they had begun an hour earlier, Dictus brushed the earth from the knees of his robes and turned his attention to the splitting of logs and driving of nails that was part of the expanded stables and corral project Sir Arans's men had started two days before.

After all, if there was to be a permanent company stationed at the Temple of the Seers—and Dictus had every intention there would be—there needed to be a proper place for the horses.

Barracks for the knights would have to wait. Dictus did not want to draw undo attention to the larger scope of his plans.

Not just yet.

He had initially bemoaned the loss of Farvon to the castle—and railed against Dylwyn and Talorous's attempts at using the scholar-monk to undermine Dictus and Vitus's plans for reinsertion of the Seers into the politics of Glittereye. Recently though, he had come to see that he could turn the bargaining chip they had tried to create back to his own advantage.

"This is a welcome sight," Vitus said, appearing from behind the tall stalks of mid-Spring corn that were nearly ready to harvest. "Sir Arans was a brilliant choice, Brother. I applaud you."

"Where is our recently acquired champion?"

"He is praying in the chapel," Vitus answered, pulling a pair of plums from his shoulder bag. "Care for a taste? They are marvelous. My personal tree. Sullus frowns upon it, but I grew it from a pit three autumns ago. I have nurtured and tended it on my own time, my own prerogative, so why should I not take full advantage of its fruits?"

Taking one of the proffered plums and devouring half of it with his large, crooked teeth, Dictus said, "Nowhere is it said that you and I are equal to the others. We have greater responsibility, nobler aspirations, and a surfeit of radiant piety. Now we have Sir Arans. When we sit with him for our talk after the evening meal, be sure to have a few of these juicy beauties to share." Sucking the remaining half of the plum off its pit and noisily down his throat, Dictus, tossing the pit to Vitus, added, "And plant this with a prayer. Two personal plum trees are always better than one."

"Olive, my young one—you are holding the knife too tight. That is why your dog looks like a bear. Relax your hand. All of you—this is supposed to be done with love. So treat your whittling like you would your Ma and Da."

Chrystan had been watching from the back of the room as Gregory moved amongst the dozen or so children who had come to learn the craft of turning wood into wondrous figures through the subtle manipulations of a knife.

When the session was over, the former knight turned baron grasped a broom and began to sweep into a pile the curls of whittled wood littered on the floor, despite Gregory's protestations.

"I am happy to do it," Chrystan replied with a smile. "You have been the most popular instructor at the Academy for nearly a week. I have spoken with Elder Marsham, and he is equally impressed. I would like to speak to you over a meal in my home this evening about staying on here beyond the work on the stables. As part of the Artisan's Guild. Surely, a man so adept at teaching children could teach grown men to work with wood as well. Create some healthy competition with the artisans in the east."

In another place, at another time, with a history far less bloody and barbaric than his own, Gregory would have jumped at the chance. His popularity with the children had not only won over the baron and many of the instructors—the music teacher not included (making her the wisest of the lot)—but some of the older sisters and younger widowed mothers had been arriving early and lingering after class. A few had brought bowls and baskets to his quarters of food far richer and more satisfying than any he could remember.

Thoughts of a wife and child had begun to fill his mind. A simple, nonviolent life as an artisan and instructor was the story he had been writing in his precious idle hours.

Which was why he could no longer wait to spill the blood he had come here to spill.

Later that evening, as he hid beneath a castle-bound cart in a secret compartment he had constructed over several nights while everyone else was sleeping, he would mouth over and over the words that Chrystan had said just before Gregory Gamelsin, assassin of the Shadow Knife, had buried his blade in the baron's neck:

"If you will allow me, Gregory, I shall give you a life that appears to me long overdue and certainly earned by a man as skilled and earnest as yourself."

Focusing on the sound of the wheels as they bumped on the ruts in the road, Gregory went to sleep, leaving all thoughts of such a life as the recently bled-out baron had offered sinking like slugs in the muddy road behind him.

On the day Sir Prima arrived at Castle Silveth, it was not with the hundreds of Western Barony knights he had initially planned on bringing. He arrived alone, carrying the shield and pennoncelle of his murdered son, Eric—three yellow circles on a light blue field. His own shield, with two yellow circles also on a light blue field, lay strapped upon his back.

Linead, Peecwyl, and Connar, the Chief Knight of the Eastern Barony, rode out to meet him. A simple salute in silence was all that they shared.

After an evening of meager soldier's food and quiet reflection, the four knights sat, along with Lan, in a far corner of the Great Hall. Linead stood beside a map of Glittereye and the larger world around it, painted upon cowhide and tacked with daggers to the wall, while the others sat in a tight semi-circle, intent on his every word.

"Sir Corvit shall remain in the north," Linead said, his voice tense and full of purpose. "An attack from the barbarian tribes—perhaps with Mellyan reinforcements and leadership—cannot be far away. Even if they had planned to wait for the larger assault, their defeat in Vaelsport shall have their blood enflamed. I have sent him three hundred knights to reinforce the garrison. As per my orders, the trade wardens from all five baronies now have marshal responsibilities. When our chief knights are away from home—such as Prima and Connar presently are—their trade wardens must remain in their baronies to coordinate local defense."

Prima raised an arm. "Sir Glenmore is a veteran, capable knight. With a portion of Corvit's men holding the desert to the north, the Western Barony is, at present, the safest. I therefore request permission to call for two hundred of our knights to join me here within the week under the arrangements we discussed at Spiltrow."

The knight-marshal nodded. "Send for them as soon as you wish. I appreciate your delaying as long as you did. Sir Connar, I know Sir Abbas is equally capable, and the east has already felt the sting of an attack, making your men all the more ready to fight. Still in all, I wish you to return to the east tomorrow morning. Although the west is for now secure, the villages and forests under your care remain vulnerable. The forests are secretive places, and we do not know how Aldemere and the northerner are faring. The Greybaer must be aided, although your first priority remains the people of the barony."

With Connar's acknowledgment, Linead turned the war council over to Lan and Peecwyl, who reported on the evolving plans to protect the castle and fortify the approaches to the lakes.

"It is my desire to ride with you to Mellya," Peecwyl said, remaining standing as Lan took a seat. "Sir Navvic was chief knight in the past and Baron Chrystan will no doubt be of help in the weeks to come, beyond his political duties."

"I welcome your experience," Linead answered, before turning again to Prima. "And what of Baron Ralin? Will he don a sword and be a leader of men beyond politics? Has he the discipline? Can he forfeit his need for drink?"

"He does and he can," Prima sharply answered. "We have spoken at length on many an evening since the evil event in the east. You need not worry. Although I question the sense in encouraging two of our barons to place themselves in further danger. It seems we are growing, as a country, callous to the loss of our best. This war shall pass, and the barons shall lead us forward, along with King Dylwyn, in peace. Or have we now resigned

Aldemere's Dilemma

ourselves to the spectre of constant war and the casual slaughter of our own?"

"I assure you, Sir Prima, that none of that is true."

All stood at the voice of the king, accompanied by Elde and Talorous. "We have a new opportunity to prove it. A hawk has just arrived. Baron Chrystan has been murdered, and the assassin has not been found."

"You!" Gadrun Grundling bellowed, thrusting his stick into the fire he was tending, sending a shower of sparks into the night as he saw Stanchion Pilon approaching. "I was recently told that you were rotting away in a Mellyan prison. Although I came all this way—*by sea* no less—half of me hoped it was not true and the Human would return without you. Now that you are here, what are your intentions?"

"I do not expect you to understand, Gadrun, why I left or what has happened to me since, but I do now realize that my duties lie in Mettlec. I realized it not long after I arrived in the city of Amdar. I found myself a prisoner before I could correct my error. I had been making arrangements to return, but certain parties made it impossible."

Gadrun felt his heart softening toward the prince, and quickly commanded it not to do so. "I wish I could believe you, but it is beyond my comprehension how the son of the king could have ever become confused about where his duties lie. There is no such confusion on Dramel's part."

"I am sure Dramel has not let our father down," Stanchion said, bowing his head, "but now my mind is clear, and I am ready to join with my family with Hawkclaw in my hand to make our stand against the Mellyans."

Gadrun knelt before him. "You have reversed your decision at a crucial time. Although my sole reason for coming here was to find you, on the king's behalf I have made an alliance with the Greybaer and those in the lands to the south and west of Tombal. Mellya prepares for war and we must be ready to fight. *Why?* Because of *him*!" Gadrun stood and pointed at Nakret Sailweaver as he stepped out of the shadows and stood beside the fire, flanked by Janzalon and Hathom. "The Dwarves of Mettlec shall forever call you Nakret the Betrayer, you Eretian bastard," Gadrun continued, thrusting the charred, pointed end of his stick at Nakret's face. "Why have you come to Tombal? Was your seat at Nadrim's side not adequate for your ambition? Do you wish to add the moniker of *spy* to your list of blasphemous titles? Or did the cliffprince no longer need you once you handed over your people's precious Stone?" Dropping his stick, the red-faced Dwarf raised his hand to strike Nakret a blow, but Stanchion stayed it with his own.

"We must not become like those whom we shall fight, Gadrun," the prince advised. "Let him answer the questions you have posed, if his handlers will allow it."

Grunting with frustration, Gadrun did as Stanchion instructed, although he stood ready to grab the Eretian should Nakret attempt to flee.

"He has thus far given us no satisfactory answers," Janzalon answered. "You will get no argument from us if you need to take more persuasive steps to extract them."

"Well, then, Nakret?" Stanchion hissed, stepping between Gadrun and the target of his questions. "What have you to say in your own defense?"

Nakret look at his accusers defiantly, one by one, before settling his fiery eyes on the tribune. "I did not give Nadrim the Stone. How could you think that of me? I have never seen it, never touched it, as you are well aware. I did my duty, which included investing in the sacredness of the Stone." Softening his gaze and turning to Hathom, he said, "Please—you have to understand. I loved your father, saved his neck—and his ship—and his reputation—on more than one occasion—and he would have let me *drown*! Can you not understand my anger? Perhaps I am lucky to have only lost an arm... but for a helmsman, to be relegated to sailweaver, the job of women and children..."

"Do not ask me for compassion," Hathom answered. "My father had a duty as captain of the *Salt-Serpent* to save his ship and crew. You claim to believe that the Stone is sacred. The Ruenai choose the captains, giving them great power and immense responsibility. I understand aspects of your anger—his promotion to grand captain was ill timed, but also well deserved. He loved you as much as you loved him. I stand witness to his offers of aid, all of which you dismissed with a sneer. Your jealousy has led to betrayal. Even if you did not give up the Stone, there is much for which you are guilty."

Nakret shook his head. "It is true that I sought audience with Nadrim through his brother, Calrain Crickback. I thought only to oversee their shipbuilding, which I had no reason to believe they would turn to the making of war upon our people. In the end, it was all of it pointless... Rather than accept my offer, they instead

275   *Aldemere's Dilemma*

coerced Millet Ronng. They cast me aside, just as did your father! I was in prison, awaiting execution, when the Human reluctantly freed me."

"Again you spit out your bitterness! Do not use the gallant and appropriate actions of Athes Ungerfil, greatest of our captains, as an excuse for what you have brought upon the lands of Mynoweth, you bastard!" Janzalon suddenly shouted, shoving the one-armed Eretian backward several feet. *Did you tell them about the Stone?*"

"Janzalon—your actions are inappropriate here in Tombal." Simon and Gidon had been watching from the treeline, and now came forward, the Regencymage's voice simultaneously peaceful and powerful. "From what you have told me of your station and traditions, this is not the behavior of a tribune of the seas. I understand betrayal… but you must not let your emotions rule your actions."

Janzalon nodded. "You are of course correct, Regencymage. I apologize."

"What is to be done with him?" Gadrun Grundling asked, secretly sorry that he had not put his hands on the Eretian traitor the instant he had the chance.

In a quiet, measured voice, Janzalon said, "He shall return with us to stand trial in Llafen Eret, which shall no doubt have to wait until the war is over. The Admiralty shall mete out his punishment, as seen fit by my fellow tribunes and me, according to the will of the Ruenai. In the meantime, Nakret, you shall look for opportunities to, in some small way, redeem yourself. While you do so, keep away from those you betrayed."

As Janzalon walked away, he heard Nakret softly sobbing.

"If you can spare a moment, I am anxious for news from the west."

Kal-Gadras placed his newly restrung bow to his side and smiled at his long-awaited friend. "In every corner, of every building, of every village and barony, and in the whole of Glittereye and Marlooq Fer, our peoples ready for war. You have not missed a thing, at least politically and militarily, in your time away from home. It is true that we have all become adepts. Used to the condition of war. Children run in the streets fighting each other with swords made of sticks, and maces made from tightly compacted mud. They laugh as they fall, as if death were not so serious. It is inspiring to behold."

The smile Kal-Gadras was wearing was so at odds with his tone and the meaning of his words that Aldemere wondered for a moment if he was engaging the wrong Elf. This sounded more like Izmen.

Then the contradiction became clear.

"You are being sarcastic," he said, picking up the bow and sitting beside his friend. "You should not be. It is wordplay fraught with peril. Leave that to us Humans."

Kal-Gadras shook his head. "I thought such things as irony and sarcasm were the wise Human's way of dealing with stressful situations... An alternative to anger and panic."

"They are," Aldemere said, patting the Elf on the knee. "Although you are wise, friend Kal-Gadras, what you are not, for which I am grateful, is Human. Nor should you aspire to be. It is the Humans of Mynoweth who have brought war and despair upon all the other races—the Elves just only recently. I fear I have gotten the best of the bargain from this complex bond we share."

Kal-Gadras did not argue. Instead, he said, "My mother and High Lord Petror have found my spirited, abruptly changing moods and emotions difficult to deal with. I have learned, however, some valuable things that will be useful when peace returns. Make no mistake—some Elves are all too Human in their actions, and a mystical bond between them and one from the north of us has nothing to do with it. Or mostly nothing..."

Once upon a time, Aldemere would have insisted upon clarification. Now he welcomed the ambiguity. Kal-Gadras had clearly chosen not to identify the subject of his statement, and his friend respected the tactic.

Aldemere suddenly realized he was thinking like an Elf.

Having so much to contemplate, they sat awhile in silence, which Kal-Gadras gently broke. "What do you make of Nadrim and the militant state of Mellya?"

"They are one and the same. That is the essence of his reign. He nearly pulled my teeth from my gums in a torture chamber that appeared frequently and ruthlessly used. He is horrific to his brother, who suffers from physical maladies that leave him hunched, weak, and in constant pain. He controls the military and his political advisors—who are naught but puppets—through fear and brutality, pitting them against each other. Worst of all, he enjoys it, how they all compete to match him. He is Garamin times twenty."

"Can we defeat such a foe, my friend?"

How Human the Elf still sounded. It made the captainguard shudder.

"I honestly do not know," Aldemere whispered, turning away and focusing on the curve of the Elven bow. "The children of Mellya—or at least of the capital city of Amdar—do not play at fighting. Their fathers train them from a very early age. They see all other races as threats—and their fellow Humans in the Centerlands as inferior and weak. They condemn us for denying them their rightful place. How and why, I have not yet discovered. We need to trust the northerner. Frederick knows the history, context, and gaps better than do our scholars. I need him to return to Glittereye with me, after a final war council here in Tombal. I long to see Anastasia, to feel our child moving inside her, and if I could, I would have been on my way already. But now I must be selfless." Handing the bow to Kal-Gadras, he asked, standing, "How is your mother?"

"She is improving. My adventure with the witch was certainly not for naught."

"I am quite relieved to hear it. We are overdue at home. Let us call the council, so we can then be on our way."

The sun was just appearing above the swells that met the horizon when the *Salt-Serpent* and *Sea-Sprite* entered the docks at Llafen Eret. Despite the early hour, a sizable crowd had gathered to see them home, including Warden Hefflar, Carra-shaman, and tribunes Kaelhul and Mastmin.

Giving the order to secure the ship, Captain Thaker Ungerfil called together his first officer and navigator, as well as Dramel Pilon, so they could leave the ship as a unit, coordinating their debarkation with Dorrin Waelsbun and his officers, followed closely by Prince Affram the Second and the Trinity Council.

"Welcome home to Llafen Eret," Warden Hefflar said with a smile, placing a hand on each of the captain's shoulders. "I trust the Ruenai guided you home without incident?"

"They did indeed," Dorrin said, looking toward the tribunes and around the dock for his father. "Has the *Sea-Sword* yet to return?"

"It has not," Tribune Mastmin answered. "Although there is no reason for concern. I am sure your father and Undersecretary Ungerfil are fine."

Stepping aside and bringing his arm toward their visitors, Thaker announced, "I am sorry to change our heading, as it were, but I wish to present the contingent from Mettlec. This is the Trinity Council. Three identical brothers, they serve as advisors to King Buttress Pilon. They shall serve as ambassadors through the duration of coming events." After the nervous threesome and the Eretian dignitaries made an exchange of formal greetings, Thaker continued. "These are two of the king's three sons—Prince Affram the Second. And Prince Dramel."

By his shift in tone from dismissive to reverent, it was clear to all present which of the two princes Thaker held in higher esteem. To all, that is, except Affram, who was busy fiddling with his double-bladed axe.

"We look forward to holding council with you all," Warden Hefflar said, "following a fine feast to welcome home our crews. We shall have accommodations prepared in our most elegantly appointed rooms."

"We do not require much," Dramel said with a bow. "There is much in need of doing. We shall begin offloading the new iron prows and weapons of war as soon as you wish."

While the captains and members of the Admiralty spoke with the Dwarves, Carra-shaman approached Silbern.

"Might I have a word, First Officer Skarling?" she asked, motioning to a spot behind dozens of barrels and crates.

Once they were out of earshot, Silbern asked, "Does this have to do with Nomma? Because she and I have broken no rules. My honor—and hers—are intact."

Raising her brow and smiling, Carra said, "You certainly are direct—as I know the best of our officers are. I shall be as well. I have had visions of the future. Of the war to come and of dark and dreadful things that shall happen as a result, and I—"

"Silbern Skarling! You are needed on the ship!" came a voice from the dock.

"This shall have to wait," Carra said softly. "Visit me in the Vessel the first chance you get. If I am able, I shall arrange for Nomma to have time with you as well."

"That is much appreciated, Carra-shaman," Silbern said, heading for the dock. As Carra followed, she saw stevedores rolling several devices, made of iron and set on wooden carriages with oak and iron wheels, down ramps from the *Salt-Serpent* and *Sea-Sprite*. "What are those?" she asked Thaker, cold sweat beading on the back of her neck.

"The Dwarves call them thunder guns. They work similar to our catapults and rail-mounted crossbows in the sense that they hurl projectiles, but they use a controlled explosion in the back of the iron tube that forces out a solid iron ball with tremendous speed and power. A single ball can devastate a ship when properly aimed."

Aldemere's Dilemma

"What accounts for the explosion?" asked Carra, sweat now trickling down her back.

"A black powder developed by Dwarven alchemists," Thaker answered. "The contents of which none of our passengers claim to know."

Recalling some of the scenes she had witnessed in the bowl, Carra whispered, "If these devices shall win the war, then the Ruenai shall bless their use, although such destructive inventions as these shall not be employed without a price. So use them wisely, Captain Ungerfil, with great humility and, as soon as you are able, send them back from whence they came and forget that they exist."

Thaker was about to answer when he was also called away.

Carra clutched the bowl, secure within her robes, and knew what she must do.

Whether or not the Ruenai would permit it, she had no way to know.

PART THREE

CHAPTER ONE

"With all due respect, Your Highness, the fate of this kingdom—and of Mynoweth herself—must not rest upon the shoulders of a single individual, no matter how skilled and indispensable Captainguard Aldemere has proven himself to be."

King Dylwyn looked out amongst those gathered in the throne room—the members of the Academic Council, Sir Linead and a handful of the kingdom's most trusted knights, including Sir Peecwyl and Sir Lan, and the monarch's trusted advisor, Elde. All were nodding in agreement with Sir Prima's pointed warning.

Heralds had sent word to the other four baronies regarding the murder of Baron Chrystan and the need for heightened security around Ashlin, Tooras, Ciloto, and Ralin. No one had thus far been able to identify the assassin. Despite Sir Linead dispatching units from the castle and Elsmore with the sole focus of finding and apprehending what they presumed was a single man, they had uncovered not a clue.

"Do not misunderstand me, Sir Prima," Dylwyn said, rising from his chair. "I do not place our fate solely on the shoulders of our captainguard. But the intelligence he has hopefully gathered will make us stronger, and we should wait a little longer to have it."

"*Swords and horses and plate and resolve*," Prima answered, with a tone that caused many in the room to avert their eyes. "Those things make us strong! Petty machinations have rocked us further and further backward since Filgrith and Garamin first began to plot. If our destiny is once more to be our own, we must delay no longer. Let us take the fight to them, as I have been urging since the murder of my Eric!"

Dylwyn could sense that Prima's stance was popular with many in attendance and would only be more so amongst the knights of Glittereye. It was clear on the faces of Linead, Peecwyl, and Lan. They were men of action. Chrystan's death had made it as personal for Linead and Peecwyl as Eric's had been for Prima and Lan.

In Peecwyl especially, who had given his eye and more in defense of Glittereye, Dylwyn saw a burning that intensified with every minute that passed.

"We will not ride for Mellya until Aldemere has returned and made his report," Dylwyn said, the set of his jaw and intensity in his eyes defying anyone to argue.

Aldemere's Dilemma

"And what of Frederick?" Talorous asked, puffing calmly on his pipe. "Do we trust him? Will we follow his counsel should he return and offer to give it?"

"Where is this fabled northerner?" Prima asked, softening his tone but not his gaze. "I know many of my comrades vouch for his sincerity, but he is off in the eastern woods—under guard by Lesster and his men, as Linead wisely ordered. He still has not answered for the wrongness of his assessment of the situation at Eerbell, which led to needless deaths. Must we now wait on him as well? What of the Elves? Must we also—"

"*Stop*." Sir Linead's voice was the edge of a sword run upon a whetstone deprived of water. "We understand your loss. Now we bear another. We have lost many—you are right. I shall not dishonor any of them, however, by using words like *needless*. We hold our titles because of their deaths—you, Peecwyl, and myself. Others shall ascend to replace us when our time arrives to die, although we do not serve the dead. We serve the king, and he has spoken. What good has ever come of a soldier forgetting his place?"

"Sir Linead speaks wisely and well," Elde said quietly from the floor before the throne. "I am no knight, but I know an array of dangers await you in the mountains before Mellya. Nadrim craves a provocation. He jabs at us from numerous fronts, inviting us to charge in blind, with fury masking our vision. That is reason enough to refrain. We still have much to do. If Sir Linead feels it prudent, call for your men, Sir Prima, but do what you must to ensure that Baron Ralin remains safe. We cannot afford to lose him. If willed so by the Deities, both Aldemere and Frederick shall soon return to Silveth. We know that Kal-Gadras sailed for Tombal. The Elves will follow his council. You shall have your vengeance soon enough."

In the stillness that followed Elde's effective eloquence, Linead said, "We must see to the last rites and offer a final farewell to our murdered comrade, Chrystan. Once we lay him to rest, we shall ready for the fight. Let us be united. Let us then prevail."

As tensions mounted in Glittereye, all those gathered in Tombal took their seats at White Rocks for a final council before going their separate ways.

When everyone was still, Gidon Greybaer offered a simple welcome and motioned for Aldemere to stand and address the assemblage. "As captainguard of Glittereye," he began, "I am authorized to speak for King Dylwyn in all matters pertaining to his safety and the safety of those residing in Castle Silveth. We must not permit Nadrim of Mellya to further his violent aims. He possesses an army, well trained and eager to fight, and his ships are almost certainly ready to sail. I was not able to get a look at them—not that I would know what I was seeing beyond anchors, sails, and hulls, but it is clear that he wishes to wage war upon the water as well as upon the land. With this in mind, I call upon Nakret Wilsbern to share his expertise with the council here assembled."

The expected grunts and groans from the two attending Dwarves echoed off the rocks as the contingent from Eret shifted apprehensively in their seats.

Shooting Aldemere a look of embarrassment, Nakret cleared his throat and stood. "Thank you, Human, for acknowledging my expertise." He did not break eye contact with Aldemere as he spoke. "Millet Ronng was, as my fellow Ereti know, our most accomplished shipbuilder. Before he died, he shared his knowledge—under torture and fear of death—with the Mellyans. A death they delivered when he refused to tell them anything about the Stone of the Ruenai. For a time, I oversaw aspects of the construction of their ships, and I will tell you, they are—with the exception of having rudders not made of Tirili ore—as seaworthy as though they were built by our ablest craftsmen."

"There is another distinction! Those ships are not blessed by the Ruenai!" First Officer Eglin Bront shouted, standing, although he was well aware that to interrupt a speaker at White Rocks was a serious breach of protocol. "You speak blasphemy, Nakret One-Arm. It is a fool who thinks your council will be accepted by any of us!"

"Although I am a jester, in the family tradition," Aldemere interjected, "I am no fool. Do you believe we can afford to refuse even a single ally, First Officer Bront, if they are willing to fight... to lend their strength and skill to our cause? I may not know ships, but I know trained and able soldiers, and the Mellyan army has both. I do not question the might of your deities—we have our own, and daily beseech their blessings—but make no mistake. The Mellyans are a dangerous, perhaps unconquerable, foe."

Gidon Greybaer nodded at Aldemere to let him know that he approved of how he had handled the interruption and to continue as he wished. Waiting until Eglin Bront and Nakret Wilsbern took their seats, the captainguard continued. "We now know that Nadrim has bargained with the tribes of the Unsettled Wilderness and shall use them to enter Glittereye while his armies move south and his ships sail for their targets—which I am certain include the sacred shores

Aldemere's Dilemma

of Tombal and even Marlooq Fer. I have come to believe Nadrim has been using the barbarians in his machinations for years, although I am still parsing exactly how."

Watching Aldemere take his seat, Gidon motioned for Simon Keymage to speak.

Looking upon all those gathered at White Rocks—Aldemere and Frederick and their Human companions, the four Eretians, the two Dwarves, and the Elf and his formidable bowmen—Simon bowed his head, inhaling deeply and holding the breath inside his chest before releasing it with a huff. Keeping his head down, he said, "All of us, as representatives of our races, must make an alliance, which you then must bring to your leaders for ratification. Time is short and the cliffprince will be moving with much greater haste now that his most precious prisoners have escaped. Do not doubt anything that Aldemere and Nakret have said to us today."

Saying their goodbyes and promising to do what Simon requested, the Eretians and Dwarves headed for the *Sea-Sprite*, and their return to Llafen Eret. Aldemere, Lesster, and the other knights and Frederick and his companions, Christoph and Martin, after making a similar promise, prepared to head west with Kal-Gadras until they reached the River Mirra, which he alone would follow south to Marlooq Fer. His bowman were returning home in their single-masted ship, but the Lord of the South Shore wished to hold further council with Aldemere and Frederick.

As Aldemere mounted Poet—whom Sir Tagen had wisely taken excellent care of in his absence—and prepared to depart, he thought of the words Gadrun Grundling had said to him, bowing, before he left. "You are truly a noble Human, Aldemere. As are your companions. We knew of your race only through the machinations and cruelties of the Mellyans. It is my hope that our two countries will grow our alliance in times of peace as well as throughout the coming months of war."

Bringing Poet alongside Kal-Gadras's borrowed horse (which Aldemere had taken from the Mellyans), the captainguard said, "It seems as though your mother's visions of our future are now beginning to manifest. I pray we are up to what our deities demand."

"Do not lose your faith, friend Aldemere," Kal-Gadras responded. "They know better than us what roles we are destined to play, together and apart."

Although he had no desire to sail the seas, Nadrim had always felt more alive with the salt air that pervaded the shoreline in his nose.

Although the decision to build Amdar on the eastern shore of the bay was a strategic decision on his grandfather's part—protected as it was by the hooked and fortified spars of land known as the Raven's and Falcon's Prongs—Nadrim believed that Ravin had felt it too. Although the Ereti had repeatedly refused to share their shipmaking expertise with the Mellyans, there had always been an attempt, however feeble prior to Nadrim, to have a presence upon the seas.

Looking out over the harbor in the Bay of Philod—filled as it was with the thirteen three-masted and eighteen single-masted ships he would soon release to the winds to begin his long-awaited war—Nadrim could feel his grandfather, as well as his great-grandfather, Rogen, beside him on this most glorious of days.

"Do you wonder what father would think of your plan?" Calrain enquired, struggling up the makeshift stairs that led to the platform from which Nadrim would address the crews before launching his lethal armada.

The cliffprince expelled a barbed burst of air and answered, "No, I do not. Other than naming the bay for himself, he lacked the vision for such an audacious endeavor as this. He and mother could think of little else other than your deformities. Needless worry, as it happens. You are doing absolutely brilliant, brother, are you not?"

Better than you know, Calrain thought, leaning his weight on the podium to relieve the strain on his legs. "Perhaps… although I am certain my troubles are fewer than yours."

"How so?" Nadrim asked, wishing he had not engaged his sibling in conversation.

Calrain brought his swollen, crooked fingers to his chin in mock contemplation. "Let me see. Although you make a great show of things with your harbor filled with warships, Millet Ronng is dead, the sailweaver has escaped, and not even one of your ships has a rudder of Tirili ore. Worst of all, you have given little to no thought as to how wood from the forest of Tombal will behave when your men o' war approach the realm of the mystical Greybaer and come within range of their magic. You could have asked their Keymage, but he made his escape with Nakret and the Dwarf. Who is a *prince*, no less. And you have come no closer to acquiring the Stone of the Ruenai."

Nadrim, who had weathered his brother's verbal storm by the very slimmest of margins, resisted the urge to push Calrain from the platform. "Anything else?" he enquired, the look in his eye daring his brother to answer.

287   *Aldemere's Dilemma*

"Only this," Calrain said, lowering his voice as the Amdarian nobles and military leaders began filing onto the platform. "Without the Stone, the triple deities might very well dash the ships to pieces as they reach the shores of Eret, despite the pains you have taken to train your crews. There are no gods on your side in this, my brother."

Instead of answering, Nadrim turned away to receive congratulations from the growing mass of men upon the platform. Calrain looked with satisfaction at the bright red patch of heated skin on the back of his brother's neck.

"Good day to you, Lord Crickback."

Calrain maneuvered his inflamed torso around with the least amount of flinching and twitching he could manage to face his detractor, whom he knew to be Carlis Stratten, captain of the Guards of Amdar. Beside him was the man he had replaced, Davus Purloch. Ignoring the current captain, Calrain asked, "How go the renovations to the prison, Captain Purloch?"

"As I continually remind you, my lord," Purloch replied, indicating the insignia on the left breast of his uniform, "I am merely a lieutenant."

"Old habits," Calrain replied, smiling through his pain. "And future hopes."

"Progress is satisfactory, at best," Stratten interjected, pushing his way past. "Pray you are never chosen for occupancy in one of my cells, Lord Crickback. It is not the wine cellar for the royal family that it once was."

As Captain Stratten joined the other military commanders gathered in groups around the platform, Purloch put his mouth to Calrain's ear. "I do not know what game you have in motion, my lord," he whispered, "but you are risking these men's wrath. You would be wise to still your tongue." Straightening his jacket, he added, "If you will excuse me, my father arranged for my presence here today. I had best be by his side."

Like all Amdarian officers, Purloch was the son of a nobleman. Garven Purloch was as powerful and wealthy as Nadrim permitted an Amdarian to be. Having made his fortune in stone quarries and plaster manufacturing, he headed several committees and oversaw a large swath of acreage south of the city.

It was for these reasons that Davus still lived and breathed.

When the attendees had assembled and seated themselves, including the five ministers of Mellya—the castrated men who had sacrificed future family for their posts—Nadrim took his place at the podium. Below him, more than a thousand naval officers and sailors stood at attention while the Mellyan flags snapped in the breeze at the tops of their masts.

"Today is a day often dreamed of and planned for by the long line of my Damonessa predecessors," Nadrim began, his voice deep and resonant with confidence and pride. "It was Feiring Damonessa, over two hundred years ago, who first saw that Lyseum had been corrupted, its once-great ideals—forged as they were by generations of Damonessa ministers—had been twisted for the purposes of fortune and ego and idle artistic and pleasurable pursuits by the self-appointed Mountain Regents, the Fragenoars. My great-grandfather continued the work that Feiring had started to correct these atrocities. He also founded our capital city and named it Amdar after expelling the decadent regents from their opulent den of degradation, the palace of Knorr-Fraga. We must not forget to honor my grandfather, who eradicated the remnants of the rebels of Lyseum and, by burning her libraries, freed our people from the memories and propaganda of the tyrants of the past."

Nadrim paused as applause erupted from below and behind him.

"This fleet I see before me is both magnificent and mighty," he continued, after letting the clapping go on for a full minute longer than Calrain thought any reasonable speaker should, "and our newly commissioned sea captains and their crews, and the land forces that shall accompany them, committed and capable. Soon you shall depart—some of you for Llafen Eret and the shores of Mettlec, to conquer countries who have dictated to us for far too long where we can go and with whom we can trade! They have laughed at you, my proud people of Mellya, but not a single moment more! Others of you will go to Tombal and on to the lands of the Elves, both of whom use unnatural and unholy energies to manipulate Mynoweth, a practice they taught to wizards who lived amongst the Lysean usurpers. The rest will go to Vaelsport, to eradicate the abomination of cross breeding that is the Eretian–barbarian population, and to secure one of the strategic gateways representing the threat to our future that is the Centerlands of Glittereye. What you will find in all of these places is the half-hearted defense that accompanies cowardice. These races that we are compelled to conquer rely on ancient, misinterpreted myths of the supposed power of gods who do not exist. Why? Because they have no faith in themselves or their so-called leaders! They may put up a fight as their priests pray and their females offer incense and animals' blood upon sterile, odiferous altars, but, in the end, we

Aldemere's Dilemma

shall easily overcome them. How could we, who rely on ourselves alone for our prosperity and safety, be defeated? Prepare yourselves and your ships, my proud sons of Mellya, for upon tomorrow's tide, you sail to claim what is rightfully ours! And when you return to this bay—which I re-name today, in your honor, Victory Bay—you shall be hailed as heroes and draped in the spoils of war!"

As the harbor erupted in renewed applause, Calrain sat in wonder—with a guarded but palpable, inescapable admiration—at his brother's facility with words. In a handful of minutes, he had deified the Damonessas—all but their father, whose name he had erased not only from history, but geography—and disemboweled all the other countries of Mynoweth with a single thrust-and-slice of his poison-tipped knife of blatant lies, all while whipping his own countrymen into a frenzy of bloodlust and bravado.

It was clearer than ever to Calrain what his mother and father's ghosts had been urging him to do through signs, shadows, and whispers since their deaths.

The only questions were: when, where, and how?

Moktar Caveraider shifted his position to relieve the pressure of the sharp ambir outcropping digging into his mid-section as he considered the movements of the leader of the northern army of the Humans—the weak-built race that once wore shiny plates on their torsos and fought in bunches that made them easier to kill than deer. They had changed their ways when the one with the colored shapes on his shield had arrived. The one whose men had killed the chieftains of all three tribes, ending their months-long war.

The one that he now watched—called Corvit—moved with an agility and purpose that he had lacked in the time when his men sat amongst their dying horses and their own waste in their camps while the barbarians made their uncontested raids. The one from south of the mountains had transformed him—made him again a warrior.

Nadrim had not been pleased.

Moktar Caveraider disagreed. With the other chieftains dead, it now was Moktar's time. Then the Mellyan had forced him to wait.

He bristled at the waiting. Now the waiting would end.

Moktar pulsed with anger. Anger at having to journey to Amdar, to sit in servitude to a Human whose head he could easily crush to powder between his hands. His and that of his brother, to whom Moktar also bowed, even though this Human could barely walk and could not lift a warrior's shield.

The Caveraiders would have killed such a weakling at birth, leaving the carcass for the wolves. Not even a Riverskab would devour the flesh of a cursed and twisted creature such as Crickback.

Moktar had gathered his warriors and left the Mellyan capital soon after Nadrim's insults and slaughter of the messengers that brought word of the defeat of the barbarian horde at Vaelsport. It was only the cliffprince's agreement to let the tribes attack the mines—as was their overdue right—that prevented Moktar from drinking his blood.

The time would come when Nadrim would pay for his threats and insults.

Moktar's father, the former Caveraider chieftain, had been foolish to talk his Krag and Riverskab counterparts into doing Nadrim's bidding. The Mellyans had nothing to offer, Moktar told him. All the nomads needed, they had always taken on their own.

His father repaid his disagreement with an hour of kicks and blows from the chieftains and their lieutenants.

It mattered not to Moktar. Cuts and bruises heal. What pained him still was the fact that his father did not live to see the nomads' defeat, to see his son was right—that he had failed the Caveraiders twice.

Melak's raid by boat of the faraway home of the corrupted nomad relatives had not been, in Moktar's unusually coherent mind, a wise decision either. Word of Melak's defeat had come as no surprise to Moktar. A good warrior, but a dim-minded, reckless leader. That was Melak.

Had he returned, Melak would have made a challenge. So why should Moktar mourn him? The Caveraider chieftain had more urgent occupations than taking the time to slaughter a friend determined to take what was his.

Releasing a stream of gas, Moktar wondered: Had it been the Human leader of the *knights*, as they called themselves, this Corvit he now studied, who had ended Melak?

If they survived the initial attack, Moktar would take from him the answer before taking from Corvit his life. The answer would determine the mode of the Human's death.

Shielding his green, grey-flecked eyes from the blinding midday sun, the Caveraider chieftain ranged his vision across the mountains and the sprawling mining camp. The sounds of winches and pulleys and the attention the Human workers showed to their tasks masked the movement Moktar sought. The movement into

Aldemere's Dilemma

position of the Riverskabs and Krags who would rain down spears and flaming arrows at Moktar's silent command.

They had appointed no new chieftains in the absence of Kull and Bokk.

Moktar now was chieftain of all the nomad tribes.

Chieftain here, and chieftain to the members of the three tribes who now lay in wait to the west, beyond the mountains, in the Unsettled Wilderness (which the nomads called *the dirt*), where the Humans had a pair of strongholds. The rising smoke from the burning garrison below them would be their signal to strike.

A daytime attack, in windless, stormless weather. A coordinated assault with the three tribes intermixing their weapons, tactics, and methods of brutality. The Humans, who had learned well their former ways, would not know who it was that was hitting them. They would have no context, no experience, as in the days before the Mellyans.

In the days when the nomads were free.

Watching as Corvit lit his pipe and perched a boot upon a tree trunk, Moktar raised his hand and signaled his men to descend.

Helkirk Nagelbrau, captain of the Shadow Knife, was exiting his rooms after a prolonged and potentially fruitful session with Deanna Callenhor, when he spotted Calrain Crickback lurking like a wraith within the shadows beyond his doorway.

"Are you enjoying the privileges that come with your station, captain?" Nadrim's brother enquired, poking his tongue through his teeth like a jackal.

"It is not your business to ask," Nagebrau replied. "You are breaking tradition by coming to my quarters. The Shadow Knife have earned our boundaries, which are not to be disrespected by a cripple such as you."

"Indeed," Calrain replied, making no move to depart. "Boundaries are important, and not only for the Shadow Knife. They exist for the ruling family and the families of our nobles. These boundaries extend, in spirit, if not law, to the lesser nobles as well. Even to the dead ones."

"Someone's been telling tales," Helkirk hissed, taking a step toward his accuser. "Supposing you tell me who?"

Calrain urged his body upwards to meet Helkirk's hateful gaze, despite the shock of pain it sent surging through his pelvis and legs. "What is the point of employing spies if you give them up for slaughter after a powerless request such as yours?"

Without averting his eyes, Calrain attuned his senses to see if Helkirk's hand was flexing in anticipation of moving toward the multiple weapons he knew he hid beneath his cloak.

If it was, it was subtle, like a coiled viper seconds before it struck.

"What makes you think I am powerless against anyone but your brother? Look at yourself, you wraith—you can barely walk. What power do you believe you wield here?"

Helkirk leaned in a little closer.

"Simple," Calrain said, savoring each syllable as he spoke it. "The Shadow Knife cannot harm, much less kill, someone of my station without express command of the cliffprince. If it ever comes to my brother wishing me dead, he shall do it himself."

"What is it you want?"

"To have the respect that I am due. And to ask you to give me the girl."

Helkirk laughed. "Do you want to *borrow* her?" he asked, his eyes demonic in the torchlight. "You should have asked up front and skipped this ridiculous posturing. The answer, regardless, is no. Although, when I am fully finished with her, and she has delivered to me a son, I shall gladly *sell* her to you. For a night or two at least."

Calrain matched the captain's laugh while placing a blade beneath his chin. "You shall not live to see a child born, should she hold your vile seed, which I pray is not the case. So I ask for the final time—release Deanna to me."

Lowering his head so the point of the knife pierced the skin of his neck, Helkirk whispered, "What I might do to you in my own defense has nothing to do with the safeguards you have been spouting about, you worthless *crickback*. Now is not the time to make a play against me. Not with operations in Glittereye already underway."

Calrain hesitated—just a moment—before lowering the knife. "Is that so?" he asked, wiping away a spot of blood that clung to the tip of his blade with a corner of his cloak.

Helkirk produced a smile as the blood flowed down his neck. "It is indeed. The baron was dispatched and the assassin is on to Silveth."

Calrain stepped backward several feet, sheathing his knife and twisting his body into a bow. "Then you are wholly correct, Captain Nagelbrau. I have no business here. Your star is on the ascent. I shall seek a trained and eager female somewhere else."

"A noble try it was... Lord Calrain," Helkirk answered, stepping past his visitor's twitching form. "If you will excuse me, I have worthier places to be."

293

Watching Helkirk walk away and noting well the strut in his step, Calrain whispered, "I am the most able of my spies. Thank you for the news. I shall put it to excellent use."

Dawn was breaking beyond the treeline to the east of the River Skillen in the Forest of the Black Light as Kal-Gadras prepared his borrowed horse to make the turn south along the River Mirra and home to the lands of the Elves.

"I wish I could say that I was looking forward to the next time we meet, friend Aldemere," he said, grasping his spirit brother's shoulder. "Soon it shall be that my mother's vision is fulfilled."

"You and I, leading the Human and Elven armies," Aldemere said, half to himself, as if speaking the vision's contents were akin to willing them out of existence. "I do not know the circumstances under which it will happen. I am captainguard of Glittereye. My duty is first and foremost to the king at Castle Silveth."

"Sir Laurel would be proud of you, reciting as though you were teaching a class on duty and honor to squires."

"Would he?" Aldemere quietly asked.

The ever-expanding legends of Sir Laurel omitted most of his humanity, as the King's Book of Games and other volumes of recorded histories and ancestries always did for heroes. Aldemere, however, had seen the great champion and former captainguard in his quiet, reflective, and outright doubtful moments. He had been with him as he died and had seen the questions in the fading light of his eyes.

Questions he had seen in others' eyes as well.

"What troubles you, my friend?" Kal-Gadras enquired. "I think it bodes ill for us to part with such a look upon your face."

"I fear what shall be asked of me—of us both. Of us all. Anastasia is with child. Your mother is still recovering. The Rebellion brought a harsh and evil winter. What shall Nadrim's ambitions bring?"

"The sooner we part ways and see to things at home, the sooner we shall know," Kal-Gadras answered, fastening his cloak, adjusting his bow and shoulder bag, and climbing into the saddle. "But I have to say, it is good to hear you asking so many questions. My old friend has not completely disappeared… At last he shows his face!"

Aldemere attempted to suppress a smile. Instead, he let it be. "He still has his uses. Safe travels, friend Kal-Gadras. Regards to your mother and High Lord Petror. No matter the dire conditions when once again we meet, I shall therein find my strength."

Several minutes later, Aldemere climbed upon Poet's saddled back and watched his friend riding eagerly for home. As Lesster, Frederick, and their men prepared their horses for departure, Aldemere felt Sir Laurel suddenly beside him, and recalled his final words: *You will be a great leader of men, Sir Aldemere of the Motley, and they will serve you well. Do not dwell needlessly on my passing, but honor my memory, and the memory of what we did this day.*

"Did you know of the days to come, my fallen commander?" Aldemere quietly asked, urging Poet on toward Glittereye with a tensing of his thighs.

Baron Chrystan's funeral pyre was little more than a mound of red-hot coals and grey and somber ashes when Sir Linead excused himself from the circle of knights congressed in silence around it so he could speak with Sir Arans before returning to Castle Silveth.

It had been a difficult, bitter decision, but in the end, the knight-marshal determined it was best for King Dylwyn and Jester Elde to stay within the confines and protection of the castle and not make the journey to the Temple of the Seers. He had ordered Sir Lan to remain at the castle as well, much to his chagrin. Linead had also sent word to the three remaining barons and the baroness to remain within their additionally fortified homes. The kingdom could not bear the risk of further losses amongst its leaders.

The Seers had been surprised to receive only a small delegation of Chrystan's family and closest advisors—including a few of the teachers from his academy and its headmaster, Elder Marsham— and Linead, Peecwyl, Prima, and Navvic, who had arrived with the family and half a dozen knights who served as an honor guard. Navvic would return with the contingent from Elsmore within the hour.

Only a handful of the one hundred knights stationed at the Temple had attended the ceremony and lighting of the pyre. Sir Arans had not been amongst them.

Linead entered the barn to find the target of his ire eating. "Was your supper of such importance that you failed to pay your last respects to our comrade and former commander?"

Stabbing a fork into an egg-sized fried potato, Arans replied, without looking up, "Of which comrade do you speak?"

As Arans crammed the potato into his mouth with a satisfied moan, Sir Linead kicked over the hogshead on which the plate of the arrogant knight was perched.

295   *Aldemere's Dilemma*

"I have to wonder," Linead said, drawing his sword as Arans rose and did the same, "why you did not stand with Garamin in his rebellion."

Spitting out a half-chewed portion of the potato, Arans replied, "Because I knew he could not win. My decision had nothing to do with any belief in Chrystan—when he was a warrior instead of a *politician*, which is how he died—or Laurel or that whelp of a jester's pup. If Garamin would have offered to *me* what he chose to bestow upon Pallin—that perennial second-best—perhaps his rebellion would have prevailed."

Laurel glared in disbelief. "Do you dare?" he asked, his voice guttural and full of fury.

"Best to be honest, yes? Is it not our knightly duty?" Arans kicked away his plate, while adjusting his grip on his longsword with his rough and sizable hands. "Chrystan ceased to be our comrade when he assumed the mantle of baron. Are you next in line for the honor? If so, you are not worth my breaking a sweat."

"The king has yet to decide who will be named in Chrystan's stead, but I have no interest in leaving the knighthood," Linead responded, shifting his stance and eight and strengthening his grip on his sword in anticipation of Arans's attack. "Since we are being honest... I find your position inconsistent. What is the purpose of your setting yourself up at this Temple like a warrior-prince if not the desire for political influence?"

Instead of an answer in words, Linead received a slicing swipe from Arans's blade that the knight-marshal easily blocked, signaling that Arans had meant it as a warning. Nodding in acknowledgment, Linead widened his stance to begin their combat in earnest. As they fully engaged, trading thrusts and parries with obvious intent to kill, the area just inside and outside the stable steadily filled with knights, including Navvic, Prima, and Peecwyl.

"Enough of this now, the both of you!" barked the one-eyed knight, although he made no move to draw his sword or place his body between the combatants.

"This is holy ground!" Dictus shouted from behind him, pushing past a row of Arans's knights with Vitus at his side. "Sir Linead, Sir Arans—stop this madness at once!"

As the two knights disengaged, sheathing their swords in reluctant compliance, Linead turned and addressed the Seers. "You hold no authority over me. But I do hold authority over *him*." He pointed to Arans to make certain his assertion was clear. "Pray I do not exercise it and recall him to Castle Silveth for discipline and demotion."

Opening his mouth to retort, Dictus felt Vitus's grip on his arm and stayed his tongue.

"Forgive our comrade and commander," Sir Prima said, turning to address the crowd of knights and Seers as Linead left the barn. "He is overcome with grief at our loss, and his mind is filled with dark and bloody thoughts. Having recently lost my son, no one knows how he feels better than I do. I understand as well his anger at Sir Arans, who has demonstrated unforgivable disrespect by not attending Sir Chrystan's funeral. I praise the handful of knights who defied him. Should any of you wish to serve under the banner of the West…"

"You hold your tongue, you bastard, or it shall feel the sting of my blade!" Arans hissed, grasping the pommel of his sword. "How dare you refer to a *politician* as *sir*!"

"Enough, Sir Arans," Vitus warned. "And you as well, Sir Prima. You have said your piece. It is best to let it be."

Prima nodded. "You Seers have done your duty with a grace we have come to expect."

Eyeing the unfinished expansion of the stables as he and Prima exited, Peecwyl remarked, "Your skill with a carpenter's square is enviable, Arans. It is a relief that such talents are unneeded during battle, or you would be missed amongst the men."

As Peecwyl and Prima ran to catch up with Linead, Dictus dispersed the rest of the knights. Digging the heel of his sandal into a pair of pristine potatoes, he said to the seething Sir Arans, "Clean up this mess immediately. Then seek me in my rooms. We have much to discuss."

Silbern Skarling, first officer of the *Salt-Serpent*, sat in the third pew on the left side of the Vessel, unconsciously tapping out the rhythm of a sea chantey on the weathered wood extending from either side of the section where he sat.

Silbern had thought of little else since the *Salt-Serpent* had docked in Llafen Eret but seeing Nomma and hearing what Carra wished to share before his duties called him away. Captain Ungerfil had kept him frustratingly busy prepping the ship for battle while the available captains convened day after day at the entrance to the harbor, learning to load, aim, and fire the Dwarven war machines Prince Dramel referred to as "guns."

As far as Silbern was concerned, their weight, rigidity, volume, and violence had nothing to do with a sailor's life at sea. He was therefore relieved to learn that the *Salt-Serpent* and *Sea-Sprite* would each have an assigned master gunner and crew of six, allowing him to stay as far away as possible from Dramel's damnable, deadly devices.

Such were his thoughts when the doors to the Inner Temple opened, revealing a smiling, wide-eyed Nomma.

"Silbern!" she whispered with no dearth of feeling as he entered the aisle and embraced her near the altar. "I was starting to worry you would not come!"

Breaking the embrace and eyeing the doors to the Inner Temple, Silbern said, "Perhaps we should seek some privacy. Is it safe here? Do the others know?"

"They are deep in meditation," Nomma answered, giving him a tender kiss and leading him down the aisle toward the pool of water in the center of the Vessel. As the bluish-purple flame that burned in its sacrificial brazier attracted Silbern's eye, Nomma suddenly stopped.

"What are we doing?" he asked. "I was hoping we could find a place to be alone before I meet with Carra. We are in danger of being seen."

Nomma shook her head, placing her finger to Silbern's lips. "We are meeting with her together, in this very spot. She shall join us in a moment. There is something she has seen, something that greatly concerns her, although she has not yet shared the details."

Sitting on the edge of a pew, Silbern clenched his jaw. "If it has to do with the war, she should speak with the grand admiral, or Thaker and the rest of the captains. I have zero authority in any matters in which your priestess is involved."

"Not in larger matters of State. That is true. But when it concerns your fate—and Nomma's—your authority is unsurpassed."

Silbern swung around at the sound Carra's voice. He had not heard her approach, nor seen her exit the Inner Temple. It unnerved him.

"Nomma's sisters in the Ruen-Eret will not be occupied indefinitely. I appreciate you coming, Silbern Skarling. Let us begin without delay."

"Begin what?" Silbern asked. "Why have you asked me here?"

Nomma placed a hand on his arm. "Silbern, please. In the Vessel, you should address the priestess as Carra-shaman, and show her due respect."

"It is alright, Nomma," Carra said, gliding past them and dipping a bowl she produced from her robes into the water. "I have always known that Silbern struggles with finding his faith in the Ruenai. He therefore sees no reason to treat their priestess with respect."

"Is that why I am here?" Silbern asked, shifting his shoulder so Nomma's hand fell off his arm. "Must I display full faith in order to have your blessing with regard to my love for Nomma? Must the Ruenai govern every aspect of our lives? Even love?"

Although he saw sadness and pleading in Nomma's eyes, Silbern continued, the wound to his pride acting like a prevailing wind on a full array of sails. "I am an officer in the Eretian fleet because I earned it. I refused a captaincy because of my love for Nomma and the rules the Ruenai impose. I have put in thousands of hours with book and chart, compass and astrolabe, studying in a tiny room night after night until the flame of my candle sputtered and extinguished in a pool of melted wax. And the days I have spent on the water! From dinghies to barges to single- and three-masted vessels, scarring my hands with rope, hook, and pike. Sea salt fills my nose, hair, and blood to such a vast degree that I shall never again be free of it! But my heart—my heart is full of love for the seafarer's life and for my beautiful Nomma, which has naught to do with your Ruenai."

Standing in silence as Silbern's chest rose and fell from the exertion of his speech, Carra whispered, after a moment, "I happen to disagree. As I am sure Nomma must as well, but there is no time for debate." Holding up the water-filled bowl, she said, "I have had visions using this bowl. Visions of the future, of which you must be made aware."

Silbern raised his hands as a bulwark against the bowl and its supposed visions. "I do not believe in your magic, Carra. Carra-*shaman*. Even if I did, I do not care to know the future. I will plot it, as does a navigator, taking the seas, be they fierce or fair, as they alone decide to come. Did you know about his, Nomma?"

"She did not," Carra said, returning the water to the pool and placing the bowl within her robes. "But if you force me, Silbern Skarling, I will show her what she must see without you there to share it, to soften the terrible shock of it. Is that what you call love?"

Aiming his finger at Carra's face like a whaler's barbed harpoon, Silbern said, "Leave us be, accursed witch! Do not attempt to turn Nomma against me as an offering to your Ruenai. We shall defy you all." Ignoring Nomma's attempt to stop him, Silbern walked briskly down the aisle and out the Vessel's door.

Aldemere's Dilemma

"I am sorry, Carra-shaman," Nomma whispered, tears welling in her eyes. "I should never have given such a faithless person my heart. I see that clearly now. But it is hard, because I love him, despite his angry words and lack of faith."

Taking Nomma in her arms, Carra whispered, "You have nothing for which to be sorry. It is not faithlessness that makes Silbern Skarling a threat. It is his excess of *misplaced* faith in himself that shall ultimately undo us all."

Dinner had just been served in the Scholars' Room at Castle Silveth when Dictus and Vitus, unannounced and uninvited, entered.

"Talorous, we must talk!" Dictus shouted, picking up a chair from the corner of the room and grabbing a thick slice of bread from a basket. "Can someone bring us some ale? Standard will do in a pinch, although honeyed is preferred."

Talorous nodded at the library apprentice holding station by the door to indicate that he should do as the senior Lord Seer requested.

"Brother Dictus," Talorous began, pushing aside his bowl of untouched cabbage and carrots and producing his pipe from his cloak. "We do not barge in upon you during mealtimes. To what do we owe this show of disrespect?"

Taking advantage of Dictus's mouth being full of bread and a sizable hunk of cheese, which he had taken, along with some cabbage, from a nearby scholar's plate, Vitus placed his hands firmly on the table around which the scholars were gathered and answered, "Do not speak to us, Talorous, of barging in and disrespect! The knights of this castle—led by that pompous ruffian Linead—have more than barged in on *us* disrespectfully as of late! They have desecrated the grounds of the Temple with their vitriol and violence!"

Nodding his head and lighting his pipe in a single motion, Talorous responded, "We have heard of the unfortunate incident to which your generalizations are—in a roundabout way—alluding." He paused to stoke the pipe with a series of shallow, rapid puffs, while holding his thumb just above the rim of the bowl. When the blue-black smoke was nearly obscuring his face, he continued. "Arans was wrong to boycott Chrystan's service. You know this to be fact. For you of all the Seers best understands hierarchy and the exercise of rights and respect as they pertain to it." Changing the focus of his gaze, Talorous said with a shake of his head, "You have missed a bit of cabbage, Dictus. It is hanging from your cowl, like an eel peeking out of a cave."

The others in the room—Laurianna, Farvon, and Elder Marsham amongst them—watched in amusement as the wise old tutor handled the Seers' intrusion with a practiced, dignified calm laced with harmless humor.

Leaving the cabbage where it lay, Dictus ran his gaze across the assembled faces like a carpenter planing a plank.

"*How dare you.*"

Raising his brown, patchy brows in surprise, Vitus whispered in his superior's ear, "Lord Dictus, I do not advise—"

"*Me.* You do not advise *me*, Brother Vitus. Not any longer. Nor does the king's overeducated minions. It is I alone who speaks directly with the Deities. Who has supplicated myself for decades to keep their favor. I have repeatedly—*endlessly*—interceded on behalf of this kingdom during its innumerable rebellions, wars, and childish machinations. Therefore… I demand that you respect me. Each and every one of you."

Puffing his pipe in contemplation over Dictus's cutting rebuttal, Talorous leaned back as Laurianna abruptly stood.

"It is clear you are incensed. So tell us, Lord Seer—how can we make this right?"

"*You*, you vixen—you have done plenty already!" Dictus answered, rising to meet Laurianna's gaze with one foretelling the storms to come. "Filling Farvon's beguiled head with nonsense. Using your feminine wiles to confuse him even further. I have seen the way our dull-witted inkblot of a second-rate scribe stares at your face. At your—"

"You shall not dishonor this innocent woman!" Farvon shouted, rising to his feet. "Not when I have seen *you* staring at her with the most impure of thoughts etched upon your lecherous, leering face! I am fulfilling the king's request with Laurianna. That is all. I am applying my skills before the Deities with humility and effort, as my parents had hoped.

Dictus's face, as he looked upon the Keeper of the Scrolls, was an untempered mask of disdain. "This is what your living amongst the bookworms has done! I shall reacquaint you with humility at the Temple. Pack your things, Brother Farvon. We are soon to be returning. I am no longer in the mood to speak with our misled king."

Farvon and Laurianna turned as one to Talorous, an urgent plea for intervention in their eyes.

"Settle yourself, Brother Dictus," warned the kingdom's senior scholar. "You have clearly taken leave of your senses. Farvon shall remain here, as per the arrangement you so eagerly embraced. Unless, of course, you have brought Arans and his hundred in exchange... No? Then you had best keep your appointment with King Dylwyn and leave us bookworms to our meagre cabbage and carrots."

Regretting his treatment of Vitus as the chief incantor turned away rather than defend him, Dictus stood his ground alone. "When we are rightfully restored to the castle, after the war is won—or, more than likely, before—I shall see this room remade into one of supplication, where those whose egos have caused them to incur the Deities' wrath shall make penance for hours a day, in ways that shall rectify what the Seers endlessly endure at your hands. I choose this room as a boon to you, Talorous, since you practically live here already. I would not fully displace you, as we were displaced by the Fragenoar!"

"Thank you, Brother Dictus. You have always been considerate. It is one of your few remaining strengths."

All heads turned at the sound of the king in the doorway, although none swiveled quicker than Dictus's.

"Your Highness," the Lord Seer chirped, bowing lower than required. "I was just on my way to see you as requested, when I was delayed by the arrogance of Talorous and his blasphemous tangle of bookworms. You have no doubt heard of the disrespect the Seers and Sir Arans recently suffered at the Temple..."

Dylwyn raised his hand. "Do not speak to me of what happened at the Temple, Lord Seer, unless you are willing to pay dearly for your part. I have summoned you here to bless the soon to be appointed interim baron. Directly after, you shall leave. You and Vitus both. And you shall go alone."

Knocking the still-red dottle from his pipe, Talorous asked, "Shall I summon the appointee to the Chapel of the Trying Soul, Your Highness?"

"There is no need of that, old master," Dylwyn said, moving to the far side of the table and placing his hand on Elder Marsham's arm. "He is already here amongst us."

Davus Purloch crouched within the shadows of Helkirk Nagelbrau's sitting room, focusing his night-diminished sight on the knife he held in his left hand and the key he held in his right—both of which were supplied to him an hour earlier by Calrain Damonessa, clandestinely transferred as they passed in a crowded hallway at a pre-appointed time.

To keep his mind from wandering as he waited out the minutes, Purloch ruminated on the myriad events—and the personal set of secrets—that had led him to this room. For weeks, Calrain had exploited every opportunity to amplify Davus's feelings of betrayal and frustration. Purloch reveled in the fact that the brother of the cliffprince was wholly unaware of the extent to which the former captain was permitting him to do so.

"I am underestimated by them all," he whispered, partially to drown out the conflicting sounds of male lust and futile female resistance coming from just beyond the door that remained locked a few feet away.

Calrain had chosen the time with care, knowing the effect that it would have.

Davus Purloch had first met Deanna Callenhor when he was nineteen and she was fourteen, at a party given for nobles at the home of Purloch's parents. He was a standout cadet in the Amdarian Academy for Military Studies. She was the pink-bowed, silken-gowned debutante who had asked him to dance three times during the course of the evening.

For the next two years, they exchanged letters and danced at similar events on the rare occasion Davus's superiors permitted him to attend. There was never talk of marriage—never even a lingering kiss—but Davus was as devoted to Deanna as any future spouse.

Then, three years ago, the nightmarish news had arrived that a fever had taken her life.

Davus, then a lieutenant and commanding a patrol to the south of the city, could not secure permission to attend Deanna's funeral. Those twin wounds had recently reopened, when he had heard from Captain Stratten, while the bastard was in his cups, that Deanna's father had been murdered as a warning to other nobles who might be considering speaking out about Nadrim's policies.

Ever since, he had lived in silent grief. A grief made increasingly precious to him in the midst of all he had endured since the escape of Tun and the others.

It had been the evening of the cliffprince's bayside speech to the fleet—an evening that had provided endless opportunity for Captain Stratten to humiliate him, while his father wordlessly watched—that Calrain had told him who it was that Helkirk Nagelbrau was keeping as his plaything within his inner chambers.

Aldemere's Dilemma

"She is alive? And nothing more than a means to produce an heir?"

"The truth is much more ugly, my friend," Calrain had answered, producing the key to Nagelbrau's rooms. "Helkirk is a monster. He is inflicting increasing amounts of pain—not only physically but to her close to shattering mind—although she need not endure it much longer." He then produced the knife. "If you are willing to use these tools."

Purloch had silently accepted the knife and the key, knowing exactly what accepting them meant.

The anger he was feeling heated them both in his hands.

Gripping the knife, with its curved, serrated blade, tighter in his hand at the memory, Purloch strengthened his stance as he heard the bedframe groan as if in accordance with Deanna's sobs of shame and relief that the evening's ordeal was over.

"You shall never again endure it," Purloch whispered, waiting at the ready for the bedroom door to open.

"Be certain to let him see you," Calrain had whispered. "*If* you are committed to ending his life. Enjoy his surprise when he sees that a lowly lieutenant in charge of the Amdarian dungeons is paying him in blood for the jokes he makes with Stratten. Recall their derisive laughter as you carve him into bits."

The laughter he could endure. But not the knowledge that his delicate Deanna—whose death had been a lie—had been the monster's prisoner all these weeks. Davus therefore let Nagelbrau see him as Calrain had suggested, stepping into the weak pool of light from the candlestick her tormentor held as he exited the bedroom.

Davus did not speak as Helkirk's eyes went wide. Steel, not stories, would suffice. Words had too often failed him. Instead, Davus brought the blade across Nagelbrau's throat two times in succession before plunging it into his chest half a dozen times.

Struggling for life, Helkirk eyed the key that Davus clutched. Mouthing the syllable *Crick* as bright red blood bubbled between his teeth, the head of the Shadow Knife expired, knowing exactly whom it was that betrayed him.

"Leave the knife inside him," Calrain had coached. "It belongs to a man who shall take the fall—a member of the Shadow Knife who so memorably challenged his captain—unsuccessfully—for his title six months ago who lived to tell the tale. Minus his ears and an arm."

"The left one, I hope?" Davus, who was right-handed, had asked.

"The right one," Calrain corrected. "So be sure to use your left. The Shadow Knife inspectors will closely examine the wounds and the spray of blood upon the walls."

"And what of Deanna?" Davus enquired, placing the knife and key in a compartment in his satchel, without enquiring how Calrain had procured them.

"Do not let her see you, at least for now. Who knows her state of mind? She might attack you in a panic, or shout for the guards. Leave the way you came. If anyone should enquire as to your whereabouts—though why would they?—I shall say you were assisting me in designing a new chair for my water closet, so impressed was I with your work on the cells and so familiar had you become with working while knee-deep in shit."

Davus, sticking the knife into and dropping the key on top of the gory mess that was Nagelbrau's chest, considered for a moment following Calrain's instructions, but there Deanna was, standing in the doorway, her hair disheveled and a blanket thrown absent-mindedly about her shoulders, leaving little to Davus's adrenaline-fueled imagination.

"Davus?" she whispered, as though they were sharing a dream.

"Is there a window in that room?" Davus asked her, stepping past to see for himself. Fate and luck were finally with them! Several feet above the bed was exactly what he required. Pulling the blanket tighter around her shoulders, and doing his best to ignore the disheveled, reeking bedsheets, he whispered, "Put on your clothes, Deanna. Your nightmare has finally ended. I shall bring you somewhere safe."

CHAPTER TWO

As tired and sore as Aldemere was after the hours-long ride he and his companions had made across the Eastern Barony and into the central farmlands, he was quick to smile upon seeing the glint of the fire and glass signaling system from first the southern and then the northern guardposts on the far ends of the Minor Sentinel Lake. He rested a little easier knowing that, within minutes, a heavily armed party would ride out to meet them, same as they would for a band of intruders.

The previous night, as they took their rest in the garrison barracks of a unit ten miles west of Eerbell, Aldemere had spoken with Sir Abbas, trade warden of the east, who told them about the assassination of Baron Chrystan.

"Linead will be screaming for blood," Lesster replied. "As shall we—is that not right, my loyal sons?" Faxx and the others shouted their agreement. "Do you think it wise to bring the northerner and his companions to the castle?" he asked of Aldemere. "No offense meant to Frederick, of course. I stand convinced that he is trustworthy, but Sir Linead is going to need time, especially now. And bringing these others with you…"

Aldemere had dismissed Lesster's suggestion with a wave of his hand, rendered speechless as he was over the news of Chrystan's death.

Now, ten hours later, as he heard the approach of a dozen heavy horses, Aldemere wondered if perhaps Lesster had been correct in his concern.

"Sir Aldemere!" Sir Navvic, trade warden of the Central Barony, who led the guard unit, shouted as they approached. "Welcome home, Sir. You as well, Sir Lesster. Welcome to you all."

Greetings exchanged, Aldemere took Navvic aside. "You have to tell me—what is the mood of the knight-marshal?"

"Determined, Sir, of course," Navvic answered, jutting his strong, cleft chin, recently shaved, toward Frederick and his cohorts. "You ask because of them, do you not? We guessed that Frederick would be with you. Sir Linead shall want your assessment."

"He shall have it," Aldemere replied, wishing he had his garter and shield and Crow Feather strapped to his side so he might better play his role. "But shall he listen?"

"You shall have to see for yourself. For my part, I am sick to death of the pointless politicking. Baron Chrystan was the best of us

Aldemere's Dilemma

all. I am duty-bound to avenge him. If Frederick and his friends are strong and brave and shall help us win this fight, I say we need to bring them into it."

He went on to tell Aldemere of the incident at the Temple, and Sir Lan and Sir Ambil's war of wills over the scheduling and manning of the tower's watchmen.

Laurel and Chrystan would not have let this happen, Aldemere thought, a cold frustration further tensing his muscles. "Thank you for the news," he said, reining Poet toward the group. Frederick immediately engaged him as they headed for the castle.

"If you would rather Christoph and Martin and I remain at the guardpost until you have spoken with Linead..."

"I would not," Aldemere said, as the party moved past the southern end of the lake. "I shall speak on your behalf, as shall Lesster, Faxx, and Tagen, but you must also be beside me, for it is important to speak for yourself." Grasping Frederick's forearm, he added, "If there is anything you are concealing, now would be the time..."

Staring at the Eastern Tower of Silveth in the early morning light, Frederick said, after a considered moment of silence, "Nothing that matters to the immediate task at hand. Once we have vanquished Nadrim, you and I shall speak of the rest. You must trust me, Aldemere. Now is not the time to tell you everything I wish to. That I need to."

Knowing he had no choice, Aldemere acknowledged Frederick's terms with a simple nod of the head.

If the northerner was not whom the captainguard thought, the price for trusting him in the weeks and months to come would be his alone to pay.

Sir Corvit fought hard to catch his breath as his men at last obtained the advantage, pushing back the relentless waves of barbarians that had been assaulting the mines with arrow and club and spear the past three days and nights.

Although the assault had caught them unaware—the nomads had never attacked in excellent weather, nor with such well-coordinated and impressive numbers—the constant drilling and discipline of the war-hardened knights of the north had prevented a total rout.

Looking to the west, Corvit saw far less black, billowing smoke than he had seen since the initial attack on his position—a glut of flaming arrows that felled a dozen men around him as the sky above the far-off mines had also filled with smoke.

They had been well into the first day's exchanges of mutilation and death when Corvit's lieutenant, Sir Goudry, had sent a messenger from beyond the mountains further north who confirmed that they were also under attack—by Caveraiders, Krags, *and* Riverskabs. All at once. The three tribes, historically at odds and ever-reluctant allies, were working together in what appeared to be carefully coordinated maneuvers.

Into the afternoon and through the night they had fought—the miners putting out the flames and shoring up the lines with axes, picks, and shovels when the barbarians threatened to breach them. Neither side could fight on horseback on the uneven, chaotic terrain, so phalanxes were the mode in which the knights defended, digging in at the foot of any incline providing a wide enough ledge as the nomads came charging down the mountainside toward the arrow-weakened formation, crashing into the knights in a cacophony of leather, bone, iron, wood, and steel.

Resting throughout the morning, with dozens of maimed and moaning men crying out from amongst the piles of the dead, the two sides resumed the fight through the following afternoon and evening, as reports reached Corvit of stalemates—with grievous losses all the same—in the west and to the north.

Now, on the third afternoon of the engagement, the tide was turning in Corvit's favor.

"Push them hard, my defenders of the north!" he shouted, rotating his aching, swollen hand high above his head so the sword it gripped gleamed through the blood that bathed it like a beacon in the sunlight. "The bastards' lines are ready to break!"

In answer to his call, the units under his command, bloodied and exhausted though they were, pushed foot by foot up the mountain. First four feet, then another three, where they dug in for a time in loud and lethal combat.

Then Moktar was in view, fast approaching the lines.

Does he want a parlay? Corvit wondered, until he saw Moktar's massive, double-bladed axe rising high into the air.

No. He wants my head.

"Let their leader through!" Corvit cried, hoisting his shield and readying his sword.

As Moktar closed the gap, Corvit noticed the chunks of flesh and innards draped on his arms and shield.

Aldemere's Dilemma

There was nothing random about them. He arranged them to make men cower.

"You do not frighten me, Chieftain Moktar of the Nomads!" Corvit yelled, suddenly understanding what Moktar had achieved.

"Moktar frightened of no one," came the guttural reply.

"Nor am I. So it seems we shall fight to the death," the Chief Knight of the northlands answered, knowing those words might be the last he ever spoke.

Then Moktar dropped his axe, and his forces began to retreat.

The *Sea-Star* and *Storm-Star*'s sails had not yet been secured nor their precious cargo of Tirili ore begun to be off-loaded when their captains were summoned by messenger to a meeting at the Admiralty. Leaving instructions with their respective first officers, captains Kaelhul and Railhull made their way through the masses of wagons, provisions, and equipment littering the docks and thoroughfares to the Admiralty building's entrance.

"Have you given additional thought to what I told you as we readied to sail out of Vaelsport?" Knot Railhull asked his counterpart, adjusting his sash and epaulets in anticipation of a meeting with the grand admiral and warden of the waters.

"As much as my duties on a cargo-laden ship quick-bound for home would allow," Kelvan Kaelhul replied, not bothering to adjust his uniform or sash. "I see no harm in enlightening the Human to the properties and value of the ore. It has never been a secret. The Dwarves do the metalsmithing. Come to that, the Elves refined the process, and you know how they love the Centerlanders."

Knot shook his head. "I fear you are missing the point. This Corvit fights for a *different country* of Humans. There the differences end. They are identical to the Mellyans. Warmongers. Land ravishers. You showed poor judgment and disloyalty to the people of Eret indulging his bloodlust and falling for his calculated praise."

Stopping before the doors of the Admiralty building, Kelvan placed his hand on his comrade's shoulder. "The Humans of Glittereye saved Vaelsport from annihilation. Its inhabitants are more of our blood than they are of the barbarians'. There were Kaelhuls and Railhulls on board that shipwrecked vessel—same as for all the other seafaring families. So whom have I betrayed?"

After stepping away to re-adjust his epaulet where Kelvan's hand had knocked it askew, Knot opened the doors and silently ascended the steps—repurposed from a retired vessel—making it clear the discussion was over.

Minutes later, they entered the conference room to find Grand Admiral Ungerfil, Warden Hefflar, and captains Thaker Ungerfil, Dorrin Waelsbun, Capstan Mastmin, and Sterrin Wilsbern listening intently to a Dwarf in chainmail who wore an ornate sword running three-quarters the length of his body sheathed upon his back.

Upon seeing the new arrivals, Warden Hefflar held up his hand. Gently, as everyone noticed. "Apologies, Prince Dramel. These are captains Kaelhul of the *Sea-Star* and Railhull of the *Storm-Star*, newly returned from Vaelsport. Before you continue with your plan for the harbor's defense, I ask that you let them report."

Nodding in agreement, the Dwarf bowed to the captains and sat beside Thaker.

"Where are Staelhuk Ronng and Jesper Bront?" Knot asked, referring to the captains of the *Spear-Shaft* and *Sea-Seeker*.

"Blunt as always, Captain Railhull," Grand Admiral Ungerfil answered. "They are patrolling the southern coast with several single-masters. Kaen's Point is at present an area of vulnerability, although we are working to remedy that, with Prince Dramel's help. Did you find success in Vaelsport?"

Deferring to Kelvan to make their report, Knot watched the brows of those assembled furrow with concern as they absorbed the gory details. He felt his stomach tighten as Kelvan finished, without making mention of their meeting with Sir Corvit.

"It was Captain Railhull's decision to leave a portion of the crew behind to train the Vaelsportians in shore defense using the ships the deceased barbarians provided."

"Well done, captains," Warden Hefflar exclaimed. "It sounds as though you have won us the opening fight of the war."

"With the help of the Humans," Knot added, silently amazed at how Kelvan had shaped the truth of their mission to ensure his cooperation. "A knight called Corvit and his men displayed impressive heroism... and humility. They proved to be worthy allies."

Later that evening, as they dined aboard the *Sea-Star*, Kelvan attempted to thank Knot for backing his play and presenting a united front.

Filling their mugs with ale, Knot shook his head and muttered, "I shall have no problem blaming you if your gamble turns out to be wrong and the Centerlanders prove unworthy of what you have credited them with. I sincerely pray it is not."

Aldemere's Dilemma

"Not since the years of the Unity Wars have we faced such an all-pervasive threat to the Elven homeland. *That* is why you have been summoned, Lord Val-Dirgas."

High Lord Petror, dressed in his finest etched-silver chain-and-plate armor and a hoodless ebony cloak, stood at the head of a rough-hewn oaken table in the fortress of Nal-Firran, Lord of Ahkete-Val.

"This should be entertaining," Nal-Koyyan, Sublord of the South Shore and Nal-Firran's only son, whispered in Kal-Gadras's ear. "You would think that we are Human, the way they are carrying on."

Kal-Gadras silently nodded. Although the seven lords of Marlooq Fer had been meeting for an hour, they had accomplished next to nothing, thanks to a barrage of pointed statements made in large part by Val-Dirgas, Lord of the Two Rivers. He had released his latest like an arrow. "No one gave you the authority, High Lord Petror, to *summon* us on a whim."

Kal-Gadras clenched his fists beneath the table. Although Val-Dirgas was technically correct, this was no time for technicalities. Besides, it was the Lord of the South Shore's report to Petror and his mother upon his return from the Forest of Tombal that had provoked the summons the High Lord had sent by hawk to the other Elven lords.

Although no one had declined, some lords were incensed that Petror had dared to ask. In the long history of Marlooq Fer, the lords, appointed by family lineage, served for life and did so autonomously. While Petror governed in conjunction with Nemmerle's guidance on pressing matters of state, such as the decision to aid Dylwyn's grandfather and Dylwyn himself during the Unity Wars and again during the recent Rebellion, each lord ruled supreme in the geographic area for which he alone was responsible.

"Is the threat so great that you deemed it permissible to herd us here like cattle?" asked Tal-Mondras, Lord of the Forests.

"How dare you ask that question!" Dal-Seernan, Lord of the Sea of Silence, retorted. "Every one of us was *summoned*, were we not? Why else would we have come? I trust you, High Lord Petror. I have no doubt that you consulted at length with Nemmerle, who consulted even longer with the Sacred Mother, before you sent your missive."

Given the unstable state of Nemmerle's mind and her low opinion of Humans, Petror had chosen *not* to take that step, but to admit so would end the meeting, which he could not allow. Instead, he turned to the sole remaining lord who had yet to voice an opinion.

"What of you, Gal-Holvan? Does the Lord of Qa Fer disagree with what I have done?"

Thoughtfully running his fingers through his shining shoulder-length hair, which looked to Kal-Gadras as though the queen of the spiders had spun it, Gal-Holvan replied, "Make an undeniable argument, High Lord Petror, and I shall not turn against you."

In answer, using all that Kal-Gadras had told him, High Lord Petror laid out for the increasingly enrapt attendees what he knew of the intentions and capabilities of the Mellyans. He ended with a reminder of each lord's duty to the whole of Marlooq Fer.

When he was finished, Nal-Firran, who had offered his fortress as proof of his support, looked upon Val-Dirgas. "Has this succinct and sobering speech softened your stance? The Mellyans shall come by ship, heavily armed, putting all of us at risk. Should they best the forces in the Forest of Tombal, they shall come by the Sea of Silence, Dal-Seernan," he continued, shifting his gaze, "and here to the Valley of the Horses, and then to the southern shore. Should we three fail to stop them—a dark probability we cannot afford to deny—they shall travel up the Qa Fer and into the River Mirra to attack the Eastern Barony of Glittereye. Show me you understand this!"

Nodding in solidarity with Nal-Firran, Gal-Horvan announced, "I stand behind the decisions High Lord Petror now must make. You must do so as well, Val-Dirgas. We seven must leave here united."

Covering his eyes in contemplation, Val-Dirgas answered, "High Lord Petror. All of the resources of the House of the Two Rivers are at your command and disposal."

"I wish King Dylwyn's flock of petulant barons could have witnessed what took place in your father's fortress," Kal-Gadras said to Nal-Koyyan twenty minutes later as they prepared their horses for a fast-paced ride to the south. "Three days hence, the Humans would still be arguing. They are most likely doing so as we speak."

"Lord Kal-Gadras! May I have a moment?"

Kal-Gadras turned his attention to the carriage stopping beside him, which carried Lord Gal-Holvan, as well as a beautiful Elven girl.

"I am at your service," Kal-Gadras stammered, his eyes affixed against his will on the face of the lord's companion.

"I wanted to take the opportunity to introduce you to my daughter, Landuleni. She has long desired to meet the one who bears the Mark of Gal-Rashand."

Taking Landuleni's offered hand inside his own, Kal-Gadras felt the mark begin to pulse.

Although the sky was devoid of dragons, the Lord of the South Shore felt a fluttering in his heart that was comparable to what he had felt when he and Aldemere had battled Flemvemor on the Isle of Bounting.

As the carriage went on its way, Kal-Gadras continued to watch it—and its breathtaking passenger—until they were out of sight.

Nadrim Damonessa stared with a look bordering on boredom at the Shadow Knife lieutenant whose left arm—the sole arm he possessed—he had ordered bound tightly to the prisoner's torso with a double pass of heavy iron chain.

"Anstil Abrams! What say you to the charges of murder and kidnapping brought against you by your fellow officers in the Shadow Knife and my dutiful brother, Calrain Crickback?"

As the prisoner raised his hairless head, marred by two ugly scars where Helkirk Nagelbrau had ripped his ears from his skull during his ill-fated challenge for command six months before, Calrain, who was seated to the right of his brother in the throne room, felt his heart begin to pound. Nadrim's apparent lack of interest in the proceedings boded poorly for his plan.

His concerns were soon to be justified.

"It was a fair fight," Anstil answered. "Not like I jumped him from the shadows. He was armed and clearly aware of my intentions."

"*Tsk tsk,*" Nadrim replied, banging his tongue against his teeth. "The report clearly states no weapon was found upon your captain. Only *in* him." Tapping the rolled up report on his knee, Nadrim shifted in his chair, as if attempting to stay awake.

Anstil chuckled. Calrain started to panic.

"Of course my fellow lieutenants would remove the captain's weapons. I do all the work, then they set me up and one of them ascends to the captaincy. One of them not man enough to take the position traditionally and with honor, as I attempted to. *Twice.*"

Throwing the report aside, Nadrim stood and approached the defendant, removing a key from his pocket as he did so.

"Your points are valid, Lieutenant Abrams. One simply has to look upon your grotesque head to understand why you would want a second chance. And that is to say nothing of your lost appendage." Nadrim's boots produced a sharp staccato in the nearly empty room as he slowly circled his prisoner. "But I have to ask—why not a formal, public challenge in the barracks like the first time? As *tradition* and *honor* demand?"

Hidden beneath the floorboards beneath his bed, Calrain kept a few precious books his father had saved from the burning Lysean library. One was a procedural manual for the vanquished country's courts. Judges called what Nadrim was doing "leading the witness."

Calrain's hands began to sweat.

"Simple. The first time, a pair of loyal lieutenants restrained me. I had already lost my ears... but the captain was clearly weakened... ready to succumb. I lost my arm—and victory—because of their interference. This time, I made certain it was only he and I."

"I see," Nadrim said, dangling the key, which hung from a chain that was a miniature of the one wrapped around Anstil Abrams. "You see this key? I shall use it to release you. *If* you tell me what became of the girl the corpse once known as Nagelbrau kept in his private chambers."

Tracking the key, which Nadrim swung rhythmically back and forth, with his sharp, crow-like eyes, Abrams answered, "Found her clinging to life. He had starved her, hit her... Visited horrors upon her body night after night. I brought her out of that hellhole with the intention of seeing her healed. Thought maybe, if she saw me as her savior, she might accept an offer of marriage. She died on the way to a doctor."

"And?"

"I buried her in the woods."

"Then take us to the body!"

Nadrim quickly turned at the sound of his brother's voice.

"Calrain," he said, wrapping his fist around the key, "my inquisitive, inquisitive Calrain. It is impolite to dig up the dead. The poor girl suffered abundant horrors at Nagelbrau's groping hands. We shall not subject her to more. Let her have some peace."

"And what of this murderer?" Calrain pressed, although he already knew the answer.

"Murderer? Have you not heard Captain Abrams's answers to my questions?"

Calrain mouthed the title, but could not give it voice.

"Yes. Yes, Calrain, I said it, and so it shall be." Unballing his fist, Nadrim fed the key into the lock that bound the chain, helping Abrams to his feet as the heavy iron links slid noisily to the floor. Glaring coldly at Calrain, Nadrim said, "It is my finding that *Captain* Abrams acted within the rules set forth by the founders of the Shadow Knife. His fellow officers did not. How you choose to deal with these conspirators, Captain, is solely up to you. You showed strength and cunning in your challenge and, although compassion is

Aldemere's Dilemma

a frowned-upon trait in elite warriors such as ourselves, your attempt to save the girl proves that you have honor. Put your things in the captain's quarters when you wish. That is all."

As Abrams walked away, earless head held high, Calrain forced a smile.

If Nadrim were to see his disappointment, he would never get the chance to move beyond this setback, and Calrain fully intended to do so.

"Two ships upon the horizon, with nary an indication they are ours!"

Billec Skarling's eyes shot open from beneath the blanket he had just crawled beneath in the stern of the *Sea-Sword* as he heard the watchman's report. Making his way through the synchronized dance of the mass of moving sailors it took to keep a ship in trim to where the navigator, Lapstrake Hefflar, stood at the double wheel, Captain Skarling took the spyglass offered to him by First Officer Eglin Bront, who had hurried to meet him from the bow.

"Our crow's nest lad be right!" Billec exclaimed, adjusting the lens on the spyglass to get a clearer look. "Two ships, three-masted, nearly identical ta ours, but crewed by Humans in armor. The Mellyans have started their war, an' Millet Ronng gave 'em the means ta do it right! We are in fer a fight, me lads!"

As he returned the spyglass to Bront, the captain nodded in acknowledgment as Tribune Waelsbun and Undersecretary to the Warden of the Waters Hathom Ungerfil joined him. Just behind them, groggy and wearing a scowl, was Gadrun Grundling.

"What is your strategy, Captain?" Tribune Waelsbun enquired.

Tightening his sash and the foot-long braids in his beard, Skarling replied, "They were lyin' in wait, knowin' we had ta come near or through the Isles a' Kirr, which means they knew we were in Tombal. That one-armed sailweaver bastard is sure enuff a spy!"

"There are other explanations," Hathom offered. "Though we should set that aside for now. Their ships may look like ours, but their crews are inexperienced."

"Mayhap that be true," Billec Skarling replied. "Tho' advantage be theirs fer now."

Tribune Waelsbun shook his head. "Enough with the sailor's yammer! The Admiralty abandoned it ages ago. I ask you again, Captain Skarling—*what are your intentions*?"

"Let me ask *ye* a question, Tribune," Billec responded, his voice full of seaweed and sand. "Have I broken a law? Am I bein' relieved? 'Cause if it be neither ye have zero authority on this ship ta be askin' questions or interferin' wit' me duties, or those a' me men. An' this *yammer* as ya call it be the patois a' the sea. 'Tis how we aughta speak!"

Wishing he were back in his office in Llafen Eret, the tribune answered, "You have broken no laws, nor are you relieved. I just wish to know your plan."

"The plan be simply thus. They be comin' at us full sail an' fuller intent, sose our best course a' action is ta outmaneuver 'em as long as we can, an' mayhap then outrun 'em if I first can get us past 'em, but morrin likely, we be facin' a fight!"

The tribune calmly nodded, despite the feeling that an unseen boatswain's mate was working block and tackle in his belly, as Skarling issued orders to the crew.

"We knew this day would come," Hathom whispered. "If it is to be a fight, I shall not hide like a coward below."

Not half an hour later, the two Mellyan ships were upon them, their bowsprits tipped with spiked iron spheres, aimed at the *Sea-Sword*'s hull.

"They are not maneuvering right," First Officer Bront observed, the spyglass pressed to his eye. "Either their helmsmen lack the skill or they lack Tirilian ore."

"I wager a bit a' both," Billec responded. "An' them heavy, awkward bowsprits ain't a bit a' help. Look at 'em dip an' shudder! Gives me an idea." Clasping Lapstrake on the shoulder, he asked, "Can ye stop us in a hurry?"

"I can and I will," Lapstrake answered, adjusting his grip on the wheel. "I shall see her safely maneuvered a moment before they arrive, if that is your order, Captain."

"Aye, me talented lad. 'Tis *exactly* that!" Turning to face the crew, Billec shouted further orders. "Full sails me fearless lads, and onward to our fate!"

As the Mellyan warships approached, they further angled their prows, making it clear that their intention was to ram the helpless *Sea-Sword* on either side of her bow, driving their spiked iron spheres deep into her hull. Waelsbun watched in admiration as the crew of the *Sea-Sword* stood, steely eyed and stalwart, in the face of the coming destruction.

"Take cover, everyone! There are projectiles in the air!" Gadrun Grundling shouted, as dozens of arrows filled the sky, more than half with their tips aflame.

"Ready with the buckets!" First Officer Bront shouted as the deadly arrows descended, embedding in the deck or tearing flaming

Aldemere's Dilemma

holes in the sails. The tribune watched in admiration as the bucket crews quickly and efficiently extinguished a dozen fires.

Then he heard the screams.

All around him, sailors knelt and lay upon the deck as their fellows worked to remove the arrows that had found a living target.

"Another flurry approaches!" Stanchion Pilon warned, joining his fellow Dwarf as the arrows began to fall. "For the love of Father Boldac, find yourselves some cover!"

The bucket crews once more doused the flames, and there were no new screams.

"Keep her steady, Lapstrake," commanded Captain Skarling, his blood aboil at the sight of his bleeding crew, and scorched and hole-poked ship. "Water, wood, and wind!"

The ship was nearly silent as the enemy approached. When the twin bowsprits were a dozen yards away, Billec called for the release of the anchors. Lapstrake finessed the wheel to ease their sudden stop, as the two Mellyan ships smashed their bulwarks together in a shower of splinters and sparks at the spot where the *Sea-Sword* should be.

"Bravo, Captain Skarling!" shouted Tribune Waelsbun, righting himself from the prone position he had been thrown into on the deck when the *Sea-Sword* came to a halt. "Brilliant bit of wheel work, Navigator Hefflar!"

"Another round of arrows—and spears as well, my lads!" Gadrun Grundling shouted, overlapping Billec's order to raise anchors and pull hard to starboard before the enemy vessels recovered.

First Officer Bront rushed to his captain as two arrows and a spear simultaneously entered his chest.

"Ne'er ye mind me wounds!" Billec hissed, clasping his teeth against the pain and the gush of blood in his throat. "Ye'd damned well better outrun 'em, if ye wish ta see her safe!"

Nodding as he steeled his resolve, Bront stood and issued his orders. "Stay low as you can, my lads. Navigator Hefflar… make for Xaer's Point as fast as she will go. Praise the blessed Ruenai! Water, wood, and wind!" Turning to the tribune, he said, his eyes shining with tears, "Do what you can for my friend—and if that bastard Nakret One-Arm shows his face on deck, keep him away from me, and in the path of the arrows."

"Listen to me, Officer Bront," Gadrun Grundling said, grasping the acting captain by the arm. "Boldac's Blade is a good deal closer. Should they be foolish enough to follow, they shall encounter a surprise that I know will lift your spirits."

Nodding at Lapstrake to sail them toward the Blade, Eglin Bront stood in silent defiance as another barrage of arrows rained down on the struggling ship.

The essence of war is ugly, incessant noise, Thaker Ungerfil thought, making his way from the makeshift harbor at Kaen's Point, where the *Salt-Serpent* was docked after its recent patrol of the southern shore of Llafen Eret, to a new observation platform amidst a miles-long line of growing fortifications, the construction of which Prince Dramel was overseeing.

The forging of bladed steel and iron weapons in the blacksmith shops, the practice firing of guns aboard ships and upon the land—with only the strange concoction that caused the explosion, but no projectiles—and the heavy clank and thump and ear-piercing whistle of weapons swung about at high rates of lethal speed were setting Thaker's teeth on edge. He longed to be out at sea, where the swell of the waves against the hull, the creaking of the deck, the tapping of block and tackle, the sea chanteys and night songs, and the swish and flap of the sheets were the only sounds a sailor heard.

Preparations were evident everywhere he went. The Admiralty had decreed that the Ruen-Eret remain sequestered in the Inner Temple of the Vessel, engaged in constant prayer, making amends for the havoc the war was already wreaking. Thaker was convinced that the thick black smoke from the forges and the discharging of the guns was offensive to Braen, the Lady of the Winds. Just prior to the Admiralty's decree, Carra-shaman had suspended the daily ceremonies in the Vessel, by order of the Ruenai. As for the men comprising the ruling body of Eret, they were locked to their desks and conference tables navigating requisition orders, reviewing allegations of misconduct by those using the unsettling times and new maritime policies for personal gain, and ensuring that Thaker's father, the grand admiral, had the resources needed to adequately defend their shores.

As for the citizens of Eret, they were doing their duty with solemn resolve. Dramel Pilon oversaw carpenters, farmers, and artisans brought into service to construct the fortifications at the points where the River Tere flowed into the seas of Natere and Nau in the south and north, and the Riven Fen into the Sea of Nau in the east. Similar operations were underway in Admiralty Bay, the Western Reach, and Vael's Point to the west and right before Thaker's eyes in Llafen Eret and on the Horn of Braen. Pilon's brother, Affram, was instructing the sailors and students at Admiralty Mast in the use of close-quarter weapons, grappling hooks, and the packing of bottles with oil, cloth, powder, and fuse that they would hurl to set fire to the decks and sails of approaching enemy ships.

"Welcome back to land, Captain Ungerfil!" Dramel said with a smile, sitting himself upon a pile of burlap sacks filled with sand and taking a long pull on a waterskin, which he then offered to Thaker, who politely declined.

"I do not recognize my homeland," the captain lamented, taking a seat beside the Dwarf, who was a head taller and far more muscled, making Thaker feel so small.

"I know it is hard to see," Dramel answered, pulling Storyteller from its sheath and retrieving a whetstone from his pocket, which he doused with water from the skin before putting the stone to rhythmic work on the brilliant silver blade. "But it is going to save your people from a brutal, bloody end. Better to have these fortifications marring the landscape than charred pits and acres of unmarked graves. Nadrim knows all he needs to of boatbuilding. Whatever has become of your sacred stone, about which I have heard your leaders whisper, he knows it is not in Eret. Which makes your people essentially worthless. At best, you shall be enslaved and at worst summarily slaughtered. So try to see what is before you, ugly as it seems, as preferable to what I have just described."

Thaker found himself pulled in and lulled into trance by the rhythmic pitch of the whetstone upon the blade. "Can you teach me to fight with a sword?" he asked, only realizing what he had requested once the words had left his mouth.

"Aye, Thaker Ungerfil. You and all the captains and your officers as well. Early this morning, a single-master departed for Port Alum from the Horn of Braen to bring back from the five forges of Mettlec proper weapons for you all. I also requested additional guns. I shall teach you the song of the sword. How to respect its violence, and how to know when to use it and when to leave it silent and sheathed."

"Naught shall ever be the same," Thaker muttered. The realization sat heavy upon his heart like a grey–black midwinter storm.

"That is the central aim of evil, my no-longer-innocent friend. To seek out what is kind, beating burning, and biting, until its battered, broken prey behaves like evil itself."

To remain unseen when everyone is searching for you—that is the assassin's truest test.

Gregory Gamelsin was a master of remaining unseen.

Abandoning the wagon several miles from Castle Silveth on the day he murdered Chrystan, Gamelsin hid in a cornfield throughout the night and into the morning's early hours. Hiding in a grain silo's upper storage section later in the day, as the field hands ate their lunch, he feasted on pockets full of grapes and almonds from a farm he had traversed the previous night.

Knowing he had plenty of time to accomplish his objective, Gamelsin watched for two more days as supply and farmers' wagons and hourly patrols passed on the road an eighth of a mile from the silo. He could sense an urgency in their comings and goings, without the slightest sign of panic.

Overconfidence in your defenses shall lead to your defeat.

As he waited, he was witness to pairs and trios of soldiers searching a wagon or questioning a traveler about the matter of the baron's murder. This happened dozens of times. He watched many a senior knight, his colorful pennant carried by a squire, engaging in haphazard, imprecise questioning of obvious innocents, because the Mellyan operations had forced their minds to focus solely on the tasks of war.

It was primarily an artifact of Gamelsin's actions. His commander—and the cliffprince—would be pleased.

If they ever discovered the details of what he had accomplished. Because chances were good that Gregory Gamelsin might not return to Amdar to make a final report.

Twelve hours prior, under cover of a cloud-filled sky that masked the Night Guardians' glow, he had abandoned the silo and taken to the treeline to the west of the main road to Silveth. Taking the opportunity to rest on a bed of moss, he emerged half an hour later beside an empty paddock, near a livery and smithy's shack.

Creeping along their western walls, he found himself within half a mile of the Horseshoe Sentinel, the manmade water defense that protected the back and sides of Silveth. Pulling a foot-long length of hollowed, reinforced reed from his boot, Gamelsin entered the chilly water. Placing the reed securely between his teeth and partially down his throat—he had gagged the first few hundred times during his training, although he felt no discomfort now—he submerged himself, making his way across the water, careful not to disturb the surface.

After all, he had all the time in the world. Sentries do not notice individuals when orchestrated events force their attention elsewhere.

Aldemere's Dilemma

That was another of the assassin's tests.

One he had already passed.

Aldemere felt the weight of the Clausmer like the embrace of an old, trusted friend as Anastasia hung it around his neck the third morning after his return to Castle Silveth, just before they rose from bed to start on their separate tasks of the day.

"It was my wish that you keep this with you," Aldemere said, fingering the sacred symbol of the jester-knight. "Should anything occur in the weeks and months to come—"

Placing a finger to his lips, Anastasia whispered, "It would make no difference if I were wearing it or it was handed to me by one of your proud lieutenants tasked to bring me the news of your death."

Aldemere moved away rather than respond, putting on his shirt and lacing up his boots. When he could no longer find a task to keep him from talking, he said, "The burden of being with child is hardening your words. The day of its birth shall be blessed in more ways than one."

Slamming her fist on her bedside table and crossing her arms in protest, Anastasia shouted, "It could be nothing other than my pregnancy causing the edge to my words? You are no better than the rest of the men I daily have to deal with—to say nothing of my mother! You all see me as weak... But I chose to marry you, despite *your* iron words and knotted thoughts! Shall the birth of our child soften you as well? Shall knowing you are leaving your child in addition to your wife make it more difficult for you to abandon us at the slightest sign of trouble, or shall the crying and competition for my attention make you all the more eager to ride away?"

Rather than answer Anastasia's barbed barrage of questions, Aldemere buckled the Garter of Glittereye onto his thigh and grasped the Mellyan sword and scabbard.

Watching her husband prepare to depart, Anastasia felt like screaming. Instead, while gathering a pile of unwrapped bandages into a basket, she asked, "When shall you once again wear Crow Feather and not the sword of our enemy?" Taking the basket, as well as a box of labeled medicine bottles, toward the door, she stopped as Aldemere answered.

"Once I have the time to sit with my father for more than a few bites of food or to review the reports of the daily patrols. This sword shall serve me for now."

"People are whispering, husband. You have yet to relieve Sir Lan..."

"He has done an exemplary job."

"You do not wear your sword…"

"Which I have just explained."

"You do not wear your motley cloak…"

"The weather has been warm! Is your quill full of arrows exhausted?"

Anastasia did not resist as Aldemere hugged her from behind, although she kept a tight grip on the box and basket rather than hold his hands in her own, as she normally would.

"It appears to me that it is. At least for now. Allow me to do things as I need to, Anastasia. In my own time. For my own reasons. I want this war to be over before you deliver the baby. If I avoid distractions, and follow my training and instincts, perhaps I can make that happen."

Anastasia pulled away. "Countries are not dragons, nor rebels you have known all your life. They are not cooks scared into foolish shows of principle or kitchen maids easy to bribe with a smile. This Mellyan savage ordered the murder of Baron Chrystan, from thousands of miles away. You tell me little of your time there, but I see the clouds it casts upon your countenance. You have my support to do as you must, Aldemere, as you always have. Granting me the same is all that I require. At least for now."

Reviewing the status reports from the westernmost mines a fourth and final time, Sir Corvit stretched his shaking, weary legs across the length of his cot, satisfied that he had not missed anything that would cost additional lives. Rubbing his tired eyes, he turned to Sir Goudry, who had arrived within hours of the nomads' mysterious retreat and then sat in patient silence for half an hour while Corvit did his work.

"If you know why they retreated, then tell me," Goudry finally said, navigating a tankard full of ale beneath a bulky swath of bloody gauze covering half his face.

"I shall," Corvit replied, "but you are sworn to secrecy. Above all, Milani and Ciloto are not to know the truth."

"Agreed. Although, being married to their sister, you put me in an awkward position."

Lighting a pipe full of strong tobacco he hoped would dull the ache in his spent and twitching legs, Corvit adjusted the rucksack behind him so he could lean against it.

"I am certain Lady Elssa will understand. When the barbarians sounded the signal to retreat up the mountain, Moktar's weapon

Aldemere's Dilemma

was on the ground. I knew it was not a sign of surrender, but perhaps a request for parlay. To test my intuition, I did the same, ordering the surrounding knights to secure the mines, see to the wounded, and above all, eat and rest. I invited Moktar to my tent—he sat where you are sitting—and asked him as plainly as I was able just what it was he wanted."

Goudry leaned in, like a curious child. "Which was?"

"First, to confirm what was already clear—he has unified the tribes under his authority. Unprecedented in their history, as far as he knows—a fact of which he is exceedingly, understandably, proud."

Reaching for a bunch of grapes Corvit had left on a table, Goudry enquired, "Why did he not kill you? Is it so important that you know what he accomplished? And, now that you know, how is it you remain amongst the living?"

"Because, my friend, there is something more he wants, besides my knowing. Besides King Dylwyn knowing. Moktar wants respect."

Spitting the seeds from a mouthful of grapes just outside the tent-flap, Goudry laughed. "Does he not need that from his own—whatever the beasts are called—to keep the tribes united? I would think your pretty skull would be excellent for that…"

Corvit also laughed—to make it clear he was uncomfortable. "If I did not know you for as long as I have, Goudry, I would think you had consolidation ideas of your own with your persistent enquiry into why I am not dead. Leave that aside for now. What he has done… What he is *doing*, with my help… is exactly what the situation demands. Leadership amongst the tribes is obtained and retained through fear—*not* respect. If I understood him correctly—and with his groans and grunts instead of common speech, this is merely a guess—he managed it by not replacing the chieftains killed, he presumes, during the attack on Vaelsport."

"You were there," Goudry responded, once more navigating the tankard beneath the bandages, "is his assumption correct?"

"Partially," Corvit answered, relighting and puffing his pipe. "Kull of the Krags was killed in the raid. Melak—the one we captured and from whom I attempted to extract information—killed the Riverskab chieftain before they reached the port, in a successful play for power. Moktar was pleased to know I prevented Melak from returning. All in all, he was sufficiently grateful that I played my part in his historical ascension."

"You cannot be serious!" Goudry said, adjusting his bandages, which made a series of nauseating sounds as he unstuck them from the mix of blood and ale beneath them. "Your story is becoming incredulous."

"To no one more than me, although every word is true. Here is the hardest part to swallow, which is also the answer to your question of what Chieftain Moktar wants." Corvit hesitated, looking this way and that to make certain no one was listening as Goudry raised his brow. "Once he was assured I had no hand in killing his father, he told me in detail—as much detail as his mind could muster—about just how deeply involved Mellya has been in the maneuvers of the nomads." Leaning forward, he grasped several pages of parchment from the foot of his cot. "I have detailed it all in this missive, which I must take to Silveth as soon as we are finished. As to *why* he told me... I see the question forming on your lips... Moktar thinks highly of himself and is, in child-like terms, put out at the lack of respect this supposed cliffprince has shown him."

"I understand," Goudry replied, picking blood from his pointed goatee. "To a point..."

Corvit rose gingerly from the cot, willing his unsteady legs to keep him standing. When they failed, he grasped the tent's maple centerpole. "Now that he has made a show, to his own warriors and to the Mellyans by attacking, he pledges to fight on our side... provided we allow him to carve a drinking bowl from Nadrim's disrespectful skull."

"Abrams is supposed to be *dead*, Lord Calrain—not captain of the Shadow Knife! Your machinations are quickly turning to dung!"

Davus Purloch was pacing the second-story walkway of the canvas-covered scaffolding erected as part of the ongoing renovations to the dungeon, pausing intermittently to peek between the flaps to be certain they were alone.

Calrain, wedged between a pair of angled scaffold supports half a dozen feet beneath his agitated co-conspirator, grabbed a mallet and banged heavily on the planks on which Purloch paced before releasing the tool as his hand began to spasm.

"Settle yourself, Purloch!" Calrain hissed. Cradling his hand between his bicep and torso, he added, "I was also surprised at my brother's decision, but I am no longer vexed. Now that I understand it, I am planning a cunning countermove."

Leaning over a railing, Davus asked, "What could you possibly understand about what has taken place? Abrams knows the truth... that makes him a risk. Unless your *cunning* countermove involves a sharp knife and that damnable liar's throat, I do not see—"

Aldemere's Dilemma

"Stop this childish caterwauling, for the love of my fragile sanity!" Calrain's injured hand was sending jolts of white-hot pain directly to his eyes. His condition was deteriorating. He had no time for Purloch's panic. "I should have seen it coming. The Shadow Knife is a vicious institution answerable only to my brother. It exists above the law. After all—they were the means by which my family seized control. If the newly promoted Captain Abrams proves to be a mistake, Nadrim shall order him to fall upon his sword. But he shall not be… Anstil is the only one amongst the lieutenants ever to challenge Helkirk. Nadrim had little use for that one—the taking of his fingers after the failed attack on Glittereye was proof enough of that. I doubt Nadrim cares a whit just who it was that killed him. Abrams is now in debt to my brother for no less than his life. And Abrams's lieutenants—those replacing the ones he tortures as we speak—shall dare not make a move on the one-armed, no-eared slayer of their formidable former captain."

If Calrain had intended to alleviate Davus's fears, he had failed.

"Think of it this way," continued Calrain, changing course at the frustrated exhalation of air he heard above him. "There was already a mishap as of late, in this very building—for which you, my demoted friend, are paying a pretty price. Nadrim could not weather another. Not as his armies prepare to march on Glittereye."

"How did you fail in your calculations?" Davus asked, wondering the same of himself. The prisoners' escape had sent his life on a downward spiral ever increasing in speed.

"What does it matter, Purloch!" Calrain screamed, his throbbing hand at last exhausting his patience. "Helkirk is dispatched, you are free from suspicion, and we managed to save the girl. Let Abrams enjoy his victory. All it cost him was a pair of ears and an arm."

"What of Deanna's recovery?"

Calrain had not been pleased to see that Davus had brought Helkirk's former plaything to his door the evening of the murder. Deferring his demand for an explanation until he had Deanna safely tucked away in the storage lofts above his suite of rooms, Calrain listened to Davus's story of a hysterical, insistent girl who threatened to scream for help if he chose to leave her behind. He had accepted the lieutenant's decision with a nod.

Calrain was now questioning if that was wise. "She is being treated and watched by a midwife I can trust. As a precaution against possible pregnancy, she administered a double dose of a potion that never fails. Deanna weathered a dozen hours of heaving, tremors, and sweats, but knew the pain was worth it. She shall soon be fit to travel."

Davus nearly asked what Calrain had planned for Deanna, but decided not to do so.

Not while he was formulating a cunning countermove as well.

Silbern Skarling had felt the poisonous serpent of ill omen begin to slither in his stomach the moment the summons to see Grand Admiral Ungerfil in his office was delivered by way of Tribune Mastmin, who had been going from ship to ship to deliver copies of and review with their captains and junior officers the decided-upon rules of engagement.

Wanting to stow away somewhere quiet until the serpent went to sleep, but knowing it would not be proper for one of his rank, Silbern walked as quickly as he could toward the offices of the Admiralty.

What had been a subtle scratching became a churning, roiling pain as he read the heavy expression upon the admiral's face.

"Have a seat, son," the veteran seaman whispered, indicating a teakwood chair opposite his desk that once resided in his captain's quarters on the *Salt-Serpent*. "I just received news from the fortifications at Boldac's Blade. The *Sea-Sword* arrived there two days ago, moderately damaged by fire and arrows, chased by a pair of Mellyan men o' war, which were sent to the sea-bottom by balls from the Dwarven guns."

Silbern closed his eyes as the serpent flicked its tongue against his innards. "You do not seem to be celebrating the victory as you should be, Admiral," he said, knowing with certainty that the news he had just received was naught but a stalling tactic. A half-hearted stab at context. A generality designed to prolong the shift to the personal. "Something has befallen my cousin Billec—is that not why I have been summoned?"

"It is," the grand admiral answered. "They made for Boldac's Blade, not because of the garrison there—we have a gun of our own at Xaer's Point, of which they were aware through the use of messenger birds—but because it was closer and they had suffered two dozen wounded and another dozen dead. Captain Skarling was amongst the worst of the wounded. The Dwarven physicians did all they could for the tough old son of the sea, but his loss of blood was great... The *Sea-Sword* is heading home and, rest assured, your cousin shall be buried at sea with highest honors off the Horn of Braen."

Standing, Silbern said, "If you will excuse me, Admiral—"

Aldemere's Dilemma

"Sit yourself, Silbern. News of your fallen cousin is only part of why you are here." The grand admiral's voice was firm, although his face showed something kinder. Father-like. "The *Sea-Sword* needs a captain. You are the logical choice. You should have accepted a captaincy out of Admiralty Mast... I have never understood why you—"

"Personal circumstances, Admiral," Silbern said, throwing back his shoulders, "which have recently changed."

The grand admiral managed a look of relief, despite the larger circumstances. "Meaning, you shall captain the *Sea-Sword*?"

"I shall captain her, Grand Admiral Ungerfil, but she shall always be Billec's ship."

Standing and saluting, the admiral answered, "Understood. I am sending word to all command crews to convene later today to share what I have told you. Until then, Captain Skarling..." Reaching into a drawer of his desk, the admiral produced a pair of pristine gold-colored epaulets. "Wear these for now, until I can get you Billec's."

"Aye, sir," Silbern answered, taking the epaulets in hand as childhood memories of staring at them with envy whenever Athes or Billec were near came flooding in. "One last thing, Admiral. The *Salt-Serpent* now has need of a good first officer."

"It is already in the works, Captain Skarling. Clear out your on-ship quarters so you shall be ready for your transfer the minute the *Sea-Sword* arrives."

Clutching the epaulets tightly in his fist, and taking his leave with a solemn salute, Silbern began to wonder if he was wrong to refuse to listen to what Carra had wanted to tell him—about what she had seen in that damned and dangerous bowl.

Would it have altered his course? Saved his cousin from death? Would it have helped to prevent him from breaking Nomma's heart?

Finding himself equidistant from the Vessel and the *Salt-Serpent*, Silbern was, for a moment, unsure of which way to go.

As he resumed his path to the ship, all the questions he had asked himself offered their inarguable answers, and he found himself at peace.

"Recall the fleet, My Cliffprince! To ignore my request is madness!"

General Hespen DeSpan, leader of the twenty thousand Mellyan troopers tasked with invading Tombal, did not retreat, nor did he drop his iron gaze as Nadrim, dressed for battle and sitting tall upon a chestnut destrier, turned his head in anger at the general's insolent words.

"The war being waged upon the water is none of your concern," Nadrim shot back, his fists twisting the reins, causing his horse to buck. "I knew we would lose some ships. Initial losses are inevitable. Within weeks, we shall have the Eretian fleet—what remains of it—as the basis from which to rebuild. How quickly you lose your faith."

News of the loss of the two three-masters near the Islands of Kirr could not have come at a more inopportune moment—just as the Mellyan land forces were readying to depart. Only General DeSpan and Vice Admiral Gorget Bailey, commander of a dozen shallow-draft, single-masted ships and three triple-masted men of war, capable of navigating the rivers, were with him when Calrain had brought the news.

"What mechanism did they use to sink our ships?" Bailey asked.

"No one lived to tell," Calrain answered. "The message was sent by a Dwarf in my employ, from their fortifications at Boldac's Blade."

"Is the news to be believed?" DeSpan enquired. "Perhaps the ships were captured—the crews imprisoned, or enslaved…"

Nadrim had dismissed the notion. Dwarves had no love of the sea, and even less of ships, although their homeland was an island.

DeSpan's agitation had continued to grow, reaching the point of anger as they sat on the plain just south of Mellya for a final review of his troops.

"Our men of war, dispatched to Eret, Tombal, and Vaelsport, shall continue on course, DeSpan," Nadrim hissed, a desert adder disturbed beneath its rock. "Whatever weapons the Dwarven forge-masters have devised, they shall not share with our enemies. The Eretians lured our ships to their shores. Boldac's Blade was an isolated incident, I assure you. Will you do your duty, or shall I order a reorganization of the officer's corps?"

Touching his right fist to his left shoulder, DeSpan shouted, "Yes, My Lord!"

"Then go forth and bring us victory."

As the men, horses, and materiel of war made their southern start with a cacophonous swell of sound, led by their dressed-down general, Nadrim stared ahead at the disciplined array of marching death as a rider approached to his right.

"It is quite the breathtaking sight, is it not, brother crickback?" Nadrim asked, keeping his eyes on the lock-stepped mass of men. "I hope you are strapped securely onto that horse. Think of the embarrassment—for both of us, of course—if you were to fall."

Adjusting his cramping arms before the pain made itself manifest in his eyes, Calrain moved his horse closer to Nadrim's. Beneath his cloak, the hilt of a poison-tipped misericord pressed against his abdomen.

It had been there, ready to draw, to use, during their last several meetings, but Calrain had refrained. Not out of love, or fear, but out of the need to strengthen or obtain the support of several key people before he could kill the cliffprince. Progress was steady but slow. Nadrim had done a breathtaking job of portraying Calrain as naught but his deformities.

Calrain knew he was more. His assets, although currently insufficient, were growing every day. He was familiar with the weapon that sank the ships at Boldac's Blade. He had seen the Dwarven guns in the Mettlec forges and had kept it to himself. He had Davus Purloch, and, through him, his father and his ilk. He had Deanna Callenhor, and once her murdered father's aristocratic allies heard her story, Calrain would have them as well.

Then, once he had ascertained the level of loyalty to their new captain of Anstil Abrams's Shadow Knife lieutenants, and identified a replacement more conducive to his plans, he would make known in key quarters that Abrams had lied about Nagelbrau's death.

Sitting higher in his saddle despite the ache it caused in his hip, Calrain reflected on the possibility of being able to sway the head of the army—Hespen DeSpan. A few strategic losses and the already agitated general would be open to alternatives. DeSpan was more Philod's man than Nadrim's, which the cliffprince failed to see. The renaming of the bay had been an affront to their father's friend. Calrain had seen it in the set of his jaw for just a moment, as Nadrim announced the change, but a moment was enough.

Then there was the assassin in Glittereye, the manipulation of the barbarians, and the truth of Garamin's rebellion. What to do with those little chestnuts, and when, were questions that steeled his resolve.

"It is quite the sight indeed," answered Calrain with a smile. "It signals a change in Mynoweth like none that has come before. The Damonessa name is soon to be writ large in all the histories of all the countries of the world. I am honored to witness its birth."

Reining his horse toward Amdar and urging it into a gallop, Nadrim shouted over his shoulder, "It is the least I could do for my half-man, all-crippled brother."

Please continue to think so, Calrain thought, his fingers playing provocatively over the pommel of his poised and poisoned knife.

CHAPTER THREE

Aldemere entered the Council Room to find Linead, Prima, and Peecwyl huddled together over a map of the known lands of Mynoweth, and another of Glittereye, while Frederick and his companions stood off at a distance, awaiting their turn to speak.

"What is the word?" the captainguard asked, as the king and his father entered the room behind him.

"We have just received a report from Sir Connor's advanced scouts in the east. They have spotted a large army—perhaps as many as twenty thousand—traveling southeast," Linead answered, looking past Aldemere to the king. "And they shall be supported by ships, which are currently in the upper reaches of the Mirra River."

"Have the scouts made an estimate of the number and the type?" Elde enquired.

"Perhaps a dozen single-masters," Linead replied, handing the report to Dylwyn's chief advisor.

"If they are designed like the ship Kal-Gadras and I acquired in Vaelsport, they shall navigate the river with ease," Aldemere said. "They could enter through Mirra Pass into Glittereye, and then to the River Skillen and finally into the Forest of the Black Light."

"They shall do it all," Frederick added. "Cabral shall be vulnerable within a week, same as Eerbell. Let me send Martin and Christoph north and east to assist and advise your commanders. They know much of Mellyan tactics and have experience with ships."

"The forces in the north have already been weakened by the recent nomadic attacks," the king whispered, thinking aloud. "Sir Corvit has once more won the field, but he shall not be able to withstand the fury of a combined onslaught such as we expect. Sir Linead—I sanction Frederick's request. Shall you do the same? You must dispatch at least a thousand men to the immediate aid of Cabral. Martin can travel with them."

"If that is what you wish of me, Sire," Linead said, his tone making it clear that he was not at all in agreement, "I shall see it done. Shall we send reinforcements to Connor?"

"Not at present," Dylwyn answered, placing his finger upon the map. "The eastern garrisons are heavily fortified, and it shall take a few days longer for the invading army to pose a threat to Eerbell. The ships shall have no choice but to stay in proximity to the army, for protection and supplies. Christoph shall leave immediately to advise Sir Connor on an effective plan of action."

Following a nod from Frederick, Martin and Christoph took their leave.

"I appreciate your faith, Your Highness," Frederick said with a bow.

"What of this one?" Linead asked. "Where would you have him go?"

"He shall stay with you at present," Dylwyn answered. "When Martin and Christoph report, you shall be side by side, working together to put the information to its most strategic use and to coordinate the armies. Speaking of, what are your immediate plans, in light of current facts?"

Asking Elde to join them, Linead motioned to the map. "I am sending Sirs Peecwyl and Prima to serve as the advance. They will each take up defensive positions with two thousand men, fifty miles east of Elsmore and twenty-five miles north of Eerbell, respectively. Sir Navvic shall be responsible for enhanced defensive positions twenty miles east of the castle. He shall also have authority over the one hundred men beneath Sir Arans. They shall remain for now at the Temple of the Seers, although, should Sir Navvic decide they are needed elsewhere, Arans will comply without question or delay."

"I shall send word to Dictus to that effect," Elde the Jester said. "And then I shall navigate his vigorous protestations."

"His feelings on the matter are of no concern to me, Jester Elde," Linead snapped. "Nor should they be to you. Should Arans prove to be stubborn—"

"Let us deal with him, Linead," the king replied. "Tell me the rest of the plan."

Sir Linead did as the king commanded. "We received word last evening from High Lord Petror that the Elves are preparing for war. Not unlike ourselves, they are setting up both defensive positions as well as providing an advance guard that shall coordinate with Sir Marvis in the south."

"We have in turn apprised them of the ships sailing down the Mirra River," Sir Peecwyl reported. "They are already prepared for an attack from the open waters, and they shall no doubt move swiftly to protect their trio of river borders."

"Excellent," the king remarked. "Do we anticipate a threat by way of Vaelsport?"

"Thanks to Sir Corvit, I believe it is secure," Linead answered. "His forces shall hold both Seafarer's Gap and Firoth Pass, and, should things devolve, Sir Glenmore, Sir Prima's trade warden in the west, shall send reinforcements to the north."

"That only leaves the castle," Elde said, looking at his son. "I trust you are further reinforcing our defenses and making additional preparations, Captainguard Aldemere?"

"If you will excuse us," Sir Linead interrupted, "we have much to do. I have the utmost faith in Aldemere. If you could continue this conversation without us…"

"Of course," Elde the Jester replied.

As the rest of the commanders departed, Aldemere spoke, choosing his words with care. "The castle's defenses are well in order, Father. With your permission, I wish to allow Lan to continue as our captainguard. He has acquitted himself well, and a changeover in command at such a moment as this could be dangerously disruptive. I am of best use to my kingdom and my king by applying my skills on the battlefield. Certainly, with the army so divided, I can be of greater service elsewhere."

Dylwyn shook his head. "You have just returned, Sir Aldemere. Silveth is where you belong. While I agree that Lan has admirably executed his duties, he does not have the respect of the men. Not at the level that you do. May I suggest that you put Lan in charge of the perimeter defenses. It is time he left the castle and learned to lead from the front."

Deciding for the moment to refrain from further argument, Aldemere bowed. "As you command, My King."

Once Aldemere was out of earshot, Dylwyn turned to Elde. "History tells me that this is not the last we shall be hearing of Aldemere's wish to ride headlong into the fray. Am I wrong to keep him from doing so?"

"That depends, your highness. If you are doing so as a king who is managing his resources best as he can, then the choice is wise. But if it is as a future grandfather who wishes to protect his son-in-law in times of war, I must remind you that there are hundreds of son-in-laws who are destined to draw swords and breathe their last breaths in the weeks and months to come, because they have no such powerful advocate."

"I shall keep your council in mind. For now I am certain, with all the faculties I possess, that Aldemere's place is at Silveth."

"I do not disagree. I must advise you, however, that Mellya may still hold him. He has yet to come to me for Crow Feather. He is still wearing a sword he procured in the course of his mission. I shall speak with him this evening. Has Anastasia offered insight to you or the queen?"

Dylwyn shook his head. "Nor do I expect her to. Their love is fierce, my friend, but it is also unusually complicated. Do make time to talk with him. We need his mind to be clear, and his commitment to the castle to be fully without question. Despite our extensive preparations, I fear that Castle Silveth shall once more fall under siege."

Word of Billec Skarling's death and Silbern's promotion to captain of the *Sea-Sword* swept through the fleet and the crews on the docks like a merciless northeast wind, shocking no one so much as Thaker with its knotted rope of circumstances.

It was not until after the *Sea-Sword* arrived—a sober, solemn moment as she sat wounded in her slip, not a soul in motion around her as a dozen sail-draped corpses were carried off, followed by Billec's burial at sea off the Horn of Braen—that Thaker had an opportunity to talk with his former first officer.

"I am sorry I was absent when you came to pack your things," he began, as they sat in his quarters aboard the *Salt-Serpent*. "I was practicing with this damnable sword with Dramel. You shall be issued your own sword soon—as shall all of your officers."

"They shall gladly take them now," Silbern answered, wishing he were elsewhere to avoid the awkwardness of this exchange. "I suppose it has always been my wish to carry a practical means of defense rather than rely on religion and superstition."

"For what it is worth, I am in favor of your appointment," Thaker replied, avoiding the subject of Silbern's thoughts about their wrong-headed reliance on the Ruenai. "You should have accepted a captain's commission in the first place."

Sitting back in his chair and closing his eyes, Silbern sharply exhaled. "I am tired of hearing those words... Who is your choice to replace me? I would be happy to make suggestions from amongst the current crew, but your father said there is already something happening..."

"There is," Thaker said. "It was settled yesterday evening."

Thaker had been studying a trio of charts for the voyage to Tombal's shores, to which the *Salt-Serpent*, *Sea-Sprite*, *Spear-Shaft*, and *Sea-Seeker* would be sailing once they had assembled and secured the additional guns arriving from Mettlec, when his father entered his cabin. Without greeting or preamble, the grand admiral shared his recommendation, upon which Thaker immediately acted.

"May I have a moment?"

Prince Dramel was practicing his swordplay upon a thick, unyielding pylon at the end of the pier when Thaker had approached.

"You may," he said, sheathing Storyteller on his back in a lightning-quick motion that Thaker paused to admire. "I was finishing my drills. Have you been doing yours?"

"Every morning and evening, as ordered," Thaker said, patting the sword that hung from his hip. He was still getting used to its unnatural, deadly weight. "I feel like I did as a child learning my sailor's knots—awkward, awful, and a little bit ashamed."

"It shall come to you with practice," Dramel said, taking a long pull from a waterskin and wiping his brow with his sleeve. "What is it you need?"

Thaker took him through the earlier conversation with his father—the reasons and rationale behind what was an unprecedented, and in some ways unthinkable, offer.

"Me as your first officer?" Dramel asked, repeating the words to give them substance.

"That is our request. Do you accept?"

Dramel lowered his head for a moment's consideration. "I do."

"Then I shall gather the paperwork and have you fit for a uniform."

"How can you do this, Captain? He knows nothing of the sea. He and his kind are—"

Thaker, hopeful the hard part was already past, found himself caught off guard by the unexpected voice.

"There is no need for vitriol, Navigator Neergarn," Thaker said, facing his critic with a scowl. "We do not need another expert seaman. We are the flagship of the Eretian fleet in times of war, and you, Corbit, are the best of our helmsmen. When it is time to engage with the enemy—and that time is nearly here—I can think of no one I would rather have beside us than the prince. Can you?"

Thaker waited patiently while his helmsman thought it over.

"You put it that way, Captain, I cannot defend my complaint. Not after seeing the *Sea-Sword*. I shall be the first to welcome aboard with the best of wishes First Officer Pilon. I meant neither of you any offense."

Crisis averted, Thaker turned to his quartermaster, Messut Kaelhull, who had been lurking in the shadows. "We shall be running drills as soon as the guns are loaded onto our decks and those of the *Sea-Sprite* and *Sea-Seeker*. See that the crew is prepared."

Aldemere's Dilemma

"They shall be, Captain Ungerfil," the quartermaster shouted. "Those bastards shall pay in flesh by the pound for the *Sea-Sword*!"

"A month ago, this would all be unimaginable," Silbern whispered, shaking his head in the present in Thaker's cabin on the *Salt-Serpent*.

Thaker silently nodded, rendered speechless by the maelstrom they fast approached.

Captain Anstil Abrams, leader of the Shadow Knife, was removing the saddle from his horse after an inspection of the training grounds when two of his lieutenants approached.

"A word, sir," Petr Ryoch growled, as his companion, Hans Kauffer, closed and locked the stable doors.

"You dare to challenge me so soon?" Captain Abrams asked, dropping the saddle on a bench and drawing his sword. "Two at a time is not the way it is done."

"Nor is ascending by a lie," Kauffer answered, drawing his sword and approaching. "When the challenge comes, I shall do it right and proper. Consider this a warning—although it is more than your earless face deserves. Your story does not hold water. Captain Nagelbrau would not have succumbed to a cut-up thing like you."

Abrams widened his stance as Ryoch drew his sword behind him. "The cliffprince is more than satisfied—do you think you can convince him otherwise?"

"You have no lineage in the Shadow Knife," Kauffer hissed, spitting into the straw at Abrams's feet. "Everything you claim, you have stolen. That does not sit well with us."

Kauffer spoke the truth. Ryoch and he were descended from Shamman Ryoch, who had left the Shadow Knife captaincy to become minister of public policy in 945 before Felzban Fragenoar assassinated him eight years later, and Siegl Kauffer, who became a general in the army after Felzban assassinated Elaric Gamselsin. Abrams had no such lineage. A Shadow Knife lieutenant had chosen him for his speed and agility, plucking him off a mountainside as he chased a pair of goats he had mistakenly let out of their pen.

He sometimes wondered if his parents thought a wolf had claimed their son.

It was, in fact, the truth.

"I have stolen nothing," he said. "What I possess, I have earned. You both can see the price. So who more truly belongs? You men would be wise not to pursue any further this ill-timed play for power.

Opportunities are rife in times of war. Should General DeSpan die on the field of honor, Kauffer, you could easily take his place. And you, Ryoch—perhaps a seat in the Ministry. Honor your ancestors by adhering to our code. Stay loyal to me, and help me convince the rest of the doubters to do the same, and I shall see it done. It must be clear to you that the cliffprince finds me of value."

He sensed the grip on their swords ever so slightly loosen. He was getting through.

"Where is Gregory Gamelsin?"

Abrams smiled. Now he understood why they had moved on him so soon.

"I did not kill him, if that is what you are asking."

Kauffer stepped in close. "If he still lives and breathes, then where in blazes is he?"

"I cannot divulge his location."

Abrams felt the tip of Ryoch's sword press against his tunic. "Is it because you do not know, or you refuse to say?"

"It is both. The cliffprince wants the broad strokes of his mission kept a secret, and I do not know the particulars of his whereabouts. The cliffprince and I—and, of course, Gamelsin—are the only ones who know what he is about to do. Rest assured, though, it is a mission of great importance, which is why Nagelbrau sent Gregory instead of either of you. Our former captain did not value you. Would you not prefer that to change?"

An hour after the lieutenants had left, Abrams was eating dinner on a bench outside the stables when a new pair of men approached.

Raising his head to see their faces as they stepped into the torchlight, he was less sure he could handle them as well as he had Kauffer and Ryoch.

Although, if he valued his life, it was essential that he do so.

Silbern Skarling was settling into his quarters aboard the *Sea-Sword* when he discovered a hidden note.

He had just unpacked his sea chest, which included a painting that his great, great grandmother had done of the port of Llafen Eret that had hung in his childhood bedroom, then his dorm room at Admiralty Mast when he was a cadet, and most recently in his quarters aboard the *Salt-Serpent*.

Scouting for a place to hang it, Silbern noticed that his cousin Billec had papered the walls with sea charts, duty rosters, and copied pages from his logs. Silbern was determined to leave every

Aldemere's Dilemma

single piece exactly where it hung. He was about to place the painting beneath his bunk when his eye was drawn to a crude drawing of a single-master tacked amongst some manifests.

Pulling it carefully from the wall, and holding it near a candle, Silbern noticed writing on the back.

To the new captain a' the *Sea-Sword*, whoever ye may be (tho' I know full well who ye be):

If yer hands be upon this paper, an' yer eyes upon these words, I have either been lost at sea or somehow lost my command. I pray with all my heart, within earshot a' the Ruenai, that it be the former, fer my years as Capt'n a' this fine vessel, an' her even finer crew, have been the best a' m'life.

Pay heed ta this tale a' the sea, fer I would wager my last coin it shall prove a' help ta ye.

The ship on the reverse a' this paper, a fine, if not worn an' weathered single-master used fer the trainin' a' cadets, now sits at the bottom a' the bay, thanks ta a brash young sailor who thought bein' an officer meant not seekin' advice, nor any compromise. He was determined ta practice that view as much as he could as a cadet.

A storm durin' trainin', which he thought he could handle, but could not, lost that fine ole trainin' ship, an' very nearly seven lives.

He spent an extra year at Admiralty Mast fer that one, an' could have done with two, but that sailor—an' yes, of course, tis me—learned his lesson well.

Best ta learn it from this paper, my successor, my worthy cousin Silbern (aye... I know it ta be you) than on the rough an' stormy sea.

Serve well your crew an' they shall well serve you—

Capt'n Billec Skarling

Tho' I know full well who ye be... My worthy cousin Silbern...

Was this what Carra wanted so badly to tell him? That he was fated to be a captain, at the expense of his cousin's life?

Reading the writing again, and twice more after a period of gut-wrenching contemplation, Silbern was tacking the message back up amongst the other maritime flotsam and jetsam when a shadow fell over his door.

He could tell by its delicate lines that it did not belong to a member of the crew.

"You should not be here, Nomma," he said in a tone not in alignment with the expression on his face, so he did not turn around. "Especially not at this moment."

"Nor should you, my love."

"That is what you came here to say?" he asked, facing her with eyes ablaze. "This is where I belong! I was stupid not to see it. Now I know the truth… I had no choice! Your damned Ruenai *arranged it*. Billec's blood is on their hands… and mine! Those evil bastards punished me for refusing a ship. I did that because of *you*!"

Nomma shook her head. "What you are saying cannot be true…"

"Stop being so naïve! You do not belong here, Nomma. You belong in the Vessel, praying for the safety of our crews. Each of us has our duty. They do not intersect. We were young. Confused. Selfish. It is time we both grow up."

"I love you, Silbern. I know that you love me. Does anything matter more?"

Before he could answer—and what he might have said, Silbern would spend years pondering, the answer morphing with his mood and experiences—Carra was at the door.

"Nomma. It is time for us to go. You said what you came to. That was our agreement."

"The fault for all of this is *yours*, you *witch*!" Silbern yelled, moving past Nomma, to confront this unwelcome third. "You knew my cousin would die!"

"Aye! But that information came too late. There is more. Events that we *can* alter or prevent. Will you not listen to me, Silbern?" Carra asked, as Nomma fled past them in tears. "Your decision is based on your refusal to hear what I have seen, instead of on the information you could glean by taking advantage of it. I am not responsible for that."

"Did you see *this* in your bowl?" Silbern asked, his voice about to break.

"Yes… if you mean your breaking Nomma's heart."

"I have no time for your silly mysticism! Keep your visions to yourself. I warn you. Look after Nomma and the rest of the Ruen-Eret. Pray your prayers and do not get in my way. What I have done is solely to fulfill my duty. It had nothing to do with you."

"Very well, Captain Skarling," Nomma said, turning to go. "But this is not over. It has only just begun. I have seen more in the bowl than your breaking Nomma's heart. So, know this, Silbern Skarling. You have broken into only its initial fragments the heart of that innocent girl."

Aldemere's Dilemma

Moving to close the door, Silbern softened his tone. "Nomma shall heal, with your assistance. I shall consider what you said."

As Carra walked away, Silbern locked the door. Seeking to temper his mood, he turned his gaze to the sketch of the single-master. Pondering the heavy words it hid, he lay upon his bed and exhaled a long, tortured breath before willing himself to sleep.

When he was ten years old, Gregory Gamelsin was like any other boy born to poor parents outside the citadel city of Amdar. He helped his father with the harvest and their pitiful collection of thin goats, sluggish rabbits, molting chickens, and a cow that was unable to give milk most mornings, no matter how urgently her udders were coaxed.

Gregory knew that, when he turned twelve, a few short autumns away, some low-ranking officer would enter their yard, and after some chitchat about the sorry state of their thin goats and molting chickens, would offer a handful of coins—barely enough to purchase half a winter's cordwood—in exchange for Gregory's service in the Mellyan army. His parents, without any pretense of thinking it over, would agree. The officer would return the following week and take him away in a wagon, to train in the mud and the cold with the hundreds of half-starved sons of other failing farmers.

Gregory knew it would happen, and exactly how, because he had witnessed it three of the four past autumns with his older brothers, none of whom he had heard from again.

Gregory could not wait for his recruitment day to come.

In preparation, in his rare idle hours, he ran the hills around their cottage, lifting stones as big—and then bigger—than his head, climbing trees, and swimming the river.

That is when he learned to hold his breath beneath the water. Starting slowly, building up his lung capacity and confidence, he went a little farther below the surface each time, until he was sinking his feet to the ankles into the sludge at the bottom of the river, where the eels and bottom-feeding fish brushed against his shins. The struggle to escape the sludge ensured several additional seconds in the dark, murky water, before he could head for the surface, his lungs aflame, before he began to drown.

Air was a precious commodity. Something not to be wasted. Something no one should take for granted.

His hard-earned ability to hold his breath for half a dozen minutes was what he used to demonstrate his prowess on the first day of training with his fellow future soldiers. It was what got him noticed by an officer of the Shadow Knife, who was amused at the sight of two sergeants plunging into the lake's cold October waters when Gregory failed to emerge with the others.

"What is your name, lad?" the Shadow Knife officer had asked, tossing him a cloth with which to dry himself and sending the two angry sergeants off with a look far colder than the water in which they had needlessly submerged themselves.

"Gregory Gamelsin, sir."

"Gamelsin…" A look of surprise brightened the officer's scarred and weathered face. "Any relation to Davin Gamelsin?"

Gregory nodded. "He is a cousin, sir. Though his parents and mine do not speak."

"You know much about your family?" the officer asked, opening his rucksack and removing a hunk of cheese and some bread that he passed to the grateful recruit.

"No sir, I do not," Gregory answered, pushing the cheese into the soft, spongy surface of the fresh baked bread and jamming it into his mouth.

So it was that he had learned about his ancestor, Elaric, a fierce, capable general who had been viciously murdered by a Lysean coward by the name of Felzban Fragenoar.

That accident of ancestry, coupled with his ability to hold his breath longer than any other recruit beneath the frigid water (how he had built the skill was of interest to his interviewer), secured him a place amongst the privileged few who hoped to one day be chosen as members of the Shadow Knife.

Such were his memories as Gregory Gamelsin emerged from the still waters of the Horseshoe Sentinel in the middle of the night. He had spent the past several hours watching the comings and goings at Silveth's rearmost doors, from a spot where he had hidden within some harlequin blueflag that those in charge of the castle's defenses had foolishly let grow to waist height along the supposed sentinel's banks.

Emerging when no one was near, he pressed himself against the smooth stones of the castle's western wall. Here he would remain in wait, knife in hand, for an opportunity to subdue and take the place of some soldier returning from the stables who, after crossing the King's Bridge, would round the corner to have a piss before joining his companions.

He had repeatedly watched it happen.

Taking advantage of the enemy's repetition and habits was another of his skills.

Three hours had passed before a soldier suitable in size and accoutrements made his way to the wall. As he concentrated on relieving his bladder, Gregory did not hesitate. He worked, silently and efficiently, stabbing the man in the back, puncturing a lung so he could not scream. He then removed the soldier's tunic, sword, and boots.

Weighting the soldier's remaining clothing with stones, Gregory dropped the body in the water, watching it sink below the surface. After slipping on the soldier's boots—he had put his own on the corpse—and tucking his pants to hold them secure—the man had outsized feet for his height—he donned the tunic. He then pulled on his vest, to cover the pancake-sized circle of blood on the back of the tunic, and buckled on the dead man's swordbelt. Opening the string on his pants as he heard a few others approach, he straddled the dead man's pool of urine and contributed a stream of his own.

"Put your poultry away and get inside with your comrades, you motherless dog!" a grizzled commander shouted in his direction. "We are locking the doors for the night!"

"Aye, sir," Gregory said, mimicking perfectly the subtle accent of the Centerlands, while pulling tight and double knotting the drawstring of his pants before heading for the pool of light cast by a gatekeeper standing beside the commander. "I could use a bowl of hot," the assassin grumbled, keeping his face turned just enough away from the flame as he passed them to not arouse suspicion.

Entering the rear gatehouse, Gregory allowed himself to smile.

He was now within the castle where his target kept their bed.

As Gregory Gamelsin hid himself away in a storeroom at the rear of the castle and settled into sleep, Captainguard Aldemere was climbing the Watch Tower stairs. They had missed passing one another outside the royal family's rooms by only a matter of minutes.

Pausing at a window halfway up the stairs, Aldemere felt his scalp begin to tingle and his heart to increase its beating as he caught a glimpse of the Ambir Dragon's tail disappearing behind a gathering of grey and threatening clouds that resembled the Adjudicator in Amdar—the bladed taker of heads.

Placing his fingers upon the Clausmer of the Jester-Knight, Aldemere made a decision—one with ramifications that further stressed his heart and brought a flood of tears to his eyes.

At dawn, after reclaiming Crow Feather from his father, he would do what his destiny demanded.

He would ride at the head of the army, as Nemmerle foretold.

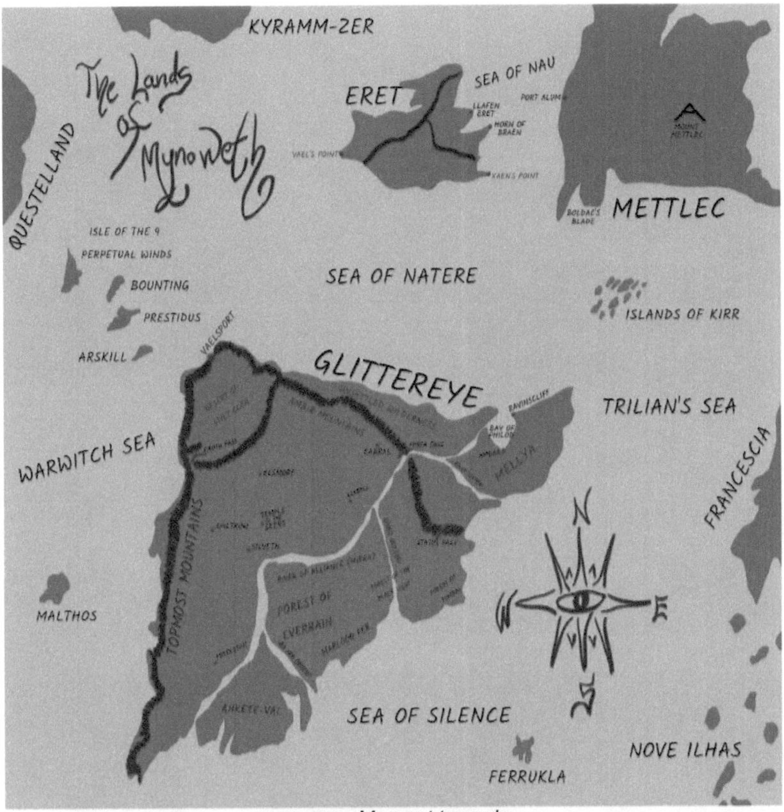

The Lands of Mynoweth

KYRAMM-ZER

ERET

SEA OF NAU

PORT ALUIG

LLAFEN ERET

MORN OF BRAEN

MOUNT METTLES

QUESTELLAND

VAEL'S POINT

VAEN'S POINT

BOLDAC'S BLADE

METTLEC

ISLE OF THE 9 PERPETUAL WINDS

SEA OF NATERE

ISLANDS OF KIRR

BOUNTING

PRESTIDUS

ARSKILL

VAELLPORT

GLITTEREYE

TRILIAN'S SEA

WARWITCH SEA

TOPMOST MOUNTAINS

MALTHOS

FOREST OF EVERRAIN

FRANCESCIA

N E S W

SEA OF SILENCE

NOVE ILHAS

FERRUKLA

Map not to scale.

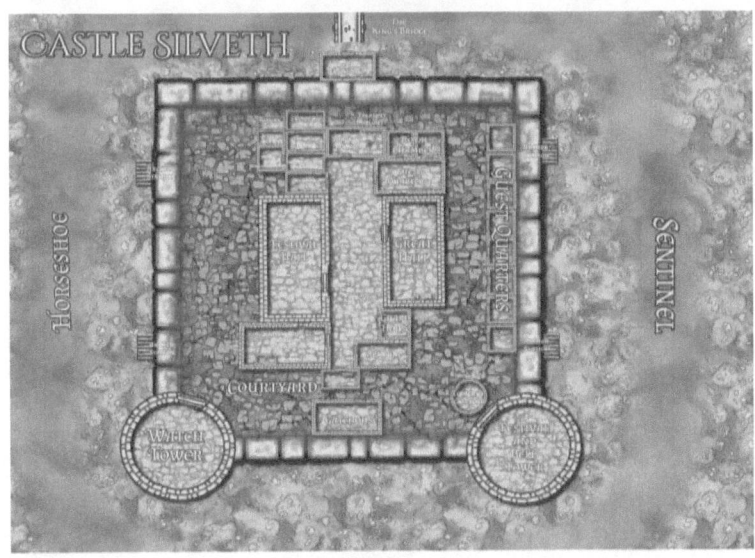

CASTLE SILVETH

THE KING'S BRIDGE

HORSESHOE

GUEST QUARTERS

SENTINEL

COURTYARD

WITCH TOWER

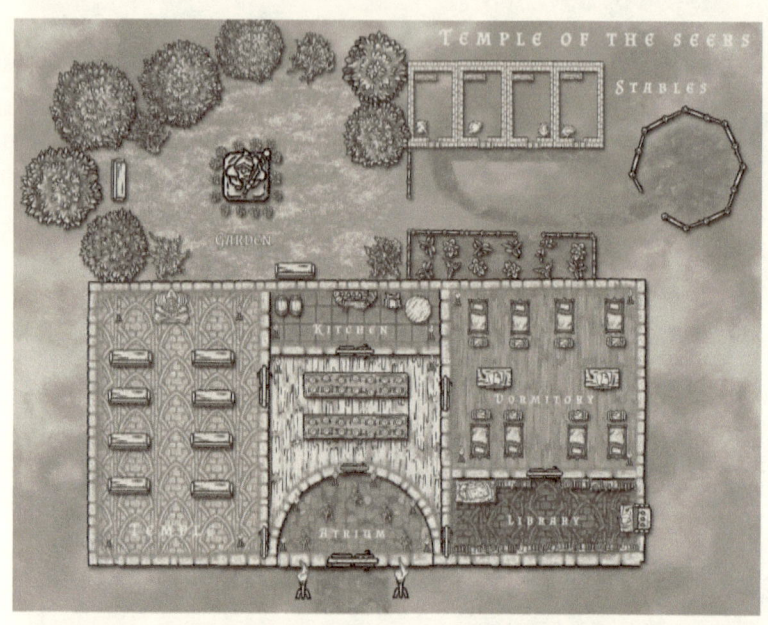

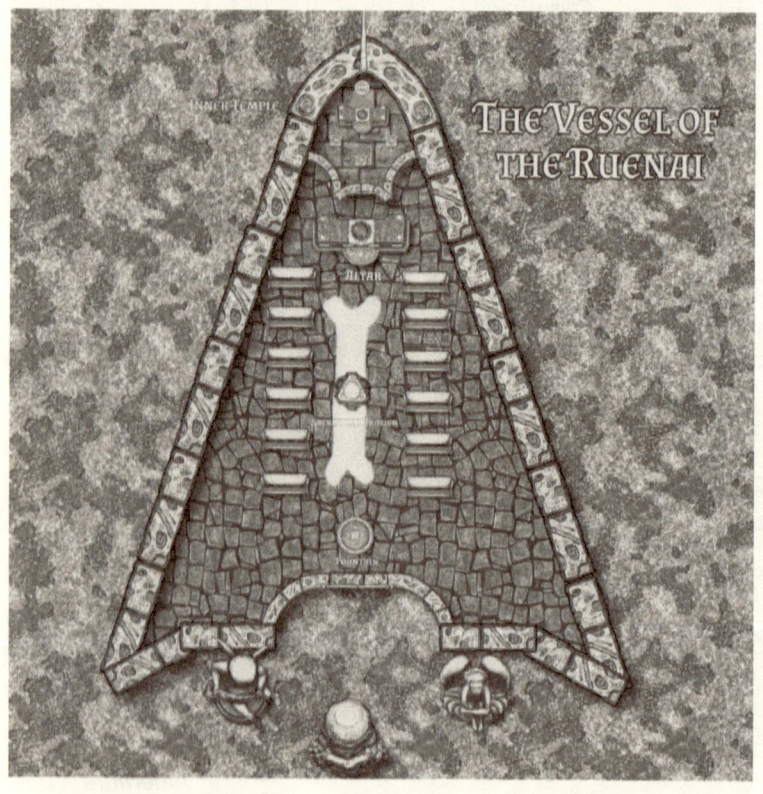

THE VESSEL OF THE RUENAI

ABOUT THE AUTHOR

Joey Madia is a writer, actor, director, podcaster, educator, and historical education specialist. He works with publicists, agents, producers, and production companies as a story analyst, consultant, script doctor, immersive experience designer, and freelance writer. He has written the narrative and designed the puzzles for four Escape Rooms (and has consulted on several others), one of which won a national tourism award in Scotland in 2023, and is the writer of several award-winning screenplays and stage plays. As a Chautauqua scholar, he has portrayed Allen Ginsberg (with cooperation from the Ginsberg Estate/Allen Ginsberg Project), Ernesto "Che" Guevara, "Black" Samuel Bellamy, Mariano Vallejo, Edgar Allan Poe, and Captain Louis Emilio. His one-man show and four novels on the Golden Age of Piracy, "The Cannon and the Quill," have been entertaining and educating audiences since 2016. He has been featured in the *North Carolina Travel Guide* (2018 & 2023), *Carolina Coast*, and other magazines and on television in Japan. Joey has written five books on using theater in the classroom and two books on his field investigations and experiences with the paranormal.